LONG GONE

ALSO BY ALAFAIR BURKE

LONG GONE

A NOVEL OF SUSPENSE

ALAFAIR BURKE

HARPER

An Imprint of HarperCollins*Publishers*
www.harpercollins.com

HarperCollins books may be purchased for educational, business, or sales promotional use. For information, please write: Special Markets Department, HarperCollins Publishers, 10 East 53rd Street, New York, NY 10022.

FIRST EDITION

Designed by William Ruoto

Library of Congress Cataloging-in-Publication Data has been applied for.

ISBN: 978-0-06-199918-5

11   12   13   14   15   OV/RRD   10   9   8   7   6   5   4   3   2   1

In memory of David Thompson

LONG GONE

PROLOGUE:
THE KISS

Alice Humphrey knew the kiss would ruin everything.

"You've heard what they say about pictures and a thousand words."

She looked up at the man—Shannon was his last name, the first hadn't registered. He was the one with the faded, reddish blond hair. Ruddy skin. Puffy, like a drinker.

She didn't like sitting beneath his eye level like this. In this tiny chair at her kitchen table, she felt small. Trapped. She mentally retraced her steps into the apartment, wondering if the seating arrangement had been planned for catastrophic effect.

Shannon and his partner—was it Danes?—had been waiting on the sidewalk outside her building. The two of them hunched in their coats and scarves, coffee cups in full-palmed grips to warm their hands, everything about their postures hinting at an invitation out of the cold. She, by contrast, hot and damp inside the fleece she had pulled on after spin class. She'd crossed her arms in front of her, trying to seal the warmth in her core as they spoke on the street, the perspiration beginning to feel clammy on her exposed face.

Shannon's eyes darted between the keys in her hands and the apartment door before he finally voiced the suggestion: "Can we maybe talk inside?"

Friendly. Polite. Deferential. The way it had been with them yesterday morning. Only a day ago. About thirty-one hours, to be precise. They'd said at the time they might need to contact her again. But now today they suddenly appeared, waiting for her on the sidewalk without notice.

"Sure. Come on up."

They'd followed her into the apartment. She'd poured herself a glass of water. They declined, but helped themselves to seats, selecting the two kitchen bar stools. She opted for the inside chair of the two-seat breakfast table, leaving herself cornered, she now realized, both literally and figuratively. But hers was the obvious choice, the only place to sit in the small apartment and still face her unannounced guests.

She'd unzipped her fleece, and found herself wishing she'd showered before leaving the gym.

They'd eased into the conversation smoothly enough. Initial banter up the stairs about how they should both get more exercise. Just a few follow-up issues, Shannon had explained.

But there was something about the tone. No longer so friendly, polite, or deferential. The surprise visit. Her heart still pounding in her chest, sweat still seeping from her scalp, even though she had finished her workout nearly half an hour ago. Maybe it was a subconscious shaped by television crime shows, but somehow she knew why they were here—not the reasons behind the why, but the superficial why. Even before the kiss, she knew they were here about her.

And then came their questions. Her finances. Her family. The endless "tell us agains": Tell us again how you met Drew Campbell. Tell us again about this artist. Tell us again about the trip to Hoboken. Like they didn't believe her the first time.

But it wasn't until she saw the kiss that she realized her life was about to be destroyed.

Shannon had dropped the photograph on the table so casually. It was almost graceful, the way he'd extended his stubby fingers to slide the eight-by-ten glossy toward her across the unfinished pine.

She looked down at the woman in the photograph and recognized herself, eyelids lowered, lips puckered but slightly upturned, brushing tenderly against the corner of the man's mouth. She appeared to be happy. At peace. But despite her blissful expression in the picture, the image shot a bolt of panic from her visual cortex into the bottom of her stomach. She inhaled to suppress a rising wave of nausea.

"You've heard what they say about pictures and a thousand words."

She'd pulled her gaze from the picture just long enough to look up at Detective Shannon. His clichéd words echoed in her ears, her pulse playing background percussion, as her eyes returned to her own image. There was no question that the man in the photograph was Drew Campbell. And even though the cognitive part of her brain was screaming at her not to believe it, she had to admit that the lips accepting his kiss were her own.

She ran her fingertips across the print, as if the woman in the picture might suddenly turn her head so Alice could say, "Sorry, I thought you were someone else." She felt the detectives looking down at her, waiting for a response, but she couldn't find words. All she could do was shake her head and stare at the photograph.

Alice Humphrey knew the kiss would destroy her life because thirty-one hours earlier she had stepped in Drew Campbell's blood on a white-tiled gallery floor. She'd fumbled for a pulse, only to feel doughy, cool skin beneath her trembling fingers. And until she'd seen this picture, she would have sworn on her very life that, other than a handshake, her palm pressed against his still carotid artery was the only physical contact she'd ever shared with the man.

She'd had a crappy year, but had never paused to appreciate the basic comforts of her life—its ordinariness, the predictability, a fundamental security of existence. All of that was in the past now.

Alice had no idea what would happen next, but she knew the photograph would shatter everything. And she knew this was only the beginning.

PART I

TOO GOOD TO BE TRUE

CHAPTER ONE

FOUR WEEKS EARLIER

Most of the best things in life came to Alice organically. Not because she asked. Not because she looked. Not because she forced. They happened because she stumbled onto them. The high-flying philosophical question of whether the pieces of her life fell into place through luck, randomness, fate, or unconscious intuition was way above her pay grade, but somehow things usually worked out for her.

She ended up an art major because a course she took on the art of Italian Renaissance courts turned out not to count toward her declared history concentration. She wound up back in Manhattan after college because she followed a boyfriend home. She'd found her current apartment when she overheard a man sitting next to her at a bar tell his friend that he'd been transferred to the Los Angeles office and would have to break his lease. The opportunity Drew Campbell handed to Alice came not only when she'd needed it most, but also in a way that felt exactly as it should—natural, discovered, meant to be.

The gallery was in the Fuller Building, one of her favorites. She paused on her way in to admire the art deco features dotted generously inside and out. The opening reception was the artist's first public appearance in a decade, so she expected the exhibition to be packed. Instead she found plenty of room to pace the spacious gallery, wineglass in hand, as she leisurely studied the overlapping abstract shapes, layered so meticulously on the canvases that it seemed they might leap weightlessly from the wall and float away into the sky.

She noticed him before he ever approached her, flipping through the price list as he admired one of the larger works, a carnival scene in oil. Beneath a few days of fashionable stubble, his face was very severe in a way that was both handsome and out of place in a froufrou gallery, but his clothing signaled he was in the right spot. She watched him speak to the emaciated, black-bunned woman she recognized as the gallery's owner. She wondered what he'd be paying for the canvas.

Alice was pleased when she felt him looking at her. Optimistic enough to meet him halfway across the gallery, she paused in front of an abstract of layered triangles and then smiled to herself as he made his way over.

"It's a shame there aren't more people here," he said. "Drew Campbell."

She returned the handshake and introduction.

"So, Alice, what are your theories about this dismal turnout?"

"It's crazy, right? You know some gallery down in Chelsea is packed tonight for a gum-chewing punk just out of art school who doodles celebrities. Meanwhile, this man could have been Jackson Pollock, and it's like Mormon night at the vodka bar in here."

The artist, Phillip Lipton, was at one time a recognized figure in the New York school of abstract expressionism, a contemporary of Pollock, de Kooning, Rauschenberg, and Kline. Apparently none of this was lost on her new acquaintance.

"I know an art dealer who used to represent him. You would not believe the player the old man used to be. You've heard of picky guys who only date skinny girls or blondes? Well, he supposedly only dated ballerinas, and yet—despite that very narrow limitation—always managed to have a new nimble babe at his side each week.

There was a joke that he must have been fattening them all up with steak and ice cream so the New York City ballet company would have to replace them one by one. He'd hold court in the Village at One if by Land."

She could picture the younger version of the artist there, smoking cigarettes, wearing that fedora he always seemed to sport in the few photographs available of him in that era. Now Lipton was a ninety-one-year-old man whose sixty-year-old wife was brushing away crumbs from his jacket lapel at an underattended exhibition with, so far, only two "sold" tags posted, including the one the gallery owner had just slipped next to the carnival painting Drew had been admiring.

"So you're interested in art?" Drew said.

"Until recently, it was my profession." She told him about her former job at the Met, truncating the long personal story behind her dismissal. It was easier to chalk her current unemployment up to the museum budget cuts and layoffs that had made newspaper headlines.

The conversation between them came easily. He had a good, natural smile. Earnest eye contact. The appearance of a genuine interest in what she had to say. It was strange: there was nothing sexual about it, and yet she felt herself getting pulled in, not by the man's looks or charm but by the refreshing feeling of being treated as if she mattered. Not merely as her father's daughter. And not like an out-of-work single woman whose petals had already begun to wilt.

As she felt herself brightening in a way she could barely remember, it suddenly dawned on her how eight months of unemployment had taken their toll. Without even recognizing the transformation, she had started to see herself as a loser.

Alice never meant to be a thirty-seven-year-old woman without a career, but she knew that plenty of less fortunate people would question the choices she'd made along the way. Even in the beginning, she hadn't gone to one of the intellectually rigorous prep schools that happily would have had her, opting instead to be with her more socially inclined friends. But, unlike most of them, she worked hard. She went to college—and not just a party school with a fancy reputation, but an actual school known for its academics.

Granted, it was a funky liberal arts college and not an Ivy League, and then followed by the few requisite years of postcollege floundering that were were typical for her crowd. The two-year stint as a publicist for a cosmetics company. That disastrous three-year marriage in St. Louis before she'd realized her mistake. But she'd started over, returning to school for her master's in fine arts. And when she was finished, she'd gone to work in the development office of what she believed to be the most impressive building in the world—the Metropolitan Museum of Art.

Now, in hindsight, she realized how silly and indulgent all of those choices had been. Her parents spent a fortune on high school tuition just so she'd land at an even more expensive college that no one aside from a few tweed-jacketed PhDs had heard of. Then she double-downed with that graduate degree.

When she'd landed the job at the Met, she'd been stupid enough to believe she'd earned it. Maybe if she had been hired for merit— her knowledge of art, her ability to raise money, her marketing experience, a demonstrated skill at something—she'd still be there in her cubicle above Central Park, quietly drafting the pamphlet to announce the upcoming Chuck Close exhibit to the museum's most generous donors.

Or if she had at least recognized the truth, maybe she would have predicted that a decision in her personal life would affect her employment. She would have realized how ridiculous she must have looked when she'd announced to her father that she no longer wanted his help. No more rent payments or annual "gifts." Her absolute insistence: *No more help, Papa.*

Well, unbeknownst to her, some of his help had being going to the museum, and when the donations dried up and the Met had to make layoffs, she was among the first on the chopping block.

It wasn't until she updated her résumé that she realized that her adult life didn't exactly add up to the perfect formula for employment in the current economy. In the eight months that had passed since her layoff, she had been offered precisely one job: personal assistant to a best-selling crime novelist. A friend who knew of Alice's plight was among a fleet of the man's rotating companions and suggested her for the job. She warned Alice that the man could be frugal, so when he wanted Alice to return his half-eaten carton of yogurt to the deli because he didn't like the "seediness" of the raspberry flavor, Alice had sprung for the new $1.49 carton of smooth blueberry. The friend had also warned Alice of his "nonconformist" ways, so Alice compliantly agreed when he'd asked her to restrain him atop his dining room table so he could figure out how his character might escape his predicament. But she had finally pulled the plug when the boss's two questionable characteristics merged together in a single request: that she personally participate in a three-way with him and a hired escort so he could collect "quotidian details" of the experience without paying double.

Alice promptly resigned, but still kicked herself at the manner in which she'd done it—blaming it on his erratic hours instead of raising her knee directly into the glorified subject of most of his research. Maybe it was because she'd been thinking about that short-lived job—and the belittlement it still invoked—that she wanted to believe the part of the conversation with Drew Campbell that came next.

"Would you be interested in managing a gallery of your own?"

Normally, she would have choked on her wine at the absurdity of the question, but Drew floated it past her in a way that felt as natural as an observation about the weather.

"Of course. I always assumed I'd work in the art world in some way or another. I think I just underestimated how hard it was to get and keep this kind of work."

The art world, as even tonight's featured artist exemplified, was a young person's domain. And Alice was a woman. And she wasn't even an artist. And at thirty-seven, she was already past her prime.

"I'll have to check on a few things, but you might be the perfect person for a new gallery I'm helping with."

"What kind of position?"

"Manager. It's a small place, but we need someone who will really pour themselves into it."

She was unemployed. Her last job was fetching coffee for a sociopath who should probably be on a sex offender registration. It was hard to believe anyone legitimate would hand her the keys to a gallery. Her skepticism must have shown in her face.

"Now don't go picturing a gallery like this. And I should probably warn you, it's a bit of a risk as far as employment goes. I've got a client—a guy I've bought art for—he's what his friends call eccentric. If he didn't have money, they'd call him a nutcase."

"Eccentric? I've fallen for that line before."

"Trust me. It's nothing weird. This is one of my oldest clients. He was a friend of my father's, actually, so he's been letting me help him out for years. With time, he's come to really trust me. Turns out he's a quiet old guy who likes the company of younger men. He treats them well, and they provide companionship, if you know what I mean."

"Not exactly subtle."

"Anyway, his most recent friend has been in the picture longer than most, and I guess my client is ready to provide a more substantial level of support. He wants a modest little gallery to showcase emerging artists. Of course one of the artists will have to be his friend. This kid's gotten his work in a few group showings, but he still hasn't landed a solo exhibit at a New York gallery."

"But thanks to your client, he'll soon be a featured artist."

"Exactly. And I'm sure he'll be very grateful to my client for the support."

"You keep referring to him as 'your client.'"

"Trust me. You've heard of him. And while there have been rumors about his personal life for decades, it's all unconfirmed, so I'm not about to out him. But, I kid you not, he is a serious collector. That piece I just held is for him. If I can find the right space and the right person to run a gallery, he won't get in the way. He won't even take credit for owning it. But he'll want it to be a place he'd be proud of. Cutting edge. A little antiestablishment, but really good stuff. This would be a good opportunity for someone in your shoes."

"Sounds like a good opportunity for anyone."

He shrugged. "I've quietly spoken to a few people, and they wouldn't pull the trigger. They're worried the owner will move on to some other passion project—a gallery today, a gourmet hamburger stand tomorrow. Then there's my client's consort to worry about. He can't be thrown to the wayside like any other artist."

"Not everyone would be so forthcoming about the backstory."

"I'm not willing to burn bridges to satisfy the whims of a fickle old man, even if I do love him like my own closeted gay uncle. Some of the more established people I've approached just aren't willing to take the leap under the circumstances. You might not have the luxury of their worries."

"If that's a nice way of saying beggars can't be choosers, consider yourself begged."

Like a teenage girl going home after her first concert, Alice left the gallery with a signed brochure from the exhibit and a feeling that the person she had met there just might change her life.

CHAPTER
TWO

Becca Stevenson had a secret.

Two secrets, really, tied together by the shiny gadget held between her fingertips.

C'mon. Just a little peek. I won't tell anyone.

She'd read those words over and over again. Only a minute or two had passed since they'd first appeared on the screen, but the stillness felt like an eternity. Not that there was actual stillness. She heard the New Jersey Transit guy announce, once again, the delay of the train arriving from Hackettstown. Heard the toddler on the next bench pester his mother for more Goldfish crackers. Heard the woman across from her "whispering" into her cell phone, insisting that the person on the other end of the line explain why he hadn't picked up last night, even though she hit redial until two in the morning.

But despite the noise of the train station, Becca felt stillness. In her head. In her hands. In her heart. She and Dan had been texting for nearly two weeks now, and they had developed a quick rhythm, responding to one another within a few seconds. Or, at least, she responded within a few seconds. So did he, usually. But like any conversation, even the best ones, their back-and-forths had to stop sometime. There had been occasions when she was tempted to be the one who cut off the banter—maybe politely, with a "gotta go" or "bye for now"—but it was always Dan who called it quits, suddenly falling quiet without warning. But he always came back, to her initial surprise and now delight.

She hadn't deleted a single entry. Their list of messages, cataloged in neat little green and white boxes of text, numbered well into the hundreds. Sometimes at night in her bed, she would scroll up to the very beginning and relive the entirety of their printed relationship on the backlit screen.

There had been so many sweet and funny and clever moments in their clipped exchanges, but probably no single message was as exciting as that first pop-up on her screen. The first text message she had ever received, just two days after pocketing her secret toy.

Sophie gave me your number. Do you mind? You seem fun. P.S. This is Dan Hunter.

Dan Hunter? Dan Fucking Hunter was texting Becca Stevenson? She'd been watching him silently since the seventh grade, when he was the first kid to download My Chemical Romance on his iPod. He'd been cute and funny even then. Now he was a jock who had dated three different cheerleaders, but she always sensed that he had another side to him. He listened to eighties punk music. Wore a lot of black, at least for a basketball player. And he was one of the first guys in school to get a tattoo. The fact that he was interested in her just proved he hid a little "alt" in him.

When he first contacted her, she didn't know what to think or feel, let alone say. She'd finally opted for casual and a little cool.

No problem. Sophie's my girl.

Of course, despite the chill attitude of her texts, she'd immediately chased down Sophie for the details.

"Holy shit, Becca. I looked up from my locker, and Dan Hunter and all his sweeping hair and blue eyes and big muscles are staring back at me, fucking confusing me, you know?"

Sophie was such a nerd with her baby-length bangs, black-framed glasses, and ridiculous SAT words, but deep down, she was pretty much the best friend Becca had ever had.

"And, what? He just asked for my number?"

"He said he saw you sneaking glances at your phone all the way through history class. I can't believe you haven't gotten busted for that yet. You know the school's zero-tolerance policy."

"Can you please skip the lecture? I seriously need every detail."

"There's no detail to give. He said he saw you fiddling in class and wanted to text you. He said you were cute."

"He said I was cute?"

"Oh, Jesus. Who swapped my friend with Hannah Montana?"

It hadn't been easy, but Becca had finally gotten Sophie to admit that Dan did have a special spark. And his texts were so . . . not what she'd expected. Cool. Almost kind of deep.

And it hadn't just been the messages. They'd been meeting. First behind the mall. Once at his house when his parents were out of town. There'd been a few times at the baseball field, kissing and whatever. But then three nights ago, it had been an invitation to meet him in the city. And his friends had been there. Friends from the team. Even a couple of cheerleaders. Becca had been nervous at first. She couldn't possibly fit in. But they'd been pretty cool with her. Dan was already talking about going to the city with her again.

And now Dan was asking her for more: *C'mon. Just a little peek. I won't tell anyone.* She found herself tempted. Liked the idea of being the kind of girl who could titillate a guy like Dan Hunter. Just a little peek.

She could slip into the ladies' room. Make sure to reveal the background. Make it a little raunchy.

A new message popped up on the screen. *You know you want to.*

He was right. She did.

No. It was better to make him work for it a little longer. Play hard to get. Make sure this was for real before giving him what he wanted.

She typed a response: *Very tempting. And very soon.*

That should serve its purpose. Buy her a little time.

In the meantime, she had someone else to meet. She saw the minivan pull up in front of the train station. Her ride was here. She had two secrets. Dan Hunter and the man whom she'd been meeting here nearly once a week for the last two months. They both made her feel special in ways she'd never known before.

CHAPTER THREE

Four days after Alice first met Drew Campbell at the Fuller Building, the conversation that once held life-changing promise now seemed like nothing but heady party talk.

"I hate to say I told you so." Lily's dark green eyes smiled at her over the rim of the Bloody Mary she was sipping on the other side of the tiny bistro table.

"Oh, yes. I know how much it pains you to be right. I mean, as pain goes, having to say you told me so is way up there: hot tar, waterboarding, the iron maiden."

Lily had skipped out of work early to meet her for a late lunch at Balthazar. Unfortunately, they weren't the only New Yorkers with fantasies of a leisurely afternoon spent lounging at a Parisian-style brasserie, authentically re-created in SoHo. Even at three o'clock, they'd had to wait thirty minutes for their postcard-sized table. Still, as Alice broke off another chunk of baguette, she had no regrets.

"What is an iron maiden anyway?" she asked.

"No clue," Lily said, tucking a loose strand of her pixie cut tightly behind her left ear before reaching for another *moule*. "At the very least it inspired years of big-hair, leather-pants metal music. Torture enough as far as I'm concerned."

"Thanks for kicking out of work early. You sure you won't earn the Gorilla's wrath?"

Lily was an editor for a travel magazine where her boss was so notorious for picking at her every move that he'd earned a special nickname. "Are you shitting me? There's no such thing as a wrathless half day. When he saw me walking out with my coat, he made sure to tell me he needed that piece on Florence tomorrow morning when it wasn't supposed to be due until Friday. Good thing for me it's pretty much done already."

Alice had met Lily in a spin class at her gym last summer. Their friendship had started with occasional groans about their shared discomfort as they grew accustomed to all that time spent bouncing on a bicycle seat. Then they'd moved on to casual conversations in the locker room after class. Once they realized they were both single and lived within a few blocks of the gym, they exchanged cell phone numbers with a promise of meeting in the neighborhood for a spontaneous drink.

Usually those "sometime we should" occasions were nothing but idle talk—imagined time people might spend if their lives weren't already cluttered and prescheduled—but Lily had actually called. About three drinks in that first night, they figured out that they'd spent their lives only a few degrees of separation from each other. Lily was three years older than Alice and was raised in Westchester, but had traveled in the same rebellious circles as Alice's older brother.

Now, six months into their friendship, Alice felt like she'd known Lily for years. And it was a comfortable kind of friendship. Unlike a lot of her other friends, Lily took Alice's last name in stride. She never asked for screening videos, for an autograph, or that annoying question that made Alice want to throw something: "What was it like to grow up with your father?" And unlike Alice's friends with similarly privileged upbringings, she had never once told Alice to run back to her parents for financial support. Most importantly of all, Lily Harper was honest. She was one of those rare friends who would tell someone what she needed to hear, not what she wanted. And when Alice had first called her after leaving the Fuller Building that night, Lily had told Alice that Drew Campbell was full of shit. Now, four days later, they were rehashing the case against him once again.

"I mean, you just happen to be unemployed, and he just happens to have the perfect job for you? A wealthy anonymous benefactor who will pay for the studio but allow you to run it? The kept young artist who has captured the closeted old man's heart?"

"I know, I know. You told me so. It was too good to be true."

"Well, I do hate to say it. The guy was just trying to get in your pants."

"Black pencil skirt actually. With tights."

"Fine, then—up your skirt and down your Spanxie pants. I swear, Alice. I might have to take away your sisters in cynicism membership card for this one. You can't tell when a guy's running a line on you?"

"You had to be there. He seemed legit."

"The good ones always do. How many women on the Sunday-morning walk of shame are saying the same thing? Tell it to the nurse at the STD clinic."

With the cacophony of the brasserie in full effect, Alice would not have known about the incoming call had she not felt the subtle vibration of her cell phone from her handbag against her thigh. She was about to ignore it but knew that if she didn't at least check the screen—as she had every twenty minutes for the last four days—she'd spend the rest of her lunch with Lily wondering maybe, just maybe.

She felt a tiny glimmer of hope when she read "Blocked" on the caller ID. Any of her usual callers—mom, brother, Jeff (who escaped all meaningful labels)—would have popped up in her directory. Lily nodded at her to take the call.

"Hello?" She used her index finger to plug her unoccupied ear and ignored the irritated stares of her fellow diners as she made her way to the front entrance.

By the time Alice returned to her table ten minutes later, Lily had finished her Bloody Mary and was playing a game on her phone. Alice's other friends would have either scolded her for disappearing so long or dropped some passive-aggressive comment about the boredom during the wait.

Not Lily.

"That call certainly put a smile on your face. I could see that goofy grin all the way from here. Jeff back in town?"

The unlabeled relationship she shared with Jeff Wilkerson had more ups, downs, and lateral turns than she could track over the years, but had last been on an upswing before he'd left town for a one-week trip to the West Coast.

"Nope. That, my dear friend who hates to say 'I told you so,' was the one and only Drew Campbell, art collector to the rich and famous."

"Let me guess: the gallery fell through, but he thought you might want to meet him for a drink anyway."

"Nope."

"Okay. He's dangling the job in front of you and wants to meet for dinner to discuss it further."

"Nope."

"My guesses are up. Just tell me."

"His client wants to go forward, and Drew wanted to know if the new manager—aka *moi*—can meet him at a space he's about to lease in the Meatpacking District."

Lily said nothing as a busboy added their empty plates to his already chest-high pile of white dishes.

"This is where you remind me he's full of shit, right?"

"I didn't say anything."

"You're supposed to warn me that when I get there, he'll have some story about the gallery falling through. Or the space will be unavailable. Or there will be a delay in the financing. But then he'll happen to know about a great bar nearby for a little chat."

"Sounds like you're doing a good enough job warning yourself."

"Maybe I should call him back. I can just say I found another opportunity."

"When does he want you to meet him?"

"Tomorrow at eleven."

"A.m.?"

"Of course. I really would deserve to lose my membership card if I fell for a business appointment near midnight."

"And that's it? He wants you to see the gallery space?"

"And to bring a résumé so he can do the requisite due diligence. All official-like."

Still, Lily said nothing.

"Go ahead and say it."

"What? I didn't say a word."

"You don't have to. I've got to admit, I'm thinking it myself. It's too good to be true. We've been running through all of the many reasons to blow this guy off for the last four days. Remember?"

"I remember."

"But?"

"But nothing. It's totally up to you."

"There has to be a catch, right?"

"Seemed so when the asshole wasn't calling. Now the asshole's calling with the perfect job."

"Jesus, you are such a contrarian."

"Am not," she said, sticking out her tongue.

"So, all right. I'll meet the man tomorrow. With my sisters in cynicism membership fully updated. Bullshit meter on high alert."

"And Mace," Lily added. "A little Mace never hurt anyone."

As she did more often than she would have liked, Alice allowed Lily to leave enough cash on the table to cover both of their meals. In the pattern that had developed, Alice would soon return the favor, but at a less expensive establishment.

"Oh, and Alice?" Lily's tone softened as she placed a reassuring hand on Alice's forearm. "I really do hope this is the real thing."

CHAPTER
FOUR

Hank Beckman watched the digital numbers change on the pump, careful to add only five bucks to the tank. He felt his stomach growl, and then stole a glance at his watch. Three in the afternoon, and nothing today but two cups of coffee.

He'd already paid for the gas—cash, just in case—but dashed back into the station to grab something to tide him over.

"Forget something?"

Just his luck. He stops for gas—at the high-traffic mega station outside the Lincoln Tunnel, no less—and happens upon the one and only gas station attendant in the country who could place a customer's face. Gold star for attentiveness. He raised a hand, both in a wave and to conceal his appearance. Damn, he was overdoing it with the paranoia. "A man's got to eat."

He turned away from the register to peruse the aisles. The usual convenience-store crap. Candy. Chips. Those weird, soggy sandwiches stored in triangular plastic containers. Fried pork rinds? He grabbed two granola bars and then a bottle of orange juice from the refrigerator case. Laid a five on the counter, then slipped the change into the plastic donation bucket on the counter, this one bearing a picture of sad-looking shelter animals.

He heard a bell chime against the glass door as it swung shut behind him. Tucking the OJ in the crook of his elbow, he ripped open one of the bars and ate it in three bites before getting settled behind the wheel of the Crown Vic. As he inserted the key into the ignition, he thought about turning around, driving back through the tunnel, and making his way downtown early.

He'd gone nearly two months without checking in on him. Two months since he'd been warned. Officially disciplined, as it had been put to Hank. But not one day had passed in those two months when Hank hadn't thought about the guy. Wondered what he was doing. Imagined how pleased the guy must have been without Hank around to monitor him.

But it was precisely because Hank had been on good behavior that he was willing to risk this brief check-in. Back before he'd been hauled out to the proverbial woodshed, he'd been watching the subject at night. His intentions had been noble—personal time for personal work—but the guy had noticed the pattern. On the upside, if the guy were still checking his back for Hank, he wouldn't be suspicious in the middle of the afternoon. No, this was the perfect time. Hank's field stops had gone faster than planned. He could easily steal ninety minutes out on his own without anyone asking questions. He'd already bought his one-point-six gallons of gas for the round-trip drive to Newark, just in case Tommy wondered about the fuel level when Hank returned the fleet car.

As Hank removed the ring of translucent plastic from the cap of his orange juice, he thought about Ellen. Poor Ellen. He hadn't realized it when he'd had a chance to make a difference, but his sister had been an addict. No different from the sad sacks he'd encountered (and judged) for years—junkies who told themselves they'd get off the needle next week, career offenders who said they'd retire after one last big score— Ellen had let something other than herself become a necessary part of her identity. In her case, that something was alcohol.

He remembered his sister commenting—usually with pride, but often in a resentful, teasing way if she'd had a glass of chardonnay or two—about his extraordinary discipline. "My little brother is the abstemious one in the family." "Hank will live to be a hundred, the way he takes care of himself." "My perfect baby brother."

He had missed the signs of addiction in his sister, but wondered whether, if Ellen were alive, she would spot them in him. Like a drunk on the wagon never stops craving the bottle, he had managed to restrain himself in the two months that had passed since the reprimand, but he had never stopped thinking about the man who killed his sister. And like an alcoholic assuring himself that this drink will be the last—even as he knows in his heart that he has no intention of ever letting it go—Hank started the engine, telling himself he would cruise down to the apartment in Newark, just this once, just to make sure the man hadn't gone anywhere without him.

CHAPTER
FIVE

There was a time when the name of Manhattan's Meatpacking District required no further explanation. It was the district where the meat was packed. Not only was the name self-evident, so was the neighborhood itself. Refrigerated trucks backed up to open warehouse doors, ready to transport the hanging carcasses that would become the city's finest steaks. Butchers—the real ones, with thick smears of pink wiped across their aprons—promised the early morning's finest cuts. The cobblestone streets, left untended since the notorious days of the Five Points slum, were fit only for industrial vehicles and the most seasoned pedestrians, who knew from years of experience precisely where to step to avoid a tumble. Even the air was tinged with the bloody odor of raw meat.

Now the neighborhood's name was simply a tip of the hat to history. On Alice's route from stepping off the 14D bus to the address Drew Campbell had given her, she passed an Apple store, the Hotel Gansevoort (site of the most recent bust of a celebrity offspring for drug dealing), and the Christian Louboutin boutique. She did notice as she made her way south that the luxuriousness of the surroundings became relative. As the $700, seven-inch heels at Louboutin faded from view, she passed a modest little wine bar, then a D'Agostino grocery, even a rather ordinary-looking brick apartment complex.

Despite nearly a lifetime in the city, she always got confused in this neighborhood. She'd spent her childhood in the Upper East Side. Stayed at her parents' townhouse on trips home from Philly in college. Lived with Bill for two years on the Upper West before the wedding and subsequent move to St. Louis. Briefly back to the folks' place postdivorce before she'd taken an Upper East Side studio of her own during the MFA program.

Even though she lived downtown now, she was still in the numbered grid, where streets ran east to west, avenues ran north to south, and the numbers on the grid always showed the way. This morning she was turned around in the tangle of diagonals known as Jane, Washington, Hudson, and Horatio, all labeled streets, yet intersecting with one another in knots.

She pulled out her iPhone and opened up Google Maps. After a right turn past the D'Agostino, she found herself on Bethune and Washington. She recognized the intersection, just one block from the dive Mexican joint that served pitchers of fume-exuding margaritas at sidewalk picnic tables.

Her inner naysayer—that voice in her head that kept warning her that Drew's offer was indeed too good to be true—tugged at her peripheral vision, forcing her to notice that she'd left the swank of the Meatpacking District and was heading away from the better parts of the West Village. A Chinese restaurant called Baby Buddha was boarded shut on the corner, the words "CLOSED Thanks you for your bussiness" spray-painted across the wood.

Past the boarded-up storefront, across the street, stood a prewar tenement with iron gates securing the lowest three floors of apartment windows. She suspected that if she walked a few more blocks, she'd eventually run into a joint needle-exchange, condom-distribution, check-cashing tattoo parlor. She summoned an image of herself, like Lucy in the *Peanuts* comic strips, sitting beneath a whittled wood sign bearing the words "Modern Art, 5 Cents."

But as she passed a closet-sized retail space featuring highbrow clothing for spoiled dogs, her outlook began to brighten. She spotted a For Lease sign in the next front window. She took in the remainder of the block. An independent handbag designer. A UK-based seller of luxury sweatshirts, which people now collectively referred to as "hoodies" to justify the prices. A flower shop. High-end shoe store. A ten-table restaurant run by a former finalist on *Top Chef*. Not a check-cashing tattoo parlor in sight. She crossed her fingers inside her coat pockets as she squinted at the approaching numerals waiting for her above the unoccupied space.

Jackpot. This was the spot. The address Drew had given her. She pressed her forehead against the front glass, cupping her hands at her temples as she peered into the empty space. The ceilings were at least fifteen feet high. Exposed heating ducts, but in a cool way. Smooth white walls, just waiting for art to be hung. She could picture herself there, wearing one of her better black dresses, gesturing toward oversize canvases that would provide the space's only color.

She jerked backward as a tap on her shoulder startled her from her daydream. She heard a faint *beep-beep* as Drew Campbell pressed the clicker in his hand, activating the locks of the silver sedan he'd parked curbside.

"So this is it, huh?"

"You sound disappointed," he said.

For some reason, people thought Alice was down even at her most enthusiastic. She had a theory that this was somehow attributable to a childhood spent with false hopes. She had been raised by parents who told her at every opportunity that she was better, she eventually realized, than she actually was. They'd had the best intentions, but their unconditional, unrealistic praise had in fact groomed her for disappointment. Having to serve as her own reality check had made Alice her own harshest critic.

Even now, she was incapable of feeling pride or excitement without immediately focusing on all the reasons she would eventually fail. She flashed back briefly to those comments she'd received periodically during her annual evaluations at the Met. Saw those signals she should have picked up on. Tried to push them into her past as Drew Campbell looked at her with impressed, expectant eyes, ready to give her a fresh start.

Drew tapped six digits into the keypad of the lockbox on the front door, and then caught the key that fell from the box. "I haven't signed the papers yet," he said. "Figured the gal who's going to run the place should have final approval."

As she watched him slip the key into the lock and push the door open, she tried not to draw the metaphorical link to a new chapter opening in her life. She tried not to get her hopes up. She told herself it still might not happen. But already she could picture herself with that same key in her hand, pushing open that very door, making a name for this still-unnamed gallery in the limitless world of art.

"What do you think?"

Admiring the polished white tile floor, Alice tried to play it cool. "It's small," she said, "especially if we need space for storage, but it's intimate, which would be right for this neighborhood. I like that it's off the beaten path of the usual Chelsea galleries. This area still has a lot of untapped potential."

"All those fashionistas need art for their luxury apartments, right?" Drew fiddled with a Montblanc pen as he spoke.

"One would hope."

He slipped a half-inch-thick laptop from a black leather attaché and opened it. "Let's see if we can't freeload off a neighbor's wireless signal. Yep, here we go." She watched as he maneuvered the cursor. Several windows opened simultaneously on the screen. The images flashed too quickly for her to process, but she caught black-and-white glimpses of exposed flesh, a nail, beads that made her think of a rosary.

"So I was pretty sure you'd be happy with the location, but as I warned you, there are a couple of catches."

Alice felt herself ground back down into the roots of reality. She heard Lily's voice—and her own running internal monologue—tugging at her once again. Too good to be true. No such thing as good luck. She tried her best to sound carefree. "So go ahead and break the news to me. There's a brothel running out of that back room, right? Something niche? Midget transvestites. Am I close?"

"Maybe I'm overselling the negatives, but just hear me out, okay? As far as I'm concerned, there are two little hitches. And, no, that's not a reference to two tiny cross-dressers. First"—he held up a thumb—"my client has a name for the place. The Highline Gallery."

"Nowhere neeeaaar the hurdle I was imagining."

"Boring, though."

Dickerings about the name of the gallery were small-time compared to the perils she'd been imagining, but the Highline moniker was pretty white-bread, the brand for both the new aboveground park running above Ninth Avenue and an adjacent multilevel concert hall. The Highline was to the Meatpacking District as Clinton was to Hell's Kitchen—an innocuous, sterile name created by real estate agents to whitewash the dust and blood and scars from a neighborhood's history.

Drew continued with the disclosures. "As you're probably wise enough to expect, the second catch is more of a doozie."

He turned the laptop to face her and wiggled his index finger along the touchpad. The staccato flashes of black-and-white images she'd previously glimpsed reappeared on the screen. "This, Miss Humphrey, is our toupee-covered bald spot, our makeup-covered wart."

Four separate images popped into view: a man's hairy thigh with crucifix-shaped welts scratched into his flesh; a fifty-cent plastic doll of the Virgin Mary dangling from a hangman's noose of cotton fiber; a metal fish—the kind she associated with evangelicals—with hot pink balls dangling from its gut; and a Bible headed into a steel shredder.

"Oh, Jesus."

"Nice word choice," Drew said.

"Please don't tell me this is the work of my silent partner's paramour."

"I'm afraid so, dear."

"It's like Mapplethorpe—only without the talent."

Drew shrugged. "Like I said, the man's a longtime friend, but I realize the wrinkles. No pun intended. If you want to pull out, I wouldn't blame you in the least."

She took a second look at the images. Alice had been raised in a wholly secular existence. She could count the number of times she'd been to church on two hands, and then only on holidays and for weddings. And yet even Alice had a visceral reaction to these images. They had no beauty. They were interesting only because they provoked. They were wrong.

"And what exactly is the Highline Gallery's loyalty to this artist?"

Drew used his index finger on the mouse to close the image files and open a Web site called www.hansschuler.com. A photograph of an attractive, early-thirtyish man with light brown curls occupied the screen. "Your first showing has to feature this idiot. Then two or three exclusive shows per year—maybe three or four weeks each—after that. In the interim, you can do whatever you want, but you'll still have to sell the guy. He's the weak link. All I ask is that you look before you leap. It's one thing to tell my client now that this might not happen. Quite another to search for someone else two months from now because you bailed."

Alice had known in her gut that something about this whole thing was too good to be true, but now she at least knew her enemy. If she took this job, Hans Schuler—artist-slash-paramour—was likely to be the constant pain in her ass for as long as she enjoyed her employment. She reminded herself that the best things in her life had come to her organically.

"Okay, I'm in."

"Really? All right, then. I can let the leasing company know I'm ready to sign the paperwork now. You want to come with? They're out in Hoboken, but it's a nice day for a drive."

Given the gallery owner's desire to remain anonymous, Alice supposed that Drew was going to be the closest thing she had to a functional boss. After she'd been laid off from the museum, one of her former coworkers let slip that Alice, unlike her colleagues, hadn't gone the "extra mile" by participating in activities outside the formal job. It couldn't hurt to start putting her best foot forward at the start.

"A drive sounds good."

CHAPTER SIX

Drew accelerated through the loop into the Holland Tunnel. She could tell he enjoyed the way the BMW handled the curves, low and tight. She felt like she should say something impressive. Something about torque or suspension or German engineering. All she came up with was, "I can't even remember the last time I drove a car."

Growing up, her parents had a chauffeur for the family in the city, so her only opportunities to drive had been at their house in Bedford or on an infrequent visit to her father's place in Los Angeles. She went through the teenage ritual of obtaining a license but had never been particularly comfortable behind the wheel. Now she preferred her nondriving existence, tooling around Manhattan by foot, subway, and the occasional taxi in bad weather.

"That's what happens when you grow up in the city." Drew hit his fog lights as the sedan hit the tunnel. "You grow up in Tampa, Florida, and you drive. My friends say I'm crazy for keeping a car in the city, but I like the freedom to hop behind the wheel and go whenever and wherever I want."

She didn't recall telling Drew she'd been raised in Manhattan. He must have Googled her before offering her the job. Lord knew she'd entered her own name in search engines before, simply out of boredom-induced curiosity.

On the spectrum of Google-able names, Alice Humphrey fell somewhere between Jennifer Smith and Engelbert Humperdink. Most of the hits belonged to a scientist who had written what was apparently a politically divisive book about global warming. More recently, sixteen-year-old Alice Humphrey of Salt Lake City had been kicking butt and taking names on her high school soccer team. But this particular Alice Humphrey had her own online existence. Unfortunately, most of it was not of her own making. Sure, there was her Facebook page, as well as a couple of mentions for her work on museum events. But any marks she had made out there in the virtual world as Alice Humphrey the woman were far outweighed by mentions of Alice Humphrey, former child actress and daughter to Oscar-winning director Frank Humphrey.

She was tempted to ask Drew whether it made a difference. To ask whether she would have gotten the job if she had been just plain old boring Alice Humphrey, with, say, a schoolteacher mother and an accountant father. But to ask that would be unfair, both to Drew and to her. There was no correct answer, and no appropriate response for her to then offer in kind. She no longer wanted to take anything from her father, but she was in fact his daughter. That was never going to change. And so far, Drew hadn't uttered one word about her family. For her to raise the issue, just because of an innocuous comment about driving, would officially make her the freaky thin-skinned girl.

"So what exactly do you do, Drew?"

"Well, I've got two possible responses to that question. One—the answer I might give to a woman on a first date—is that I'm an entrepreneur. Are you suitably impressed?"

"Honestly? I'm not sure I've ever understood entrepreneurship as a job description."

"Which is why there's a second option—the one my mother might give you. If my mother were here—and not mixing up her it's-finally-noontime martini down in Tampa—she'd probably tell you I'm a spoiled kid living off his family's money."

Apparently she wasn't the only person in the car with delayed-cord-cutting issues. "Well, if those two versions are your only choices, I'd stick with the first."

"Somewhere between asshole and pathetic daddy's boy lies the truth, which is that I live a really great life and figure out ways to make people money in the process. Like, say I go to a tiny little restaurant with a young chef who's doing everything right; I'll see if he's the kind of guy with bigger dreams that might require investors. Then I try to get a deal done and take a little commission for myself in the process."

"Why does your mom give you a hard time?"

"Because usually the people I turn to for the seed money are the same two guys I've been working for since I was mowing lawns for the snowbirds as a kid. And they happen to be my dad's friends, which makes them only slightly less despicable than the AntiChrist."

"And one of these men is my new boss?"

"To the extent you have a boss."

Drew pulled next to a parking hydrant in front of a rehabbed town house and hit the emergency blinkers. The ground floor's front window was lined with commercial real estate listings. He was out of the car before she'd even unbuckled her seat belt. He tossed the keys on the driver's seat before shutting his door. "You can drive, right?" he hollered from the curb. "Just in case?"

"Yeah, sure."

She watched through the glass as he spoke first to the receptionist, then shook hands with a leggy woman with spiky black hair. She walked to a file cabinet and returned with some paperwork. He removed a pen from his sports coat pocket and gestured toward the car. Spiky woman was looking at her now. Was Alice supposed to wave or something? She pretended to fiddle with the car stereo, then saw Drew leaving the building in her periphery with the paperwork.

He hopped back into the driver's seat, placed the documents on the center console, and began a rapid-fire signing of pages that had been pretabbed with hot pink tape.

"Creepy in there," he said as he scrawled. "Those girls are all way too pale and tall. I felt like a field mouse dropped into the middle of an anaconda tank."

"So you said you find ways to make other people money. Does my new boss see the Highline Gallery as a hobby, or is it actually supposed to turn a profit?"

He snapped his Montblanc into his coat pocket and tapped the contract against the steering wheel. "Excellent question, Alice." Stepping out of the car, he glanced back at her. "I guess we'll find out, won't we?"

CHAPTER
SEVEN

Joann Stevenson felt a tongue between her toes and jerked her leg back, letting out a high-pitched squeal.

"Sebastian!"

Her shih tzu matched her yelp as he leaped to the floor, then back onto the bed near her head. She couldn't help but giggle as his fluffy nine pounds bounced around her pillow.

"I thought you said we had to be quiet."

She felt a warm mouth against the back of her neck. This time, the kisses were definitely not Sebastian's.

"We *do* have to be quiet."

"Mmm, you sure about that?"

She felt Mark's bare skin against hers beneath the sheets. Felt his knee rub against the back of hers. She turned to face him. Saw him smile before he kissed her.

"Very sure."

"Absolutely certain?"

She raised a finger to his lips. "Be very, very quiet."

She fumbled for one of Sebastian's smooshy toys from the top of the nightstand and tossed it across the room. He happily followed.

"Good dog," Mark whispered.

She hadn't been kidding about the need for silence. They stifled their giggles and adjusted their bodies as necessary with each squeak of the mattress, each knock of the headboard against the bedroom wall. She struggled to choke back her own sounds at that crucial moment. Bit her lip so hard she thought she might bleed.

Afterward, they shared silly, silent, sweat-soaked grins. She nestled her way into the crook of his right arm and placed her head on his chest.

"I don't want to move."

"Me neither."

"You're a scientist. Can't you invent a machine that lets us hit pause and stay here naked for a week while the rest of the world remains still?"

"I adore you, Joann, but I don't think either one of us would be faring very well if we kept this up for a week straight."

"We could pause for showers and nourishment."

"Now *that* sounds like a plan."

A monotone beeping erupted beside her, and she let out a pained groan as she slapped the top of the alarm clock.

"Do I even want to know what time it is?"

She gave herself twenty minutes between snooze alerts, and the latest round of beeping marked the end of the third respite. "Eight o'clock."

"Crap. I need to be on campus by nine. So how are we sneaking me out of here?"

After fifteen years as a single mother, Joann had never—not once, not ever—allowed a man to spend the night in her bed while Becca was home. Sleepovers in front of her kid were a strict no-no on Joann's list of self-imposed rules. But she'd known the previous night that Becca would be out with her friends until ten. And things with Mark had heated up when she'd asked him inside after the restaurant. She'd known him for two months now. Had hit double digits in dates. And he was—well, he was different.

So she'd broken her own rules. As if she were the high-schooler and Becca the parent, Joann had sneaked Mark into her bedroom before Becca returned home. Left Becca a note in the kitchen: "Decided to hit the hay early. Knock if you need anything. Apples and really tasty cheddar in the fridge if you want a snack. Love, Mom."

Now she had to sneak the boy out.

She climbed from bed and pulled on her dog-walking sweat suit. Sebastian hopped excitedly at her feet. She cracked open the bedroom door, listening for the usual household sounds. Becca's sleep schedule was unpredictable. Sometimes she sprung from bed at the crack of dawn to surf the Net or to catch up on whatever TiVo'd show she wanted to kibitz about with her friends at school. Other times, she was truly her mother's daughter, hitting the snooze button until Joann had to drag her from bed.

The house was silent.

"Coast is clear," she whispered.

She admired the leanness of Mark's body as he pulled on the jeans and striped shirt he'd worn the previous night. Forty-five years old, but the man looked good. She waved him into the hallway, past her daughter's room. At the top of the stairs, he took her hand and pointed to the first step. They took each step in synchronicity, walking with a single gait. She gave him a quick good-bye kiss at the door, then watched him through the living room window, making his way to the Subaru he'd parked on the street, two houses down.

She heard a low growl and looked down to see Sebastian with one of her UGGs in tow.

"Hold your horses, little man." She leashed him up, then paused at the bottom of the staircase, wondering whether to wake Becca before their walk. Becca could get dressed in ten minutes flat when necessary, and it was good to see the girl get some much-needed sleep.

She and Sebastian kept their usual pace on the usual route around the usual block. Most people—and dogs for that matter—would have tired of this morning routine long ago, but she liked to think that both she and Sebastian appreciated this ten-minute ritual as "their" time. Between raising a kid and working full-time as a re-cords clerk at the hospital, life tended toward chaos. At least she and Seb could count on their walks.

Unlike too many of her mornings, Joann found her thoughts during this particular jaunt to be peaceful. In the fifteen years she'd been trying to build a life for Becca, Joann had been lonely. She had a few friends at the hospital, but they were married with younger children and didn't have the need for friendships that extended past working hours. She had met some men along the way, but none of them ever stuck. She had a kid, after all. She had all of her rules as a result. Not many men were willing to abide. And the few who had? None had ever turned out to be worth what felt, to Joann at least, like an awful lot of effort.

Until Mark. She'd met him at the prospective-students reception she had forced Becca to attend. Becca fostered fantasies of attending design school at Parsons in New York City, but Joann certainly couldn't afford the tuition, and the last thing she wanted for her kid was to be unemployed and saddled with debt at the age of twenty-two. She was hell-bent on getting her into a state four-year college.

Even with her single-mother status hanging out there for all to see, given the nature of the event, she'd been certain Mark was interested. He'd gone out of his way to catch up to her and Becca after the panel discussion to speak to her about the university's physics department. Becca barely hid her indifference, but Joann feigned a deep interest in the school's brand-new lab facilities. When she finally said good-bye, she was disappointed he didn't ask for her number. But two days later, there he was, roaming the hallways of St. Clare's Dover General Hospital in search of the records department.

"Are you lost?" she'd asked.

"Not anymore. Call me old-fashioned, but I just couldn't hit on you in front of your daughter. It's okay I'm here, right? If not, if I read things wrong the other night, I can—I don't know, awkwardly excuse myself with some ridiculous cover story?"

"As curious as I am to hear what you'd come up with, no, a cover story is definitely not necessary."

They were two months in, and nothing about Mark had once felt like work. They talked, dined, walked, kissed, and made love effortlessly. She kept reminding herself to take it day by day, but she found herself imagining a future with him.

And it wasn't only her love life that was falling into place. After a few rough teenage months, Becca seemed to be back to her normal self. No more skipped classes. No more missed curfews. She'd even set aside some of her more rebellious ways, hanging out with a few of the popular kids at school.

As they approached the house, Sebastian—as usual—pulled against his leash. She let go, allowing him to drag the thin brown strip of leather behind him as he ran to the door. She opened it for him and followed him inside.

"Becca," she called out as she hung her keys on a cat-shaped hook in the entranceway. "Time to get up."

Nothing. Sebastian beat her to the top of the stairs and scratched at Becca's door.

"Come on, sleepy girl. I'll drive you, but we've both got to get going."

Still nothing.

She opened the bedroom door, expecting to find her daughter in that same sleeping position she'd used as a toddler—on her side at a diagonal, head rested on her forearm, one leg straight, the other bent like Superman taking flight, blankets and pillows scattered across the bed.

But the bed was empty.

She knocked on the bathroom door down the hall. Nothing. Opened the door. No one.

She walked back to the bedroom for another look at Becca's unmade bed. Was it her imagination, or were the sheets bundled into the same knot as when she'd quickly pulled the door shut last night to hide the mess from Mark? Same with the bathroom: Becca's paddle-shaped hairbrush was tossed on the right side of the sink counter, and the adjacent bottle of gel was capless, despite Joann's repeated reminders about the cost of dried-out hair products.

Joann tried to convince herself she was wrong. Becca must have woken early and left for school already. Maybe she realized Mark was over and snuck out to give them privacy.

But as much as her brain tried to create a simple explanation, somehow Joann knew—truly *felt* the truth, at a cellular level. Her daughter had never come home last night. And the explanation wouldn't be simple, if it ever came.

CHAPTER
EIGHT

"**P**lease tell me this is one of your practical jokes."

It had been three weeks since Drew Campbell had signed the lease for the Highline Gallery. Now she stood, one night before the grand opening, feeling tiny beneath the eighteen-foot ceilings and next to Jeff Wilkerson's six-foot-three frame.

Jeff's comment was a reference to her long-standing habit of testing what she called his Indiana goodness.

"I know," he would sometimes say, "I'm gullible."

But *gullible* was not a word Alice would choose to describe Jeff. To call a person gullible was to imply he was stupid. But Jeff was no dummy. He'd been a top student at Indiana University, both as an undergraduate and then in law school, moving to New York City to work at one of the world's largest firms. But after seven years of slaving away at billable hours, he realized that life as a big-firm partner wouldn't bring any monumental changes, so had hung out a shingle on his own.

No, nothing about Jeff was gullible. He was well read and refined, brilliant even, as much as Alice hated the overuse of that word. But he still had that Indiana goodness. He was trusting. Earnest. Vulnerable. He wasn't the kind of person who even contemplated the possibility that others would fabricate facts for mere entertainment. Jeff was good. And his vulnerability made him sweet. It also made him a tempting target for people like Alice.

She'd lost count of the number of times he'd fallen for her ridicu-lous stories: that some breeds of cats could grow their tails back, that a car's stereo would stop working if the transmission fluid fell too low, that she'd had a bit part in the Aerosmith video for "Janie's Got a Gun." As for that last one, even when he called to complain he'd watched the entire clip on YouTube without spotting her, she only persuaded him to watch a second time as she listened, stifling her giggles.

Granted, her pranks had occasionally misfired. To this day, Jeff was convinced that her father disliked him because, on her recom-mendation, Jeff had eschewed the usual handshake on their first introduction, opting for a flash of the peace sign instead. Her father was bemused by the episode, but Alice saw no point in disabusing Jeff of his impressions, because in truth her father did not like Jeff, but for entirely different reasons.

She kept expecting Jeff to stop falling for her jokes, but he insisted she had a poker face that could break a casino. He'd express disbelief, and like Lucy with her football, she'd persist that *this time* she was serious. She suspected he often feigned the credulity, but even so, her white lies and his Indiana goodness formed one of the few patterns that had cemented in their ever-fluid relationship.

Unfortunately, this was not another occasion for leg-pulling. They stood side by side, Jeff with his hands on his hips, Alice with crossed arms, perusing the series of black-and-white photographs.

"Those of us in the art world would refer to this as high concept," she said.

"Nice try for your consumer base, but you forget that I know you. And I know that *you* know this is a bunch of pretentious crap."

She tried out her most authoritative gallery-managing voice. "The artist refers to the SELF series as a portrait in radical introspection. By examining the baseness of raw physicality, we reveal our true selves and can therefore achieve a higher level of inner reflection." She'd been diligent throughout the day in referring to Hans Schuler as "the artist" and to these photographs as the "SELF series." As she stumbled through the words, she realized it might take more than a day to overcome the bad habits formed over the last two weeks, when she continually referred to Schuler as the "German Boy Toy" and to his pictures as her "porn collection."

The centerpiece of the series was a photograph he called *Fluids*, featuring a taffylike strand of drool stretched from his lips to the bloody bite marks in his wrist. His hairy wrist. Prior to seeing the diverse variety of exposed Schuler flesh in close-up, she had no idea that one body could contain so much fur. She posed next to the *Fluids* photo in mock contemplation, placing the hook of her index finger beneath her chin.

"Can you picture me now on the cover of *New York* magazine? I can already imagine the tagline: 'New Highline Gallery Seeks to Mainstream Radicalism.' "

He shook his head. "That is scary. You could actually pull that off, Al. Maybe you should have been an actress after all."

She usually hated all iterations of shorthand for her already short name, but for some reason, when Jeff had taken to calling her Ally and then Al when they'd first met seven years ago, she had never minded.

"I feel like I'm selling snake oil. Radical introspection? What does that even mean, and why would we want to mainstream it?" She found the photographs aesthetically unappealing and intellectually vapid, so had simply pulled catchphrases from the artist's Web site when drafting her own materials for the exhibit. "Please remind me I just have to make it through this first show, and then I can start highlighting actual artists."

According to her deal with Drew, the Highline would open with an exclusive three-week showing of Schuler's SELF series. She would have to continue selling Schuler's work afterward, but could move on to showcasing other works.

"Just hang in there, all right? This is a good gig. You're going through the rough patch now."

She grimaced. "I don't think I like the idea of anything *rough* or *patchy* with our friend Hans here."

"So what is the man who bites himself bloody like in person?"

She plopped herself down on the low white leather banquette at the center of the gallery space and clucked her tongue. "You see. Now *there's* the catch."

"You mean to tell me that Hans's hairy porn *isn't* the catch?"

"Just a part of it, I'm afraid. Schuler apparently read one too many J. D. Salinger obits and has decided he's a recluse."

"Salinger went into hiding because he couldn't stand the public attention anymore. Does your guy realize no one's even heard of him?"

"First of all, he's so *not* my guy. And yes, of course he realizes this, but he thinks being a supersecret man of mystery will give him an allure. Drew tried to persuade him otherwise, but he says the only appearances that matter are the images he chooses to reveal in film."

"But you'll meet him at his show?"

"Nope. He's not coming."

"That's . . . well, that's ridiculous. How does he expect to sell anything?"

"That's where we get to the mainstreaming part. How much do you think a Hans Schuler will run you?"

"Clueless on that, as you well know."

"Guess."

They'd had countless discussions about the randomness of art prices. Art was worth whatever a buyer was willing to pay in an arm's-length transaction on the open market. "I don't know. I guess it depends on how many photographs he's printing and signing. Assuming he runs a series of—what, a couple hundred?—I'd guess you're charging at least a few thousand dollars."

"Seven hundred bucks."

"Dudes in Union Square Park charge more than that."

"That's why he says he's mainstreaming radicalism. He's making high-concept art available to any and all. And there's no limited print run. Take a look at that lower right-hand corner there."

Jeff did a half-raise forward to get a closer look. "What a cheese-ball."

Instead of marking each piece 1/some number to indicate where a particular print fell in a limited numbered series, Schuler had penciled "1/∞" onto every photograph to indicate an infinite run. According to him, there was no need to restrict art's supply to make it precious. The very advantage of photography as a medium, he pontificated in the artist's notes that accompanied the prints, was the ability to produce identical replications. By lowering the price, he would make his work accessible to more people, making him more influential than any artist who sold only a handful of pieces, no matter the price.

Alice suspected that Schuler himself didn't believe a word of his trite puffery. The plain fact was that Schuler's plan, if successful, would pocket him far more cash than a traditional showing for an unknown artist could possibly hope to yield.

She walked to the low white desk at the front of the gallery, removed an item from the top drawer of the steel side-return, and tossed it in Jeff's direction.

"Nice catch."

He inspected the tiny thumb drive. "Self," he said, reading the simple personalization aloud. "So what is it?"

"Yet another piece of Schuler's gimmick. Every buyer gets one of these stupid thumb drives. Everything you could possibly want to know about Schuler is then uploaded to the buyer's computer."

She unplugged the gallery's own computer, a slim Mac laptop, and resumed her seat next to Jeff. "I guess if customers want to know more about him, I'll just refer them to the thumb drive and his Web site." She pulled up a familiar bookmark.

Jeff moved closer to get a look. They'd known each other so long that his knee against hers, his arm around her shoulder—they weren't signs of passion or romance, but a level of familiarity and physical intimacy that remained between them regardless of where they were in their on-and-off experimentations with coupledom. "Not much of a site if that's going to be his only venue."

The home page was a stark black screen with Schuler's name in white block letters, along with three links: New Work, Galleries, and Bio. She clicked on each link so Jeff could get the idea. The New Work page featured thumbnails of the photographs now surrounding them in larger proportions. The Galleries page referred to the Highline Gallery, with a promise of "additional venues to be announced." The bio, supposedly a short version, listed training at an art school in Germany, some group exhibitions around Europe, and even a few grants.

"Someone gave him money to support this garbage?"

Maybe Jeff did have some skeptical bones in his body.

"Oh, who knows? Those grants could all be coming from our mutual benefactor, for all I care." She gently clicked the laptop shut.

There was a moment when neither of them filled the silence of the empty space. When his knee was still against hers. The arm still around the shoulder. Eye contact.

"Look, I know you'll be fine, but just be careful not to make any affirmative representations to your customers about his background. Limit your talk to his work. If anyone wants to know his credentials, steer them back to the art itself."

"Well, for a seven-hundred-dollar photograph, I doubt I'll be getting the third degree about his bona fides."

"I just don't want to see you get sued for fraud."

"Got it, counselor."

The moment between them had passed. She slipped the thumb drive into her jeans pocket. Retrieved their coats from the backroom. Tucked the tiny laptop into her gigantic purse. Took in the majesty of this space—*her* space, sort of—one last time before flicking each of a long row of light switches like dominoes, rendering the cavernous room dark but for the hints of street light fading through the front glass.

Jeff held the door open for her. "You're lugging that laptop around with you?"

"It's a hundred times faster than my dinosaur. A perk of the job."

"You're excited, aren't you?"

"Of course." She managed her tone of voice as if the gallery opening were no big deal, but inside she felt the same way she had as a child, clicking her knees together in the dressing room as her mother instructed her to sit still for the nice makeup lady. Something big was about to happen. And she'd be at the center of it.

CHAPTER
NINE

Thanks to the radio station's Two-for-Tuesday playlist, Hank lost track of time tapping on the steering wheel to the beat of "Satisfaction," followed by "Shattered." *Sha-doo-be. Shattered, shattered.*

He was pulled back into reality as the DJ with the corny voice introduced a block of Steve Miller Band. All he needed was to have "Abracadabra"—the worst song in history, by his ear—stuck in his head for the rest of the day. He switched off the radio, looking up for a double take at the redhead cruising up the sidewalk on the opposite side of the street. She wore those oversize Jackie O shades women went for these days, the heavy collar on a peacock blue coat flipped up around her face. Sky-high black stiletto pumps, the kind that look French and expensive. She might be a real bow-wow beneath it all, but she was rocking a look all right. Classy but with a little edge.

He looked at his watch. Crap. He'd been parked here for over twenty minutes, waiting with his camera for something worth photographing. Stupid. He could be spotted. Or someone downtown might wonder why he had so much solo fieldwork this week. Or, thanks to his little gas stops, Tommy in the garage might eventually notice that Hank was getting some damn good mileage out of the Crown Vics.

Hank had told himself four days earlier that the afternoon drive to Newark was a onetime deal, a harmless peek to make sure he could find the man if necessary, just in case. But this was his fourth detour in as many days. During yesterday morning's drive, he'd sworn it would be the final drop-in. And Hank really believed he had meant it. But then he saw the car. A BMW. As in Big Money Wagon. Granted, it was a 3-series, not one of the super-high-end ones. Still, it was a better ride than this scumbag should be sporting.

He'd seen the guy—he didn't like to use his name, not even mentally—walk from his crappy building to the apartment complex parking lot. But then instead of the man's familiar blue Honda, he'd headed for the gray BMW. Hank had hoped to follow him. He'd even been willing to miss an eleven o'clock debriefing if necessary. But the guy had simply opened the driver's side door and then closed it again, forgotten iPod in hand.

When Hank got the skinny on the plates, he'd felt a familiar rush of adrenaline—that feeling he experienced whenever he was in the hunt. The BMW's registration came back to Margaret Till of Clifton, New Jersey. Maybe the guy's new mark. Maybe Hank could warn her before she fell too deep.

When he finally gave up on the apartment yesterday, he'd buzzed by the woman's address in Clifton instead, eager to learn Margaret Till's connection to the man in Newark. He'd spotted her in the front yard, tending to begonias off the brick walkway with a tiny shovel and lime green canvas gloves, accepting a peck on the top of her head from the man of the house, still pulling on his suit jacket, late for work. A freckled girl with two missing teeth played jacks on the sidewalk. And beyond the girl was a gray BMW sedan, parked in the driveway next to the Lexus coupe that the happy husband was crawling into.

With one look at the car, Hank knew Margaret Till was not the man's latest mark. It wouldn't have been the first time a Mrs. Wholesome June Cleaver type stepped out on her family, but the problem was the BMW's license plate: he recognized it, but it wasn't the one that belonged on Margaret Till's BMW. Last time he'd seen that combination of numbers and letters was two months ago, on the bumper of that scumbag's blue Honda.

When Hank returned to the man's apartment complex today, his BMW was still parked in the lot, adorned with Till's stolen license plates. The switched plates probably meant the car was hot. Hank was tempted to drop the dime on the guy with an anonymous call to the locals, but car theft was chump change. Hank wasn't about to risk exposure of his unauthorized stakeout missions for some chippy Class C felony that would get bumped down to probation on the county criminal docket.

Now he'd wasted twenty minutes parked on the street in a white Crown Vic in full view. This wasn't exactly the hood, but someone might still make a G-man on the lookout. He was about to call it a day, maybe even for good this time, when he noticed the redhead again. Big shades. Blue coat. Looking great. Making her way up the steps with that same confident stroll she'd owned on the sidewalk. Right to his guy's apartment door.

He ducked even lower in his seat.

Knock, knock, knock. The door opened. A quick kiss on the lips, and then the redhead walked inside.

Figuring a woman like that would hold a man's attention for the near future, he stepped from his car, walked through the apartment complex parking lot to the BMW, and searched for the vehicle identification number through the front window. A folded copy of *New York* magazine blocked his view of the dash.

He thought about trying the door, but knew in his gut it would be locked. It was all about the risk–reward ratio. Low odds of reward. Medium to high risk of setting off a car alarm. Basic math told him to let it go for now.

He made his way back to the Crown Vic. Felt his pulse beat quicker than expected as he imagined a nosy neighbor calling 911 about the stranger near the BMW. Kept the key in the ignition just in case he needed to roll.

Nothing happened for the next forty minutes.

Nice car. Pretty girl. He'd spent so much time thinking about this man over the last seven months that he fancied himself something of an expert about his fundamental nature. And his expertise was telling him that his time watching Travis Larson had not been wasted. There was something here after all.

CHAPTER
TEN

Alice remembered a time when the sultry baritone of her mother's determined voice could cut through a crowded room like a diamond through glass. She didn't know whether a woman's voice simply faded with age, or if changes in a woman's life somehow worked their way into vocal cords, but now she found herself leaning in to hear her mom over the din of the busy restaurant.

"You should have seen our girl, Frank. She was just wonderful. The way she talked about the artwork, she had those people in the palm of her hand."

Alice had no problem making out her father's booming words from across the table. "Alice has always been good at anything she tries her hand at. I've told her that from the time she was born."

"Still, you should have been there to see it firsthand."

Alice caught her mother's eye and gave her a quick shake of the head, but it was too late.

"Obviously I would have liked to have been there, Rose, but our baby girl's all grown up. She doesn't need her father looking over her shoulder all the time. Wouldn't want to make it all about the old man now, would we?"

Tonight had been the official opening of the new Highline Gallery, and Alice was celebrating at Gramercy Tavern with Jeff and her parents. To anyone overhearing the conversation at their table, they would have sounded like any normal family, two proud parents fawning over their daughter, the mother taking a shot at the father's absence from the main event.

"Of course you could have gone, Papa."

Frank Humphrey had never wanted to be called Daddy or Dad. In fact, Alice suspected he had never even wanted children or a marriage. His habit of casting, and then bedding, his leading ladies probably could have kept him content for life. But he'd managed to knock up the acclaimed up-and-comer Rose Sampson during the production of their second film together, *In the Heavens*.

These days, unwed pregnancies were a Hollywood norm, but in 1969, even the film crowd still followed the traditions of the old nursery rhyme—maybe not about first-comes-love necessarily, but certainly about marriage coming before the baby carriage. When Frank Humphrey and Rose Sampson wed, *Life* magazine pronounced America's most sought-after young director and the actress he'd twice directed to best actress nominations "The King and Queen of New Hollywood." Five and a half months later, Alice's older brother, Ben, was born.

Where was Ben? Alice now wondered. He'd been a no-show at the gallery, texting her that he'd meet them at the restaurant. Fifteen minutes into cocktails, his seat at the table remained empty. She tried to write off the pit in her stomach as a byproduct of his past.

"We're so proud of you, dear." Her mother patted her gently on the shoulder as she spoke, but with her gaze still directed at her husband. The silence that followed was awkward.

Luckily, Jeff was there to fill it.

"Great turnout tonight. Did you sell much?"

"Not everything's about money, Jeff."

Had she been seated next to her father, she would have nudged him under the table. Poor Jeff. She was certain he would have preferred to be anywhere other than the "celebratory family dinner" her mother had been determined to organize, but he had insisted on accompanying her after Lily had come down with a stomach flu.

Alice had been careful to engineer the seating arrangements at the round table: her father next to her mother, then her, then Jeff, and then Ben was to be the buffer between Jeff and her father. But thanks to that empty fifth seat, her dad had a clear shot at Jeff. And, as always, he'd taken it. And, as usual, Jeff deflected the bullet.

"Of course not, Mr. Humphrey."

Alice jumped in before the discussion could escalate. "It's actually a good thing my friends turned out, or the place wouldn't have looked so full. We had pretty good publicity leading up to the opening—mentions in *Time Out* and *New York* magazine—but about half of the crowd were people I know."

"Gee, I wonder how all your friends heard about it," Jeff said with a smile.

She filled her parents in on the joke. "I sort of buried every person I've ever met with Evites, Facebook alerts, and every other form of spam so they'd at least show their faces."

"That's what it's all about," her mom said. "You've got to create that opening buzz. It's just the same with movies, you know."

Alice could count on a single hand the number of acting jobs her mother had lined up since Alice's birth, but the film industry was and would always be the lens through which Rose Sampson saw the world. This was, after all, a woman who'd stayed locked in her bedroom for a week when a much younger Alice had finally stopped trying to be a star herself.

"I only sold a couple of prints tonight, but I was checking online orders, and we were about to cross into the triple digits when I left the gallery."

Jeff's eyes widened above his highball glass. "You're kidding me." Coming off her adrenaline high from the successful opening, she'd been so busy gushing to Jeff in the cab about the various mucketymucks who'd shown up to the gallery that they hadn't had a chance to talk numbers.

"Is that a lot?" her mother asked.

"You saw the pictures, Mom. Hans Schuler's a little off the beaten path."

"Good," her father interjected. "Too much art is sterile and commercialized. If you're representing fresh work, you can be proud regardless of whether you make a single dollar."

Now her father was proud. He hadn't actually seen the crap she was pushing, and couldn't resist that dig to Jeff about art not being measured by money, but all he needed to hear was that the photographs were weird, and suddenly he was on board. This from the man who watched his opening weekend grosses like a hawk, even as he insisted that studio executives were hacks who cared only about their bottom line. Her father wasn't consistent, but he was definitely predictable.

Predictable enough that she foresaw his response when the waitress interrupted to ask whether Mr. Humphrey preferred to wait for the last member of his party before ordering.

"If we waited to eat every time my son ran late, the whole family would have starved by now. Go ahead, everyone. Let's order up." Her father had spent so much of his life in charge of other people on set that he refused to tolerate tardiness, especially from his flaky son, Ben. It probably did not help that everyone at the table was imbibing while he sipped club soda, twenty-five years after he quit drinking (but not craving, as he liked to say). "I'll have the duck," he announced, handing the waitress his unopened menu. "Get the duck, Jeff. They do a great duck."

Just as she knew that the family dinner would be at Gramercy Tavern, the restaurant her father always insisted on when he came to "her neighborhood" (meaning south of Thirty-fourth Street), she knew he'd order the duck. She also knew that, even though Jeff would have preferred beef, tonight he would opt for duck.

She wished she could persuade Jeff to stop trying to appease her father. She wished she could explain why her father would always be hard on him. But any discussion about her father's disapproval of Jeff would inevitably lead to a discussion about the history of Jeff's relationship with her, and that might end the friendship that meant so much to her.

After the waitress departed, Alice continued calculating her sales results for the day. "We'll have brought in over seventy thousand dollars by morning. I have to admit, I thought Schuler was full of it, but maybe he's onto something. The online orders came in from all over the world. Instead of targeting the tiny pool of customers who happen to show up in a New York City gallery, anyone living anywhere can buy this stuff. Granted, I don't understand the appeal of it, but—"

Her mother tipped her pinot grigio in Alice's direction. "To each his own, right?"

She noticed a small groan from her father and felt like she was thirteen years old again. She'd been about that age when she'd first learned to recognize—to label—the tension that had always existed between her parents. Her mother's resentment of her father's successes. Fights that coincided with his time spent on location. Her father's barely veiled boredom as her mother filled him in on the mundane details of days he missed from his family. His snorts—like the one she'd just heard—when her mother wasn't sufficiently creative in her choice of words.

With any other couple, she might have wondered why the two of them bothered to remain married. But she always assumed—or maybe, as their daughter, she'd just wanted to believe—that there was some sticky bond of love between them that outweighed all of the apparent imperfections. The rumors about her father? She'd always written them off as precisely that. Her mother trusted him, and therefore she had too.

But they weren't rumors. She'd learned that last year. And yet Mom still didn't leave. Someone had to say something to him. And so Alice had been the one. She had finally cut the cord, at least as much as she could without destroying her mother. Then she'd lost her job at the Met. Now she'd finally landed on her feet and didn't know whether to see her father's absence from the show as punishment or exactly what she had asked of him.

She took another sip of her vodka martini, allowing the alcohol to warm her stomach, feeling it form a fuzzy cloud around her face.

Ben never did show up that night. It would be two more days before she realized why.

CHAPTER
ELEVEN

Joann could not help but feel she was somehow being punished for every mistake she had ever made as a mother. As a woman. As a person.

The last fifteen years hadn't always been easy. Pregnant at twenty-one by a guy who was not only uninterested in being a father, but who proved to have no idea what he wanted out of life even for himself. Working retail as the mother of a toddler, getting laid off for missing hours every time her kid was sick. Taking part-time classes at the university, then juggling full-time waitressing once Becca started school. A college degree and the hospital job had given her sick time, benefits, and all the security that came with the territory, but it had taken years of saving, a housing market crash, and a lot of luck before she'd finally been able to buy them this house.

But as much as she had managed to improve life for the Stevenson girls, she had never rectified her original sins. In fact, she had only managed to compound them as her daughter got older and began to ask the inevitable questions a child asked of a single parent. Lineage. Biology. History. Pedigree. As if the desire for answers were ingrained in the very DNA whose origins we could not help but explore.

It was bizarre to watch this police officer—this stranger—roam room to room through the home she'd worked so hard to create.

She could see him making judgments with every observed detail. The boxes of sugary cereal on the linoleum kitchen counter. The crappy DVDs on the living room shelves, mostly two-star romantic comedies and buddy action flicks, far outnumbering the books, declaring she was no intellectual. The clutter. The piles of papers. Unopened mail.

Tidying up had been the last thing on her mind since Becca had gone . . . missing. She could still barely stand to imagine that word and its significance. So she hadn't straightened the place. As a consequence, she now wondered whether this cop had irreparably categorized her as one of "those" parents.

She would have expected the detective to be older. Dover, New Jersey, was a small town, the kind of place the movies would depict with a seasoned sheriff. Grizzled, even. With a southern accent, no matter the actual locale.

This particular cop was younger than she was. Probably in his early thirties, even though he could pass for his twenties in a different context. When had she gotten so old that a police detective investigating a missing child could be younger than her?

"How did Becca feel about your having company that night?"

"I told you, Officer Morhart. I mean, Detective." She looked at the business card he had handed so purposefully to her upon his first polite step through the door. Jason Morhart. Detective Sergeant. Town of Dover Police Department. "Becca didn't know."

He lowered his gaze. She was now not only a slut but a lying liar. The kind of woman who snuck men into her bed without even noticing whether her own kid came home for the night.

No, she had no doubt how the situation looked to this fair-haired, blue-eyed, strong-jawed officer. The teenage child of a single mother. The recent dip in Becca's grades. Attendance problems at school. The phone call from the guidance counselor, asking whether there had been any changes in Becca's home life. Joann, struggling to balance a full-time job with motherhood and a new boyfriend. The teenage girl missing just as the boyfriend spent his first night in the family home.

"You sure there's not someone else your daughter might be stay-ing with? Maybe she just needed a break."

In other words, you're one fuckup of a mother, and your daughter finally made a run for it. Suck it up or go cry to your boyfriend, lady.

But Joann knew the truth behind the stereotypes that were dom-inating this police officer's conclusions.

Joann had already called every last one of Becca's friends. Ac-cording to them, she'd gone to the library that morning, just as expected, to finish her chem lab report with her class partner, Joel. Went to Sophie's house afterward, just as she told Joann she would. The girls met Sophie's boyfriend, Rodney, at the Rockaway Town-square mall to check out the new gadgets at the Apple store, then headed back to Sophie's again to pick up Becca's backpack. Sophie, whose parents (unlike Joann) could afford to buy their daughter a car, offered Becca a ride, but Becca (as was often the case) wanted to burn a few calories with the five-block walk. No one had seen Becca since.

These were the facts Joann knew. Not only knew, but trusted. Would swear by. Because Joann, unlike this cop, had known Sophie Ferrin for three years. Had carpooled her around through junior high. Had stayed up in her pajamas with her and Becca for late-night gossip sessions over chocolate-chip cookie dough. Joann, unlike this cop, knew Sophie wouldn't lie to her.

Becca had been frustrated, even angry, at her mother for failing to give her the thorough explanations she was looking for about her childhood. About her very existence. And she had gone through a troubled few months as a result. And Joann—as always—had more on her plate than any one person should have to handle alone. But Joann, unlike this cop, knew something else: she and Becca had a bond.

Sure, they were mother and daughter, but they were also friends and confidantes. Becca would know how the sight of her empty bed in the morning would affect Joann. She would know that just one look would devastate her. Break her to the core.

As angry as Becca could sometimes be with her mother, Joann knew her daughter—her best friend, her everything—would never voluntarily destroy her this way.

Joann had made mistakes as a mother, there was no question. And she would work every last day of her life to remedy them, if given a chance. But at that moment—as she watched a police officer run his fingertip along the edges of the baby photos on her mantel—all she could do was close her eyes and pray that she be the one punished—not her baby, not her Becca.

Please, God, not my precious Becca.

CHAPTER
TWELVE

Alice blew hot breaths into her cupped fists, trying to warm her fingers before they numbed. With a puff of warmed air trapped between her hands, she'd then rub her palms together before balling them into her coat pockets once again. She'd been in this rotation system since she stepped out of the gallery ten minutes earlier—warm breaths, brisk palm-rub, coat pockets—but there was no curing the chill that had already set in.

She finally gave up and tried following the advice Ben used to give when she was young. She must have been about nine by the time her parents entrusted her older brother to escort her around the city on their own, and Ben took full advantage of every opportunity to roam Manhattan on foot.

"Stop hunching. Just relax your shoulders and let the cold in. You'll adapt. I promise."

Ben could stroll for miles in single-digit temperatures with that strategy, but Alice inevitably wound up with her shoulders near her ears, her arms folded against her body, fighting desperately for every single degree of her body temperature. Since then, she'd adopted her own coping skills. Heavy wool coat. Thick socks. Warm boots. Good gloves.

Where the hell were her beautiful gloves—the crocodile-embossed leather ones, with the cozy fur lining she blissfully chose to believe was faux? She'd rather lose a kidney than those gloves.

Alice had yet to take a break or leave the gallery before eight o'clock, until today. For three weeks, she'd lived with the frenzy of launching a new business. Renting the furniture. Hiring painters and a cleaning service. Connecting to Con Ed and Verizon. Communicating with the diva Hans Schuler via his chosen medium of text message. Finding a mover specializing in art to deliver hundreds of Schuler's prints from a warehouse in Brooklyn to the gallery's stockroom. Getting one of each print from the SELF series framed for display. The press releases. The phone calls. The online marketing. Until opening day, Alice had been a one-woman manager-slash-decorator-slash-publicist.

But after last night's fanfare at the opening, she was looking forward to finding a rhythm to her new employment at the Highline. This morning was marked by the bus ride to Ninth Avenue, a Starbucks stop, and then crouching down, brass key in hand, to release the lock on the pull-down security gate. She loved the clacking sound of the old gate as it retracted.

Inside the gallery, she'd finished her coffee while checking the Web site for new online orders. She'd been worried about keeping up with the shipments as a one-woman operation, but she quickly had the packaging process down cold: tightly rolled print, one of Schuler's thumb drives, and a letter to explain the concept, all tucked inside a cardboard tube to be picked up by Fred the UPS guy before two o'clock. Other than walk-ins, the rest of the time would be her own. She planned on splitting it equally between publicizing the gallery and researching emerging artists for the happy day when she could show her own selections.

Alice had been glued to the gallery for the last three weeks not only out of necessity, but also because she loved being employed again. She had missed having a place where she was needed. She'd missed having a schedule. All those months of waking up and knowing that no one cared where she went, what she did, or whether she changed out of her pajamas had worn her down in ways she hadn't realized at the time. Maybe one day she'd go back to being like everyone else. She'd have mornings when she wouldn't want to work. She'd complain about the job.

But maybe not. Maybe she'd continue to come in early and stay late, simply out of gratitude.

Lily had been the one to insist that her new routine include the occasional break. According to her, the patterns of employment set in early. Breaks were use 'em or lose 'em, she said. If the boss got too accustomed to her constant presence at the gallery, he'd come to expect and then require it.

Alice had tried to explain to Lily that Drew wasn't exactly checking in on her, but her friend had finally persuaded her to go for a walk when she e-mailed her a link to the day's Wafels & Dinges schedule. One small but significant upside to Alice's unemployment had been her discovery of the culinary wonders that are served from the windows of New York City's food trucks. Tacos. Burgers. Dumplings. Cupcakes. And, in the case of Wafels & Dinges, Belgian waffles made to order. The truck's online announcement that it would be parked mere blocks from the gallery had done the trick, proving once again that Lily Harper knew her well.

"I'll have a waffle with strawberries, bananas, and butter, please?"

She would have killed for a scoop of ice cream on top, but it was just her luck that the first time she gave herself a break from the gallery, the temperature would suddenly drop back into glove-wearing weather. And her, with no gloves. She shook off the thought as soon as it formed. No more bad luck. No more beating herself up.

She felt a buzz from the cell phone in her coat pocket. It was a text from Lily. *Fresh air yet?*

She typed in a return message: *Fresh, freezing air. Yes.*

Waffle?

Just ordered. Strawberries & nanas.

Ice cream, woman!

Too brrrrr . . . Bye. Waffle here!

Alice returned her phone to her pocket and grabbed her lunch through the truck window, grateful for the warmth against her fingers. Even more grateful for the mixture of the sweet flavor of fruit with the crisp buttery waffle.

She resisted the temptation to swallow the thing whole. Despite the cold, she walked to the Westside and parked herself on a bench before allowing herself further bites. She tried not to look too pleased with herself as panting joggers glanced enviously in her direction.

She had polished off her meal and was halfway back to the gallery when she felt a buzz in her pocket. It was Lily again.

Hey look: You left the gallery & the world didn't break.

You were right. Thanks. She typed in a smiley face, a colon followed by a dash and a closing parenthesis.

The world may not have broken, but something had changed back at the gallery.

When she first spotted the small crowd huddled together on the sidewalk, she couldn't believe the uncanny timing. She had somehow managed to hang out her "Be Right Back" sign just as a burst of walk-in activity arrived. She tried not to chalk it up to her bad luck. But then she saw the signs and knew that impatient customers were not the problem.

What can 311 Online help you with today?

Those were the words staring at Alice from the laptop screen as Alice tried to decide whether to make the call.

Child abuse isn't art.

Highline or Hell's Line?

God hates pornographers.

Those were the words staring at Alice from the placards held by protesters lining the sidewalk outside her gallery. A few of the signs referred to biblical passages whose significance she was in no position to recognize.

Despite his warning that he wanted no involvement in the day-to-day happenings at the gallery, she had tried phoning Drew. He wasn't answering his cell, so she'd called Jeff. Jeff was the one who suggested calling 311, New York City's nonemergency help line.

The Web site made it sound simple enough. *What can 311 Online help you with today?* Well, you could help me kick the Bible-belting, freedom-hating nut jobs away from the only gainful employment I've had in a year. Wouldn't that be nice?

Still, Alice hadn't called immediately. Controversy and attention were nourishment to these kinds of people. A police presence would only support their narrative: good, holy people oppressed by the godless bureaucratic machine of New York City.

So instead she tried to ignore them. She tallied up another round of phone tag with John Lawson, an artist who incorporated Mardi Gras beads into his sculptures, trying to persuade him once again to commit to a showing this summer. She updated the gallery's growing Web site to include the latest blogosphere references to the opening. She even added a new, meaningless status to her Facebook profile: "Wafels & Dinges!"

It was the NY1 truck that put her over the edge. She watched as an attractive correspondent stepped from the passenger seat. She recognized her from television. What was her name? Sandra Pak, that was it. She was followed shortly by the jeans-clad, bearded cameraman who emerged from the back of the van.

Sure enough, the man she'd pegged as the protesters' ringleader made a beeline to the camera. The man could have been anywhere between fifty and seventy, depending on how he'd lived his life. About six feet tall, but that was taking into account the hunching. Thin. A little gaunt, in fact. Hollowed cheeks. His frame curved like a human question mark.

She watched as the man scurried to the reporter, the crown of her dark hair bundled into a shiny poof, the chubby cameraman struggling to keep pace, even though he wore sneakers and she balanced in ambitious four-inch platform pumps.

She had to put an end to this.

Three . . . one . . . one. Four rings before an answer, followed by a series of recorded messages about the opposite-side-of-the-street parking schedule. Had she really expected a sugary sweet voice to greet her with, "What can 311 help you with today?"

When a live operator finally picked up, Alice explained the situation. Gallery manager. Protesters. Name-calling signs. She did her best to include the buzzwords she thought would make a difference. *Disruptive. Harassing. Blocking the entrance.*

"Has anyone trespassed on your property?"

"Um, no, they didn't actually enter inside the property. Yet."

"Have they engaged in any physical contact with you or anyone else, ma'am?"

Ma'am. Alice knew that being called ma'am by a government employee was not a good sign. "Well, no, nothing physical. But they're creating a public disturbance."

"Please hold."

Three minutes until she returned. "If these people are exercising their rights to free speech, I'm afraid there's nothing we can do for you."

"But they're creating a public disturbance."

"Ma'am, you're running a business in New York City. What you think of as a public disturbance, some people call the city's flavor. You know what I mean?"

"Would you be saying that if I were calling from Citibank instead of some fledgling art gallery in the Meatpacking District?"

"Please hold."

Three more minutes. The cameras still rolling outside.

A male voice came on the line. That in itself bothered her for some reason.

"Miss Humphrey?"

She wondered if her actual name was a promotion from ma'am or simply an escalation. "Yes."

"If you'd like to go to your local precinct to file a report, the address is—"

"I don't want to go to my local precinct, because I'm at work trying to run a business. I am calling you because these extremists are disrupting that business."

"I realize that, ma'am, but—"

"Shouldn't someone at least come out here to see what's happening and decide whether it's legal or not? I mean, I'm not a police officer. I don't know the difference between protected speech and public nuisance. Isn't that what police are for?"

"Please hold."

Alice looked at the time on her laptop. Minutes ticking by. Camera rolling outside.

She heard a long, solid beep over the Muzak piped in by 311. The other line. It could be Drew. She stared at the buttons at the phone, realizing she had no clue how to click over to the other line without disconnecting the call. Fuck.

"Highline Gallery. This is Alice."

"Good, you're still at your desk."

She recognized her father's voice.

"Hey, Papa. Can I call you back?"

Up until last year, her father had been a regular caller. Too regular, in fact. Regular enough that she'd made a point never to mention her cell phone number.

"Don't say anything to those cocksucking reporters."

"Excuse me. What?"

"I've been pulled into this game before. Don't do it. Stay away from the vultures."

"Wait, this mess is out there already?"

"Your mother called me. It's on New York One as we speak." The magic of live television. "A group like that will want to paint you as the bad guy. Same as *Daily News* and the *Post*. Cable news might be the same if it goes national. They're all trying to outfox Fox. I've fallen for it, and I've been burned every time. You need the *New Yorker*. Maybe the *Times*. The libertarianish blogs would be good. Huffington Post would be terrific. Make it all about free speech. Theirs and yours. The more speech, the better. That's the high ground."

It had been a long time since she'd felt like this with her father. Symbiotic. Comfortable. Papa to the rescue.

She heard the long, solid beep again. Maybe Drew had finally picked up her messages.

"I gotta go, Papa. But thanks. Really . . . Highline Gallery, this is Alice."

"Hi, Peter Morse from the *Daily News*. I was calling about your Hans Schuler exhibit?"

She recited a few of Schuler's bullet points. The SELF series. Self-introspection. Mainstreaming radicalism. She left out the part where she herself had spent a good couple of weeks calling the stuff pornography.

"Sounds like it's right out of the artist's brochure. Between me and you, I'm looking at this guy's stuff online. Is there really any art to be found there? The Reverend George Hardy of the Redemption of Christ Church certainly thinks not."

"The value of art—and speech—is in the eye of the beholder and the ear of the listener. Mr. Schuler has a right to free speech, and we've been happy to help showcase his provocative images." She found herself grateful for her father's advice. "Whether people enjoy them or not, if the pictures get the community thinking and talking, we think that's all for the bett—"

"And what about the allegations that the photographs contain pornographic images of minor children?"

"Excuse me?"

"The Redemption of Christ Church alleges that one of the models in Schuler's series is a teenage girl. That would make the photographs in violation of criminal law, unprotected by the First Amendment."

She immediately swiveled her chair to face one of Schuler's photographs, the one called *First*. The flat chest. Thin, boyish hips. Flawless pale flesh.

"No comment."

CHAPTER THIRTEEN

Alice had been hunched over her laptop so long that the small of her back ached. When she lifted her wrists to work out the kinks, she saw a crease in her skin from the pressure of her forearms against the edge of her pine breakfast table.

Despite all of her online digging, she still had no one to contact about the growing public relations disaster besides Drew Campbell, who was not answering his phone.

As a car commercial faded out on the television, she heard the familiar staccato theme music of the Channel 7 news. She reached for the remote control to crank up the volume.

A male anchor in a light blue suit with a plastered mushroom of thick black hair introduced the story. "City officials and local religious leaders are weighing in on the elusive line between art and obscenity tonight, thanks to a controversial exhibit at a new gallery in Manhattan's Meatpacking District. The Highline Gallery has not yet been open a week and already has the city in an uproar."

The screen flashed to images pulled directly from Hans Schuler's Web site, and the audio switched to a female correspondent's voice.

"Blood. Saliva. Nudity." The camera tightened in around each referenced image, cropping any nudity they could not air. "Unknown artist Hans Schuler calls the photographs in his SELF series 'a portrait in radical introspection.' A growing chorus of critics, however, say Schuler has crossed a line into obscenity."

Flash to a female protester. "Those pictures are disgusting. They shouldn't be in a gallery, and they shouldn't be on the Internet."

"Of course, nudity in the art world is nothing new," the correspondent announced. "The Museum of Modern Art created headlines last year with a show featuring live nude models, but the only point of contention was making sure that observers didn't touch the art. The image that brought these protesters to Manhattan is this one, called *First*, which the protesters claim is an image of a minor."

The screen cut to the gaunt man who led the protests, the caption identifying him as George Hardy, Pastor, Redemption of Christ Church. "Just looking at the picture is enough to raise questions about the age of that so-called model. But the artist won't answer those questions. The lady at the gallery won't come outside, won't answer the question, and won't assure us she's *not* selling child pornography. Well, my daddy always used to tell me, where there's smoke there's fire. If they've got nothing to hide, they could put this thing to rest right now."

Now the screen changed to a pan across the piece of art in question. The correspondent narrated. "We at *Eyewitness News* have blocked out almost the entire photograph because we have also been unable to confirm the age of the depicted model. Some local officials are calling for the exhibit's removal pending verification of the model's age."

The multiple black bars pasted across the photograph created the impression of more tawdriness than the collage actually contained.

"The manager of the Highline Gallery declined our request for an on-camera interview, but the gallery did release a written statement: 'The Highline Gallery promotes the work of provocative, cutting-edge artists who, like Hans Schuler, create art that makes us think, react, and sometimes even become uncomfortable with our own thoughts and reactions. We of course condemn and would never agree to display indecent depictions of minor children, but we have heard no evidence to support these disturbing allegations. Absent some articulation of a good-faith basis for the accusation, we respect the First Amendment rights of our artists.'

"For now, it sounds like the city's mayor agrees."

Alice wanted to believe she was managing the public relations aspect of this disaster as well as could be expected, on her own, isolated from the information that actually mattered. She had issued the written statement. She had stopped answering the gallery phone, letting all calls go to voice mail with the same statement recorded as the outgoing message. Last time she checked, she had received not only that first call she had answered from the *Daily News*, but also calls from the *Post*, *Times*, *Sun*, *Observer*, and a place called Empire Media.

The film cut to an image of Mayor Michael Bloomberg stepping from the backseat of a town car. "This isn't the first time someone's been offended by art. I support artistic freedom, and I support the First Amendment. If there is evidence that laws have been broken, we will take that evidence seriously and prosecute offenders under the law."

"It seems the one person who *isn't* commenting tonight is the artist himself. According to his Web site, Hans Schuler communicates with his followers only on the Internet so as not to taint the world's perception of his art. Although the origin of this photograph might still be a mystery, one thing is certain: with this level of controversy, Hans Schuler isn't likely to remain unknown for long."

"We'll keep an eye on this one, Robin. Sounds like it could turn into a real wrangle."

"Sure thing, Andy. One interesting side note about the gallery. Its manager is Alice Humphrey, the daughter of Frank Humphrey and his former leading lady, Rose Sampson."

Great. Apparently there was icing to go on the cake.

"Oh, sure. She was the kid in that show about the single father—what was it called?—*Life with Dad*."

"Before my time, I'm afraid, Andy, but importantly, Alice Humphrey's own father is no stranger to scandal. His acclaimed film *The*

Patron was boycotted by the Catholic Church for its depiction of a steamy affair involving a Catholic bishop. It was his long and seemingly devoted marriage to the beloved actress Rose Sampson that often softened a public persona defined by his explicit films and controversial public statements, but of course that all changed when several women came forward last year with evidence of multiple extramarital affairs with Humphrey over the years. So far, his wife has been standing by him, and the family had begun to fade from the headlines until this new story involving his daughter—"

Alice couldn't stand it any longer. She hit the mute button and was relieved when the broadcast moved on to a story that appeared to be about the beneficial health effects of red wine.

She returned her attention to her computer.

Schuler had not responded to any of her many texts, and a call to the number she'd been using for their texts went unanswered. She'd made no progress finding additional contact information for the artist online. Other than his Web site, the man was a ghost.

More creatively, she'd been trying to track down the gallery owner using the few facts she'd gleaned about his biography from Drew. Moneyed. Maintained a part-time presence in Tampa since Drew was a kid, making him a considerably older man. Plagued by long-whispered rumors about his sexuality. Presumably here in New York. Sufficiently well known for the name to be familiar.

She prided herself on pretty clever Googling skills, but so far, she'd come up with squat.

She tried Drew's number for the umpteenth time. Straight to voice mail once again.

Moving her cursor to the search window, she typed in "George Hardy," and then clicked to review recent news articles. The first cluster of hits linked to stories covering that afternoon's protest outside the Highline Gallery. But as she scrolled through a series of pages, she learned more about the Reverend Hardy and his Redemption of Christ Church. Based out of southern Virginia. Founded by Hardy only a decade earlier. They'd made a name for themselves protesting seemingly everything—abortion clinics, "antifamily" movies, same-sex commitment ceremonies, and the funerals of American soldiers for defending a depraved nation that had lost its way.

Her cell phone rang. *Blocked call.* She answered.

"Hey, it's Drew."

"Thank God. I've been calling you all day. I put out a statement, but we need to reach Schuler. Call the gallery owner. Make Schuler prove the model's age."

"There's something I need to tell you. I'll meet you at the gallery tomorrow morning. Early. Seven, okay?"

"Wait. I need to know—"

But somehow she knew in the silence of the receiver he was gone. "Drew? Hello? Are you there?" She called his cell, but once again, she immediately heard his outgoing message. She hit redial for another hour until she finally forced herself to go to bed.

CHAPTER
FOURTEEN

Hank Beckman made it to Jersey before the crack of dawn, determined to return to the city with the vehicle identification number of Travis Larson's newly acquired BMW. He parked across the street from the apartment complex, tucked the slim jim up his coat sleeve, and stepped out from behind the wheel.

He kept his eye on Larson's front door as he made his way into the parking lot. He was within fifteen feet of the car, slipping the slim jim from its hiding place, when he saw movement at the top of the stairs.

Saying a silent thank-you for the pricks who still drove gas guzzlers, he dodged behind a GMC Yukon and bent down next to the tire, faking a tie of his shoelaces in case a neighbor caught a glance. He heard Larson's footsteps move quickly down the stairs and across the concrete. Larson wasted no time hopping into the driver's seat and firing up the BMW's engine, not bothering to signal when he pulled out of the lot.

Hank trotted back to his own car, flipped a quick U, and headed after the BMW. By the time he reached the T at the end of the road, Larson was already gone. Hank played the odds and hung a right, heading for the city.

It was just past six in the morning, but traffic was already starting to accumulate outside the Lincoln Tunnel. His eyes scanned the lanes of cars lined up to pay their tolls, searching for the gray sedan in what seemed like a sea of light-colored luxury cars.

Then he thought again about his previous glimpse through Larson's dash. He prided himself on his photographic memory. He could pull mental images from his past and display them like a virtual snapshot against the blackness of his closed eyelids. How many times had he pictured Ellen beaming across the table from him, a bright smile above her wine glass, as she announced her engagement to the man sitting beside her? The man who just hadn't rubbed Hank right. The man who was too young. The man whose name turned out not to be Randall after all.

He shook the image away as if it were sand in an Etch A Sketch and instead pulled up a visual of Larson's front window. Pictured the *New York* magazine, the one with the funny looking black-and-white dog on the cover, concealing the VIN. Saw the gray pebbled console. The black rearview mirror. And the unoccupied glass around it.

Larson hadn't had an E-ZPass, the automated toll-payment device users mounted to their front windshield. Hank moved two lanes to the left, pulling himself closer to the Cash Only toll lanes. He spotted Larson two lanes over, about six car lengths in front of him.

No problem. Hank inched up, watching his progress against Larson until he merged into his E-ZPass lane.

By the time the gray BMW emerged from the tunnel, Hank was lingering in the right lane, ready to pull in behind him.

He worried about the man spotting him. Hank had made the trip in his personal vehicle, confident from his past rounds of surveillance that Larson would be dead to the world this early. He found comfort in Larson's speed. He didn't seem to be paying attention to traffic around him. He didn't act like a man worried about a tail.

Larson drove north on Sixth Avenue, then curved into the West Village on West Fourth Street. Hank forced himself to remain a block and a half behind the BMW on the narrow streets, still quiet this time of morning. When he spotted the glow of Larson's brake lights midblock past the stop sign at Bank Street, he immediately hit the button to roll down his window as he pulled to the curb on Washington. He watched as Larson parallel-parked. Leaned his ear outside as Larson hopped out of the car, looking both ways before crossing the street. He saw Larson disappear into a storefront, but couldn't identify the business from this vantage point.

Hank pulled forward to the stop sign, hung a left on Bank, and then circled around to park north of the BMW and head south on foot. He took the red wool scarf he'd brought for the occasion—remembered Ellen giving it to him for Christmas—and wrapped it around his cheeks. Slipped the slim jim up his coat sleeve.

He paused at the curb beside the BMW. Did a quick visual of the interior. Nothing. He was relieved to see that Larson had removed the magazine from the dash. He had a clear look at the VIN and jotted it down.

He felt the slim jim against his forearm. It was an unnecessary risk, but he was moving too fast now to rethink his decision. He hadn't heard the *beep-beep* of an activated alarm when Larson left the car. The sidewalks were still empty. It was now or never. Just one quick peek.

He forced the slim jim past the rubber seal of the driver's side window. Allowed himself to exhale when no alarm blasted the neighborhood silence. He began to jiggle, counting off the passed seconds in his head. One, one thousand, two, one thousand. He had vowed to give himself only fifteen seconds before hightailing it back to his own car.

Thirteen thousand. He felt the lock release.

Still seeing no one, he popped the glove box. Completely empty. Pulled the lever for the trunk, shut the door, and headed to the rear of the car. Also empty.

He clicked the trunk shut and made his way north to his Toyota Camry. Made three left turns: Greenwich, to Bethune, and back onto Washington.

As he cruised past the parked BMW, he checked out the storefronts across the street. He identified what looked like a flower shop and a shoe store as candidates for Larson's location, a closed-down storefront separating the two.

Nice car. Pretty girl. Early-morning drives. And absolutely nothing in his ride, not even an owner's manual or registration.

The next step was to run the VIN.

CHAPTER
FIFTEEN

Her apartment had to be cold—it always was in the winter, thanks to the lousy furnace and cheap windows—but Alice woke up with the covers kicked from her body and a thin sheen of perspiration coating her skin. She was thankful to be one of those people who could never truly remember her dreams. Although the details of last night's sleep were fuzzy, they'd left behind a shadow of anxiety still lingering in her core.

Even as she shuffled into the shower, images from her sleep flashed through her mind. Hans Schuler's photographs. The protesters. Those ugly words plastered onto their signs. News cameras. Standing at a podium before an auditorium full of reporters. The white lights of flashbulbs blinding her. A hush covering the room as she began to speak. Looking down at her notes to find nothing but blank paper. A thin, balding man chasing her. In her dream, she imagined he was Hans Schuler. Or maybe he was the Reverend George Harvey. Or perhaps he was no one—just a physical representation of the horrible feeling she carried in her subconscious about yesterday's protest at the gallery.

She held her head beneath the spray of hot water, as if she could literally wash away the thoughts from her mind and send them spiraling down the drain.

Even after the long shower, she had too much time on her hands before her meet-up with Drew. She used the extra minutes to check the online situation.

She entered "Highline Gallery Hans Schuler" into her search engine and hit enter. As the computer did its thinking, she hoped against hope that she would find no new results since the previous night.

No such luck. As she'd suspected, the story had gone viral. What started as a local New York story had been picked up on the wires, was spreading blog to blog, and was now being "retweeted" across the Web with irreverent headlines like "Hans Smut-ler" and "New York Art Show: Mainstream Radicalism or Old School Porn?"

On the *Daily News* Web site, she was happy to see that the story of a missing girl in Dover, New Jersey, had replaced the gallery for top billing. No surprise. Alabaster skin, full lips, a few freckles for good measure. Becca Stevenson's photo beneath a banner declaration—MISSING—made good newspaper copy. Alice felt a pang of guilt as she registered her hope that the media vultures would latch on to the missing girl story instead of her own saga.

She moved her cursor back to the search window. This time, she searched for her own name, plus the words "Highline Gallery." Maybe Channel 7 would be the only outlet to play up her family background.

Despite her hopes, she found story after story identifying the gallery's manager as the daughter of Frank Humphrey and Rose Sampson. Almost all of them alluded to the controversies her father had created with his own work. Most also mentioned his recently exposed infidelities—the "casting couch" allegations, the scandalous ages of the women involved. Then she reached a news update that she found herself rereading.

> **Alice Humphrey is only the latest member of her family to find herself at the center of controversy. In addition to her father's reported extramarital and perhaps even coerced sexual activity going back decades, her brother, Ben, was arrested last weekend for drug possession. According to two**

separate NYPD sources, Ben Humphrey, 41, was arrested after police found marijuana in his possession while investigating a noise complaint outside of a West Village bar.

She remembered Ben's unexplained absence from the gallery opening. Recalled her parents' anxious expressions, wondering whether he was back to his old ways.

She quickly pulled up his number on her cell, but heard only his familiar outgoing message: "This is Ben. You know the drill." Even when he was clean, Ben was not the type to answer a phone this early in the morning.

As she disconnected the call, she caught the time displayed on the screen: 6:34. Shit. Time to meet Drew. Her brother's problems would have to wait.

She found herself working the metal of the gallery key between her bare fingers inside her coat pocket like a worry stone. If it weren't for those ridiculous protesters, she would have had time yesterday to pick up a new pair of gloves to replace the ones that were still missing. One more reason to hate the fuckers.

Alice wasn't proud of this aspect of her personality, the complete inability to harness free-floating anxieties. She was the kind of person who could not sit still once she realized an unsent piece of mail still lingered on her desk, who would wake in the middle of the night with a recollection of an unreturned phone call.

Her relationship with stress was one of the reasons she had never felt at ease with the acting career her mother had so desperately sought for her. The standing around, biding time before the next scene. Wondering if the director was going to alter the dialogue or the order of filming. Waiting to know whether the powers that be would pick up the pilot or approve the dailies. The constant uncertainty had left her feeling unfocused and insecure, never able to find peace within herself.

The irony that she had chosen a safer path only to find herself out

of work for nearly a year was not lost on her. Now she had finally
landed not only a job, but a fabulous one at that, and once again she
found herself trying to anticipate what would happen next.

As she continued to rub that key between her fingers, she resolved that her involvement in this nightmare would end today. She
would not spend another night as she had the last, tossing and turning in bed while those awful images rushed through her mind. She
would take control of this situation, or at least her role in it. She was
through with Drew's middleman smokescreen. She would simply
refuse to end this morning's meeting until he put her in direct contact with Schuler. And if he couldn't connect her to Schuler, she'd
insist on speaking with the gallery's owner. And if all else failed, she
would quit. She'd go back to being jobless. She'd break down and
ask her parents to help, if it became necessary.

But no matter what happened, her anxiety about those photographs would be assuaged. Hopefully, it would be a simple matter
of verifying the model's age and identity. A quickie press release,
and all would be forgotten. And if the verification didn't come,
she'd take the omission as a sign that the Reverend Harvey might
actually be onto something, and she would walk away. Regardless,
she would no longer be part of this story by the time the day ended.

She found comfort in that knowledge. She'd found a small ele-
ment of control.

As she approached the gallery, she spotted brown butcher paper
lining the previously unobstructed glass. Drew had been quite the
busy bee this morning. She let out a frustrated sigh. She was as
upset about the protesters' allegations as anyone, but covering the
windows like some seedy peep-show emporium was a little over
the top. Knowing—okay, not knowing at all—but based on her assumptions about Hans Schuler, she wondered if this was the artist's
way of generating even more controversy, along with the attendant
publicity.

The security gate was unrolled over the glass entrance, but when
she bent down to unlock it, she found it unsecured. Drew must have
pulled it down behind him. She rolled the gate open and found the

front door also unlocked. She pushed it open, ready to find Drew waiting for her at the desk. Instead, the lights were off. The space black.

"Drew?"

He must have stepped out for coffee. If she was going to continue to work here, she'd have to talk to him about leaving the place unattended, even at this early hour.

She made her way through the gallery space, struggling to adjust her vision to the dark, wondering who the genius was who installed the light switches in back. She was relieved when she finally felt the rear wall. She ran her hand along the now-familiar row of switches, but nothing happened.

Damn it. She had no idea where the fuse box was in this place.

She worked her way toward the fire exit, one hand against the wall. Fumbled with the bolt until she felt it release. She was disappointed when only a gray ray of morning light crept through the propped open door.

She knew immediately when she turned to face the interior of the gallery again that something was wrong. It was one of those unexpected realizations. A dawning of awareness at a cellular level. The rhythms of this space had already become ingrained. Even in the dark, her brain was wired to expect certain shaded forms—the low leather banquettes dividing the gallery in half, the glass-topped desk toward the front door, the very objects that she'd been careful to avoid bumping into as she'd worked her way to this place. But she saw nothing but evenness in her field of vision.

"Drew?"

Her voice sounded different in the room. Louder. With a touch of an echo.

Every sense was telling her that something had changed. She fumbled inside her purse for her cell phone and activated the screen for a tiny pocket of light. Did a 180-degree scan of the room. Saw an empty floor where the benches had been. Saw uninterrupted blank space on the wall where Hans Schuler's *First* had hung.

Fuck. She had assumed the brown paper on the windows was

a cheap publicity stunt—a very public effort to obscure their so-called pornography from public view—but now she realized Drew had been even busier this morning, and even more overreactive, than she'd first assumed. It looked like she wouldn't be calling the shots about how the end would go down. Obviously the owner was pulling the plug.

She was tempted to walk out the door and leave the entire experiment behind her, but thought Drew owed her an explanation. She assumed, based on the open gate, that he'd be returning.

As she walked toward the front of the gallery, she noticed a shadow on the floor—some sort of pile. She took each step carefully, as if the sounds of her footsteps might disrupt it. Fifteen steps from the pile. Now ten. Five.

Despite her caution, she felt the sole of her boot slide beneath her on the floor. Felt her weight pulling her down backward. She reflexively stuck her hands beneath her, forgetting all those old ski lessons about protecting your wrists in a fall. She heard her cell phone tumble to the floor.

Her body hit the ground, palms first, and then slid against the tile. Wet. Warm. Sticky. Paint?

She pulled herself to her knees and crawled toward the form on the ground. Used a tentative hand to tap what she recognized upon touch as some kind of fabric. A rug? A large canvas?

She patted the form's edges and jerked upright when she finally identified a texture with certainty. Hair. Coarse human hair.

She scrambled on the slick tile, fumbling for her phone. Found the button at the bottom. Aimed the tiny beam of light toward what she now suspected was a body.

Drew Campbell lay on his side, a magenta pool forming beneath him despite the bundling of his winter coat. Her hands and knees and shins and forearms were soaked in his fresh blood.

She felt her fingertips stick to the glass screen of her phone as she dialed 911.

CHAPTER SIXTEEN

> **This page has been blocked. Please try again later or contact your network administrator for assistance.**

"God damn it."

Detective Jason Morhart hit the enter key on his computer once again, this time so hard he thought it might not pop back into place.

> **This page has been blocked. Please try again later or contact your network administrator for assistance.**

"Fuck."

"Cursing's for the uncreative. They say 'Frack!' on *Battlestar Galactica,* and everyone still knows what it means."

Nancy had appeared at his desk about six presses of the return key ago. Her job was to process file requests. In her mind, that plus a few software classes at the community college made her the resident computer expert at the police department. No one had the heart to disabuse her of the notion. He knew for a fact that Nancy could out-cuss a cussing contest at a sailor's convention, but that wasn't going to stop her from ribbing him about his temper.

"Cursing's also for the seriously pissed off, Nancy. And I'll let you in on another secret while I'm at it: *Battlestar Galactica*'s for nerds. You're never gonna land a man quoting a nerd show."

"Now, for *that*? You really do deserve to have your mouth washed out with soap. Let me see that keyboard again."

She reached across him and typed in the Web address he'd been trying to pull up: Facebook.com. Hit the enter key.

This page has been blocked. Please try again later or contact your network administrator for assistance.

Tony Rollins passed behind her and rolled his eyes, but Morhart just shrugged. Nancy could drive folks crazy, but her heart was in the right place.

"You want me to call Gary?" she asked. "You know all roads eventually lead to Gary."

Gary Moore was the town's technology guru.

"No, I'll call. The fucking town's blocking all the good Web sites again."

Two years ago, after it was discovered that eight of the ten most-frequented Web sites on the town network were sex-related, the town had finally started tracking Internet traffic, issuing warnings and threatening to go further for inappropriate usage. Apparently the Big Brother tactics didn't go far enough, however—at least not for the accountant who racked up nearly thirty hours a week watching online porn from his desk. When the local news broke the story, the higher-ups demanded stronger action.

Now poor Gary Moore had to foresee all of the idiotic ways town employees might squander their time online and block all the fun stuff in advance. Jason knew from experience why he was getting that frustrating message about the Web site being blocked. He'd received the same error alert a few months ago when he was investigating a sex offender who groomed his victims by enticing them to look at pornography with him. Every time Jason tried to pull up one of the sites listed in the suspect's browser window, there went the alert.

He picked up his phone and dialed Gary Moore's number. "How can I help you, Detective?"

The town's network was for shit, but the caller identification seemed to work just fine.

"First you block my porn. Now it's Facebook? Pretty soon we'll be down to nothing but National Geographic and the weather channel. Oh wait, they might show bikini shots for the weather in Miami."

"Don't get me started about the smut on National Geographic. Some of those baboons are pretty kinky."

"Seriously, Gary? Facebook?"

"I know, it's ridiculous. But the order came down from on high."

"Too many hours spent on *social networking*?" The name struck Jason as the ultimate misnomer. Socializing for the asocial. Like Happy Hour at a skid-row bar.

"Definitely. Major online time suck. But with this particular Web site, the blocking was personal. You didn't hear it from me, but apparently thanks to Facebook, the mayor's wife got a little too cozy with one of her ex-boyfriends from high school. Now he's got his panties in a bunch over it. No town employee can access Facebook from a public computer."

Morhart had met Dover mayor Kyle Jenson. And he'd seen his smoking-hot wife in those reelection ads. If she was stepping out on her husband, Facebook had nothing to do with it.

"Jesus. Seems like half our cases pull us online, and half of those run me right into one of these blocking problems. Can't you exempt the detectives from this stuff?"

"Yeah, right. You mean to tell me Rollins had a work-related reason for every single one of those replays he hit on the Miss Howard Stern page before I got appointed the town's cyber czar?"

Leave it to Rollins to mess it up for everyone.

"Well, can you at least unblock me? I got a missing girl and need to check out her Facebook page."

Morhart heard a clucking noise in his earpiece.

"I saw that on the news this morning. My wife and I were sort of hoping it was a runaway kind of deal."

"Might be, but I don't think Jenson wants me telling the girl's mother I'm not really sure because her mayor got cuckolded by his wife and won't give me access to the resources I need to find her daughter."

"No, I don't imagine he'd be happy with that explanation." Morhart took the sound of keyboard tapping on the other end of the line as a good sign. "All right. I unhooked you from the nanny system. Run. Be free. But don't let Rollins near your computer, okay?"

Becca Stevenson had eighty-two friends.

Eighty-two friends sounds like a healthy number. To maintain eighty-two relationships required a certain degree of social activity and mutual care. But on the Internet, where "friendship" meant nothing other than the click of a mouse, eighty-two "friends" was nothing. Eighty-two friends for a high school sophomore made Becca something of a loner.

Funny how it was the loners who went missing.

Eighty-two friends might not be much in the world of Facebook, but it was too many people for Morhart to track down on his own. He was about to narrow down the field.

He clicked first on the tab for photographs, hoping to find an array of photos matching full names to smiling faces, the high-tech equivalent of a "question these witnesses first" list. Instead, he found only two photo albums. One, labeled "Profile Pictures," included one shot, a photo of Becca's little dog. The other, labeled "Big Apple," featured grainy phone-quality pictures of what looked like Manhattan, posted three and a half weeks earlier. Water. Buildings. Graffiti on brick. No people. No smiling faces. Based on what he'd gathered about the girl's disposition, he assumed she was trying to be artsy.

He read the postings on Becca's Wall, the page where her friends could leave messages for her.

The entire first page consisted of messages submitted since Becca's disappearance had been made public.

Linwood High misses you. Come back soon and safe!

OMG, Becca. Hope you're just off being wild.

We love you, Becca, and pray that you're well.

Morhart suspected the trite sayings had been scribbled by class-mates who hardly knew the missing girl. He scrolled down further, searching for posts written prior to Becca's current claim to fame. The level of posting activity suddenly dropped. He read from the bottom up, taking in the earliest posts first.

Four weeks ago, she posted a status update: "I know I shouldn't, but I do love me some Glee."

A girl named Sophie Ferrin posted a response: "And you say I'm the dork."

Sophie Ferrin. Morhart knew the name. Best gal pal. Last to see her around.

Sophie's post was followed by a second response. "That show is totally gay." Authored by Rodney Carter. Morhart recognized that name, too. Boyfriend to Sophie. Accompanied the girls to the mall that same night.

He scrolled further up the page, skipping over the postings re-lated to the nonsense games people played on Facebook. Squirreling up loot in one virtual world. A promotion to captain in another. The fertilization of nonexistent farms.

He was only thirty-four years old but felt like a cantankerous old geezer, shaking his head with scorn at the rotting brains of today's teenagers.

A few days after the *Glee* posting, Becca had posted another update: "Heading to the city tonight. Woot!" The date matched the upload date for the city images he'd seen in her photo album.

"Have fun, girl, but not too much fun!" The response was from Sophie, meaning Sophie hadn't accompanied her friend on the photography trip into New York. Morhart made a mental note to follow up on that.

He clicked again on the album of images from the city and no-ticed that Becca had "tagged" someone named Dan Hunter. Not a name Morhart had come across until now.

Morhart knew that tagging was used to identify people depicted in pictures posted to Facebook. It was also a way to make sure that the photographs would also be displayed on the tagged person's own page.

He clicked on Dan Hunter's name. His profile photo showed a sandy blond teenager in a basketball jersey shooting a free throw. Morhart scrolled down until he found the postings of Becca's photographs. "Dan Hunter was tagged in a photograph." Tiny thumbnail images of Becca's pictures appeared on Hunter's virtual wall.

The posting of the images had triggered a comment from an Ashleigh Reynolds, another unfamiliar name. Ashleigh had typed only one word, but it was enough to place her at the top of Morhart's priority list.

Slut.

CHAPTER
SEVENTEEN

How did this happen?

It's a question most people ask themselves at some point in their lives. For some, the question comes when they wake up one morning, look at the person sleeping next to them, and realize—all at once, for the first time, but with unambiguous clarity—that they no longer want to be married. For others, it's a glance in the mirror at a face lost beneath years of self-neglect. Or the bank foreclosing on the house. Or a body that has lost its strength.

Most people experience a singular moment when they pause to take a hard look at their lives and don't recognize what they see. For Alice Humphrey, that sobering moment came when she saw Drew Campbell's body being carted through the narrow gallery door to a medical examiner's van waiting at the curb.

An ambulance had previously arrived, just after the first marked police car. But the paramedics hadn't bothered moving the body. Drew was that dead. Now his body was simply evidence. She felt herself flinch as the side of the metal gurney bumped the door frame.

That was the moment.

And, like anyone confronted with the fact she had been living a life she couldn't recognize, she asked herself, How did this happen? And like anyone trying to answer that unanswerable question, she kept rewinding the clock, struggling to identify the second when the path of her life veered in this direction.

Maybe if she hadn't walked into the gallery this morning, none of this would be happening. In retrospect, it made no sense that the front entrance had been unlocked, yet the windows covered with paper, when she had arrived. Maybe she ought to have walked away right then and there. If she'd gone home and forgotten all about Drew Campbell and this place, someone else eventually would have ventured into the gallery and been the lucky winner. Slipped in the blood. Called 911.

Or better yet, what if she hadn't come to the gallery this morning at all? What if, instead, she had marched over to her brother's apartment the second she saw that news story about his arrest? What kind of sister keeps a meeting at work when her brother might be in trouble? If she had tracked Ben down instead of simply trying his phone, maybe then, things would be different.

But eventually she would have been pulled into the investigation. She worked at the gallery. She had keys. She ran the place. She'd still be an essential part of the story of a man's murder.

So she rewound the clock. How did this happen?

How did this happen? She took the job. It sounded dumb even to say it, but she was swept off her feet by Drew—not romantically, but professionally.

So if Alice was trying to figure out how all this had happened, she'd have to rewind the clock pretty far. Far enough so that when Drew Campbell first came along, she would have smiled at his generous offer and politely declined. She would have to have been in a position not to take the bait. She could have returned to her comfortable job as a teacher, or as a banker, or maybe as a wife and mother. She would not have become the proud manager of the Highline Gallery. She would not have walked into the gallery that morning to find the entire inventory missing. She would never have been forced to see those awful wounds. And she would not be sitting on a street curb, looking up at a detective and his note pad, while she could still feel the warm, sticky shadows of Drew's blood on the palms of what her brain knew were now her cold, dry, clean hands.

"Was it usual for Mr. Campbell to be at the gallery this early in the morning by himself?"

"Um, no. I mean, nothing's really *usual*. We only opened two days ago. But in theory I'm the only one who's here. Drew hired me but wasn't really involved going forward. And we don't even open until eleven." She caught the detective locking eyes with his partner and realized she was rambling. "We had something of an emergency—some religious protesters yesterday because of the nature of the work we were displaying. When I finally got hold of Drew last night, he told me to meet him here this morning. When I got here, well, you know what I found."

She watched the detective's head nod. She fiddled with the business card he had handed her. His name was John Shannon. Had Detective Shannon known about the protests before he arrived here? Or was he just now drawing the link between this location and a news story to which he'd paid only vague attention? Was he wondering about a connection between the protesters and Drew's murder?

She found herself wishing this were an episode of one of those hour-long crime shows she loved on television instead of her new reality.

"Alice!"

She looked in the direction of the voice to see Lily bounding from the back of a cab, all long, skinny limbs and that baby-bird blond hair. A police officer immediately stepped in front of her to block her rapid movement toward the gallery.

"That's my friend. I called her after I called 911."

The detective made a beckoning motion toward the younger man in the uniform as an all-clear, and Lily ran to the curb, giving Alice a quick squeeze of the shoulder before settling down beside her. The detective acknowledged her with a polite nod but nothing more before continuing his questioning.

"We didn't find a wallet or any other possessions on the body. Was that your experience with Mr. Campbell?"

"Um, no. Well, I guess I don't know for sure." She tried to clear her thoughts to think rationally. "No, he carries a wallet. When I first met him, he asked me for a card, but I didn't have any. He wrote my number down on the back of some piece of paper from his wallet. And keys. He should have keys to a gray BMW." For the first time, she realized Drew's car should have been parked on the street in front of the gallery when she'd found the door unlocked before her arrival.

If she'd noticed the discrepancy then, would things be different? So many thoughts she had now that she should have had an hour earlier.

She saw the detective's gaze follow hers up and down the street. She watched the detective make notes on his pad. No BMW at the curb. No keys or wallet in Drew's pockets.

"And you say that when you left last night, the gallery wasn't vacant like this?"

"It definitely wasn't vacant. It was an open, functioning gallery. There was art and a desk and a computer and furniture."

"And I assume this art was valuable?"

She had no idea how to answer his question under the circumstances. "Our current showing featured reprints of photography with a potentially limitless run, so the price point was relatively low—seven hundred dollars for a photograph. But I had more than a hundred copies already printed and ready to ship in the stockroom. I also had, I don't know, probably ten canvases from other artists in the back, ready to show, once we were done with Schuler's initial run."

She realized she would need to call the artists whose works she had acquired for showing and explain that the paintings were gone. She had trusted Drew that the gallery was insured, but now had no idea whether she'd be able to make it up to the artists.

She watched as the detective scribbled more notes in his pad. She imagined the gears of his mind at work, churning through the possibilities. Religious protesters looking for vengeance? Art heist?

"What else can you tell me about the deceased?"

She had no idea what he meant. "I'm not sure what you mean."

"Date of birth? Family? Friends? Without his wallet, we don't even have an address for him."

She shrugged. "I don't know. I met him at a gallery a few weeks ago, and he hired me to manage this place."

"So he's the owner."

"No, he was an intermediary." She explained the backstory of Drew's anonymous business contact, motivated by his relationship with the elusive Hans Schuler, and noticed the detective's pen moving furiously in his notebook. He may as well have said it: rich, spoiled perverts.

"And you have no idea who the owner of the gallery is, or how to reach this man, Hans Schuler, other than through his Web site?"

"I've texted with Schuler and can give you that number, but that's all I've got. I'm sorry." Why was she apologizing?

"The place is pretty cleared out, as you know, but we did find a few of these on a shelf in one of your back storage closets." He held up a clear plastic bag filled with the personalized thumb drives that served as freebies with every Schuler purchase. "Are they yours?"

"Not *mine*, technically, but, yes, the gallery's. They were part of the promotional materials for the Schuler exhibit. Instead of a paper catalogue or other documents, each purchaser received one of those. You know, interactive stuff featuring the artwork. High-tech. Greener than paper. It's sort of a gimmick."

"So what about your paychecks? Where were those coming from?"

She fished through her handbag. One blessing of treating one's purse like a sack of garbage: lingering remnants of recent business. She retrieved a torn pay stub from the one and only check she had received as manager of the Highline Gallery. Eleven hundred and change, paid to the order of Alice Humphrey, from the account of ITH Corp. She had been so happy to have a check to cash, she had never paused to wonder about the origin of the name.

"Can I keep this?" the detective asked.

"Of course."

"Alice?"

She looked once again in the direction of her name. This time it was Jeff, emerging from the back of a taxi.

"Sorry," she said to the detective. "I sort of called everyone I could think of after I called you guys." Including her brother. She still hadn't heard from Ben.

She watched as the detective—what was his name again?—waved Jeff through the inner sanctum enfolded by the growing array of law enforcement around them. Jeff nodded toward Lily and kissed the top of Alice's head before joining them on the curb.

The detective continued to ask his questions, and she continued to answer them, but as much as she tried to ground herself in the severity of this moment, she found her mind wandering.

A man was dead. A life was lost. Drew hadn't been her husband or family or even a friend. This wasn't about her. Not in any way. So what if she lost a job? Who even cared that she had been through the shock of finding his body? Who cared about her junkie brother falling out of sobriety once again? She knew at a cognitive level that nothing about this situation involved her. Yet the feeling of Lily and Jeff on either side of her shivering body meant the world to her.

How did this happen?

Alice Humphrey had no idea.

She also had no idea the police would soon identify the person who had created ITH Corporation, the company named on her pay stub. She had no idea whose index finger would match a latent print that a crime scene analyst was currently pulling from the gallery's bathroom door. She had no idea that, two hundred yards away, on the corner of Washington and Bank, as Alice answered a question about Drew Campbell, a police officer working the routine perimeter search for a discarded weapon had just found a pair of black leather gloves with mink lining resting on top of a discarded half bagel in a trash can. He thought about passing them on to his girlfriend, but then placed them in a plastic evidence baggie just in case. She had no idea that this same detective and his partner would be at her door the following day with a photograph that would change everything.

CHAPTER EIGHTEEN

Hank threw an offhand wave toward Charlie Dixon as he passed Dixon's cubicle on the route to his own. Ever since the shit hit the fan two months ago with the reprimand, Hank felt like he was walking the gauntlet each time he padded through the narrow corridor formed between the makeshift light gray walls erected around the agents' identical faux-grained desks. It was as if a wave of whispers rippled behind him as he moved through the open-air hallway. He knew it was mostly his imagination, of course, but mostly was not the same thing as entirely.

With Dixon, though, things were different. He'd always been a quiet guy. Came to work, did the job, and left. No group jogs. No lunchtime skins and shirts on the basketball court. No happy hours. But ever since the reprimand—the one that was supposed to be private but which the entire field office obviously knew about the very morning it had been delivered—Dixon had been just a notch more cordial. Intentional eye contact. Meaningful nods. Even hellos in the lunchroom. If the two men didn't start to slow things down, they might actually share an entire conversation at some point.

At his computer, Hank checked the BMW's VIN in the National Motor Vehicle Title Information System. Title information used to be maintained only by the states, meaning fifty different databases. Not surprisingly, the bad guys figured out how to use that gap to their advantage. In theory, stolen cars have limited value in a world where a routine traffic stop can turn into a felony bust in a matter of seconds. As a result, stolen cars were usually sold for pennies on the dollar to be exported out of the country or broken down for parts.

But then the bad guys figured out they could steal a car in Florida, install forged VIN tags matching an identical car from a dealer lot, and then register the cloned car in North Carolina. Voilà. Unless the legitimate purchaser of the car that was actually supposed to carry that number just happened to move to North Carolina, no one would ever know that two cars were cruising around with the same regulatory fingerprints.

The federal government had finally pulled its shit together a couple of years earlier to create this new national database. The usual privacy fanatics were apoplectic. About half of the state DMVs also refused to play nice, sensing a system that would rival the one they charged taxpayers to access. Now the system was up and running well enough to be useful in a lot of cases, but was still no guarantee he'd be free from a state-by-state search.

He got lucky. The VIN hit a match.

According to the database, the gray BMW was owned by Quick-Car Inc. Hank was familiar with the company. QuickCar members had access to cars maintained in various lots throughout the city and paid only for their actual use. Rentals could be for hours, a full day, or longer. "Quick" out of the lot and dump the car back at any Quick site in the city. He searched for QuickCar on the Internet and dialed the company's toll-free number. Even if another agent overheard the call, all he'd hear would be an innocuous question about a vehicle identification number. There'd be no need for the name Travis Larson to be spoken on his end of the line. No need for anyone to let slip to the SAC that Hank was once again keeping tabs on the man he was supposed to leave alone. *Let it lie, Beckman. As far as you're concerned, Travis Larson does not exist. Forget the man's name if you know what's good for you.*

"QuickCar."

He identified himself as an FBI agent and explained that he needed to track down the identity of the person who'd been driving one of their gray BMWs as recently as this morning. "I have the vehicle identification number."

"Can you hold for my supervisor?"

Not good.

"This is Mr. Martin. How can I help you?"

Mr. Martin obviously brought an intensity to his job as a rental car company's phone-bank manager. Hank was tempted to hang up and move on to Plan B, but went ahead and restated his request.

"I'm sorry, sir, but I'm not able to hand out identifying information about our customers on the telephone."

"This is an urgent matter in a federal criminal investigation."

"I understand that, Agent, but the company follows certain procedures. If you can fax over a subpoena . . ."

"You do realize that a fax comes over the telephone line, no different than this phone call. Anyone could doctor a piece of paper."

Mr. Martin didn't have a ready response, but he also wasn't budging.

"Never mind," he said quickly. "I just got the information I needed from another route."

He turned his attention back to his computer and pulled up another number, this time for a Quick rental location in midtown. A woman with a heavy Bronx accent answered after six rings. He could almost picture her chomping on the gum in her mouth.

Once again, he said he was an FBI agent with a VIN he needed to track down.

"Um, my manager's not here right now." He could hear someone yelling in the background about a car blocking the garage entrance. *"Hey, you! Yeah, girl in the Mazda. Can you back it up just like three feet so this guy can get out and stop yelling at the both of us? Thanks, hon!* Sorry, so, yeah, my manager's out. Can you call back? I think you're supposed go through corporate or something."

"This is an urgent matter in a federal criminal investigation."

The line meant absolutely nothing, of course, but Hank had been amazed over the years at its effectiveness. At heart, people were wired to comply with authority.

"Federal?"

"Yes, ma'am. It's urgent. My guess is, if I call corporate, they'll have me hammer out a subpoena. Not a problem, of course, but it's a delay. All I need is a name." He heard another urgent voice in the background, and added in the kicker. "We have reason to believe that, in addition to the crimes we are investigating, whoever rented that car has switched the license plates on it, which could be an indication that he's planning to use the car as an instrumentality of criminal activity. I'm sure Quick wouldn't want one of its cars to be the next suspicious vehicle abandoned in Times Square. If you want verification that I'm at the FBI, I can give you the number of my office down here at Federal Plaza, and you can give me a call back."

The voice in the background got louder. Something like, *If you'd ever get off that phone.*

"Okay, give me that VIN again?"

He recited the numbers.

"Well, this is funny. The computer says it's no longer in our inventory."

"Why would that be? Do you sell cars out of your fleet?"

"Oh. Wait. This is a gray BMW 335i sedan? Says it was last checked in at a garage on Fourteenth Street."

"That means something?"

"Oh, hell. I remember this. Some fool at that garage let some lady just run off with the keys."

"It was stolen?"

"Oh, hell yeah. Must have been around a month ago. Now, you're calling the central location, where every car on this lot's a Quick-Car, and I work directly for the company. But we keep our cars at garages all over the city, just a few cars here and there scattered at private lots for customer convenience. Not everyone's gonna pay the same kind of attention to the cars, you know what I'm saying?"

"So one of the private garage attendants let his guard down?"

"Let his *something* down. All he could say afterward was that some pretty lady was asking questions about how the QuickCar rentals worked. He left to dig out a buried car for a resident. Next thing he knew, she was gone, and so was the Beemer."

"He said it was a woman by herself?"

"Yeah. A white girl. A pretty white girl with long red hair."

CHAPTER NINETEEN

Even with his eyes closed, Morhart would have known his location simply from the squeaks and *boings* echoing down the hallway. The squeaks of rubber and the *boings* of leather against maple. Nothing sounded quite like an indoor basketball court. This particular court, down this particular hallway, was familiar territory to Morhart, but Linwood High School felt so much smaller than it had when he graduated sixteen years earlier.

Lingering inside the double doors to check out the team's practice, he recognized Dan Hunter right away from his Facebook photos. The players were in uniform, sprinting from half court to baseline, tagging the floor with their fingertips at each end. Hunter kept up okay step for step, but by the time the team was ten laps in, he lagged half a court back from the pack and would have eventually gotten lapped if the coach hadn't blown the whistle. Next were rapid layups. The students fell into line, a few paces between them, each galloping toward the basket for a one-handed reach. This time Hunter wasn't the worst, but he was no Air Jordan, apparently both slower and more prone to gravity than the average team member.

But then came the outside shots. Twelve boys formed an arc around the three-point line, hurling ball after ball after ball. Some throws ricocheted hard off the backboard. Some barely skimmed the metal rim. The coach shook his head as the number of airballs multiplied. But one kid was swooshing balls through the net, seven out of ten. Dan Hunter could shoot.

The shrillness of the whistle halted the cacophony of bouncing leather and squeaking rubber. Morhart stepped onto the court and raised a friendly wave. "Coach, you got a second?"

Not much older than Morhart himself, David DeCicco had started at Linwood High long after Morhart's own years here, but he'd gotten to know the man two years earlier when Linwood's starting center broke the wrist of a girl who dared to break up with him the day before prom. A lot of coaches would have been tempted to protect one of their best players, but DeCicco had walked into the station on his own to report that he'd once seen the player grab his girlfriend's arm when she tried to walk away from him at a postgame party. Morhart had felt the man's guilt for having looked the other way at the time. He heard later from the girl's parents that the coach kicked the kid off the team and brought in a guidance counselor to talk to the other boys about teenage dating violence.

"Water break, guys, but no wandering off." DeCicco shook Morhart's hand. "Any chance you just had a sudden urge to watch a basketball practice, Detective?"

"Something like that. What can you tell me about Dan Hunter?"

"Aw, Jesus. Hunter? He's the only man I got who can shoot from the outside. What the hell did he go and do?"

Morhart raised his palm. "Nothing like that, Coach. I'm talking to anyone who might have some insight into that missing girl, Becca Stevenson."

DeCicco made the same *tsk* sound Morhart was already accustomed to hearing after every mention of Becca's name.

"I wouldn't have thought Hunter would even know that girl."

"Why do you say that?"

He squinted. "You know how kids are. Cliques. Popularity contests. The social hierarchies, if you will. Hunter's a jock. My thirteen-year-old daughter tells me he's a cutey patootie. Her words, not mine. He's into, you know, cheerleaders and pep squad girls with perky smiles and, well, perky everything, not that I try to notice. A girl like Becca—"

He cut himself off, but Morhart urged him to complete the thought. DeCicco glanced around and lowered his voice. "I'll be blunt. She's an odd bird. Had her in American History last year. I'm sure she's a decent kid, but there's something that's, I don't know, just *off*. Sullen. Dark. Probably very insecure. Something almost broken about her, but, you know, no big behavioral problems, no signs of abuse, no obvious indications of drug use. Not positive enough to really be engaged in school, but not quite bad off enough to be one of the problem children."

"Invisible."

"Exactly. One of those invisible kids. Look, I know the reality about a lot of my guys. For most of them, these will be the heydays. They'll wind up going to JuCo at best, and they'll never leave this town. But at least they'll have their years in this building, with the cheering in the stadium and the letter jackets and the pretty girls to look back on as some moment in their lives when they were something. The kids my guys pick on? They'll wind up inventing the next electric car or something. They'll date supermodels and buy Italian villas or whatever, and will look back on this place as a joke. But then there are kids like Becca. These sad kids who don't have much happiness now and give you the feeling they'll never have anything in the future."

"That's fucking depressing."

"Needless to say, I'm a little more encouraging to my players. Save the armchair psychology for the grown-ups."

"And what would the shrink have to say about Dan Hunter if it turns out he was spending time with the Stevenson girl?"

He waited a full five seconds before answering. "He's not a bad kid, but he's not inherently good either. His ethics are, how can I put this? Situational."

Hunter sported the shaggy hair that young kids seemed to favor these days, resorting to a series of lopsided head spasms to flip his long bangs out of his eyes. He swept the back of his hand across his face to wipe away some of the sweat.

"Coach said you wanted to see me?"

If Morhart's introduction as a member of the police department made Hunter nervous, he didn't show it.

"You might have heard that Becca Stevenson never came home Sunday night."

"Yeah, I heard. Where is she?"

The kid asked the question as if Morhart would know. As if Morhart had come here to inform this kid personally what had become of Becca Stevenson. He had no idea what to make of it. Maybe the kid had been close to Becca, thinking about her, expecting to hear news. Or maybe he was just thick in the brain. He looked thick.

"Well, that's sort of why I'm here, Dan. Talking to Becca's friends. Trying to get some ideas about where she might have gone to."

He offered no response, only nodded in a slow way that warned Morhart not to attribute too much wiliness to this one.

"So would you say you were one of Becca's friends?"

Hunter shrugged. "My friends are guys, you know?"

"Did you know her?"

Another shrug. "I sort of know everyone at the school, you know?"

"Ever go out with her?"

"Go out?"

"Date. Hook up. Fuck?"

The obscenity shook the kid out of his supercool frat-boy daze. "No, nothing like that."

"But something. Maybe a little road trip into Manhattan?"

"Yeah, okay, but that was a while ago. We were sort of talking and stuff last month, but it didn't work out."

"You need to start using complete sentences, son."

"And with all due respect, sir, you need to stop calling me son. I mean, sorry, I know you've got your job and all, but just because I made the mistake of giving some screwed-up chick like Becca a chance doesn't mean I deserve the third degree."

Morhart could see what the coach had meant about the kid's situational disposition.

"I do have a job, Dan. And it requires that I walk into a circumstance I know nothing about and make some quick decisions about where best to focus my time. And right now my focus is on you, and the more attitude you show toward me, the more likely it's going to stay there and intensify like a white-hot laser beam. Now, with all due respect as you called it, please start telling me about your relationship to Becca Stevenson—who, if I must remind you, is missing and could very well be in jeopardy if not worse."

"There's not much to tell. She's kind of weird, but I've always known she had a crush on me or whatever. I was getting sick of the usual girlfriend bullshit and thought I'd try something new. We started talking or whatever, and, yeah, we went into Manhattan a couple times. It was fun. She was, like, different or whatever. But I don't know, it just didn't work out. It was no big deal."

"Why didn't it work out?"

"It just didn't, I don't know. We were too different."

"Who's Ashleigh Reynolds?"

Hunter shook his head in frustration. "That's what this is about? Yeah, so Ashleigh and I are what you'd call on-and-off. Needless to say, we were off when I was having conversations with Becca, and Ashleigh wasn't having any of it. She was talking smack about Becca."

"Like calling her a slut on your Facebook page?"

He looked at the floor. "Yeah. That was about the worst of it, really. Most of it was catty comments to her stupid girlfriends, but it was too much drama, so, whatever: that was that. No more Becca, and me and on-and-off Ashleigh are back on."

"No more Becca, huh?"

"Jeez, man, not like that."

"Where were you on Sunday night?"

"Come on, man. You've got to be kidding."

"Then humor me. Decent-looking guy like you, lots of friends— I can't imagine you spend too much time alone."

"I was on the court kicking Jefferson High's ass. You can check with the coach if you want."

"And after the game?"

"You gonna bust me if it involves some underage drinking?"

"Not exactly my priority right now, kid."

He paused, then smiled. "In that case, I was ripping some mighty beautiful keg stands in Jay Lindon's basement. His parents are out of town. The whole team was there."

Both components of the alibi would be easy to confirm—or break, as the case might be.

"Look, check me out all you want. I have no idea where Becca is, but—and I feel *bad* saying this—she was seriously screwed up, okay? Why do you think the school doesn't have banners all over the building or a twenty-four/seven candlelight vigil on the front lawn? Everyone assumes she ran away. She's long gone, and the sad thing is, no one really cares."

According to her two-month-old driver's license, Ashleigh Reynolds lived at an address in one of the more upscale neighborhoods of Dover, meaning new brick instead of linoleum siding, a smooth unmarred concrete driveway instead of oil-stained blacktop, and perfectly manicured yards. He used the shiny brass knocker on the magenta-painted door. A man in a dress shirt, sleeves rolled up but his tie still knotted, answered.

"Mr. Reynolds?"

The man greeted him with the friendly smile of a salesman, but his squint made clear he expected an introduction, which Morhart provided. "I was hoping to talk to your daughter, Ashleigh, about a girl from her school who's been reported missing. Becca Stevenson?"

"Sure, we heard about that. Sad thing. I swear, my wife's about to drive our daughter crazy watching out for her now."

"So is your daughter here?" The echoes of a Taylor Swift song from inside the house suggested so.

"She's working on her homework right now."

"It'll just be a few minutes, sir. I'm talking to everyone at the school trying to find some kind of lead. The poor girl's mother is beside herself."

Reynolds looked up the stairway behind him toward the sounds of the music. "Ashleigh's mom and I already talked with our daughter about that issue, trying to see if maybe she could offer anything helpful. She didn't know the girl, and obviously has no idea where she might have gone, or we would have called you right away."

"So if she'd confirm that for me—"

"We don't want her involved in this. Ashleigh and her friends are pretty scared wondering what might have become of that girl and whether they might be next. I heard her up pacing the house last night. She couldn't sleep because she'd had a dream about being kidnapped. Talking to a police officer will only get her thoughts back into those dark places, and for what? She doesn't know anything. I hope you'll understand, Detective."

Morhart blinked at the magenta door with the brass knocker, closed before he could respond.

By the time Morhart returned to the precinct, Dan Hunter had removed his Facebook tags from the New York photos, erasing any public evidence of the popular jock's short-term involvement with the weird girl named Becca Stevenson.

CHAPTER
TWENTY

Alice was bundled in Jeff's white terry bathrobe, her hair still damp from the shower. She turned sideways on the black leather couch to facilitate the shoulder rub Jeff had started. Somewhere along the road, she had forgotten all the simple ways he had of comforting her.

When the police were finally finished asking questions, all she could think of as a next step was to take a shower. To wash away the blood from her skin and clothing. To rinse off the smell of death. When she, Lily, and Jeff all crawled into the back of a cab, Lily had given the driver Alice's address, but it was Alice who changed the directive. For reasons she could not explain, she did not want to be in her apartment, not even in the company of her two closest friends.

Maybe she just yearned for the sterility of Jeff's ultramodern apartment. The white walls. White floors. High-gloss white cabinets. Sleek leather furniture. Steel accents. No clutter. No dust. No blood. Lightness and order compared to her shabby chic chaos.

But maybe it was more than just an aesthetic preference. Drew had been impossible to find yesterday, and then sounded panicked last night. He wouldn't talk on the phone. He had asked to meet her—in person, and first thing in the morning. And now someone had killed him. Two gunshots to the chest, is what she overheard one of the policemen say. What if she had arrived at the gallery earlier? What if whoever killed Drew saw dropping in on her as part of finishing the job?

"I feel so awful about you both taking care of me. Don't you need to get back to work?"

"My deposition was set over until next week. Had the whole day clear anyway."

The question had been aimed primarily at Lily. Travel magazines weren't exactly rolling in profits in this economy, and the Gorilla was not the kind of boss who took a missed day in stride. "Don't worry about me. I told the Gorilla my sister was in the hospital."

"You don't have a sister."

"Yeah, but the Gorilla doesn't know that. Just got to remember to add that little factoid to the work persona. Now, what's the appropriate period of mourning before we just throw down and get this woman skunk drunk?"

Lily was making herself at home in Jeff's kitchen, foraging through the bar cabinet and pulling out whatever bottles of booze looked interesting.

"Seriously, Lily. I don't think I can do it."

"I don't want to make light of your boss being dead, but c'mon, Alice, you really didn't even know the guy. He showed up at an art exhibit, offered you a job running a gallery with an anonymous owner, hooked you up with some weirdo artist you can't even get a hold of—he was obviously doing something shady. Whatever it was caught up to him. And whatever it was, the police will eventually sort it all out. You're no longer involved."

"What do you mean, whatever he was up to? Obviously, whatever got him killed had something to do with the gallery. You saw the place. It was stripped bare. No signs of life."

"Literally," Lily said, inspecting the label on a bottle of neon blue liquor. "Sorry, too soon?"

"Look. Maybe we should talk about something else for a while." Jeff had slipped off one of his loafers. "Or, better yet: Al, why don't you try lying down for a while. You could use the rest. Sprawl out and watch some TV. Or take the bedroom."

"Watch out, Alice. He's just trying to get you back in the sack."

"Jesus, Lily."

"It's fine," Alice said, placing a hand on Jeff's knee. "I don't want to go to sleep. I want to talk about it."

He was trying to protect her, but the truth was, Lily's bluntness was what she needed right now. Jeff didn't argue with her, but the shoulder rub came to an end. He was not one of Lily's biggest fans, but his usual preference to avoid her company was not a priority today.

"If we're going to talk about it, let's really talk. Alice is right. We can't ignore the fact that someone went to great lengths to empty out the gallery. The question is why."

"No," Lily said, finally opting for a bottle of Grey Goose vodka and tipping it over a glass of orange juice. "The question is why the two of you think we need to be the ones asking those kinds of questions. Unless I missed something, we're not Shaggy, Velma, and Daphne squirreled up like meddling kids on the Mystery Machine van with Scooby-Doo. Alice is a witness to a crime—an after-the-fact witness at that. Nothing more. End of story. She should worry about her own problems and leave all this to the police."

"It's only natural that she'd worry about her own safety. And figuring out what might have happened to Campbell this morning—and why—is a first step to figuring out whether she's in any danger."

"And what if she does figure something out? Did it ever dawn on you that figuring out too much is precisely what could put her in danger?"

"Hello? The third-person *she* of this conversation is sitting right here." Alice rose from the couch to accept the glass of spiked juice Lily extended in her direction.

"Good girl," Lily said. "Take your medicine."

The first sip burned. By the third, Alice wanted to retract the orange juice.

"There's nothing dangerous about talking through the possibilities," Alice said. Talking with them would keep her mind moving.

Would keep her thoughts from carrying her back to the floor beside Drew's body. Keep her imagination from conjuring flashes of her big brother in handcuffs. Keep her eyes away from the screen on her cell phone, still black despite multiple messages, begging Ben for a return call. Most of all, talking would help her feel—at least for a few brief moments, however manufactured—like she had retained some tiny portion of her agency in a world that had spiraled out of control. "So, let's play the Mystery Machine. What are the possible scenarios that could have led to what I saw this morning?"

Lily let out an audible sigh, but saw that she was outvoted.

"One," she said, extending her thumb, "theft. A large-scale jacking of the entire contents of the gallery, with Drew ending up the unlucky victim. The problems with that are: A—the art wasn't worth much compared to an established gallery, and B—why not grab the art and run? Why clear out every last stapler and pencil?"

She added her index finger to the count. "Two: the religious nut jobs who were protesting yesterday. Maybe they decided to take matters into their own hands. They couldn't track down the artist, but they could send a message by eviscerating the gallery this morning when someone showed up to open. But we've got a problem there, too. Even if they're rabid enough to try to pull something like this off, why kill Drew? I mean, if they're violent enough to shoot someone, why not just firebomb the place? A dead body in an empty gallery? Not exactly dramatic and protester-y, you know? And that, boys and girls, leaves us with option number three." Out went a third finger.

"And you said this was none of our business," Jeff said.

"I said I thought minding our own business was the best thing for Alice. And part of the reason I thought that—and still think that—is because I've been running through the options since she called me this morning, and only one of them makes any sense. Three," she continued, "that lingering feeling you had that this job was too good to be true was right on the money. Campbell was up to no good. Maybe he double-crossed the owner. Or the artist. Or maybe the anonymous owner story was total bullshit from the very start. Maybe he was the one pulling the strings, using the gallery as a front to hide stolen money. Maybe the protesters brought a little bit too much attention to the place. He was trying to get rid of all evidence of the place when someone caught up to him. Or maybe whoever he crossed decided it was lights out for both Drew and his pet project."

No one else in the room spoke. There was nothing to add. Lily was right. Three options: two highly improbable, and the third raising more questions than they could even begin to answer.

Lily added another shot of vodka to Alice's glass. "I'll help you out however you want, but if I were you? I'd consider yourself lucky you don't know more about Drew Campbell and the Highline Gallery."

Less than a mile away, in the homicide unit at the Thirteenth Precinct, NYPD Detective John Shannon told his partner, Willie Danes, they had a problem.

"I'm not finding a Drew Campbell who looks anything like our guy."

"Wouldn't be the first person to hide his bridge-and-tunnel status. Everyone who's anyone's got to live in the city these days." Danes was chewing on a toothpick. Five years into the partnership, Danes knew Shannon hated the toothpick chewing. Five years into the partnership, the chewing of the toothpick was still a daily habit.

"Except I checked Jersey, Pennsylvania, and Connecticut. No Drew or Andrew Campbells who resemble our vic. I've looked at so many DMV photos my eyes are blurring." The cell phone numbers Alice Humphrey had given them for Drew Campbell and Hans Schuler had both come back to disposable phones that were untraceable. "What about the company on the paycheck?"

"ITH Corporation?"

"Yeah, that's it. You getting anywhere?"

Danes swirled the toothpick around his tongue. "Depends whether up my own ass counts as somewhere. The company was incorporated twenty-five years ago, but I can't figure out what the hell it does. State records show the stock is owned by a trust called ITH Trust, but trusts aren't recorded, so there's no way to know what it does or who it benefits. The registered agent is one of the big services, so that's a dead end. I nearly had to give up a kidney to persuade a girl in the secretary of state's office to try to dig out the incorporation paperwork for us. She said she'd try, but I'm not holding my breath after all these years."

"You say the company was incorporated twenty-five years ago?"

"A little more. May of 1985 to be precise."

"And how old do you think our vic could've been?" Shannon asked, holding up a crime scene photo of the body.

"Granted now, death has a tendency to age a person, but I'd say forty. Tops."

"Bringing us back to the mysterious older owner whom the lovely Miss Humphrey says she never met." Shannon tapped the ashen face in the photograph. "I put a rush on the fingerprints, but so far, this guy's a ghost."

CHAPTER
TWENTY-ONE

Morhart was at Linwood High School for the second day in a row, feeling nearly like a regular when Coach DeCicco threw him a wave as Morhart passed the oblong window of his classroom door. A dimpled smile and a flash of his badge to the secretary posted outside the principal's office earned him directions to the Algebra II class on Ashleigh Reynolds's schedule. Only five minutes until classes changed, so he waited in the hallway for the bell.

Ashleigh sprung from the classroom clustered together with two other girls, the three of them chattering too furiously over each other to possibly be listening. One of them caught his eye and gave him a look he was uncomfortable receiving from a teenage girl.

"I need to have a word with Ashleigh, girls, if you don't mind."

They were still eyeballing him from their lockers like he was the head of the football team extending an invitation to prom, but he could tell from Ashleigh's dark expression that she already knew who he was.

"My father told you I don't know anything about that Becca girl."

That Becca girl. Like Ashleigh couldn't use her name. As if Becca weren't human.

"I know what your father said, Ashleigh, but you're a big girl. I wanted to hear what you had to say for yourself." Morhart knew he'd be hearing later from an angry Mr. Reynolds, but the law didn't allow a parent to invoke a child's right to silence on her behalf. Ashleigh would have to do that on her own.

But she didn't, just as Morhart had predicted.

"What do you want to know? It's not like she's my friend or anything."

"No. But she's Dan's friend. Or at least she was."

She hugged her books closer to her chest. "I don't know much about that. We took a break. He was just trying to make me jealous."

"Based on the comment you posted on Facebook, I'd say it worked."

Her gaze moved in the direction of her girlfriends. He wanted to smack the relishing smirk off her face but instead took a step to his left to block the line of sight.

"Look. Maybe I was a little harsh. But I knew me and Dan would get back together. The last thing I need is for people thinking we're somehow the same."

"And what's so wrong with being the same as Becca Stevenson?"

She shook her head as if he'd asked how to boil water. "She's, I don't know— She stares at Dan all the time but then kind of acts like she's better than everyone, like too good to go to games or parties. She's just *weird*. And then out of nowhere she's posting pictures of her little road trip with Dan on Facebook, like we're going to accept her all of the sudden."

"You called her a *slut* for posting a picture on a Web site?"

"That wasn't the picture I was talking about."

He could tell she regretted the words the instant they left her mouth.

"What picture?"

He watched her gaze move once again, but this time to a chubby girl peering out from behind her locker door.

"What picture are you referring to, Ashleigh?"

"Why don't you go ask Becca? Oh, yeah, that's right. She's a head case who ran away to get the whole school's attention. My father told you not to talk to me, Detective. I better go to class now."

• • •

The bell rang as a classroom door closed behind Ashleigh, but the girl tucked behind her locker door remained.

"How you doing, Sophie?"

Sophie Ferrin was by all accounts Becca's best friend. Morhart had already interviewed her for more than an hour when he'd first caught Becca's case.

"You were talking to Ashleigh Reynolds."

"I'm aware of that. I saw you watching us. You knew about this Dan Hunter situation?"

She nodded.

"Why didn't you say something?"

"About Dan and Ashleigh? There's nothing to say. They were pretty awful to her, but Becca was totally over it."

"What do you mean by awful?"

"At first it was just Ashleigh and her stupid friends. They heard about Dan and Becca hanging out and started saying she was a slut and that Dan was only hooking up with her because she was willing to do all kinds of freaky stuff Ashleigh would never do."

"Was that true?"

She shrugged. "I assume not."

"But you don't know?"

"Becca was pretty into Dan. I gave her hell about it. I feel so horrible now." She sniffed back a sob.

"You said at first it was Ashleigh and her friends spreading rumors. Then what happened?"

"I'm not sure on all the details. I thought Dan actually liked Becca, but Ashleigh was just relentless. I think she wore him down, and the only way he could make things right with her was to bring down Becca. He arranged to meet Becca down at Hudson Park, you know, it's where we hang out." Morhart nodded. As a cop, he'd broken up more than a few fights and drinking parties at the park over the years. "When Becca met him there, he was with Ashleigh and all their friends. He said something like, 'You haven't figured this out yet? This whole thing with you and me has been a joke.' "

He wanted to believe that kids hadn't been so cruel when he was the one meeting his friends at Hudson Park, but maybe that was how he preferred to remember the past. "Why didn't you tell any of this to me or Mrs. Stevenson?"

"Honestly? Because around here, what Becca went through wasn't even that bad. Last year, Luke Green pretended to ask some nobody girl to homecoming. She was waiting on her porch in her new dress and up-do when that whole clique cruised by in their limo jeering at her. Supposedly one of them beaned her from the sunroof with a half-eaten Big Mac. They're assholes, and they're brutal, but they're pretty much a way of life at Linwood."

"Ashleigh called Becca a slut after she posted a photograph taken in the city on Facebook. When I asked her about it today, she said that wasn't the picture she was talking about. Do you know anything about that?"

"Jesus, I knew this was going to get out."

"This is not a time for keeping secrets, Sophie. Becca's mom believes in you. She nearly fell to her knees in her living room begging me to search my hardest for her girl. And she swore up and down that she knew something untoward has happened to her daughter, because she's relying on your word. She says she knows you in your heart and that you would not hold back on her. Not now. Not under these circumstances."

Her eyes scanned the empty hallways for potential eavesdroppers. "Dan had a nude picture of Becca. One of Ashleigh's stupid friends borrowed his phone and saw it. She forwarded it to Ashleigh, and that's when they really started to pile on. Not that many people know about the picture. Becca was worried they'd forward it all over the school, but Ashleigh must have her reasons for holding on to it. Knowing her, she was going to torment Becca down the road with it. So, Joann said that? That she knew me in my heart and that I wouldn't keep anything from her?"

He nodded. "Said something about you being almost like a second daughter. Why didn't you tell her, Sophie?"

"Because when Becca comes home, I don't want her to be in trouble, either with Joann or around here."

"I notice you say *when* Becca comes home."

"It's just a feeling I have."

"Which is?"

"I don't know whether to be scared for Becca or pissed off at her. One minute my mind is racing through all the horrible things that might have happened to her, and the next, I remember how adamant she was about walking home that night. I remember how secretive she'd been with me lately. At first I assumed it was because she knew I thought Dan Hunter was a total tool, but then even after they broke up and everything went down with Ashleigh and her friends, she still had all these mystery plans. She'd get all evasive about it. Said she liked having something that was 'just hers.' That's what she called it. I guess that need for her to have something special is what led her to send that stupid picture to Dan. So, yeah, I've kind of wondered if her insistence on walking home that night might have been for a reason. Not to mention, no one's saying a bad word about her at Linwood now. Sort of an added bonus."

"Would she really put you through this? And her mother?"

"I don't know. I really hope not, but then that would mean something bad has happened. And so, yeah, I convince myself there's a side of Becca that might crave this kind of attention. I feel awful saying that about my best friend. Please tell me you won't stop looking for her. You told me not to hold back, so please don't punish Becca and Joann for it. Even if this is Becca acting out, she needs to be found. For her own good."

He nodded. "I already promised her mother."

Sophie was spinning her padlock closed when he turned back for a final question.

"You said Becca *sent* that picture to Dan? He didn't take it with his phone?"

"No. Becca took it with her phone and sent it to him."

"Her mom told me Becca doesn't have a cell phone."

"Sure she does. She got it a couple of months ago. I've called her, like, a thousand times, but it goes straight to voice mail. You mean Joann didn't know?"

CHAPTER
TWENTY-TWO

Alice was in her bed, thinking about friendship.

People go through life accumulating and occasionally discarding relationships, casually using the word *friend* to describe the human beings who flutter in and out of their daily worlds. But not everyone who can be counted on as good company at a new restaurant or an afternoon matinee or even a late-night visit to the emergency room can truly be called a friend. Only a true friend would have done for Alice what Lily Harper and Jeff Wilkerson had done for her today.

From the second they had heard about Drew, they had dropped everything. Lily, who had the Gorilla watching her every move at the office. Jeff, who was struggling to keep his practice afloat since he'd left that miserable firm only to learn that the economy had tanked months before the public realized. Despite their own responsibilities, the two of them had been there the instant she'd needed them and had not once taken a break, not for a phone call or an e-mail or even to rest. They had taken care of her the way only true friends could.

She had finally left Jeff's apartment when she found herself nodding off on the couch. She had been tempted to accept his invitation to stay overnight, but had foreseen what would have developed. The shoulder rubs. The smell of his broken-in robe as she'd stepped inside it from the steaming shower. His gestures had been in friendship, but she knew herself well enough to interpret her own responses to them. Whatever journey their relationship was on, today was not the time for a major shift in direction. When Alice insisted on going back to her own place, Lily had proven her dedication once again by insisting she sleep on the sofa.

The *ting-ting* of the doorbell halted her thoughts. She was about to call out to Lily when she heard the release of the safety chain, followed by friendly murmurs. She assumed her self-appointed bodyguard had ordered a late dinner until she heard the voices getting louder.

"She's had a bad fucking day, made all the worse by the fact that her own brother wasn't there when she needed him. She must have called you fifteen times."

And here Alice had thought she'd been discreet, feeling guilty about sneaking off for phone calls while Lily and Jeff had placed their own lives on hold for her.

"All I can say is you haven't changed a bit. Take that however you'd like." Her brother's voice was simultaneously cutting and dismissive.

Alice stepped from bed and cracked open the door. "I'm still up, Lily. It's okay. Sorry if he woke you."

"No, I was up." No complaints. No passive aggression. Just Lily, trying to stick up for her.

Ben didn't bother moving the clothes from the only chair in the bedroom before plopping down. "Jesus Christ, that girl is and always has been such a royal cunt. There's a screw loose with that chick."

"Unh-unh. Not here, Ben. Not today."

"Sorry, I just can't believe you guys are friends. Irony of ironies, you know? She was the biggest sycophant in high school. She thought she was hot shit in podunk Mount Kisco. Treated me and my friends like scum until she realized who we were, then couldn't get enough of us. You would have fucking hated her."

Alice now wished that she and Lily had never figured out the few degrees of separation in their past lives. After her mother died, Lily had been raised by her father in Mount Kisco, just south of Bedford, where Alice's family had a home. Alice and Ben had gone to school in the city, but had friends who were from local families. As best as Lily and Alice had been able to reconstruct, Lily was a year behind Ben. They were never close friends, but ran in the same weekend circles. She'd even been to their house for a couple of his parties, but had never met his little sister.

"You know what's funny, Ben? It's funny that you didn't mention all that months ago when you found out we were friends. Maybe you suddenly remembered just now when she totally called you out?"

The words were harsh, but were delivered teasingly. Alice couldn't help it. Ben could frustrate her, anger her, even break her, and somehow she always had a little smile for him, even when she was doing her best to bust on him.

"Whatever, fine. I was out of line."

"Seriously? The c-word? Under my roof? About my *friend*?"

"I said I was sorry."

"So you got my messages." She crawled into the bed and bunched a pillow on her lap.

"Yeah. I'm sorry. I should have called you about the arrest. It never dawned on me it would make the news."

"And you got the other messages? About the gallery?"

"Yeah. How's that going? I'm really sorry I missed the opening."

She shook her head. He had listened to the first message, maybe even the second, when she'd been calling about his arrest. But he'd obviously deleted the rest of them. *Ben, I've got a man's blood on my hands. Where are you?* Beep. *Jesus, Ben, you can't even call me back when there's been a murder at my job?* Beep. *I'm sorry Ben, but I could really use some family right now. And you know with Mom and Dad . . .* Beep.

"So was it true? Were you arrested?"

"You called like it was some big Medellín Cartel bust or something. There was a complaint about the sidewalk noise outside of Little Branch. Some douchebag I didn't even know mouthed off to one of the cops, so we all got frisked. I had some dope in my pocket. It's no big deal. The lawyer says I'll pay a fine and that'll be that."

"I thought your program required you to be completely clean. In the past, you've said the pot makes you more likely to slip into other drugs."

"Can you give me a break? Please? I've been clean five years, and the Humphrey family still sees me as the junkie loser son. It was just a little pot. I promise."

She looked into his eyes, wanting so much to believe him. Wanting to wash her brain of its desire to check his pulse. Inspect his forearms. Search his apartment for pipes, needles, and bloody Kleenexes. She'd have to search for all of it, because for a decade and a half of his life, Ben Humphrey had been a human garbage can, willing to dump anything and everything into his body.

"You believe me, right?"

She was about to, before he'd asked that question.

"So what's up with your dear, sweet, totally-not-a-cunt friend out there with sheets on the sofa. She get dumped or something?"

"Um, no, Ben. She's here because something really bad happened today." She told him about finding Drew at the gallery. She watched his eyes move unconsciously to the pocket that must have held his cell phone, the one she'd called so many times.

"Sorry you went through that alone."

"I wasn't alone. But, yeah, I did want my family."

"You didn't call Mom and Dad?"

"Did you call them when you were arrested? I notice you mentioned 'the lawyer.' If Dad was involved, you would've said Art."

Arthur Cronin, in addition to being one of her parents' best friends, was also the go-to attorney for all remotely law-related Humphrey family problems.

"No Mom or Dad. No Art. I guess your independent ways are contagious."

"I thought you said I was being too rough on Dad."

"You mean to tell me you haven't thought about all those women he was with? I mean, barely women at that. Jennifer Roberson, or whatever her name is? She was nineteen when she auditioned for *Smashed.* I've done the math. She was only a year older than you were at the time. I mean, our father had a casting couch—literally, a casting couch—in his office. And the penchant for photography? Not to mention the fact that all those women look vaguely like our mother. Frank certainly has a type."

"Stop it, Ben. I really am going to hurl."

"You don't even know the half of it."

"What is that supposed to mean?"

"Nothing. Just blowing off steam. Our dad's a goddamn player, and our mom's too dazed to give a rat's ass. Let's just say we're both avoiding their shit for the time being."

She and Ben had always been so different. More than twenty years after she had walked away from a promising start as a child actor, Ben was still trying to find a place for himself in the family industry, first as a screenwriter, a few times as a producer for small-time indies (with their father's money, of course), and now, more realistically, as a sound engineer recording special audio effects. She'd always been a quiet student. He was a rowdy party guy. She saw herself as a connected part of the larger world. He preferred to shrink from it. While he had the olive skin and exaggerated features of their father, Alice—with her red hair, clear, pale skin, and what her mother called a nose and lips for plastic surgeons to study—bore little resemblance to the man.

That they had found this commonality against their parents, in this tiny, disheveled bedroom, made her sad.

"So do the police have any idea who shot your boss?"

She laughed. She couldn't help it. The lack of sleep from the night before. The hunger and the stress of the day. The weight of her brother's problems, and her parents' flaws, and the completely unrecognizable state of her life. The entire fucked-upness of every-thing.

"Is that funny?" he said, joining her in the laughter.

"Who shot my boss? No, it's not funny at all. And they have no idea what's going on. Neither do I. I don't even know how to contact the artist or the gallery owner or anything. ITH Corporation. What the hell is that, anyway? So I guess I just walk away."

"What corporation?"

"Something called ITH. I assume it's the owner's investment company for these projects Drew was helping him with, but I have no idea how to contact him."

"ITH? Just those three letters?"

"Yeah. Why? Does that mean something to you?"

"No. Just seems like a random name, is all."

"You're acting weird, Ben."

"Okay, I know you've had a seriously shitty day, but you need to chill out right now. Jesus, I regret even asking about it."

"You promise? If you know something about that company, you have to tell me." She knew her brother. He wasn't behaving like himself. Was he holding something back from her? Maybe this was another sign that he was using again. Or maybe he was right, and she was being hypersensitive after the trauma of the day.

"I promise, all right? I don't know anything."

"Well, neither do I. I tried Googling that company name as soon as I got a paycheck. No luck."

"Just let it lie. Try to forget you were ever involved."

"Funny. That's what Lily said, too."

"Well, your dear, sweet friend is right."

"Are you still going to meetings, Ben?"

"Seriously, Alice?"

"I thought you went at least once a week."

"Not for a while now. Don't look at me like that. Would you want to sit around in some fluorescent-lit church basement drinking bad coffee with a bunch of addicts? Not exactly an uplifting scene."

"What about Down?" Downing Brown had been the cinematographer on some horrible indie film Ben produced back when he was still aspiring to be Frank Humphrey Jr. Everyone simply called him Down. When the other producers kicked Ben off his own project after one too many drug-fueled rants at the director, Down had introduced Ben to Narcotics Anonymous. As far as Alice knew, he was still Ben's sponsor.

"He'd like me to be at meetings more, but, yeah, we're still down. So to speak. He's sort of my own personal meeting host."

"You'll tell me if you need something, right? You know I'm here for you."

"Always. You shouldn't be worrying about me after what you've been through. You gonna be all right tonight?" He looked at his watch.

"Yeah. Thanks for coming by."

As she watched Lily replace the safety chain behind her brother and reclaim her spot on the sheeted sofa, Alice thought again about friendship. Friends were supposed to be there for movies and restaurants and maybe even hospital visits. It was family who were supposed to help you scrub dried blood from beneath your fingernails and then sleep on your sofa just in case you woke up in the middle of the night remembering how it got there.

Not only had Lily been there for her, she was also right. Alice had told herself earlier in the day—when she was staring up at that police officer, trying to recall everything she'd ever known about Drew Campbell—that his murder wasn't about her. It was awful. Horrific. Unimaginable, really. But it wasn't about her. To see it as such was vanity. And since his death wasn't about her, it wasn't up to her to figure out why Highline Gallery was closed and Drew Campbell dead. The protesters. An art heist. A business riff. The police would eventually figure it out, and nothing she could do would hasten that process or bring Drew back to life.

She'd woken up that morning determined that her involvement in the drama around the gallery be resolved. Now it was, albeit in an awful, horrific, unimaginable way. Now she was resolved to listen to Lily. *You're no longer involved,* she'd said. *Consider yourself lucky you don't know more about Drew Campbell and the Highline Gallery.*

But despite that moment of resolve, Alice would not remain uninvolved. The following day, the detectives from the gallery would arrive unannounced at her apartment asking all of their same questions once again.

PART II

NOTHING TO HIDE

CHAPTER
TWENTY-THREE

*Y*ou've heard what they say about pictures and a thousand words.

Alice took another sip of her water, but immediately wondered if the movement seemed suspicious, an obvious attempt to appear calm. *I'm hot because I took a seventy-five-minute spinning class,* she wanted to yell. *I'm sweaty because we ended with a long climb, then I sprinted home from the gym. And I just walked into this overheated apartment from the bitter cold. I'm hot and sweaty and more than a little stinky, but not because of your being here or your questions or this ridiculous photograph of me supposedly kissing Drew Campbell.*

But she could not say anything. Instead she stared at the picture. It was not the best quality. It looked like a blowup from a digital version. But the man certainly appeared to be Drew Campbell. And the woman? It was hard to make out her face in profile, but the black sunglasses pushing back her red hair looked like hers. That blue coat with the upturned collar was exactly like hers. The profile followed the same contours. Jesus, it looked like her, certainly enough that she had no doubt about why they had come to her apartment to ask her to reexplain everything she had already said to them yesterday.

And now that she'd conveyed it all once again, they apparently weren't asking any more questions. Not explicitly. Shannon had simply glided the photograph onto the tabletop, accompanied by a single sentence.

You've heard what they say about pictures and a thousand words.

The detectives' silence following that single sentence had somehow made her apartment louder. The clicking furnace. The upstairs neighbor's plumbing. The usual horns on Second Avenue below. The rattle of an accelerating bus. A distant siren growing louder, then fading once again.

She found herself wishing Lily were still here, but Alice had been the one to insist that she return to her own routine lest she face her boss's wrath. Lily would have some pithy comment to break through the awkward silence. With humor and fortitude, she would somehow persuade these police officers that, despite every appearance in this photograph, Alice Humphrey was someone they should believe.

But Lily wasn't there to speak for her. And someone in this room had to start speaking before the sounds in Alice's own head caused her to scream something she'd regret.

"I don't understand." That's it, Alice? Minutes of stunned silence, and that's what you come up with? She tried again. "If you think I've been lying to you, or hiding something from you, I swear to you, I have not. That's not me in that picture. It can't be. Who gave you that? It has to be doctored. I never, ever, ever kissed Drew Campbell."

The two detectives exchanged the kind of look that suggested an inside joke.

"Well," Shannon said with a patient smile, "did you ever kiss the man in this picture? The man whose body we carried out of your gallery yesterday?"

Your gallery.

"I don't understand," she said before realizing she'd repeated herself. "I just told you, I never kissed him. I only met him a few weeks ago. He hired me. That's all."

"That's not what you told us. You said you never kissed Drew Campbell. We're just trying to verify that you're saying you never kissed the man in this picture, despite what this picture suggests."

"I assume the man in that picture is Drew Campbell, and, no, there was nothing romantic between us."

"Did you ever know him by another name? Something other than Drew Campbell?"

"No, of course not. I would have told you."

"And how about yourself? Have you ever used any name other than Alice Humphrey?"

"Me? No. Never."

"Well, do you have any thoughts on why there would be a photograph of Mr. Campbell kissing a woman who seems to share a very close resemblance to you? If I'm not mistaken, Miss Humphrey, that's the very coat you had on yesterday at the gallery."

"I know. I find it very confusing. Maybe I reminded him of his girlfriend? That might be why he offered me the job in the first place. That's all I can think of. But I know that's not me in this picture. It can't be."

"And, just to be clear, you didn't have anything to do with clearing out the contents of your gallery."

Just to be clear? She knew the worst thing she could do right now was show anger. Friendly, polite, deferential. That's what she needed to be. "No. The place was closed up when I got there."

"But not really closed. The gate was open, I believe you said? Door unlocked?"

She nodded. That was obviously what she'd said, both yesterday and today. "By closed up, I meant that the gallery had been cleaned out."

"Miss Humphrey, is that your computer?" Shannon asked the question, but both of the detectives were eyeing the slim gray laptop that was open on her kitchen table. Her old dinosaur was closed on top of a bookcase in the living room, growing dusty since she'd starting carting around the newer one.

"Um, I guess not anymore. Drew gave it to me for the gallery. And for me to work from home. It served double duty, I guess you'd say."

"So that laptop there's the only computer you had in use at the gallery?"

"Uh-huh."

"And when we asked you yesterday, and today, whether you knew the whereabouts of any of the property from the gallery, you didn't think to mention the fact that you had the gallery's computer in your personal possession?"

"No, I didn't even think about the computer until you asked about it just now. I'm sorry. I didn't realize—I mean, you're welcome to have it. It's not even mine, and I have no idea how to even give it back, or whom I'd give it to."

"ITH. Right?" The H sounded like an A coming around Danes's toothpick.

She sighed. "Whatever that is."

They exchanged another one of those insider looks before Shannon picked up the computer.

"So just to be clear"—he liked that phrase—"you're consenting to our seizure of this computer for purposes of our investigation and consenting to a search of all of its contents: files, search histories, cookies, what not. Those techno-geeks will give it the full once-over. You're all right with that?"

Friendly, polite, deferential. Nothing to hide. "Of course," she said with a nod. "I'm feeling a little gross from the gym, if you know what I mean. Maybe I can take a quick shower?" She fanned her shirt from her body and was momentarily relieved when the detectives returned her smile.

"No problem." Once again, Shannon did the speaking, but both men stepped from their chairs. "You do what you need to do. We'll have a look-see on this," he said, holding up the laptop. "Maybe Drew had some earlier activity on it that might come in handy. And, Alice, I'm going to leave that copy of the picture right there for you to ponder. Give us a call if you have any additional thoughts about it."

CHAPTER
TWENTY-FOUR

"**L**ady, first you want me to go to Jersey. Now you tell me you don't even have an address? Let me guess: you're also paying with a credit card, right?" The cabdriver could read Alice's response on her face in the rearview mirror. "Ah, Jesus. I read you all wrong. Would've been better off picking up that crazy-looking woman wrapped in all the scarves."

"Just drive. I'll tell you how to get there once we're on the other side of the tunnel. And I'll make it up to you on the tip."

"If you say so."

The round-trip fare to Hoboken would run into triple digits, plunked onto a credit card that had been hovering at maximum for the better part of a year, but she had no choice. She'd gone to sleep last night planning to follow Lily's advice. *You're no longer involved. Consider yourself lucky you don't know more.* But the unannounced house call from the detectives had changed all that.

As the cab emerged from the tunnel, she tried to recall the views she'd taken in from the passenger seat of Drew's BMW three weeks earlier. A right turn next to the construction site. Then another right where the road came to a tee. A left to cross the overpass. Straight until downtown, then another left.

"I'm pretty sure this is the street. It should be up here on the right. There's a fire hydrant out front."

"That's very specific, ma'am."

"No, wait, this is it. I remember passing that bar on the corner."

"Crabby Dick's? You needed to see that sign to remember a bar called Crabby Dick's? Are you kidding me?"

"Just pull over, okay?"

"Wait—the fare. You owe me fifty-seven bucks. Plus that tip you mentioned."

"Look, I have a credit card, okay?" She even pulled it from her wallet as proof. "Just wait for me a few minutes."

"Jesus, lady."

"I can't exactly hail a cab from here. Just run the meter, all right?"

She left him grousing in the front seat with no option but to wait, pulled next to the same parking hydrant where she'd bided her time while Drew Campbell had obtained the paperwork to rent the Highline Gallery space. A bell chimed politely as she walked into the converted town house. Alice recognized the spiky-haired Amazon working two carrels behind the waif of a receptionist at the front desk.

"Good afternoon. I was wondering if I could speak to the woman over there, with the short black hair?"

"And your name?"

"Alice Humphrey. She doesn't know me, but it's about a retail space on Washington Street, in Manhattan in the Meatpacking District?"

She watched as the receptionist conferred with the agent, and then returned to the front counter. "I'm sorry, but she tells me that space is unavailable."

"I know that. I need to talk to her about the lease." She called out directly to the other woman. "I manage the business that moved into that space. I need to know what name the lease is under."

The agent barely glanced in Alice's direction, but did make her way to a wall of file cabinets to retrieve a manila folder. She flipped through its contents as she walked to the front of the office. Alice stepped to the side to make room for the departing receptionist.

"Coffee run, Michelle. Can you watch the front for a sec?"

Michelle with the punky hairdo nodded absentmindedly.

"Now, if you're the manager, shouldn't you already know whose name's on the lease?"

"It's probably either ITH Corporation or Drew Campbell."

"Well, okay then. There you go. Drew Campbell." She looked directly at Alice for the first time. "Is this a joke or something?"

"No, I just—"

"I mean, you're the woman who was starting a gallery, right?"

"Well, managing it, yes."

"So, okay, why would you have any doubts about your name being on the lease?"

"Me? My name's not on the lease."

"Drew Campbell."

"Right. I was hoping he gave you an address I could get?"

"Is this Who's on First or something? I'm pretty sure you know the contact information on the lease. Just like you knew the name."

"I don't know. That's why I'm here."

"Well, I wouldn't normally recite the contents of a lease to someone who walked in off the street, but, sure, I'll play along. The address is one-seven-two Second Avenue, New York." She rattled off a Manhattan phone number.

Alice felt a fog building around her. "No. That's *my* address. *My* phone number."

"Not to be rude, but, no duh. Seriously, I've got other work to do—"

"No, wait. Please. I don't understand. Drew Campbell gave you *my* address to put on the lease?"

"Of course. You *are* Drew Campbell, aren't you?"

"No. My name is Alice Humphrey. Drew Campbell is the man I was with. He signed the lease with you."

"My notes here say his name is Steve Henning. He said he was helping his girlfriend look for a gallery space, and I suggested the Washington property. When he was finally ready to sign the lease, I told him you needed to be the one to come in. But when he got here, he said you were absolutely at death's door with the flu and didn't want to infect anyone. Didn't you see me looking at you through the window?"

"Well, yeah—"

Alice heard the polite chime of the front door behind her. Stepped aside again to make room for the hundred-pound receptionist and her newly acquired cup of coffee.

"So your boyfriend assured me he was taking the lease out to the car for you to sign. He even gave me a copy of your license."

She flipped the manila envelope around to show a photocopy of what appeared to be a New York State driver's license. She recognized the photo. It was cropped from a larger shot taken at a friend's wedding the previous year. Ben had been cut out, and it had been Photoshopped against a standard background in DMV gray. Her face, her address. Drew Campbell's name.

She replayed her previous visit to this location in her mind. Drew had taken the paperwork, removed a pen from his pocket, and then gestured toward the car. The agent had looked right at her. The reason he'd offered for signing outside had played right into Alice's stereotypes of a woman who looked like this one: *Creepy in there. I felt like a field mouse dropped into the middle of an anaconda tank.*

"This license is a fake. I am *not* Drew Campbell. Drew Campbell is the man who came here to the rent the gallery."

The coffee-sipping receptionist's eyes grew wide at the sharpness of Alice's response before holding up a hesitant hand like an intruding schoolgirl.

"I'm not sure if this matters, but I copied that entire file yesterday for the New York City police department."

CHAPTER
TWENTY-FIVE

"**W**hat do you mean, she had a cell phone?"

Morhart had known the conversation would be a difficult one, but Joann Stevenson was having a harder time with the news than even he had anticipated. She was only a year older than he was, but, man, what a different kind of life she'd led. He'd never been married. Never even lived with a woman, not formally. And here was this person—pretty much the same age as him, who'd made her daughter the center of her world for as long as she could remember—learning that her baby girl had already reached the age of keeping secrets from her.

"Sophie says Becca got the phone two months ago."

"Why didn't she tell me?"

"Sophie assumed you knew."

"No, I mean, Becca. Why wouldn't she tell me?"

"Well, that's one of the questions I'm trying to answer."

"She's been begging for a phone since eighth grade. Come to think of it, she hasn't mentioned it of late. How'd she even pay for it? And don't kids need a parent or something to sign a contract? I just don't understand this."

Morhart prided himself on the quality of his witness interviews, but this woman had a way of wresting a conversation from him.

"Joann, that's what I'm trying to explain right now. The number

Becca was using comes back to a prepaid cell phone. Do you know what that is?"

Joann shook her head.

"There's no billing plan or credit cards or contracts necessary. Just any form of payment for prepaid minutes. The phone Becca had was purchased two months ago, with cash, at a Sears in Lynchburg, Virginia."

"Lynchburg? I've never heard of that. Becca certainly wasn't *there.*"

"That's what I figured. Now maybe she bought it from someone else, but that's going to be real hard to track. Our best shot is to look at the call histories."

Joann's face brightened. "Of course. This is great. Can you do that thing I've read about where you track the phone's signal, like a GPS?"

"Unfortunately, Becca hasn't used her phone since Sunday. Now, wait, let's not get ahead of ourselves here," he said when her expression fell. "She might have turned it off to save the battery. Or she could have lost it. What I want to focus on are the calls she made prior to Sunday night. Not too many, really. Mostly she was using it to text with friends. I guess kids prefer that nowadays. But she did have several calls to a number I've tracked to a church based out of Oklahoma. The Redemption of Christ Church? That ring a bell?"

"No. Becca isn't religious. Like, not at *all.* Sort of antireligion, if anything."

"No recent curiosity about it? Or some change in her demeanor to suggest a conversion of some sort?"

"Well, you know she'd been having a rough patch over the last year or so, and she did seem to have turned that around. But I chalked it up to the usual ups and downs of teenage life. She had some new friends at school, that sort of thing, but a sudden embrace of Jesus? I don't think so. Becca thought Lady Gaga was too mainstream. Does that sound like your redemption church?"

He gave her a smile. It was the first time he'd heard her allow herself some humor. "Definitely not. Don't worry. I'll be contacting them about the phone calls, but wanted to get the lay of the land from you first."

"I appreciate that."

"There's something else about the phone, Joann. And this is undoubtedly going to be hard for you to hear. But Becca was involved in some flirtatious texting activity with one of the boys at school." He broke the news to her. The texts. The nude photo. The retaliation from Ashleigh. All of it.

Joann wiped a tear from her cheek. "I'm sorry. Just the thought of her going through all that alone. I forgot how horrible teenagers can be, you know? It's like you don't want to believe your own child could be subjected to that abuse, so you repress the pain they can cause. These bullies, could they have done something to Becca?"

"I've accounted for both Dan and Ashleigh's whereabouts that entire day, so, no, I don't believe they're directly responsible for her being missing right now. But to be honest, Miss Stevenson, it does raise the question of whether Becca may have left for a while to remove herself from the situation at school." He held up a palm. "I'm just raising the possibility, because I know you want me to be honest with you. But I made you a promise that I would not stop looking for Becca, no matter what. And I plan to keep that promise, so please don't make me feel like I can't discuss what I need to discuss in order to do that."

She took a deep breath and pursed her lips. "All right. So you're saying maybe the problems at school just got to be too much?"

"You've always said that Becca leaving on her own was the best-case scenario, right? So, in a way, these problems at school might be seen as good news from that perspective. It at least gives her a reason for going."

"Other than me. Sorry," she said, obviously regretting the impulsive comment. "It's stupid, but I keep wondering, What if she ran away because I had someone in our house that night? Maybe she came home from Sophie's and realized Mark was here. That never should've happened, and I didn't even have the guts to talk to her about it first. Maybe she wanted to teach me a lesson—"

"Stop. That's not right."

"I just can't get the thought out of my head. Mark . . . well, he wouldn't even hear me out on it. I think this has all been too much for him. If I could just let Becca know that he's gone. He won't be back here again. Maybe then she'd come home."

"Just stop, Joann. You're wrong on that, okay? You've got to trust me, but you're wrong."

"How do you know?"

He sighed as his own words about honesty rang in his ears. "I asked Sophie how your daughter felt about Mark. You've got to understand, in a situation like that, any man who's close to the family—"

"I've got it."

"In any event, Sophie told me Becca was happy for you."

"But, still, the shock of finding him here. At night."

"I don't think it would have been a shock, okay? I think Sophie's exact words were, 'Becca was psyched that her mom was finally getting laid.' Sorry. Oh, God, awkward." She was smiling again, and her cheeks had flushed from something other than sobbing. "So, all righty then, I'm going to find out who at Redemption of Christ Church has been calling Becca."

"You'll be able to do that? Churches aren't private from the law or something?"

"This isn't the Vatican we're talking about here. Seems like a pretty small organization. Figured I'd start with the pastor himself. Hopefully George Hardy's a good enough Christian to help us out."

"George Hardy?"

"Yeah, looks like he started the church himself. A real Bible Belter, from what I read online."

"Detective, I'm not sure what this means, but I know a man named George Hardy. Or at least I used to." The color that had been in her cheeks had been replaced by sheets of white. "George Hardy is Becca's father."

CHAPTER
TWENTY-SIX

H ank Beckman was only forty-eight years old, but there were days when he felt old as dirt. The creeping reminders of the ever-present passage of time certainly didn't help: that little potbelly that materialized a few years back without any explanation, each move of the pin to a lighter notch on the weight machines at the gym, the pain he'd developed in his side last week when he'd bent over for the newspaper a bit too early in the morning.

But not all indications of age were physiological. He'd joined the bureau when he was twenty-nine years old, meaning he'd be eligible for retirement at fifty. In many professions, a man of his age might be hitting his stride. But law enforcement was a young man's—no, it was a young *person's* game. It shouldn't be. Hank knew more about people—their desires, their instincts, their weaknesses, their motivation—than he could have ever begun to understand as a rookie. But these days, it seemed half their cases came down to bank records, cell phone towers, and computer cookies instead of a deftly handled interrogation. He'd done his best to keep up with advances in investigative techniques, but sometimes it was easier to hand off the actual mechanics of the keyboard work to an intern.

Today's work, however, could not be delegated. He had lost Travis Larson. He needed to find him.

Hank had last seen the man yesterday morning, parking the stolen

BMW on Washington Street. After work, he'd picked up a Subway sandwich to go and headed directly to the Newark apartment complex. No lights on at home. No BMW in the lot. He'd stayed on the place until finally risking a walk up to the man's landing. The Subway buy-one-get-one coupon he slipped halfway under the front door had still been there this morning and remained there again when he'd found time between field interviews for a drop-by.

No Larson. No BMW.

If Larson wasn't home, Hank would start from his last known location. He had pulled up Google Maps on his computer, then zoomed in to the few blocks that divided the West Village from the Meatpacking District. From there, he dragged the orange figure of a man onto the map to see the location from street-level photographic view. He remembered the twenty-year-old intern who had shown him how to do it: "See? He looks like the little guy on a bathroom door." Like she was teaching a computer class at the senior citizens' center.

He dragged the cartoon man up Washington Street. It seemed that every other click, he did something wrong, shifting out of street-level view, or zooming in to a close-up of broken concrete. He started to get a hang of the movement, taking a virtual stroll past Perry, past West Eleventh, past Bank, until he found the BMW's parking spot. He rotated the view to home in on the side of the street where Larson had disappeared. He saw two empty storefronts and a laundromat called Happy Suds.

Problem was, the images on Google Maps could be several years old. He was pretty sure the shoe store he'd seen on that street yesterday morning occupied the same space as Happy Suds in this picture. He called information for the number at Happy Suds, but there was no such listing. No surprise. Retail turnover in that neighborhood was faster than the $20 tricks that used to be turned under the Highline before the gentrification. Yet another business owned by one hardworking person to service the needs of other hardworking people, probably closed to make room for a shop hawking thousand-dollar handbags.

He needed another strategy.

He "walked" his little orange bathroom guy down Washington, jotting down the street addresses that appeared at the top of the screen as he passed each of the three storefronts that lined the portion of the street where he'd last spotted Larson. Then he Googled each address to determine the current occupant of the space, wondering whether Larson might have reason to go there early in the morning. The Happy Suds address came back to the designer shoe boutique. He tried not to think about the half a paycheck he'd blown on a pair of those shoes for Jen's birthday. Three weeks later, she had moved out. He skipped the second address, which he recalled as being papered over, and moved on to the third address. It currently belonged to Pete's Flowers.

He knew no more than he had yesterday.

He went ahead and entered the address of the abandoned storefront in the middle. It pulled up mentions of two different businesses: a frame shop and a gallery.

He searched for the name of the frame shop and learned that it had moved three months earlier to Chelsea.

And then he typed the gallery name: Highline Gallery.

Interesting. Larson was a man who lied for money. Art held far more promise in that arena than either flowers or high heels.

Even as he hit the enter key, he recalled a headline he'd seen tucked into the back pages of today's paper. By the time the search results appeared on his screen, he remembered the story of a body found at a gallery that had just opened two days earlier.

He double-clicked on the first news story. Highline Gallery. Plagued by trouble since its initially successful opening. Protesters alleging child pornography. Body of an unidentified male adult found yesterday morning. The contents of the gallery missing. Windows papered over. Gallery manager no stranger to either the limelight or controversy. Former child actress. Daughter of womanizing director Frank Humphrey.

He pulled up a photograph of Alice Humphrey. Red hair. Good-looking. He could picture her with big sunglasses and hot shoes, just like the woman he'd seen enter Larson's apartment. How had the QuickCar employee described the woman who cruised away in the BMW? "A pretty white girl with long red hair."

Shit. Hank's little hobby wasn't going to remain secret much longer.

CHAPTER
TWENTY-SEVEN

The city of New York claims more than eight million residents. It is the financial and media capital of the world. Photographs of its iconic skyline are recognizable by children raised in villages on the other side of the globe. And most of the majesty—the power, the deals, the fame—unfolds on the tiny little island of Manhattan. About thirteen miles or so long, north to south. Only 2.3 miles wide at the fattest part of the island.

One might think that a person who had spent nearly her entire life on that tiny little island would have long ago memorized its every last square inch. Certainly Alice had noticed in Missouri that her ex-husband's hospital colleagues—the ones who'd been born and bred in St. Louis—could rattle off directions to any spot in the region, even the outskirts. But New York was different. In New York, where people walked to their local grocer and newspaper stand, neighborhoods still meant something. To a resident of China-town, the Upper East Side might as well be Rhode Island.

Alice had lived in the East Village since graduate school. Her apartment was less than two miles from Centre Street, but she could count the number of times she'd been down here in those eight-plus years on three fingers: once for jury duty, once to accompany her father to a radio interview on the *Leonard Lopate Show*, and once for that ill-fated karaoke party on her thirty-third birthday.

Now, though, she knew she needed legal advice.

"Here we are. Eighty-six Chambers. See how easy it is for the nice taxicab driver when you know the address?"

Alice was tempted to stiff the driver for the snarky remark, but kept her promise, tacking a 25 percent tip onto her credit card tab before dashing through the bitter cold wind to the lobby of Jeff's building. She hollered at the sight of the closing elevator doors. "Can you hold that?"

Apparently not. She managed to nudge one knee in front of the sensors, absorbing a hard blow before the doors bounced back open. The messenger inside, clad in cycling gear and tattoos, didn't even bother to look sheepish. As they ticked past the fourth floor, he threw her a glare and she realized she was clicking her nails loudly against the wall behind her.

Too fucking bad, dude.

"Wait. Drew told the property management company that *you're* Drew Campbell and *you* were the one starting the gallery?"

Every square inch of Jeff's desk had been blanketed by papers and open books when she'd arrived unannounced at his office, but Jeff somehow managed to appear as if he had time only for her.

"Yes. And the police must be buying it. They came to my apartment today and were asking me all these questions. Had I ever used an alias. Whether I ever knew Drew by another name. The cop told me yesterday that they didn't find Drew's wallet or anything else with his body. They must not have been able to confirm his identity, so now I'm wondering whether anything the man ever said to me was true. Basically, I have no fucking clue who he actually was, but now the police seem to think that I was the one who started the gallery, and I did it using a fake name."

"How could they possibly believe that? It's crazy."

"Any crazier than a complete stranger offering me a dream job with a rich, anonymous boss?"

"Sounds like it was a con. Maybe he was planning to ask you

for money to keep the place afloat but got himself killed before the ask."

"The ask, huh?"

"The grift. The pigeon drop. The swindle. The scam. I've got the lingo, babe."

"Campbell played me like a fiddle. Coming across as an art expert. Being all self-deprecating about his work, saying his client was one of his dad's old friends. He even threw in a martini-drinking mother for good measure, the ultimate bonding experience."

"Let me call these detectives and try to get a read on the situation. Maybe we can get them to see this in another light."

"I don't think it's going to be that easy." She pulled the print out of the digital photo from her purse and unfolded it on his desk.

"Is that—"

"No. It's not me. He must have found a shot of someone who looked like me and then Photoshopped it onto a picture of him kissing someone else."

Jeff squinted as if sheer will might bring focus to the grainy picture. "I don't know, Al. That's some damn good Photoshopping."

"He was also pretty good with fake IDs. He gave the property management company a supposed copy of my driver's license. Looked like the real thing except for the name Drew Campbell."

"Did you give him a copy of your driver's license when he hired you? Maybe he just scanned it and changed the name."

"No, it wasn't my driver's license photo. It was cropped from a picture of Ben and me at Christina Marcum's wedding last summer."

The bride had been a childhood friend of theirs. Jeff didn't know her personally but had attended the wedding as Alice's plus-one, back when they were officially "on." Alice wasn't particularly close to Christina, but she loved that photograph of her and her brother.

"Maybe Drew—or whoever he was—hacked your computer?"

"Well, that's what I was wondering too. But then I remembered something. May I?" She moved to his side of the desk and pulled out the keyboard tray. "Christina's sister's the one who took the picture. I only saw it because she posted it on Facebook."

Alice pulled up her own Facebook profile and clicked on "Photos."

"See? There it is." The picture had a clear, straightforward angle of Alice's face, perfect for clipping as a head shot.

"Is your profile set to private?"

"What's that mean?"

"Can anyone in the world see it, or do people have to be your friend first?"

"I honestly don't know."

He reached for the mouse and gave it a few clicks. "Your entire profile is public, so Drew definitely could have gotten the driver's license picture here." He pulled up her Wall posts, showing the messages Alice and her friends had posted to one another over the past few weeks. "Alice, this is insane to have this public. Anyone, anywhere, can read all of this."

"Who cares? 'Happy Birthday. Have a good day.' It's all a bunch of nonsense. You mean to tell me I should have anticipated that some guy using a fake name would con me into taking a fake job and then use pictures off my Facebook profile to set me up?"

"It's not just nonsense, Alice. Look, two days ago you posted 'Wafels & Dinges.' To you, that's a bunch of nonsense, but it's also an announcement to everyone in the world you're at the Wafels & Dinges truck."

"I posted it after I was back at the gallery."

"Okay? Well, how about this one? 'Fantastic opening at the gallery. Off to celebrate at Gramercy Tavern. Fifteen minutes until martini time.' "

"Please don't criticize me right now. Wait. Oh, no."

"What?"

She didn't pause to ask permission before taking the mouse from him and scrolling farther down her page. She clicked the Older Posts button at the bottom of her wall. "No, no, no, no. I was just assuming that this was all bad luck. That Drew was running a scam and decided that an out-of-work art history major was a pretty good mark. But look: the morning before the gallery opening where I met Drew? Look at my post."

Phillip Lipton exhibit tonight at Susan Kellermann Gallery. Most under-rated artist of late 20th Century.

"You think Drew went there that night looking specifically for you?"

"Can you honestly tell me that I should have any idea *what* to think right now?"

CHAPTER
TWENTY-EIGHT

It had been four weeks since Alice's last visit to the Susan Kellermann Gallery. This time, she headed directly to her destination.
She no longer had the luxury of a woman who could pause to
admire a building's architectural details.

A man in white painter coveralls carried a ladder into the gallery,
followed by an identically clad man hauling a bucket of paint and
two rollers. She caught the door for their convenience, then began
to step inside behind them.

"Yoo-hoo. Hello there. I'm sorry, but we're closed. Come back
Tuesday night. We're getting a Jeremy West exhibit ready now.
Great stuff."

From the neck up, the woman at the back of the gallery resem-
bled the gallery owner Alice had seen a handful of times: same tight
black bun, same gaunt pale face, same burgundy-stained lips. But
today Susan Kellermann wore a black T-shirt, baggy blue jeans, and
clogs. The dichotomy between her head and body brought to mind
Mr. Potato Head.

"I need to ask you a question about the Phillip Lipton opening."

"I'm afraid I don't represent Phillip any longer. I think he's a free
agent now, if you want to try to contact him directly."

"I'm not buying art. I'm looking for one of your customers."

Kellermann's attention had turned to a five-foot-diameter ball of twine being manhandled by two of her workers. "Careful. There's nothing holding that together but a few drops of epoxy. About six inches more in this direction."

"Please, Miss Kellermann. It's very important."

She peered at Alice as if she were a black speck tainting a perfectly tidy white wall, but then something in Alice's face got her attention. "Pull one string loose, and the two of you will roll that thing all the way back down to Dumbo yourselves, where I'll allow West to wrap you inside it as performance art. Got it?"

"Ah, yes, that handsome devil from opening night. Rough around the edges, but *very* charming. Agreed to purchase *Carnival One* for a client."

"He hired me for a gallery job, but now it looks like the entire thing was a con." She didn't mention the nagging fact that the man was dead. Hopefully Kellermann hadn't heard enough about yesterday's murder at a new downtown gallery to start making connections. "I need to track him down. Do you have his payment information? Maybe the address where the canvas was delivered?"

"If only I did. I'm afraid all I have is a name, a disconnected phone number, and one very pissed-off nonagenarian."

"I take it the sale didn't go through?"

"I wouldn't usually mark a piece as sold without a deposit, but he was very persuasive. He said he was acquiring the canvas for a client. Usually, dealers pay up front and then I take the art back as a return if the client isn't satisfied with the selection. Steven, however—"

"He told you his name was Steven?"

"Yes. Steven Henning." It was the same name Drew had used with the property management agent in Hoboken. "He told me he was certain the client would defer to his selection but was absolutely headstrong against letting Steven pay for a piece without his first viewing it in person. Supposedly Steven was going to bring the client in the following day but wasn't willing to risk the piece being sold in the interim, or the client would have his head for needlessly dragging him around the city. And it was all very mysterious: a wealthy man, a serious collector, like someone whose name I'd recognize if only Steven trusted me enough to share it. He made it sound like he was between a rock and a hard place with a very difficult client."

The story sounded familiar. It was the same shtick he'd handed to Alice.

"Frankly," Kellermann continued, "having spent several weeks trying to appease Phillip Lipton, I suppose I empathized a bit too much. The art market's in the crapper right now, so sometimes you've got to bend over backward to make the sale. And, what can I say, I have a weakness for a man who looks like George Clooney."

"But he didn't return the following day with the mysterious, wealthy client."

"Oh, no, he most certainly did not. When he hadn't appeared by late afternoon, I called the number he'd given me. It was a takeout falafel stand, as far as I could make out through the broken English. No art dealers on premises," she added with a wry smile. "Unfortunately, our talented Mr. Lipton was not particularly understanding. All artists have unrealistic expectations, but I think Phillip really expected this show to be a comeback that would set the art world afire. He was shocked we didn't sell out at the opening. I, on the other hand, was happy to have sold two pieces in this market, but when I had to notify Phillip that the *Carnival One* sale had fallen through, he was apoplectic. That wife of his only encourages him. Consider me one more art dealer in that very talented but absolutely insane man's long path of self-destruction. I have Steven Henning to thank for that. I suppose from that look on your face that I wasn't the only one to fall for him, hook, line, and sinker?"

CHAPTER
TWENTY-NINE

O nly forty miles of road separated Dover, New Jersey, from New York City, but Morhart's lifetime trips into the city probably still numbered in the single digits. He liked Central Park. The pizza. The lights at Christmas at Rockefeller Center. But, boy, you sure did pay a big price for those experiences. Simply put, this place had too much stuff in too small a space for his tastes. In Dover, you get outside of town and can look at miles of green hills and blue sky. He appreciated the open space. In New York, a person wasn't in control of his own movement. Cars crept inch by inch around double-parked trucks. Pedestrians gazing up at skyscrapers and down at cell phones collided into each other like bumper cars. The ability to move was what made Morhart feel free.

Now he was one of thousands of other drivers fighting to squeeze through the light at Broadway and Houston. How–stin, they called it, just inviting out-of-towners to make the obvious mispronunciation so they could whisper about stupid tourists. He was tempted to trigger his dash lights to cut through traffic but didn't want to find himself at odds with the infamously territorial NYPD.

When he heard a voice blasting from a bullhorn, he felt some of the stress leave his hands, still tight on the steering wheel. He couldn't spot the protesters yet, but they were here.

He had found a 900 number for the Redemption of Christ

Church online. The call cost his department a buck, but the pre-recorded message had given him a line on George Hardy's current location: *"We came to New York City to tackle the belly of temptation and sin. We started with peddlers of smut and the pornographers of children. Yesterday, we learned that the establishment in question had closed, proving we are on the side of righteousness. Today we will continue our work here in the name of our savior. The slope of sexuality created for our children is a slippery one, and the slide can sometimes begin with the so-called clothing that treats our young girls like objects of sexuality instead of vessels of Christ. We will converge upon Little Angels, a store that markets to our children clothing more suited for street corners than schools, at three p.m. If you are with us—even if you have not met us—if you love your daughters, and follow the word of our one savior, Jesus Christ, please join with us. We will expose Little Angels for the damage its business causes to the lives of young women. And we will continue to spread our message that each Christian is called and chosen in God to be a priest unto God, and to give of his time, strength, and material possessions to the service of the Lord. To donate to this cause, please . . ."*

Morhart did not make a donation, but did jot down the address of the church's protest du jour.

He recognized the man with the bullhorn as Hardy himself from photographs on the Internet. Based on the patches of clothing barely covering the mannequins in the front window of Little Angels, Morhart had to admit the man had a point. A flash of his badge was enough for Hardy to hand his amplifier to one of his followers.

"Someone from your precinct's already been around here with some ground rules. We're following them to the letter, Officer."

"This isn't about your protests, Reverend."

"Is this about the pornographer found dead in that smut palace over yonder? The Meatpacking District, they call it? Might as well call it the fudge-packing district, you ask me. I done already talked to some of yours about that one, too."

"This is about something else entirely."

"Well, my word, son. How many of this city's problems can y'all lay at our feet? Don't you have about eight million other folks to talk to?"

"I need to talk to you about Becca Stevenson."

A darkness fell across Hardy's face. The exaggerated folksiness was gone from his voice when he finally spoke. "Now is that right?"

"Are you really going to force me to play this game, Reverend? I know Becca was your daughter. I know you gave her a cell phone. And I know you established contact with her behind her mother's back and against her mother's wishes."

"Her *mother* had no business denying a man the right to father his own blood. Her *mother* had no right to give that girl her own last name, like some bastard child. Her *mother*—her mother's a harlot and a liar."

Joann had already filled Morhart in on the background. When she was twenty-one years old, a few years out of high school in Oklahoma, she had gotten pregnant by an out-of-work married man who started out as a daytime drinking buddy at the local watering hole and had become her lover. Would he offer to leave the wife he'd never managed to impregnate? Offer to pay child support in exchange for her silence? When she told Hardy about the pregnancy, she hadn't known what to expect.

What she never anticipated, though, was the man's anger. No, not mere anger. As Joann had conveyed it to him—all these years later—Morhart could tell that she had been exposed to the humiliating scorn and hatred of the first man whom she had trusted and loved. Meeting that man now, Morhart could imagine the words Hardy would have used. *Seductress. Beguiler. Trouble. Couldn't keep your legs shut even with a married man. How do I even know it's mine with a loose woman like you?*

The anger in Hardy's whisper was fierce. "She told me she killed it. Is there anything worse than that?"

Rather than forever entangle her and her daughter's lives with Hardy, Joann had tried to create a new life on her own. She saw Hardy one last time before leaving Oklahoma. She told him she had terminated the pregnancy. She said she would no longer continue her relationship with the still-married Hardy. She moved north to Jersey and enrolled in classes at the technical college while working full-time. She assumed that Hardy would go on with his life, with the same enabling wife, the same bar stool, and a new woman to keep him company.

But apparently that hadn't happened.

"Linda and I were almost fifty when I knew Joann."

"Joann was young enough to be your daughter."

"I wasn't the same man then. I changed. Linda never could give me a child. She blamed it on me. Said I wasn't good at much of any-thing, not even spreading my seed. I finally told her I knew she was the one who was barren. I knew I was capable of fathering a child. But that, that *woman*—I know, I wasn't kind to her when she came to me with news of the baby. But she killed our child. Murdered it. Or so I thought. I couldn't get past that. And Linda couldn't get past the infidelities I eventually confessed once I turned to Jesus Christ for forgiveness."

Morhart didn't want to hear Hardy's self-serving account of the distant past. He didn't want to understand his side of an ancient story.

"How did you find out about Becca?"

"I went looking for Joann. I wanted her to know that her decision ultimately led me to a path of salvation and redemption. I wanted her to know the love and strength and spiritual maturity that can be found only through the one true God who has revealed Himself as Father, Son, and Holy Spirit."

"So you tracked her down."

"Nineteen ninety-nine for a person search on the Internet with a full name and date of birth. Joann's birthday was Saint Patrick's Day. Easy to remember. Turns out she had a baby girl about six and a half months after she left Oklahoma. I didn't go to college, but I'm smart enough to add two and two."

"Why didn't you go to Joann and ask to have a relationship with your daughter?"

"After what she done, would you *ask*? Would you *beg* to enjoy what was yours by both man's and God's law? If so, I feel sorry for you as a man."

"So, what? You just showed up one day and surprised a fifteen-year-old girl? 'Hi, dear. Daddy's here'?"

"I e-mailed her, actually. She could have gone to her mother if she'd wanted, of course. Instead, she asked to meet me."

"I'm sure you tried your best not to disparage the choices her mother made as a younger woman."

"I laid out the truth. That I was told she was dead. That I was denied any choice for myself about a relationship with her. That her mother lied to both of us. Her mother told her I was a loser and a flake who didn't want anything to do with either of them."

Was it a lie if it had been the truth fifteen years earlier? Joann was so proud of what she thought was her close relationship with her daughter. *Not just mother and daughter,* she had told him: *Best friends.* Morhart could only imagine the pain Becca would have experienced learning, from the undoubtedly harsh words of this man, that her mother and friend had denied her the full story about her very existence.

"You're telling me all of this about yourself, sir, but I can't help but notice you haven't asked yet why I'm asking so many questions about your daughter."

"I don't figure it's my place to question the authority of a police officer."

"I didn't invite you to challenge my authority. I'd think that a father who cared enough about his daughter to track her down halfway across the country might be alarmed when a police officer came around asking questions about her."

" 'Do not let your hearts be troubled. You believe in and adhere to and trust in and rely on God; believe in and adhere to and trust in and rely also on Me.' John 14:1."

"What exactly do you mean to say to me, sir?"

Hardy smiled at him as if he were a patient man waiting for a child to tie a shoe. "I no longer try to anticipate obstacles."

"When was the last time you spoke to Becca?"

"I'm not entirely certain."

"Take a guess."

"Maybe a week ago?"

"You met with her?"

"I spoke with her."

"You suddenly seem very careful about your words, sir. Did you speak with her face-to-face? On the phone? E-mail?"

"By phone."

"The phone you gave her so Joann wouldn't know you had forged a relationship with her daughter?"

"*Our* daughter. That's right."

"I assume you're aware that your daughter has been reported missing."

Morhart saw the man's eyes shift up, then left to right, as if he were reading to himself mentally. "I saw the story in the newspaper yesterday."

"And you didn't think your recent reemergence was sufficiently relevant to warrant a phone call to the police?"

"I have been in contact with Becca for two months, so your attribution of cause and effect does not strike me as particularly rational. I have been worried about Becca, certainly. I have called her number to no avail. And I have not stopped praying for her. But, no, I did not see how a phone call to the police could help the situation. It would only ensure that her mother would prevent Becca from contacting me once she returns."

"You sound confident that she'll return."

" 'Cast your burden on the Lord and He will sustain you; He will never allow the consistently righteous to be moved.' Psalm 55: 22."

"And what would the Lord say about the fact that a man was murdered yesterday at a place of business you just happened to be protesting?"

"The police have already questioned me about that. I assured them that my people and I were uninvolved. On the other hand, 'A man who stiffens his neck after many rebukes will suddenly be destroyed—without remedy.' Proverbs 29:1."

"So the man deserved it, is what you're saying?"

There was that patient smile again.

"One more question before you go back to saving the world, Reverend. Those city police who talked to you about the murder—did you happen to tell them your daughter was missing?"

"I surely don't see the connection, Detective."

Back in his truck, Morhart cranked the heater before dialing the NYPD, asking to speak to the detective assigned to the homicide at the Highline Gallery the previous morning. Life definitely was different in the big city. Turns out the case was assigned to two detectives: John Shannon and Willie Danes, out of the Thirteenth Precinct.

"You spent the afternoon with the reverend, huh? He quote you any scripture?"

Willie Danes was a big man with big hands, a big head, and a roll of neck fat above his collar. He was eyeing the half-eaten pastrami sandwich on his desktop, so Morhart knew he should make his visit short.

"I got more preaching on a SoHo sidewalk today than I've had the last three Christmases put together." He reminded Danes again why he had called. "I don't want to step on any toes, but it seems like when one man's name comes up in two different criminal investigations, we ought to at least exchange information."

"Makes sense to me. We looked at Hardy right away. Trouble is, we got a street-level security camera showing Hardy walking into the rathole he's staying at in Chinatown around ten o'clock Wednesday night and not coming out again until nine the next morning. The ME says our vic died around six or seven a.m. Hardy's in the clear."

"I keep coming back to the fact that we've got one guy linking my missing girl to your dead body, both events going down within a few days of each other."

"Some people have shitty luck."

"I read that Hardy's church was protesting the gallery over some naked pictures?"

"The stuff seemed pretty tame by today's standards, but yeah, there was some S&M imagery, things a guy like Hardy would find offensive. It wouldn't have been much of a story, except Hardy's people claimed underage models were used in the photographs. A claim like that should have been easy for the gallery to clear up, but all they offered was radio silence. All of a sudden, Hardy's got a media hit on his hands, then we've got a dead body."

"What age kids?"

"Can't say for sure it was a kid at all, but postpuberty for sure. The artist's Web site has been pulled down. Tell you the truth, we can't even confirm the artist ever existed. Why?"

"Becca, my missing girl? She was getting hassled by some of the popular kids at school recently about some naked pictures of herself."

"Sexting, huh? I tell you, as the father of two girls, that shit makes me wish I'd had sons. So you're telling me that your case and my case not only have George Hardy connecting them, but now we've got this photograph angle, as well?"

"Plus my understanding is that Hardy didn't mention having a missing daughter when you all reached out to him about this murder. I mean, your newly found daughter suddenly disappears, wouldn't you be talking about that to any cop you could? I'm telling you, Hardy was holding something back from me. I hope you trust me on that."

Danes didn't know him from a hole in the ground, so Morhart knew he was being summed up when Danes held his gaze. "Fuck. You got some fingerprints from this girl of yours?"

"Becca Stevenson. I sure do."

"All right. Send 'em to me. We'll check 'em against the ones we pulled from the gallery. Better send those pictures you were talking about, too. We'll see if they match up with our so-called art."

Morhart left the Thirteenth Precinct knowing that his trip into the city hadn't been wasted.

• • •

Ten minutes after Jason Morhart emerged from the Lincoln Tunnel, Detective Willie Danes's phone rang. He swallowed the final bite of his pastrami sandwich before answering. The caller's name wasn't familiar, but his voice brightened when she said she was getting back to him from the secretary of state's office about the incorporation research he had asked for.

"Yes, that's right. On ITH. The stock is held by a trust, but I was hoping to find a name associated with the original incorporation in 1985."

"I should probably file a worker's comp claim for all the dust I inhaled, but I did find the original incorporation papers. I'm afraid all I've got for you is the name of the lawyer acting as counsel: Arthur Cronin."

After thanking the woman profusely, Danes searched online for the law office of Arthur Cronin and was pleasantly surprised to learn that the man was still in practice after all these years. He lifted the receiver to dial, already anticipating the upcoming conversation. *Attorney-client privilege. Lawyer's work product. No information without a subpoena.* Whoever had created this company only to turn over its stocks to an untraceable trust did not want to be found.

Still, he was prepared to go through the necessary motions. But another look at the head shot on the law firm's Web site made him pause after entering only the area code. Arthur Cronin. Something about that name. Something about the face.

He typed "Arthur Cronin" into his search engine and hit enter. Six screens into the search results, he located the article he'd seen just the previous day on this same screen when he'd been gathering background information on Alice Humphrey. It was a puff piece from three years earlier, touting the successful premiere of her father's film—his last big one, before the commercial flop about the war in Afghanistan. Before the sex scandals. In the photograph accompanying the article, the beaming director was surrounded by four people: his wife, Rose; his son, Ben; his daughter, Alice; and his lifelong friend Arthur Cronin.

CHAPTER
THIRTY

"**F**uck, I feel guilty. I sat here and bitched for fifteen minutes about my craptacular day at work with the Gorilla breathing down my neck. Meanwhile, you've spent your entire day in the middle of the Twilight Zone."

Lily had kicked off her high-heeled shoes and was bent over her legs extended on the sofa, stretching out her hamstrings.

"I don't know what to do. Jeff told me not to talk to the police anymore without a lawyer, but doesn't that just make me look guilty?"

"What do I know? Everything I know about law I learned from television."

"Well, on TV, the cops immediately suspect anyone who lawyers up. But anyone who talks always winds up digging themselves a bigger hole. It's like you're damned if you do, damned if you don't."

"I'm still not sure I have my head wrapped around all this. So you think the entire gallery story was a lie?"

"That's what it looks like. The very first night I met Drew, he supposedly bought a painting for the same mystery client who was opening the gallery, but he used a fake name and never completed the sale. He told the property management company I was Drew Campbell."

"And what's ITH?"

"The name of the corporation my supposed boss was using to fund the gallery. Jeff said he'd try digging up some information through state records. The worst part is, I don't think my involvement was random. Drew faked the purchase of the painting before he even spoke to me, meaning he was already looking to set up this con. Well, what are the odds he just happens to meet someone desperate for a job in the art world?"

"You think he went there specifically to find you."

"That's the only way it makes sense. I had posted my plans to go to the exhibition on Facebook. It would have been easy to find me there. He makes sure I see him negotiating the purchase of a canvas, so I'm more likely to buy his crazy story about the anonymous gallery owner."

"Why would anyone do that?"

"I don't know. I can't find any information about the supposed company behind the gallery. The Hans Schuler Web site has been pulled down. Now I'm not even sure who Drew Campbell really was. He told the property management company and the woman at the gallery where we first met that his name was Steven Henning. I called information, and there's like seventy listings."

"Oh, come on, woman. We can do better than that. Hand me your laptop."

Lily flipped open the screen and typed "Steven Henning" into Google.

"I already tried that, Lily. There's an accountant and a DJ and some guy who runs a lobster restaurant. I didn't get anywhere with it."

"Did you try Facebook? If he was following your profile, maybe he's on there, too."

Alice immediately felt stupid for not thinking of the possibility herself.

"Eighty-six results," she said, watching over Lily's shoulder.

"And that's not even counting the Steves. Hold on." She clicked on a button that read Filter By, then typed "New York" into the Location box.

"How are you so good at this?"

"I've cyberstalked every man I've met for the past seven years. Shit." The screen showed no Steven Hennings in New York City.

"Is there some way to try the entire New York area? Jersey? Connecticut?"

"I don't think so. We'll just have to check all of them."

They were about halfway through the search results when Alice's phone rang. She let it go to her answering machine. "Miss Humphrey. This is Robert Atkinson. I'm a journalist with Empire Media."

"Oooh, you're famous," Lily teased.

"Shhh—" Alice remembered the name of the media outlet. Atkinson had been one of the reporters who had called the gallery the day George Hardy and his Redemption of Christ protesters had shown up in front of the gallery.

"I'd like to talk to you when you have a moment."

"Maybe I *should* call him."

"Are you out of your mind? Didn't Jeff tell you to keep your pretty mouth shut?"

"It wouldn't hurt to get my side of the story out there."

"Except you might piss those cops off even more, and then you'll be locked into anything that's in print. Jesus, woman, maybe you do need to watch more TV. Do *not* call that guy." Alice didn't protest when Lily walked to the kitchen and hit the delete button on her answering machine. "There."

They finished culling through the profiles, searching for a picture resembling Drew Campbell, but it was a waste of time.

"The guy is dead, and I find myself hating him and wanting to kill him myself, and I don't even know who the fuck he *was*." She was screaming by the time she completed the sentence. "Why would someone do this to me? I'm scared, Lily. I'm scared of the police. I'm scared for my life. I'm scared of things I can't even imagine."

Alice had never broken down like this in front of Lily, and she could tell her friend did not know how to respond. Lily patted her on the leg before saying they couldn't give up. "We're just getting started. We're two smart, capable, and stubborn women. We're going to get to the bottom of this."

Alice wiped away her tears with the back of her hand and tried to regain control over her breathing as Lily turned her attention back to the laptop. She typed in "Drew Campbell" and hit enter. More than five hundred results. Alice felt herself succumbing to sobs again until Lily narrowed the results to New York City, and a manageable list of profiles appeared.

Her eyes surveyed the pictures, searching for the man who had charmed her. The man whose body she had found just yesterday morning.

But she didn't see the face of that man on the screen. It was another picture that caught her attention. A photograph of a woman. A face that could not have been more familiar.

She felt Lily's hand pushing back her own, as if to protect a curious child from a hot stove, but Alice reached the computer and clicked on the name next to the photograph: Drew Campbell.

A page of basic biographical information appeared. Sex: Female. City: New York, New York. Education: Haverford College for undergrad, MFA from NYU. Employer: Highline Gallery.

The profile picture was the same photograph she'd been handed earlier that morning by the property management agent in Hoboken. The photo of Alice at Christina Marcum's wedding. The picture that had been used to create a fake ID under the name Drew Campbell.

She felt her hand quiver involuntarily as she clicked on the tab marked "Photos."

The page was filled with photographs from her own life. Times with Jeff. With Ben. With her best girlfriends, Danielle, Anne-Lise, and Maggie. In Paris and Rome when she could afford those kinds of trips. But in every picture, the other people depicted had been cropped out—except in one photograph, which, although familiar, was not from her own life.

It was the photograph the police had sprung on her just that morning—a picture of some other red-haired, Alice-looking woman kissing the man she had known as Drew Campbell. She had known that kiss would destroy everything. It was a kiss she'd never even had.

She'd asked the detectives where they'd found that photograph, and now she knew. The police had discovered this Web site. They also had copies of the lease for the gallery. They believed *she* had been living as Drew Campbell.

Which would mean she had been lying to them about everything.

CHAPTER THIRTY-ONE

Hank Beckman felt like a dying man who had planned his own funeral. Much as a man sent to hospice for his last few months could anticipate the fallout of his eventual demise, he had known that the death of Travis Larson—and his firsthand surveillance of Larson's final days—would bring certain unavoidable consequences.

To manage those consequences, Hank needed to maneuver around three unalterable truths. The first of those truths? He would share his knowledge with the New York Police Department. That decision was beyond choice. He was not the kind of man who would place his own stature before the investigation of a murder—even if the vic was a scumbag like Larson, and even if the disclosure cost him his pension.

The second truth was that the world of law enforcement was a sprawling and inefficient bureaucracy when one needed it to be streamlined, and yet remarkably insular and incestuous when one might prefer the impersonal. Once he came forward to the NYPD, word of his extracurricular surveillance activities would migrate back to the bureau like a freshly hatched salmon to sea.

The third truth was that Hank was a man who took lumps when they were due. No weaseling, no matter the costs.

Add up one, two, and three, and Hank's decision was preordained. He waited patiently for his SAC to finish up his face time with the field office's Citizens' Academy. Like most special agents in charge, Tom Overton enjoyed the mythology of the bureau. John Dillinger. Baby Face Nelson. Ma Barker. Taking on the Gambino crime family and Sonny Barger's Hell's Angels under RICO. Newly expanded powers under the Patriot Act. In some circles, a bureau man was thought to be a stuffed suit with a stick up his ass, but the novice writers, true-crime junkies, and curious retirees who filled out the Citizens' Academy arrived at the field office with eager questions and appreciative eyes and ears. Overton returned to his office with a skip in his step and a smile on his face.

Until he spotted Hank waiting for him.

Hank got directly to the point. He knew he was supposed to leave Larson alone. It had been two months since he'd been reprimanded for his communication with the man who had "taken up" with his sister, as Overton worded it at the time. Two months since he'd been told he was lucky Larson hadn't sued both him and the bureau for false accusations and harassment. Two months since Overton himself persuaded Larson not to file charges after Hank had thrown the first punch.

"I didn't keep my word, sir. I'll hand you my resignation today if that's what you want, but what matters is that I step up to the NYPD with what I have."

"Not this again, Beckman. The guy's a low-level con man, I grant you that. But it's only because of your sister that you want the bureau—"

"It's nothing like that this time, Tom." Beckman's use of Overton's first name might have been a first between the two men. "Larson's dead. And I was watching him not long before he got popped."

Overton stared at him for a full thirty seconds before speaking. "Should I even ask whether you had something to do with this? Do we need to get you representation?"

If Hank had more sense, he probably would get himself a lawyer. Instead, he assured Overton he had nothing more to hide but would need to take the rest of the day as personal time so he could pay a visit to the detectives handling Larson's murder investigation.

• • •

Police precincts have a rhythm and a grit and a smell that mark them as a unique culture, so different from the sterile bureau field offices that could be mistaken for any office park in the country. Hank had worked enough joint task force operations to read the energy of an NYPD precinct. The second he stepped inside the homicide squad, he knew a case was hot. Detectives out of their desks. Moving a little more quickly than usual. Sheets of paper changing hands. And when the civilian aide at the front desk pointed him to an interrogation room down the hall, he knew the bustling was related to the Travis Larson case.

The detectives handling the case had covered every inch of a rolling whiteboard with scrawled notations in four different colors of ink. The small table in the center of the room was layered with documents and photographs. Piles of paper were beginning to accumulate on the floor.

An attractive blonde passed him in the narrow hallway. He was embarrassed when she caught his gaze moving to the detective shield hanging from a chain inside her tailored shirt. He was relieved when she threw him an amused smile instead of a faceful of the coffee she held in one hand.

"Let me guess: Feds?"

"Bureau."

"For Shannon and Danes?"

"That's what I'm told."

"Oh, yeah. They're gonna love that."

Hank suspected the detectives actually *would* love what he had to say. He understood the whole local-versus-feds tension. Truth be told, he wasn't certain he was always on the right side of it. Cops worked more cases in less time and with fewer resources. When the feds showed up, it was usually to cherry-pick the high-profile slam-dunks. But this time, a federal enforcement officer was walking into their yard with his tail between his legs. They'd love it, all right.

All it took was an introduction for the toothpick chewer to shepherd him out of view of the war room. "Let's have a word next door. You'll be more comfortable."

The man introduced himself as Willie Danes. Hank didn't bother holding anything back.

"I doubt the details matter, but I have what you might call a grudge against Travis Larson. I've been keeping an eye on him here and there ever since, and thought I should let you know in case anything I saw might be helpful to your investigation."

"Travis Larson, huh?"

"My understanding is you're one of the lead detectives. The body you caught at that gallery on Washington Street?"

"Sure. Travis Larson."

"I take it you didn't have an ID yet?"

"I didn't—"

"Look, man. I'm not sweating you. The guy was good at running a scam. He dated my sister for five months under a fake name, and she wasn't a stupid woman. Was he using a false identity?"

Danes's gaze moved to the hallway as if he was considering running the conversation past a partner, but something in Hank's face must have told him that for once a federal agent had come here with no agenda. "We had zero ID. No wallet. Cell phone came back to a throwaway. Even his prints were a dead end. You're telling me this guy's never been popped?"

"I hooked him up for an attempted fraud on my sister. Unfortunately, that decision happened to occur immediately after he said some choice words about her, and then I punched him in the side of the head."

"Jesus. Remind me not to fuck over your sister."

"Ellen's dead. She ran her car into the side of a triple-trailer on what was supposed to be her wedding day."

"Then I'd say Larson was lucky you only punched him in the head."

"That's not how his lawyer saw it. Or the bureau. He threatened to press charges. Started the paperwork for a civil suit. He got an apology, and all record of the arrest was purged, including his book-ing photo and prints. That's why you didn't get a match."

"You've got an address on him?"

Hank handed him his business card from his lapel pocket, Lar-son's address already printed on the backside. He also handed him six typewritten pages of notes summarizing his recent surveillance. It wasn't until he watched Danes flip through the pages that he fully realized the drive-bys were really over now. No more staring at the ceiling at night, wondering whether Larson was courting another well-to-do woman. Whether he was enjoying his life. Whether he ever paused to remember Ellen.

Hank was grateful for his death.

"You saw him in the gray BMW, huh?"

"Stolen from QuickCar last month. It's all there."

"That, we knew. Found it three blocks south of the gallery, un-locked, keys in the ignition. Someone wanted it stolen."

"Last I saw it, Larson had parked directly across the street from the gallery. And he locked it."

"How do you know?"

"Because I had to use a slim jim to break into it."

Danes chuckled, then started from the top, asking first about Hank's general knowledge of Travis Larson, then building a time-line based on his recent surveillance.

"You said you saw the redhead at Larson's home?"

"That's right. She either took the train or lives nearby, because she arrived on foot."

"Hold on a second." When Danes returned, he handed Hank a cup of coffee. Hank drank it even though it was bitter. Danes slipped two photographs onto the table. "Is that the lady?"

It wasn't the way they'd handle an ID at the bureau. Always better to use a six-pack. Multiple choices to make sure the witness isn't just rubber-stamping. One at a time was preferable to all at once. Hank took a moment to consider the images. The first was the kind of blurry that came with resizing low-resolution digital images. It looked like Larson kissing the woman he'd seen at the

Newark apartment complex. Same orangey blond hair. Even the same piercing blue coat. The second photograph was a clearer shot of the woman's face. He recognized the photograph as one he had seen online of the gallery manager. Frank Humphrey's daughter. What was her name? Alice.

"Yeah, that's her."

"Did you ever see Larson with anyone else? Maybe a younger girl? High school age?"

Hank shook his head.

"How about religious involvement? Any church groups or the like?"

"If Travis Larson was going to church, it would be to steal from the collection plate. Why do you ask?"

"Just some angles we're working. I think we've got what we need from you for now. Thanks for coming forward. I hope you're not in too deep a hole with the bureau."

"You sure that's it? Because, trust me, I probably know more about Travis Larson than his own mother, if he even has one. He's the kind of guy who's forging checks while peddling fake concert tickets and smurfing Sudafed for meth dealers, all while he's looking for a woman to pay his bills. I wouldn't be surprised if a hundred people out there wanted him dead."

Still, Danes did not voice the obvious follow-up.

Hank felt uneasy as he followed Danes down the hallway, past the interrogation room lined with evidence pertaining to Larson's murder. Hank had come here expecting a different kind of conversation. By his own statements, he had placed himself on the street outside that gallery immediately before Larson's death. By his own statements, he had a motive to kill the man. By his own statements, he had stalked him for the last week. He had served himself up as a suspect on a silver platter, and Danes hadn't taken even a single nibble.

Danes struck him as a good man. He was probably a well-intentioned cop. But Hank had seen this before. Those detectives had not even identified their victim until he did it for them, and yet they had already made up their minds about who killed him. They didn't want to know anything different at this point. They'd slot the rest of the evidence where they could to fit the story they had already written.

He threw his half-full cup of coffee in the garbage on the way out.

CHAPTER
THIRTY-TWO

There was a time when the Upper East Side was Alice's front and back yard. The townhouse on Seventy-second Street. Shopping on Madison Avenue. Burgers at P. J. Clarke's. Saturday-morning tea with her mother in the trustees' dining room at the Metropolitan Museum of Art.

In retrospect, she realized how odd it was that her lefty lib parents opted for a neighborhood where residents were occasionally wistful for the other side of the park's devil-may-care stance on blue jeans. But the Upper East Side was home to almost all the exclusive girls' schools, and her mother had always valued Alice's convenience over Ben's. Her father had never seen this part of the city as his home, but he would have deferred to her mother, since he basically lived at their country home in Bedford when he wasn't in L.A. or away on location.

Today, though, he had come into the city especially to see Alice, and he had insisted that she make herself available. She rang the doorbell and then followed the assistant she remembered as Mabel into the front parlor. Mabel was fiftyish and professional, and she looked like a Mabel. She'd appeared in place of the younger, more attractive assistant last year, just after the big blowup. The woman who'd looked like a younger Rose Sampson was out, and Mabel was in.

"Sort of silly to ring the doorbell at your own childhood home, isn't it?" Her father wore a bulky gray cardigan. She smelled fresh cedar and soap when he leaned in to kiss her cheek.

"It's a bit presumptuous for a grown woman to walk into her parents' house without knocking."

"Touché. I don't have to tell you to take a seat, do I?"

She took her usual place on a mid-century recliner and waved off Mabel's gesture toward an aperitif from the bar cart. She knew she had been summoned here for a reason, so wasted no time laying out the abbreviated version of the still-unfathomable events that had landed her and her former employer on the crime pages of the *Daily News*: "Murder on the Highline."

"You say this like it's nothing, Alice. As if this were yet another little cycle in your life—getting married, that move to St. Louis, returning home, the MFA, finding a dead body at what turned out to be a nonexistent job. Where is the shock? Where is the fear?"

"You have no right to tell me how to *act*. I am not one of your starlets for you to direct. Trust me, I feel fear and shock and terror and fury. I feel it so much that I'm numb."

"Yet you still can't call us for help. I practically had to beg you to come here and tell me what is happening. You want to punish me so badly that you'll punish yourself in the process."

"If I thought you could help, I would have asked you. This isn't late rent or a job interview. Money or a phone call isn't going to make this go away."

"So you think that's the only way I know how to help? By handing you money or throwing Hollywood names around?"

"No, Papa, that's not what I meant. I didn't want you to worry."

"We always worry about you, baby girl."

He had called her that as long as she could remember. There had been times as a teenager when the sound of it made her cringe, but she had to admit she liked hearing the term of endearment now. She liked being here in this familiar room. In this particular chair. She wanted to close her eyes and believe her father could make everything all right.

"The police obviously think I was the one who set up the gallery. And if I lied to them, and I was the one who found that man's body, I can only imagine what they must be thinking. I'm really scared, Papa. I'm scared they're going to arrest me with who-knows-what kind of evidence someone has cooked up. And I'm scared that whoever killed that man might come after me. But then if I leave town to protect myself, they'll think that's a sign of guilt. And I'm—I'm terrified that someone has done this to me. I just don't understand it." She wiped away a tear. "See? This is why I wasn't showing you that shock and fear you were looking for. It's all I can do to hold myself together."

"These police officers are probably bureaucrats who would love to make their careers by hanging this on an attractive, wealthy woman with a famous last name. They can't possible believe—"

"Papa, the contract was under what they think is my alias, with my photograph. They have a picture of me kissing a guy I swore was only my employer. What they're thinking is so damn believable that sometimes I wonder if I'm the one going crazy."

"Well, this may not be something you thought I could help with, but you know I will insist. Do not talk to them any more without a lawyer."

"Jeff said the same thing, but I think that makes me look even guiltier."

"You went to Jeff with something like this? No, you need someone good. Let me call Arthur. He was trying cases when Jeff was in diapers."

"Jeff graduated top ten percent from law school. He has his own firm. He's perfectly capable of protecting me from a police interrogation." And Arthur was with you on a few of those mile-high-club adventures on your private jet, she wanted to say. He knew all about your dalliances, and yet continued to be a friend and confidant to your wife and children. He continued to let my mother host his frequent weekends to the guest cottage in Bedford that he jokingly called his country home. Yeah, I'm going to trust Arthur Cronin.

"It's not about book smarts. It's about stature. Did you read *Outliers*?"

She shook her head.

"Well, Malcolm talks about something called 'practical intelligence.' " Since her father had struck up a friendship a few years earlier with the author Malcolm Gladwell, he had taken to frequently quoting his friend, and always by first name. "It's about the ability to read a situation. To know what to say and how and when to say it. Arthur Cronin went to some crap school in Florida, but he made a name for himself based on his work. Jeff? Jeff is a simple little boy who cares so much about his bourgeois, two-kids-and-a-picket-fence, brainwashed, cookie-cutter lifestyle that he hurt a bright, talented, and thoughtful woman. He *hurt* you, Alice. I remember you calling us in Bedford that night. We could hardly understand you, you were so distraught. We got in the car and drove to the city to make sure you wouldn't hurt yourself. Our beautiful baby girl. We were *that* worried about you. And that little asshole Jeff Wilkerson is the one who put you in that state."

"That was a long time ago, Papa."

It had been nearly three years since Jeff suddenly announced they had no future. He wanted children. She had learned during her first marriage that she could not carry any. That fact had never been a secret from Jeff, but one night during dessert at Babbo, he came to (or at least vocalized) the conclusion that a future with biological children meant more to him than a future with her. He tried to blame the disclosure's poor timing on the wine, but he could not retract the sentiment.

"It's not as if anything has changed with him. He shows up, and then he's gone again. He's in your life, then he's out. I hate to say this, but the man uses you, Alice, and it breaks my heart to see it."

"I guess you know about using women."

She regretted the words immediately and knew there was no way she could ever explain to her father why she had hurled them. Her father had always given her unconditional praise, however undeserved. When she was still acting, he would tell her she was absolute perfection, conveying more expression in a single glance than most girls her age could manage in a five-minute monologue. Anyone who criticized her was written off as a hack, too jealous or untalented to fathom the enormity of the career she would ultimately have.

He had only the best intentions. He had wanted a daughter who believed in herself absolutely and without reservation. But, at least for Alice, to be told that she was perfect when she knew otherwise only invited her to form—and then internalize—the obvious counterarguments. I'm not perfect. I'm not better than the other girls in class. I'm not pretty. I'm not talented.

Even now, as her father insisted the police must be idiots, she could only see how rational their suspicions of her actually were.

And now her father was also telling her that she was too good for someone like Jeff. Jeff, who had always been honest with her about wanting to father children. Who was still trying to find a place in his life for her despite that desire. Who had dropped everything when she had needed him at the gallery. Who, once he eventually did get married and have his children, would never do what her father had been doing—and denying—all these years.

"There is something you can help me with, Papa."

When he said nothing, she was thankful he'd accepted the change in subject.

"This is the photograph the police have of me and the man I knew as Drew Campbell." She handed him the copy the detectives had left with her. "It's either someone who looks a lot like me, or it's been Photoshopped, or both. Can you tell whether it's been doctored?"

Although her father had become famous as a director, he was also considered one of the best cinematographers and photographers in the world.

"Looking at it right now, it is hard to say offhand. I see no obvious mistakes. No missing earlobes," he said with a smile. "Seems consistent in perspective and shadow. I can take a closer look at it if you leave it here. Maybe I can let one of the visual effects people have at it, if that's all right with you?"

She thanked her father for his help before she left, and for the first time in what had been a very long year, she meant it.

CHAPTER
THIRTY-THREE

It had been five days since Becca Stevenson had disappeared, and Morhart could already feel the case losing momentum. He'd handled missing-kid reports before, but he'd always had a resolution within a day or so. With one exception, the kids had turned up, after either running away or a simple misunderstanding about so-and-so's slumber party. He didn't like thinking about the one exception, a stepmother who had faked an abduction with her lover in an attempt to extract ransom from her husband. The boy's body had been found in the Jersey City Reservoir.

Morhart may not have juggled one of these prolonged searches before, but he'd seen some of them unfold in the news. Some kids got the full treatment—the high-profile Amber Alerts, front-page headlines, and around-the-clock cable news updates. Others got one paragraph in the back pages, and then just disappeared—both in life and from the media. Anyone willing to be honest about our lingering unconscious biases could recognize the role that race played in those distinctions. Morhart couldn't recall a single case where the media took up the cause of a victim of color. But he had a relatively attractive white girl at stake, and he needed her face in the newspapers and on television if he had any hope of generating new leads.

The problem, he suspected, was the narrative. Not a cheerleader. Not an honor student. A messed-up girl with a single mother who didn't even notice her kid was missing until morning because she was busy getting nailed by her new boyfriend. Those reporters were assuming what everyone else was—that Becca had simply run away. Morhart found himself thinking the same thing, but it didn't change the fact that he wanted a resolution. He wanted to know where Becca was and why. He wanted to know if she was still alive. He wanted to keep his promise to a mother who struck him as a better woman than she was believing herself to be right now.

Five days had passed, and he felt like he was swimming in Jell-O. The bullying Becca had been experiencing at school. The secret cell phone. The recent reappearance of her father. Those illicit photographs. He could not help thinking there had to be a connection between the fact that Becca had taken a nude picture of herself and her father's subsequent allegations against an art exhibit featuring controversial photography.

He walked into the precinct to find Nancy bent over his desk, scribbling a note, her left hand still resting on his telephone. He could smell her powdery perfume ten feet away.

"I've told you a hundred times, Nancy, just let the calls go to voice mail." On calls about his cases, he preferred to hear the callers' demeanor and exact words himself. Not to mention that Nancy had a habit of switching digits around when distracted.

"Your phone rings so darn loud, I can't help it sometimes. Here you go."

He looked down at her bubbly, cursive letters. "Det. John Shannon, Homicide, NYPD," followed by a phone number.

"He said it was about Becca Stevenson."

"So, we compared those pictures you sent over to the images we have of the so-called artwork that was up at our gallery."

Morhart felt like the tide was finally breaking. The images would match. Shannon was about to confirm that Becca was the girl depicted in those photographs. He didn't know whether to be pleased or disappointed. A connection between her and the gallery would be a step toward a resolution, but he suspected it would not be a happy one in light of the murder that had occurred there.

"No match."

Morhart found himself relieved. He wanted Becca to be safe even more than he wanted answers. "Are you sure? You said your pictures didn't have any faces in them."

"The ones on display in the museum—or the gallery, I guess— just showed little snippets of bare skin, but we've actually found some other photographs that are of more interest to us."

"What other pictures?"

"Stuff that wouldn't be on display anywhere."

"Are these minors? Is it child pornography?"

"Christ, Morhart. You're worse than my partner. Can you let me get a word in, here? We've got a bunch of pictures, and trust me, none of them matches. Your girl was a little, um, softer than the girls in these pictures. But it doesn't matter, okay? You were right. There's a connection."

"I don't understand."

"The fingerprints. We had them run the latents picked up from the gallery against the prints you pulled from your vic's bedroom. We found a right index and ring finger match on the bathroom doorknob."

"She was there."

"Correct. Becca Stevenson was inside the Highline Gallery."

CHAPTER THIRTY-FOUR

"**N**ow we're at the height of our practice. Trikonasana, triangle pose."

Alice tried to keep her mouth shut, concentrating on the deep nasal breaths that were supposed to help her control her heart rate, release toxins, and center her thoughts on the present. She bent her right knee at a ninety-degree angle and spread her arms like an eagle, aiming her right fingers between her big and second toes and her left toward the sky. Her legs and arms quivered. She felt her heart racing. She did not, however, feel her past and future float away. She did not feel her worries leave her body.

Instead, she felt the oppressive heat of the 105 degrees and 40 percent humidity and the sour taste of regret for believing that a Bikram yoga class could help her escape from her reality, even momentarily.

She knew from experience that Otto, the teacher who'd affectionately been dubbed "the yoga nazi," would not allow her to leave the room. This, after all, was the man who once asked a frazzled student to name a pose, only to say in response: "That's right. Standing head-to-knee pose, not stand-in-my-front-row-and-check-out-your-hair-in-the-mirror pose."

Despite the quick, cold shower after class, she could still feel heat escaping her body when she returned home to find Willie Danes waiting for her. This time, he had not remained at the curb. He was fiddling with a BlackBerry just outside her apartment door.

"Another workout, huh?"

She immediately wondered whether all this exercise made her look guilty. She had found a body, after all. Her life had been turned upside down by information that didn't add up. Exercise was a form of escape for her, but would a cop like Danes see the trivialities of her daily routine as a sign of callousness?

"If you need something from me, Detective, you're always welcome to call."

She had meant to sound helpful, but the words came across as prickly.

"Didn't want to inconvenience you, Miss Humphrey, but I do have a few more follow-up questions. Do you mind?"

She heard her father's voice: *Do not talk to them any more without a lawyer.* She remembered Jeff's advice: *Three simple words: I want counsel.* She stood with her key in the door and prepared herself. *Just tell him you don't want to talk to him right now. Tell him you think it's best if you have an attorney involved.*

But when she turned and looked him in the eye, she couldn't do it. She knew any mention of a lawyer would immediately terminate the cordiality between them, however artificial it might be. They would officially be antagonists. It would be her versus the police. And they had power and information, and she did not. She knew she was innocent. She had nothing to hide. "Sure, Detective, come on in."

This time, she took a bar stool at her kitchen counter. No more sitting low in the corner with a cop staring down at her.

"Have you ever heard of a girl called Becca Stevenson?"

She shook her head. "Is she connected to the man I found in the gallery?"

"She's a fifteen-year-old girl from Dover, New Jersey. She's been missing since Sunday night."

"Oh, sure. I saw something about that in the newspaper a couple of days ago."

"You don't know her?" He handed her a photograph. She had dark eyes and a freckled nose. Her dark curls were blowing in the wind, but her pink cheeks looked like they'd be warm. She smiled as if she were trying to hide the tiny snaggletooth on the left side of her mouth.

"Pretty girl. No, I don't know anything about her. Why?"

"We've had some leads come up, but I'm afraid I can't discuss them."

Alice could see only one possible connection. "Wait. Do you think she's the girl from Hans Schuler's photographs?"

"No, we don't."

"So—"

"I'm sorry I can't share information with you, Miss Humphrey. But you said if we had any questions—"

"Yes, of course. I understand." She understood this was a one-way street.

"So, just to be clear, you've never met or been in the same room or spoken to Becca Stevenson, the girl in this photograph?"

She didn't like the way he asked the question, as if he were nailing her down for the record. As if he were ready to prove she was a liar. But she knew the truth, and she knew how it would look if she tried to avoid answering. "That's right."

"All right. Now I also wanted to talk to you about ITH, the company that was backing the gallery."

"Uh-huh?"

"You say you've never heard of the company before?"

"That's right."

They were back on familiar territory, but how many times were they going to ask her to repeat the same information?

"Do you have any thoughts about what ITH might stand for?"

"I don't know. I've tried digging around online, but I never found anything."

"All right. And, just to be clear, you say you never met the man you knew as Drew Campbell before?"

She tried to hide her frustration as she described, once again, the series of events that had led to her first meeting with Campbell, her meeting with him at the gallery space, her acceptance of the job, and eventually her discovery of the body. She realized she must have sounded remote as she walked him through these facts, but she had recited them so many times that they hardly seemed real anymore.

"And you're sure your father didn't have anything to do with the gallery?"

"My father? Um, no, of course not. Why would you ask?"

"Just looking at all the possibilities here. Your father is a man of means. He is part of the broader art world—"

"So is, I don't know—Brad Pitt, but I don't think he had any-thing to do with Drew Campbell or the Highline Gallery."

"There's no need to get testy."

She reminded herself why she had allowed him into her apart-ment in the first place. She was innocent. She was helpful. And she had nothing to hide. Innocent, helpful, forthcoming witnesses do not get angry.

"I'm sorry, Detective. It's just—well, it's a long story, but I've gone to great lengths to be independent of my family. Part of me thinks I wouldn't even be in this situation if I hadn't gone to those lengths, so I apologize if this is a touchy subject. My father and I had a kind of falling-out last year. If you've looked him up on the gossip pages, you might be able to figure out why."

"I'm sorry, too, if I'm dredging up something for you." They were both continuing their roles in this charade of civility. "But I have to ask: You spent nearly a year turning down your father's offers of financial assistance, and then, lo and behold, a man you've never met before comes forward and offers you this golden op-portunity to manage a gallery for a wealthy older man who would remain completely anonymous and allow you to call all the shots."

"I realize it sounds ridiculous in hindsight, but—"

"It never dawned on you that the man cutting the checks might be your father?"

She felt herself flinch at the suggestion and wondered whether

that blink she felt internally had manifested itself for Danes to witness. "No," she finally said. "It didn't."

"ITH. Didn't your father win an Academy Award for a film
called *In the Heavens?*"

These questions were taking them into subject areas she never
imagined. She knew Danes was wrong. Her father wouldn't start
a business and hire a man to draw her into it, just to force his help
upon her. Would he? And even if he would, how did that explain
Drew's death? Or these questions about a missing girl in Jersey?

"I'm sorry, Detective. I don't think I can help you any more."

"What are you saying?"

"I'm saying I don't want to talk to you any more outside the presence of counsel." She pictured Jeff, and then heard her father's voice
once again. *It's not about book smarts. It's about stature. It's about the
ability to read a situation. To know what to say and how and when to say
it.* "My lawyer's name is Arthur Cronin. Please call him if you need
to discuss anything further with me."

"Cronin, huh? That's with a C, right?"

She had already thrown back two fingers of scotch when the phone
rang. She let it go to her machine. "Miss Humphrey. It's Robert Atkinson again, with Empire Media? I'd really like to talk to you—"

She picked up the phone and screamed over the screech of her
machine. "Please stop calling me. I don't want to talk to you. If you
call my home again, I'll seek a restraining order."

She slammed the phone back onto the cradle as her cell phone
began to chime. She was tempted to hurl it across the apartment,
but checked the screen to see it was Jeff.

"Hi."

"You okay?"

"Yeah. I finally filled my dad in on everything, then went to
Bikram. I'm a little wiped out, is all." She wasn't ready to talk to
anyone yet about Danes's theory of her father's involvement.

"I did some digging around with the corporate filings for ITH. I still don't have an actual person who's pulling the strings, but I did manage to get the name of the attorney who handled the incorporation."

"That's good, right?" She felt the panic beginning to subside. ITH could mean anything. Her father had made seventeen films in his career. The matchup of the letters was just a coincidence.

"Hopefully. The papers were filed in 1985, which I guess would make sense if this is an older guy who's been using this corporation for other projects over the years. I thought I'd give the lawyer a call and see if I can get some basic information as a professional courtesy. His name's Arthur Cronin. His office was closed for the day, but I'll give him a ring first thing in the morning."

CHAPTER
THIRTY-FIVE

Alice tried to make herself small inside the tiny alcove at the entrance of her brother's apartment building. In that day's street-shopping session with Lily, she'd finally replaced her missing gloves. She'd even purchased a fake fur hat while she was at it, but no amount of bundling was sufficient to protect her from the Icelandic winds pouring up Mott.

Unlike her rental in the East Village, Ben's Nolita apartment was a condo, purchased in her parents' names at the top of the market about five years earlier. It had eleven-foot ceilings and thirteen hundred unencumbered, lofted square feet. He paid utilities and maintenance. Supposedly.

She pressed her index finger against the buzzer for the fifth floor, this time holding it down for a complete four seconds before breaking into a staccato rhythm of "ah, ah, ah, ah, staying alive, staying alive."

A pack of four girls stumbling up the street in platform wedges and miniskirts barely attempted to mask their giggles. "Sometimes he's just not that into you," one of them said, giggling, after they had passed.

"Gross! He's my idiot brother, not that it's your business. And put some frickin' clothes on. It's fifteen degrees out. You look ridiculous."

More giggles. Jesus, she was turning into one of those crazy old New York women who yell at strangers on the street. She leaned on Ben's buzzer again until she heard his voice over the intercom.

"I told you, just a second, okay? I was in the shower."

She had tried calling her father as soon as Jeff had dropped the bombshell about Arthur Cronin filing the incorporation papers for ITH. Jeff wasn't familiar with the attorney's name, but Alice certainly was. The phone at her parents' townhouse rang for two straight minutes without an answer, and her father's cell went directly to voice mail. When she tried the house in Bedford, her mother said her father had flown to Miami to scout locations for his next film.

Alice got the impression that her mother still didn't know about Drew Campbell's murder or its aftermath. She had never followed current events that were not related to culture or entertainment, and apparently her husband hadn't felt the need to fill her in on her daughter's current crisis. Alice had said nothing to change the situation, simply asking her mother whether she knew about a corporation her father might have used called ITH. Her mother did not, but said she would try to ask her father about it.

In the meantime, Alice had questions for Ben.

She gave a perfunctory tap before opening his unlocked door. She found him in the living room fully clothed. His hair was dry. The apartment was not particularly tidy. He had some reason for keeping her waiting in the cold. She looked into his face, searching for signs of drug use, but she'd never been good at detecting such things. Or maybe he'd always been good at hiding them.

"I need to ask you something, Ben, and I need you to be totally honest with me. Do you know anything about ITH Corporation? Specifically, I mean any connection between it and Dad." She told him what she had learned from Jeff about Arthur Cronin being the attorney who filed the initial documents for incorporation. "The police must also know about Art's involvement, because they were asking me whether Dad might be connected to the gallery."

Ben shook his head. "I told you, Alice, I don't know anything about it."

"But you acted weird the other night when I mentioned the company, and now it turns out Art was involved."

"I wasn't acting weird. God, not this again. What would Dad have to do with that gallery anyway?"

"I have no idea. That's what I'm trying to figure out. I'm starting to wonder whether there's anything our father *isn't* capable of."

"Jesus, Alice. It's been a year. Mom's not going anywhere. She seems fine with him. You've got to start forgiving him, too. Lighten up."

"I thought you said my independence was contagious. You didn't even call them when you got busted, and now you're defending them?"

"I didn't call them because I don't want them to freak out and worry."

She plopped herself down on his oversize sectional sofa and threw her feet onto the ottoman. "It doesn't piss you off that he spent all those years telling us to ignore tabloid lies? It was all true, Ben. All those years. All those women. It's embarrassing."

"Of course I'm pissed. And, yeah, that's part of why I'm not really down with them right now either. But with me, it's temporary. So the man's not perfect. He loves Mom. He loves us. He's just—you know, he's fucked up and has his baggage, like everyone else. Did it ever dawn on you that maybe he and Mom had an understanding?"

"Oh, gross."

"Don't be so provincial, as they'd likely say. They've always been a little weird."

They both knew that her parents' nontraditional approach to marriage had rubbed off more on Ben than on her. She'd been so eager to have a stable, regular marriage that she had dashed down the aisle with someone who proved to be entirely wrong for her. Ben, on the other hand, had been engaged twice to two wonderful women, who both eventually left when they realized he would never be able to live his life around anyone but himself.

"I'm sorry. I'm not ready to forgive him."

"Will you ever be?"

"I don't know. Why are we talking about this?"

"Sorry. I guess I want to see things back to normal with you guys. You've always been able to be my sister, even when I was sticking anything I could find in my arm. I wish you'd show the same tolerance with Dad."

"I can tell you one thing: if it turns out he had anything to do with this gallery and kept it from me, even after all that has happened, I'm done with him. I will never talk to him again."

"Well, hopefully that won't be the case, then."

She pushed her fingers through her hair. "Fuck, if the police know about Arthur they might try to ask Dad about ITH. I can only imagine how that conversation will go. Remember that time the police came to our house after that belated birthday party you decided to throw for yourself?"

"I'm surprised you remember that."

How could she forget the one time police officers had been called to their home?

It was a Sunday afternoon. Before the drive back into the city, she had been finishing a project for her sixth-grade civics class— a five-minute oral autobiography delivered in the role of the first female Supreme Court justice, Sandra Day O'Connor. Her father had knocked on her bedroom door. Two police officers in uniforms stood behind him. She remembered her father looking nervous, but in retrospect, she had probably projected her own reaction onto him. Apologetic for disturbing her, he made a point of telling the officers they were disrupting his daughter's schoolwork.

She remembered feeling small as she followed them to her father's private study. She remembered running her fingers across the nap of his new red velvet sofa—push it one way and it's shiny, then the other way for dull.

"Alice, these policemen have some questions about a gathering your brother had Friday night? Remember we were watching your movie until midnight? They just need to ask you about that."

Ben had a way of telling his parents he was "inviting a few friends over," only to wind up hosting a kegger in the backyard. This particular night was precisely one week after Ben's sixteenth birthday. Ben had wanted to celebrate the actual date with his school friends in Manhattan, but that didn't stop him from taking a second bite of the apple in Bedford a week later. By then, Ben was nearly an adult in her parents' eyes. They thought of themselves as too freewheeling to interfere.

The party had proven to be a doozie. Ben would tell her later that one girl got so drunk her parents sent her away to an all-girls boarding school.

It seemed like the police officers' questions went on forever. How many people were at the party? Could she name any of them? Did she hear or see anything unusual? Where were her parents? She ran her fingers back and forth over that red velvet—shiny then dull, shiny then dull.

She remembered wanting to protect her parents. She remembered hating her brother for putting them in a position of having to answer questions from police officers. She remembered wishing that her father's friend, Arthur, was still there, but he had already left for the city.

Were her parents going to have to go away with these men because of Ben and his stupid underage drinking parties? All she could do was tell the truth: her mother had gone to bed early, and her father hadn't paid the party any mind. He'd been in their screening room with her, watching an advance copy of *The Goonies*. He hadn't really been watching it, of course. He'd been sneaking glimpses at scripts in the dim glow of a flashlight until he had a few too many scotches and fell asleep, but she didn't see any point in adding that detail.

Her parents were the kind of people who dined with liberal senators and raised funds for elected officials, but who held in contempt the people who actually carried out the work of government. People like her parents saw police as security guards for people with "those kinds" of problems. She remembered that day because it was the day she learned that police officers—whom children naturally saw as helpers and heroes—were, to men like her father, unfit to intrude upon the private affairs of a family like theirs, unqualified to disrupt even a sixth-grade homework assignment. She would witness that attitude in her father several more times over the next fifteen-plus years, every time Ben had one of his scrapes with the law. He'd rail against the war on drugs. He'd demonize the nation's irrational emphasis upon retribution over rehabilitation. But he'd never blame Ben for blowing so many second chances.

She didn't want to think about how her father would respond if Willie Danes and John Shannon showed up at his doorstep unannounced, as they had with her.

Ben walked her to the door and gave her an awkward hug. "Try not to get ahead of yourself on this ITH stuff. Arthur represents thousands of clients at that huge firm, and that was like twenty-something years ago anyway. It's probably just a coincidence. Hang tight, and I'm sure the police will figure this out."

As she made her way to the 6 train, she passed the location of what used to be her favorite bar, Double Happiness. It seemed like only yesterday that she and her girlfriends were downing ginger martinis in the basement-level hangout—getting ejected once when her friend Danielle broke not one, but two, cocktail glasses—but she realized it had been closed now for almost five years. Terrific. First she was yelling at the group of hot party girls on the street. Now she was pining for the better-than-today places that used to be. Why didn't she go ahead and adopt a dozen cats to seal her grumpy-lady fate?

She was just about to swipe her MetroCard through the turnstile when something about her conversation with Ben began to nag at her. The man behind her rammed into her when she failed to follow the usual rhythm of the subway system.

"Sorry."

"You going or what, lady?"

She stepped out of his way, not wanting to board the train until she figured out what was bothering her. Something related to what

Ben said about Cronin. What was it that he had said? That Art had a lot of clients, and it was a long time ago.

But she had never said anything to Ben about ITH being incorporated twenty-five years earlier. She nearly slipped on ice patches three different times as she ran back to his apartment. Despite five minutes of buzzing, no one answered.

CHAPTER
THIRTY-SIX

Hank Beckman popped his third Advil in as many hours. He felt his eyes beginning to cross from the strain of reading entries on bank statements and deposit slips.

"Okay, Mrs. Ross. If we've identified every transaction at issue"—he punched a series of numbers into the calculator—"it looks like you transferred a total of $410,525.62 to Coulton since 2007. You withdrew only $35,000, leaving you with a loss of $375,525.62. Our charges against Coulton will reflect as much, and you might be needed to testify about the transactions and your communications with Coulton should the case proceed to trial."

"What about the money? When will I get the money back?" Marlene Ross was a well-maintained woman with smooth skin and immobile hair. Had it not been for access to her official date of birth, he would have placed her a decade younger than her sixty-six years. She had tastefully applied whatever fragrance had created the subtle sweetness he smelled whenever she leaned toward him.

The U.S. Attorney was on the verge of indicting Richard Coulton in what would have been the office's largest Ponzi scheme if Bernie Madoff had not blown that record out of the water a couple years back. "We'll go after his assets, but there's no guarantee, of course, of obtaining a complete recovery. The very nature of a

Ponzi scheme is that Coulton used the money you gave him to cover promises he made to clients he enlisted years earlier."

"So are you telling me that if you had just minded your own business and left him to his own devices, he would have received investment money from some other person in order to pay me back? He promised me a thirty percent return."

The newspapers made it sound like the swindlers who engaged in pyramid schemes were taking food from the mouths of gullible investors, but Hank had found it difficult to sympathize with some of the entitled people who were supposedly Coulton's victims.

He walked Mrs. Ross from the conference room. As she passed him, he noticed the ease with which she walked to the elevator in her six-inch heels, the designer red soles unscratched despite her claims that Coulton had left her "with nothing."

Back at his desk, he Googled "Highline Gallery," "Travis Larson," and "Alice Humphrey," as he had been doing obsessively since he divulged everything he knew to NYPD detective Willie Danes. No new information. He had seen the boxes of documents in the war room at the precinct. He had felt the energy and momentum of that investigation.

The police had a theory. He was certain of it. They had a suspect, that much had been obvious from their conversation. But three days had passed without an arrest. Probably some prosecutor had concluded that they lacked sufficient evidence for a trial, so now they were in that familiar holding pattern. He'd heard all the metaphors before: getting their ducks in a row; holding their cards close; letting the suspect wiggle free like a fish, careful not to try to grab it too early. Waiting for the media frenzy to die down. Waiting for another piece of the puzzle to fall into place. Waiting for the suspect to make a mistake. Waiting. Waiting.

He couldn't wait any longer. For seven months, since Ellen died, he had thought about Travis Larson every single day. Now the man was dead, and Hank—for reasons he could not identify—felt like he had seen something that would somehow prove relevant. He hated being locked on the outside, left scouring the Internet for clues like one of those housebound true-crime crazies who routinely called the bureau with so-called tips gleaned from online surfing.

He kept recalling moments from the last days of Larson's life, replaying mental videotapes from his periods of surveillance, wondering if he had overlooked the significance of something he had witnessed.

He also had an uneasy feeling about the identification process Danes had used to get him to name Alice Humphrey as the redhead he'd seen at Larson's apartment. Last year, a federal court had released a man named Anthony James Adams after DNA evidence cleared him of raping a nurse working the night shift at St. Vincent's Hospital thirteen years earlier. Hank had been the FBI agent in charge. He'd shown the victim a six-pack of photos, and after a minute of careful study, she'd identified Adams as the perpetrator. It would be more than another decade before a different man, Teddy Jackson, would tell his cellmate that he raped a nurse at a New York City hospital in 1997 and got away with it when another man took the rap. More sophisticated DNA analysis, unavailable during the original investigation, led to Adams's release.

Hank never wanted to be part of a wrongful conviction. He still woke up some nights thinking about Anthony James, and wondering what kind of life he might have had if things had been different. Hank liked to think that he had at least learned something from the experience. What he learned was that human memory was fragile. An expert in eyewitness testimony had explained to him why the nurse had erred in her identification: when Hank handed her a single piece of paper depicting the faces of six men, she had asked herself which of the six men looked the *most* like her attacker. Poor Anthony James looked more like Teddy Jackson than the others. From that day forward, the nurse simply continued to identify him—not because she remembered him from the attack, but because she remembered him as the man she had already picked out of the six-pack. The expert had shown him videotapes of subjects in her laboratory who, after choosing the wrong suspect in a lineup, would continue to identify that person even when given a choice between him and the actual perpetrator.

Hank prided himself on his ability to pull up images from his past as clearly as if he were examining a color photograph, but he realized that the clarity of an image and its accuracy were two different things.

When Willie Danes asked him about the woman he'd seen at Larson's apartment, he had handed him two photographs: one of a redhead kissing Larson, and one Hank knew to be Alice Humphrey. Hank realized now that he had simply assumed that the same woman was in both photographs. And the two images looked enough like each other and enough like the woman at Larson's apartment that he had made the ID. But if the identification process had been perfect—if Hank had not already seen photographs of Alice Humphrey on the Internet, and if Danes had shown Hank a series of photographs of red-haired women to examine sequentially—would he have picked out Alice Humphrey as the woman from Larson's apartment? He could never be absolutely certain, but he found himself doubting his own memory.

And that's why he kept searching for news updates. He wanted to know the police had more evidence pointing to Alice Humphrey's involvement in Larson's death. He wanted to be certain he had gotten it right when he'd made the ID.

For what had to be the fifteenth time in the last three days, he entered her name in Google Images. He was trying to be certain she was the same woman from the apartment complex, but he knew he'd seen so many pictures of her by now that he had simply cut and pasted her face on those remembered images that he kept replaying in his mind's eye.

If only he could see her in person, watch her walk down Larson's street in that bright blue coat and sexy shoes. Watch her arms barely move as she took the stairs. See the tilt of her head when she looked into a man's face. Maybe if he were in the same room with her, he would know.

And then he realized he might be able to get a moving image of her, right here from his cubicle.

He opened YouTube on his computer and searched for Alice

Humphrey. Nothing. Searched for Highline Gallery. Nothing. Then he searched for Frank Humphrey.

He found thousands of results. Many of them were illegally up-loaded—iconic scenes from his copyrighted films. There were also reels from *Inside Edition*, *Entertainment Tonight*, and TMZ about the many mistresses who had stepped forward last year, one at a time in a slow, painful drip of tawdriness. There was the director's exclusive sit-down interview with Katie Couric. Hank usually tried to block out celebrity gossip, but even he had been exposed to some of the ubiquitous sound bites: *I understand other people with more traditional lifestyles may not understand; This is a private matter between Rose and me; None of this affects my work as an artist; I want to be evaluated based on my filmmaking.* The interview was labeled a "trainwreck"—a patronizing non-apology from an arrogant old man.

Hank clicked through the videos, searching for images of Humphrey with his family, until he finally found a screen capture of Humphrey, hand in hand with his daughter. It was footage of him leaving the premiere of *The Burn Wall*, his last film before the scandal. By all accounts, it was a good movie, but a commercial flop due to the public's lack of interest in the story of a soldier serving in Afghanistan.

Alice's eyes darted around the glare of the flashbulbs while her father delivered the obligatory words of gratitude toward his actors and producers. As they left the red carpet, Alice looked down at her feet, delivering one awkward wave to the crowd before stepping into an awaiting limousine.

He rewound the reel, examining the woman's face, trying to re-create the appearance of the woman he'd seen with Larson. Her hair was pulled into a low ponytail at the nape of her neck, but a woman's hairstyle could change twenty times in two years. She appeared to be about the same height and weight. The woman with Larson had struck him as younger, but he had seen her from a distance, and those big sunglasses and bangs over her eyebrows would have covered the small lines on her forehead and around her eyes, the only betrayals of Alice Humphrey's age.

He rewound the clip again, knowing that something about the video was bothering him.

It wasn't her face. It was the walk. Just like Mrs. Ross gliding into the elevator, every person had a distinctive gait. When Alice Humphrey followed her father on the red carpet, she looked down at her feet, watching each placement of her feet onto the ground. Her shoes had heels, but they were three inches max—modest as far as those things went for women these days. The way she stepped— flat-footed, cautious, in tiny baby steps—reminded him of Ellen practicing in her first pair of Manolo Blahniks, or whatever those things were called.

This was not the walk of the woman outside Larson's apartment. What had initially caught his attention had been that walk—that catlike prance up the street, eyes ahead, back straight, chest forward, nearly marching in those black stiletto pumps. It had been nearly two years since that film premiere. Maybe practice had made per- fect for the once hesitant Miss Humphrey.

But maybe not.

He picked up the phone and asked for Detective Willie Danes.

"I hate to bother you, Detective, but I may have been a little too quick to call the ID on Alice Humphrey." He explained the discrepancy between the woman he'd seen and the videotape of Humphrey on YouTube.

"You're saying you saw Travis Larson with a knockout beauty of a redhead at his apartment, wearing a stunning peacock blue coat. And then his body gets found by, lo and behold, a knockout beauty of a redhead in the very same peacock blue coat, but it's not the same woman? And you're basing this on a pair of shoes the girl wore two years ago?"

"I'm not saying it's a different woman. All I'm saying is I can't be a hundred percent sure that it's the *same* woman. Not based on what I saw."

"Well, it's a good thing the NYPD doesn't operate on the same definition of a hundred percent as the FBI."

It wasn't the first time Hank had been ribbed by a local cop about the federal government having the luxury of demanding more evidence, and it wouldn't be the last.

"Can you just be sure and check out Humphrey's shoes? It's not every woman out there who can pull off the monsters Larson's girl was wearing."

"Do I look like Prince Charming? Chasing down Cinderella with the glass slipper? Tell you what, Beckman: we don't even need your ID at this point, so don't worry your head about it, all right?"

"Well, you can't have that much. I see you haven't made an arrest yet."

"I don't know you, Beckman, so I don't know how to say this to you, but your sister's dead. You couldn't save her, and the asshole you blamed for that is dead now, too. See a shrink or find something else to obsess about. I don't really care, but your involvement in this case is over."

The click on the other end of the line was like a punch in the throat.

CHAPTER
THIRTY-SEVEN

It was Alice's second trip to the Upper East Side, and the weekend wasn't even over. This time her mother answered the door herself, greeting her with a big hug and a kiss on the cheek.

"Hey, Mom. I thought you were in Bedford."

"Well, I was, but Arthur has a table tonight at some fund-raiser for one civil right or another. I thought it would be a good excuse to put on a fancy gown and eat dessert."

"Dad's going with you?" She had called in advance to make sure he had returned from yesterday's location-scouting trip to Miami.

"I'm afraid not. He's packing a bag now to head out to Los Angeles. I told Arthur I'd be representing the family tonight. Don't tell anyone, but I've already had a little martini to get me started. Would you like one?"

"No, thanks." Based on her mother's tolerance and extraordinary chipperness, Alice suspected she'd had more than one warm-up drink. She'd always found it strange that her mother continued an open affair with alcohol despite her husband's decision twenty-five years earlier to go dry, but there was no shortage of things she did not understand about her parents' marriage.

"How are things at the gallery?" Her mother looked at her watch. "Shouldn't you be there?"

"It's taken care of for now."

She felt guilty for not telling her what was happening, but Alice's mother had spent her entire life sending out signals that she did not want to be troubled by disturbing news. Maybe in a different marriage, with different hardships, she would have developed into a more complex woman. Certainly the promising actress who had won an Academy Award for her depiction of a promiscuous young widow had shown early signs of emotional depth. But at some point in her life, Rose Sampson Humphrey had accepted a permanent role as happy Hollywood wife, standing quietly and supportively by her talented husband and perfect children, always grateful for the family's good fortune.

Even when Ben was turning into a full-out junkie, she'd allow herself to be convinced that he was plagued by migraines, anxiety disorders, chronic fatigue, any explanation for his weight loss, erratic behavior, and sickly pallor. Rose Sampson was not, as she liked to say, in the stress business.

"All right. It's nice to know I've got one child I don't need to worry about for the time being."

"Ben?"

"He didn't show up for your opening last week. He told me he'd come up to the country for the weekend, but—well, he's probably busy. Have you seen him?"

"I was at his apartment last night." She'd been trying him all morning, but her calls were still going directly to voice mail.

"Did he seem okay? Everything's all right?"

"I only saw him for a few minutes, but, yeah—he was—he was Ben." Go ahead, Mom. Ask the follow-up question. Push me for more information. Because you know. You know, Mom. You know he's still got a problem, the way you know you smell like vodka and have glassy eyes at eleven in the morning.

"Well, that's good to hear. To what do I owe this pleasure, by the way?"

"I need to talk to Dad about something."

"That's even nicer to hear. Maybe the two of you will be back to normal soon." Her chipper smile fell when Alice didn't respond.

"Don't be so hard on your father, Alice. There are very few people in this world who have the power to hurt that man, and you're one of them. I haven't been a perfect wife, if that makes a difference."

She didn't want to hear her mother make excuses for his affairs. She didn't care about his sins as a father or a husband anymore. She just needed answers.

"Mom, you don't know anything about Dad somehow backing the gallery, do you?"

Her lips formed a small O. "Sweetie, I know your father gave you a hard time about wanting to do things on your own, but really—I think you're letting your imagination get the better of you."

"Did you have a chance to ask him about the ITH Corporation?"

She was here to ask her father about the company directly, but it wouldn't hurt to know what he might have said to her mother.

Her mother snapped her fingers and pointed at her. "That's *right*. You asked about that. I did not have a chance to ask your father about it. You know how hard he is to reach when he's on the road. But I did have some extra time on my hands up in that empty house in Bedford waiting for your brother to show up, so I did some digging in your father's old files."

She made her way to the coat closet near the front door and pulled out a canvas tote bag. "I found this."

Alice removed a file folder from the bag and flipped through its pages. She was no lawyer, but she could tell the document was an agreement between ITH Corporation and someone named Julie Kinley. ITH agreed to place all of its existing assets into a trust for the benefit of Julie Kinley. In exchange, Kinley agreed to release all potential legal claims against ITH and its agents, officers, and employees, both in their official and personal capacities. Alice wasn't entirely clear about that part, but she assumed it was a settlement agreement of some kind. The final paragraph of the document was a clause requiring confidentiality from both Kinley and ITH about the agreement.

"Is that what you were looking for?"

"I think so. Thanks. Do you know what ITH was for?"

"Your father has created a few different corporations over the years, hon. You know, for the film funding and what not. What's this all about?"

"Nothing, Mom. I'll talk to him about it. Have fun at your event tonight."

By the time Alice was halfway up the stairs, her mother was already at the bar cart, pouring herself another martini.

"Your mother went through my study? I don't know how many times I've asked her—"

"You were in Miami, and I needed to know about this company."

He shook his head with confusion. "You're telling me that this gallery was started under the name ITH?"

How many times would she need to go over this? "It was incorporated in 1985, and Arthur Cronin filed the paperwork with the state. Now it turns out you had this settlement agreement in your office. I assume that means you're behind ITH. I need to know whether you were also behind the gallery."

Most of the time when Alice looked at her parents, she saw them as they had always appeared to her—beautiful, strong, a little exotic. But every once in a while, she saw them through a neutral observer's eyes—not as they once were, but as they currently existed. A little thinner. A little paler. Their noses and ears a bit larger. Older. Her father was seventy-eight years old, and right now his face showed every day of it.

"This doesn't make any sense."

"I've been trying to tell you that. But I can't dig myself out of this unless you tell me everything. ITH is your company, isn't it?"

"It was a d-b-a I formed to film *In the Heavens*."

She knew that d-b-a stood for doing-business-as. It was a moniker used for small businesses that were not technically formed as corporations. "You didn't incorporate?"

"I had no idea what I was doing back then. I was a kid with a script, some friends, and a fantasy. The next thing you know, your mother and I are both winning Academy Awards. I kept the money associated with *In the Heavens* in an account I had opened under the d-b-a."

"But then you incorporated in 1985? That was fifteen years later."

"Sixteen, actually."

"And now someone has used that company name to open the Highline Gallery."

He placed his head in his hands before looking up to answer. "There was a lawsuit that needed to be settled. I still had money under the ITH name. Arthur structured the settlement so that the plaintiff accepted the assets that were already with ITH. He incorporated and then created a trust. By that time, I was a millionaire fifty times over. Arthur had probably incorporated me fifteen times since then for various projects. It's all about limiting liability and taxes and whatnot. But I haven't used that corporate name for years. And I certainly didn't start that gallery."

Her father had confirmed her suspicions about ITH, but she was no closer to the truth about the gallery's origins.

"Who is Julie Kinley?" She gestured to the settlement papers that were now resting on the desk in his home office.

"A wannabe screenwriter who claimed that I stole the idea for *In the Heavens*." The movie that garnered his first and her mother's only Oscar statues still remained his career-defining film. About a socially proper woman whose sexuality is awakened after the death of her husband, the film was labeled obscenity at the time by three attorneys general.

"You were accused of plagiarism?" Her father had long been known as a sharp-tongued, hot-tempered, arguably sexist man who didn't suffer fools, but she'd never detected any doubt in artistic circles about his intellectual integrity.

"Anyone who's had any kind of success in Hollywood gets accused with every project. Leeches slither from beneath every rock searching for publicity or an easy settlement. Kinley was a former employee and made the allegations long after the fact. They were bogus, of course, but I had enough money by then to settle. Art said it was better than taking the public relations hit. We structured the settlement using ITH, but I really haven't thought of it for more than two decades."

"I already knew that someone did this to set me up. Now they use the name of a company you started when I was twelve years old? This is obviously personal."

"Maybe this isn't just about you. I'm the one behind the corporate name."

"Someone wanted to set us *both* up?"

"I hate to think this, Alice, but I had this nauseous feeling from the minute I heard about your employer's murder at the gallery. No, even before then, when those protesters showed up at your door. I had this horrible pain in my heart—this feeling of portent—but I didn't want you to think I was undermining your accomplishment. I didn't want to take something that was for you and make it about me. I wanted to believe that this new job was exactly what you believed it to be—"

"Just say it."

"From the second that fascist preacher appeared outside the gallery with his brainwashed followers, I had a feeling that something horrible was happening. I never thought it was a coincidence that you landed this golden opportunity just to have some right-wing nuts drag your name through the mud—and in the process, let the media take a few more shots at the old man while they were at it."

"You think George Hardy's behind this? What would he get out of it?"

"These fellows thrive off of the culture wars. They have evil in their hearts, they preach hate in the name of Christ, and they have been coming after me for forty years. They already branded me an adulterer—"

"Come on, Papa." They both knew he had himself to blame for that.

"I'm not making excuses, but I am pointing out that they fanned the media flames. Arthur even dug up proof that a couple of these guys paid women from my past to come forward with their stories."

"Hardy's outfit seems pretty small-time. I mean, how would they even have the resources to pull something like this off?"

"Oh, don't you kid yourself, baby girl. Those guys pretend to be grassroots movements, tiny sects acting independent of one another. But they are organized. And they collaborate. And they have tremendous financial backing. Men with money fund their efforts. And these are not men of God. They manipulate religiosity for political, and ultimately financial, gain. If they can tie my name to child pornography, they can slap my face on every one of their fund-raising letters. And they can use guilt by association to campaign against every candidate and every cause your mother and I have ever given a cent to. When Hardy showed up at your door, I should have told you to walk out, right then and there."

"So if Hardy and his church are behind this, who was the man who hired me? And why is he dead?"

He shrugged. "He could be anyone. One of Hardy's followers who wasn't playing along anymore. Or someone they hired. You said he wanted to meet you at the gallery that morning. Maybe he was going to tell you the truth."

"A sudden change of heart?"

"Or he realized that the daughter of Frank Humphrey might be in a better position to help him than some loser like George Hardy and the whackjobs who carry his coat. I know I don't have all the answers, Alice, but you have to trust me on this one: I did not have anything to do with this. And no matter what happens, we are apparently in this together now. My special effects guys tell me that photograph you gave me wasn't Photoshopped. Whoever's behind this went to the trouble of lining up not only the man who hired you, but whatever woman is in that picture. I'm canceling my trip."

"Dad, you don't know a girl called Becca Stevenson, do you?"

"No. Who's that?"

"Some girl missing from her home in New Jersey. The police asked me about her, but I have no idea why."

"We definitely need to get Art in on this. You need a lawyer."

When Alice returned to her own apartment two hours later, she saw a green Toyota Camry around the corner on St. Mark's. The driver appeared to be checking out the posted hours for parking. She could not tell if it was the same man she'd seen fiddling with the stereo in a green Camry on Second Avenue when she'd gone on her Starbucks run that morning. She made a mental note of the license plate number and was still repeating the pattern to herself when she flipped the bolt on her apartment door and fastened the security chain.

CHAPTER THIRTY-EIGHT

"**T**his might have been a bad idea."

Alice was staring at a piece of foie gras on toast with some kind of jelly, the type of sweet and savory treat she would usually try to devour in one gob. When she had called Jeff, he had been on his way out of the office to grab a bite to eat. He had persuaded her to join him at the bar of her favorite restaurant, Eleven Madison Park. Now that she was here, she couldn't muster an appetite.

"You need to eat something. And if the food here isn't good enough for you, well, you really have lost your mind."

She forced herself to take a bite, hating the fact that Jeff was going to pay a fortune for food that she was in no position to enjoy. "Thanks, Jeff. For this. For making time for me."

"Making *time* for you? What are you talking about? You're one of my best friends, and you're going through hell. I'll do anything for you, Al. I've always been willing to do anything for you."

Friends. She wondered if the word choice was his way of clarifying what had been, for her at least, an ambiguous period in their long relationship. He had been dating a woman—Ramona was her name. She was only now turning thirty. Alice had even suspected that Ramona moved in for a while, during that period when Jeff rarely called, and then only from his cell. Six months must have passed at one point without any communication, and she had wondered if, at last, they were finished.

But then when the shit hit the fan with her father, he was back. It started with a call to check how she was faring. Then the meetings for drinks and meals and matinee movies picked up pace. There were those late-night phone calls when mutual, but not necessarily synchronized, bouts of insomnia set in. *Hey. Are you up? I can't sleep.* Not one, but two drunken sleepovers: the first accompanied by awkward apologies and a kiss on her forehead, but the most recent followed by a continuation of what had begun the night earlier.

And then he'd gone to Seattle for a week to visit his brother. And then she'd opened the gallery.

Friends, he said. That's apparently all they were. And he'd been willing to do anything for her—except examine the possibility that there might be a life without children but with his best friend.

She pushed the thoughts away, knowing they were planted by her father's words. All she needed right now was a friend.

"Your father says the photo's legit, huh?"

"I don't understand the technicalities of it, but apparently he knows some high-speed visual effects guys who can examine a photograph for inconsistencies—like a shadow that falls the wrong direction given the light, or problems with respective sizing of different people in the image. The picture's not great quality, but I guess nothing jumped out as phony."

"But it could still be doctored."

"Possibly, if someone did a good job. Or they found a woman who looked an awful lot like me."

"Because you know for certain it's not you, right?"

"You've got to be kidding me."

He flashed that disarming smile that always managed to check any anger brewing in her. "I know. I'm an asshole. Just making sure there were no intoxicated evenings with that handsome boss of yours. Maybe something you didn't even remember?"

"Absolutely not. You, my sir, are the only man I've drunkenly stumbled into bed with lately."

The woman at the next table coughed loudly.

"Very subtle," Jeff whispered. "Wait until she hears us talking about dead bodies and right-wing conspiracies."

"My father can be paranoid, but as they say—"

"Just because I'm paranoid, doesn't mean they're not out to get me."

"So do you think the amorphous *they* are out to get my father?" Her father's theory sounded crazy, but it would explain the bizarre timing of George Hardy's protesters outside the gallery just before Campbell's murder.

"Crazier things have happened. You had wondered why they targeted you for this job. If the entire point was to make your father look bad, taking advantage of you—and the fact that you needed a job—would be a vehicle to get to him."

"And yet?"

"That's a pretty complicated way of dragging you and your father through the mud. Someone had to set up a bank account, forge a driver's license with your picture under Drew Campbell's name, enlist Campbell to recruit you, create Hans Schuler's artwork and Web site, rent the gallery space, pay for the furniture, pay for the space—"

"I get the picture."

"I know this isn't exactly my expertise, but I represented some pretty amoral corporations when I was at the firm, and now I'm handling some criminal cases. In my experience? There are cheap ways to get revenge. Violence. Lies. Threats. That stuff doesn't cost a cent. People who spend money do it to earn money."

"Okay, so maybe you and my father are both right. What if there's a dual motive—some financial gain, but then leaving me and my father holding the bag was the icing on the cake?"

"How would that fit in with George Hardy?"

"Is it that hard to believe that the pastor at some fly-by-night, crazy church would be involved in illicit activity? I think I've read that story before, Reverend Ted. So what kind of operation could they be running?"

"All kinds of nefarious activities require a cover story. They could have been using the gallery to launder money. Or smuggle drugs. Or smuggle people."

"But we didn't really have any cargo. All we had coming in and out of there were Schuler's prints."

"Which you sold a lot of, right?"

"More than a hundred."

"Which is what? Like, seventy grand? By an unknown artist who in hindsight appears to be nonexistent?"

"And almost all the orders came in online. I got people into the door based on hype, but I had a hard time selling anything in person. All that money was from the Web."

"So where'd the money go?"

"I have no idea. I didn't have access to whatever account it went to, but if the police are still talking to me, my guess is the account is either untraceable or yet another thing that somehow traces back to me or my dad."

"Okay, so where did all the money come from? Why was the show so successful?"

"At the time, I wanted to believe it was because of my viral marketing prowess."

"And now?"

"I feel like an idiot. They weren't smuggling anything. The gallery wasn't a cover at all. They were selling the pictures. That's where the money to cover the operation came from."

"So how did they generate demand? Why would all those people pay seven hundred dollars for pictures that aren't worth anything?"

"Shit, we have to go."

He was throwing cash on the table before she had a chance to explain.

"It wasn't just the prints that I'd mail to the customers."

He obviously didn't remember.

"The thumb drives, Jeff. Remember? Every customer received a little stick of data about Hans Schuler. And whoever cleared out the gallery only left two things behind for the cops: Drew Campbell's body and a bag of those thumb drives. Whatever's on there, the police have already found."

"Do you still have any?"

"I don't know. I've got to look."

"That night I went to the gallery before you opened—you showed me the whole setup on your laptop and then slipped the thumb drive in your pocket when you were done. I remember."

They ran all the way to her apartment, where she found the pair of Hudson bootcuts she had not worn since she had first shown him the so-called Han Schuler exhibit. The thumb drive was still in the front pocket.

"I can't believe I didn't see through this bullshit."

She had viewed all of these files before: images of Schuler's art, an interactive game where users could cut and paste portions of the images to create their own virtual mosaics, and a program that created desktop background images from Schuler's work, complete with trite sayings about inner reflection and mainstream radicalism.

"And yet more than a hundred people were willing to pay seven hundred bucks for this crap."

"What are we missing?"

"Try downloading all the desktop backgrounds, and see if something happens."

"Like what?"

"Obviously I don't know, but there's got to be something there."

She downloaded all four alternatives, but other than the changes to the background of her laptop desktop, nothing seemed to happen.

"Maybe it's embedded somewhere." She began clicking her mouse across the various images. On the photograph called *Fluids*, the centerpiece of Schuler's SELF series, she clicked on what was supposedly the artist's lips, the saliva extending from his mouth, the bite marks in his wrist. Nothing.

She moved on to *Wince*, a similarly themed close-up of the artist biting his lower lip.

Her clicking became more random and desperate as she moved on to *First*, the photograph that had created such an uproar after George Hardy and his protesters arrived outside the gallery. It was a collage of cutouts from the image of a body that was obviously not Schuler's. Pale, smooth skin. Thin hips. A chest just starting to develop above still-bony ribs. She moved her mouse over a dilated pupil and clicked.

The full-screen image of *First* started to fly away like shards of broken glass. The screen went black.

Enter password.

They tried Schuler. Hans. Hans Schuler. Highline. Self.

Then she typed the name of the photograph that had created this passageway: F-I-R-S-T.

A list of files appeared on the screen, each named with a seven-digit number. She felt her eyes moving involuntarily from the images as she flipped through them. If there was any ambiguity about the age of the woman in the *First* photograph, there was none in these. Several of the images seemed to be of an older girl, maybe a young teenager. Her face had been cropped from the pictures. The photos seemed from another era for reasons Alice couldn't immediately identify. And slightly muddled, as if they had been scanned from physical photographs. She quickened the pace of her clicking, not wanting to see the details. There was a man in some of the photos, also faceless.

The pictures of the older girl were spliced in among other, higher-resolution photographs of children, maybe six to eight years old. Both boys and girls. Alone. With adults. With each other.

She felt the few bites of food she'd allowed herself at dinner working their way up her esophagus. Jeff placed a palm on the small of her back. She closed her laptop, harder than necessary, and heard her voice waver when she finally spoke.

"What am I going to do?"

CHAPTER
THIRTY-NINE

"**G**ood to see you again, Morhart."

Willie Danes gave Morhart a hearty handshake and extended a half-eaten bag of Cheetos in his direction like they were old friends. Morhart didn't doubt that he had earned some brownie points with these NYPD guys by tipping them off to Becca Stevenson's connection to their case, but he also suspected that he had top-down bureaucracy to thank for his presence today in the Thirteenth Precinct. He hadn't voted for Mayor Kyle Jenson since the mayor cut the town's community policing program seven years earlier, but the man enjoyed a natural ability to charm. He'd called the chief for an update on the Stevenson investigation. When he found out the road had led to a gallery in New York City, he had called Danes's deputy inspector personally. Now the NYPD and the Dover Police Department had an "understanding" that their investigators would fully share information in their separate but overlapping cases.

Morhart believed he had already delivered his half of the quid pro quo with Becca's fingerprint match. Because of him, Danes and his partner, John Shannon, knew that a missing fifteen-year-old girl had previously entered the gallery where their victim was killed. They knew that the girl's father—the one who had only recently appeared in her life—had just happened to protest that very gallery the day before the body was found.

Now he was about to see the NYPD's cards. He stepped carefully around piles of documents and disheveled boxes to take a seat in the overpacked interrogation room. He did his best to ignore the sounds of the creaking door as a young, unintroduced Asian guy walked in and out the room while Danes spoke.

"My partner couldn't be here," Danes explained. "He's down reviewing the final results of the ME's report. You ready to share the sandbox?"

"Did the ME find anything interesting?" It seemed to Morhart that medical examiners often confirmed what was obvious from the initial crime scene. A victim filled with bullets usually had died of gunshot wounds.

"Not much. We already had a short window on time of death, since the body was fresh. Two shots from a .38. Chest and stomach. He did find postmortem bruising on the genitals." Danes's bag of Cheetos shifted protectively in front of his torso, and Morhart felt his own knees clench together involuntarily.

"So whoever killed him really hated him."

"Or she was making sure he wasn't faking it." Morhart noticed the use of the feminine pronoun. "Maybe she'll eventually tell us. Anyway, from what we hear, if anyone deserved a kick in the balls even after death, it was Larson."

Danes recited the background information they had collected so far on their victim, Travis Larson. A string of insignificant sales jobs through his late twenties, and then no lawful employment since. No family. An apartment filled with stolen mail, skillfully faked IDs, forged checks, and pilfered credit card solicitations. An FBI agent who claimed that his sister was just one of many women Larson had deceived and sponged from over the years.

"From what we can tell, he started looking for a way to move his criminal activity indoors since that FBI agent called him out on the cougar-swindling last year. Our techno-geeks found evidence on the gallery computer of downloading and producing child pornography starting about five months ago." He removed a data stick from the pocket of his short-sleeved dress shirt and tossed it to Morhart.

Morhart dusted off the bright orange crumbs. /SELF. "As you may know, the feds have gotten aggressive in their enforcement against smut on the Net. If they think someone's peddling child porn online, they do an instant download, and voilà, they shut the site down. One step removed, the dirtbags might require a mail order, but again— the feds place an order, then verify the contents of the product and track down the origin of the package to make the bust."

Morhart had no personal involvement in those types of investigations, but he did his best to keep up with the times by reading law enforcement Web sites. "As much as technology has helped the bad guys, it's helped us to track them down."

"Exactly. So it's no surprise that someone might try to use a high-tech way to attract customers and build demand, but a low-tech method of delivery to evade detection."

"That's where this comes in?" Morhart asked, holding up the data stick.

"Any customer who placed an order through the Highline Gallery received one of these. On the surface, it's filled with a bunch of bullshit. But find the embedded link, and enter the requisite password, and some seriously perverted shit awaits. Our computer nerds tracked down messages going back six weeks on some of these chester chat boards, alerting them to the pictures they could buy through the Highline."

"And no one monitoring these sites picked up on it?"

"I've seen some shit the past two days that makes me want to stab my eyes out. The truth is, this stuff's like catching fish in a barrel for the feds. They chase down the easy prey—the guys with instant downloads, file exchanges, and mail-order operations. Someone who posts a link to a gallery with the promise of hot young things and a password to come later? Tracking that down takes one or two or three steps more than the easy cases, so no one follows up. It's actually pretty clever."

"So they line up their customers through these message boards, then when the gallery opens, they accept orders and ship the data sticks. Where'd the money go?"

"An offshore account. Totally untraceable."

"Where do George Hardy and Becca Stevenson fit in?"

Danes placed his hands on his hips and hung his head before looking at Morhart. "I wish we had better news for you, guy. We don't know."

Morhart intertwined his fingers behind his head and looked up at the ceiling.

"You've got nothing connecting Larson to Becca?"

"Just her prints on the gallery's bathroom doorknob. No e-mails. No phone calls. And I'm telling you, none of these pictures we found were of your girl."

"Fuck."

"Best we can figure, maybe Larson was grooming Becca to pose for him or maybe worse. Something went down in the operation and got Larson killed. It could have scared her off as well."

They both knew Danes's theory was complete speculation.

"A second ago, you said something about *she*. That *she* might have kicked Larson postmortem to make sure he was dead. You've got a suspect?"

Danes pointed to a five-by-seven photograph pinned to a rolling bulletin board behind him. "Her name's Alice Humphrey. She was the 'manager' of the gallery." He used air quotes to emphasize his skepticism. "According to her, she doesn't know shit about anything, but we've got pictures of her with Larson and evidence tying her to an alias used to start both the gallery and its bank account. As far as we can tell, she had something to prove to her BFD father. She persuaded him to start the gallery, but then hooked up with Larson and his smut to make sure she turned a profit."

Morhart looked at Alice Humphrey's photograph. He recognized it from one of the articles he'd read about George Hardy's protests at the gallery. Rare was the woman who victimized a child for her own pleasure, but even out in the sticks, he'd learned that people would do anything for money.

"Who's the big-fucking-deal father?"

"Frank Humphrey."

"The director?"

"Yep. And quite the lothario, if you read the tabloids. You'd have to ask Freud whether that has anything to do with his daughter's venture into child porn. All we know is that she apparently had a falling-out with him some time last year. Maybe this was her way of starting over, separate from her family."

"And you think Alice Humphrey killed Travis Larson?"

"Wouldn't be the first time a woman killed a lover. Or who knows? Maybe he double-crossed her. Love and money are powerful motivators. Hopefully we'll nail down the precise motive when we eventually get a confession. We can tie the gallery laptop to some of the messages that were posted in the chat rooms. We seized that laptop from her possession, but she can always say Larson posted the messages, not her. And even if we can nail her on the kiddie pictures, that's not enough to carry through to murder. The truth is, we don't have quite enough to hook her up on anything yet."

Morhart heard the creak of the door once again. This time, the Asian guy popped only his head inside. "Good news, man. Those gloves from the garbage on Bank and Washington? CSU called. Positive for GSR."

Morhart didn't know the city well, but he recognized Bank and Washington as located somewhere downtown, in the unnumbered part of Manhattan, presumably near the gallery. Apparently the crime scene unit had discovered gunshot residue on a pair of gloves found near the crime scene.

Danes pumped his fist at what remained of his waistline. "All we got to do is connect our girl to these gloves, and we just might be in business."

CHAPTER
FORTY

E ven in better days, Alice felt an intense irritation navigating the crowded sidewalks of midtown Manhattan. Cookie-cutter clones in dark suits. Street vendors pushing roasted peanuts and $3 belts. Meandering tourists staring up at the skyline, blissfully unaware of their shopping bags smacking other pedestrians in the thighs. Teenagers in flip-flops snapping cell-phone photos while they juggled two-quart buckets of soft drinks from fast food restaurants. It was just . . . too much.

"Smile, girl. Don't matter if it's ten degrees out. Every day can be beautiful." The man with the broad grin wheeled a hand truck filled with bottled water down the loading ramp of a delivery truck double-parked on Fifty-fourth Street. When he hit street level, he reached for the volume knob of an old boom-box CD player resting on the truck floor. "Summertime" by DJ Jazzy Jeff and Will Smith when he used to be called the Fresh Prince thumped over the sounds of midday traffic.

She flashed him a thumbs-up as she hurried to the entrance of the office building towering over them. She signed in with the front guard and posed for a digital camera before receiving a guest pass to proceed to the forty-third floor.

Her father was already waiting in Arthur Cronin's office, sipping from a glass of water with lemon as he sat cross-legged on the cherry-colored leather sofa. Art sat perpendicular to him in a coordinating wing chair in stocking feet. It would have come as no surprise to anyone seeing these two men for the first time that they had known each other nearly fifty years.

"There she is, right on time, the beautiful female half of the next generation of Humphreys." Art rose to greet her with a solid bear hug, then clasped her shoulders. "How is my fabulous goddaughter holding up? Huh?"

"I've got to admit, I found myself eyeing my passport this morning, wondering about the most livable country in the world without an extradition agreement with America."

"This is why artists aren't lawyers. Your imagination is getting away from you. Something is amuck here, no question, but these things have a way of getting worked out. You'll see."

She looked at her father and could tell he was working hard to appear untroubled. He was a brilliant filmmaker, but he was no actor. He rested his glass on the coffee table in front of him and used his hands on his thighs as assistance to stand. "All right. I've got a meeting with a certain hard-to-land octo-mom of an actress. I don't want to keep her waiting. She might get bored and adopt another baby."

"Dad, I thought we were meeting with Art together." When she had called him about the images she found on the Hans Schuler thumb drive, he had persuaded her it was time to get a lawyer involved, starting first with Arthur.

"Sorry, baby girl. This casting is a major get, and it was the only time she could meet me. I told Art what I know. You're in good hands now." He blew her a kiss with all ten fingers, then closed the door behind him.

"Don't be upset with him, Alice. I was actually the one who thought it might be best to meet with each of you separately."

He'd obviously notified only her father of the change in plans.

"I brought the thumb drive."

She hadn't looked at the pictures since that first manic perusal the previous night. Once she walked him through the process of pulling up the screen with the portal, clicking on the girl's pupil, and then entering the password, she made a point to check out the corner-office views. A couple clicks of Art's mouse were followed by wincing sounds. She tried not to remember.

As he browsed through the images hidden on the thumb drive, she moved her attention to a different collection of photographs, the framed ones clustered on top of his mahogany file cabinet. Art shaking hands with Hillary Clinton. Art accepting an award from the ACLU. A younger Art on a boat with her father. An even younger Art and a little gap-toothed Opie Taylor lookalike, huddled in the stands with hot dogs and matching Yankees caps.

"Who's the cutie at the Yankees game?"

"I'm sorry?" He rose from his desk and waved her back to the sitting area. "That's my nephew, Brandon. Little runt's already out of business school, if you can believe it."

She knew Art had a sister who was married, but she'd never met any of his family. She had always gotten the impression that Art considered himself more of an honorary Humphrey.

"Let's get down to brass tacks. The detectives who questioned you did not ask you anything about these pictures?"

"No, but they asked me about the missing girl from Jersey. Do you think the older girl in those photographs might be her?"

"I have no idea, but if they know about these pictures, that could certainly be a reason they're inquiring. Of course, why in the world they've imagined any connection between you and that girl is one of a number of unknowns we're dealing with right now."

"They also asked me about Dad. And about ITH. They obviously tracked down the same records my friend Jeff got from the state. Someone used the ITH name to open the gallery, and they know that's one of my father's corporate entities. They must think I was the one pulling the strings. The pictures on that thumb drive prove I've been telling the truth. Whoever opened the gallery did it to sell those pictures, and used me as the cover."

Art steepled his fingers toward her. "So what is it that *your* instincts are telling you to do right now, Alice?"

It was funny to see Art here, in this cigar-and-brandy-styled office, wearing a thousand-dollar suit, talking to her the way a grown-up lawyer would speak to a grown-up client. She had known him her entire life. She could still distinctively remember concluding that he was the wisest person on earth after he taught her not to pull her arms through her coat sleeves until she'd first put on her mittens, protecting even her wrists from the cold.

She'd seen him in less noble moments as well, slurring his speech on their living room sofa as he and her parents debated politics, films, literature, life, until three in the morning up in Bedford. Art had been a dirty old man even when he was young. The eternal flirt, always happy in the company of whatever eye candy happened to be at his hip for the weekend. She'd realized early on that Art's friendship with her father no doubt assisted his ability to land that steady stream of short-term, high-caliber escorts (not a euphemism in this context), but what she had once seen as an amusing penchant for bachelorhood bore a new level of creepiness now that she realized her father apparently shared it.

"My *instincts*? I really wasn't kidding about the running-away thing. An island and a margarita the size of my head are sounding pretty damn good right now."

"Too early to start talking about going fugitive."

She smiled but then realized he was not. "You're kidding, right?"

He shrugged. "I can't joke about these things. What do you think I say to a client who has a private jet, a passport, and enough money in an offshore account to live the rest of his days, when he's looking at a twenty-year sentence because the SEC suddenly decides corporations should be honest about the value of their own stock? Those conversations get a little dicey—not just on the ethical issues but, you know, whether or not someone's really prepared to walk away from their home, family, reputation, and country. But look, none of this applies to you. You haven't been arrested, and they obviously don't have enough evidence to make an arrest, so we have some time."

Yet, she wanted to add. None of this applies to me . . . *yet.*

"Well, if I'm not—what did you call it? going fugitive—then my instinct was for us to put together everything we have to explain how someone's framing me, and maybe you could present it to the police. Convince them to take a closer look at George Hardy, or try to find out who was really behind the gallery."

He pointed to her like she'd just answered a trivia question correctly. "See? That's why people hire lawyers, Alice. Good, law-abiding, honest people like yourself are predisposed to trust the police. You've been told all your life that you have nothing to fear in the truth. Nearly every client I have who winds up in tension with the government wants to do the same thing. But my job is to force you *not* to follow your instincts."

"But I'm actually innocent."

"That and an apple might get you an apple. These guys who've been questioning you hear the same thing from every lying, guilty dirtbag they encounter. *I'm innocent. I didn't do it. If you'd just listen to me.* All that does is inoculate them. They're trained *not* to believe you. They will twist anything you say to inculpate you further. And if you do happen to say anything that casts doubt on your guilt, they'll make it their number-one objective to go out there to rebut it. Trust me on this: you do not help yourself by talking to them."

"But shouldn't we at least tell them about these pictures on the thumb drive? What if it has something to do with that missing girl, and they don't know?"

"It's not your job to help them find that girl. And don't take this personally, if you and that dumbass of an ex-boyfriend of yours could figure out these thumb drives, I'm pretty sure the NYPD already knows about the pictures."

It was no surprise that Art shared her father's opinion of Jeff.

"So what do I do? My father thinks George Hardy and his church have something to do with all this. Seems hard to believe a church would be involved in child pornography, but I guess any nut can start himself a religion these days. From what I could tell on the Web, Redemption of Christ is just Hardy and a bunch of wackos willing to follow him around the country. I don't even think they have an actual building."

"I'll start pulling up research on them. See what we can find."

"Maybe there's someone involved in the church who had some connection to my father around the time ITH was formed."

"Why do you say that?"

"Because even if they thought he'd make a convenient political scapegoat, they'd still have to know about ITH to be able to use the company name."

"We resolved the issue without litigation by making payments over time through a trust. It's fairly standard."

"Okay, but I'm still wondering what happened to the person who originally threatened the lawsuit. What was her name? Julie Kinley? I mean, she accused my dad of stealing her screenplay idea. Is it possible she's still pissed off all these years later?"

"The allegation might seem scandalous, but it's the kind of claim that gets thrown around all the time in the entertainment industry. As it happens, I did in fact follow up on this issue already. The former employee in question passed away last year."

"Julie Kinley's dead?"

He nodded. "I had a paralegal do a public records search so we could locate her. The road stopped at her death certificate. She died last March."

"Damn. I got myself all worked into a frenzy, thinking we'd find out that she'd been following George Hardy around the country for his protests. Thought I'd sic the police on her instead."

"Afraid not. A dead woman can't exactly be trailing Hardy around on the protest circuit, can she?"

"Maybe someone else who was involved, who would know about ITH and my father's connection to it? Maybe her lawyer or something?"

"Corporate names are easier to look up than you might think, but sure, I'll think again about anyone else who was involved in that transaction and see if there's any connection to this church. In the meantime, Alice, I know this cuts against every impulse of every fiber in your being, but your number-one job right now is to do nothing. Don't talk to the police. Don't talk to your friends, at least not about anything having to do with this investigation. Don't try conducting your own investigation, because if they tap your phone or search your computer or have you followed, it might wind up looking like you have a personal involvement in this."

"I *do* have a pretty damn personal involvement."

"You haven't been listening to me, Alice. The government will interpret your actions in the very worst light. They won't think you're snooping around trying to save your own hide. They'll think you're covering your tracks. You absolutely *must* trust me on this. I have an entire firm of lawyers and investigators here. I am good at what I do. And my phone can't be tapped, and my computers can't be searched. Try to go back to your life. See some shows. Try some new restaurants. You still want to work? You know my offer to help you out on that has always been open."

She shook her head. The way she saw it, accepting help from Art was no different than taking it from her father. And yet here she was, receiving his legal counsel, arranged for by her father, when she clearly had no way of paying the astronomical fees someone like Arthur Cronin must charge for his services.

"You take care of yourself, all right?" He patted her head, as he had since she was a child. "And tell Ben I said hello. My secretary says he stopped by yesterday, but I missed him."

"He came to your office?"

"Maybe I shouldn't have mentioned it. Is there something wrong?"

He still had not returned her many messages, but her brother had somehow found time to drop by Art's. It hardly seemed to matter now how he had known about their father's company—he always had found his identity through Dad's work more than she had—but she was still worried that he was using again. He had a way of avoiding her when that was the case.

"No. Just haven't seen him for a while, is all. Should I take that thumb drive home with me, or do you need it here?"

"Better let me hang on to it for now. The harder we make it for them to connect you to those pictures, the better."

The unspoken implication was obvious. Despite his reassurances, Art was already thinking forward to a day when the police would show up at her door, arrest warrant in hand.

CHAPTER
FORTY-ONE

"**H**oly shit, you actually picked up your phone."

After a mere two rings, Ben finally demonstrated signs of life and answered his cell.

"Sorry. It's been a little busy."

"The sound business is *en fuego*, huh?"

Ben's work in sound engineering was not exactly nine-to-five employment, but she was pretty sure that he'd experienced longer dry spells between gigs than she had suffered after the museum layoff, and yet he never referred to himself as unemployed.

"Just a lot of stuff going on, that's all."

She held her free ear shut with her index finger, struggling to hear over the traffic outside Cronin's building. Ben's voice sounded flat. In someone else, she might attribute the tone to worry or distraction. In her brother, three or four controlled substances came to mind.

"I'm worried about you, Ben."

"Isn't that always the case with the Humphreys? Everyone worries about Ben. Everyone assumes the worst."

"You *did* just get arrested last week."

"Jesus Christ. I told you, it was a little weed. I'm fine."

Whenever she was tempted to write her brother off as a total fuckup, she forced herself to remember that, although siblings, they really did not have the same parents. Ben was close to five years older than she. Their father had stopped drinking when she was eleven, but Ben was already in high school by then. He remembered more. And their parents had always expected less of him as a result.

"Art said you stopped by his office yesterday. What's that about?"

"He's our godfather. Do we need a reason to see each other?"

"I'm starting to wish you hadn't picked up the phone. Did I do something wrong?"

"No. Look, I'm sorry. I wanted to talk to him. That's all."

"Was it about ITH?"

Ben was silent.

"When I was at your apartment, you said that ITH was incorporated a long time ago, but I never told you about the incorporation. And I didn't know about Dad's connection until Jeff dug up those documents with the state. But *you* knew, Ben. If you knew something about that company, you should have told me."

"I thought I remembered hearing Art and Dad talk about ITH when I was in high school. I dropped by Art's office yesterday to see if he could shed some light on who might've used the name to start the gallery. That's all."

"When you were at my apartment, you told me you'd never heard of the company."

"I didn't think I had. Then after I left, it sort of rang a bell. Are we done with the cross-examination?"

"I feel like I'm stuck in the middle of a nightmare, and I can't wake up. I already talked to Dad and Art about it, but when I brought ITH up with you, I sensed you were holding something back. And, frankly, Ben, you're not always a hundred percent honest when you're using."

"You know what, perfect little sister? I was trying to help you out by going to Art. I was making sure that he and Dad weren't the ones being selective with their information. But fuck it. Just go to hell."

By the time Ben hung up on her (and refused to answer her four consecutive redials) she was already a third of the way home from midtown. Despite the cold, she continued on foot toward her apartment.

She told herself she needed the forty-five-minute walk as exercise, but she knew precisely why she'd opted for foot travel over subway: the squandering of time. Forty-five minutes of her boots against concrete meant forty-five fewer minutes in her apartment, struggling futilely to read a book or watch a television show without thinking about Highline Gallery, Drew Campbell, or those horrible photographs. The walk gave her one less hour in the day to tie her head into knots about the trail of evidence that even she had to admit led directly to her. The walk allowed her to believe that the argument with Ben had been just another sibling tiff, and that she and her brother would be patched back to normal by nightfall.

She felt herself slow her pace as she passed Tenth Street, only two blocks from her apartment building. She usually ran past the corner on Twelfth because of all the construction noise from the new condo development that would seemingly never be completed, but today she managed to tune out the eardrum-shattering sounds of the jackhammers.

Even though she wasn't hungry, she stopped at the counter in Veselka for pierogies to go. She savored the warm pillows of dough-wrapped potato while standing, chewing slowly, buying more time.

She had finally resigned herself to a fate of sitting in her apartment, accompanied only by her worries, when she saw the green Camry roll through the intersection at St. Mark's. She caught the last three digits of the license plate. They matched the car she'd spotted twice the day before. She tried to remember now if she had seen the Camry while she'd been walking south on Second Avenue. Had the man been following her? Or was the Camry simply a car from the neighborhood that she'd never had reason to notice?

She pulled her phone from her pocket and started to dial 911, but then remembered Cronin's warnings. She dialed his number instead. His secretary cheerfully reported Mr. Cronin was unavailable but that she was happy to take a message.

She understood Cronin's point about strategy, but the third

Camry sighting in two days raised concerns that went beyond her legal situation. Someone had killed the man she'd known as Drew Campbell. She still did not know his true name, but she had seen his body and felt the stickiness of his blood on the floor.

She dialed 911.

"So . . . I'm sorry, miss, but you say you do know the man was following you, or you don't?"

The uniformed officer was polite, but she could tell from the way he smiled reassuringly at gawking passersby that she sounded like a woman who was one missed med away from screaming at the pigeons about an impending alien takeover. She tried to explain once again that she had seen the Camry twice yesterday and again today but did not know who was driving it.

"And what makes you think the man is, um, stalking you or whatever? Did he make threats toward you? Or try to follow you into your building? Or act inappropriately in some manner?"

She was tempted to say all of the above just to appear less insane. "No. It's just—I know it sounds crazy, but I'm a witness in a homicide investigation. I—I discovered a man's body four days ago and they haven't found the person who did it. So when I saw the same car three times in twenty-four hours—"

The officer was nodding quickly. She couldn't tell if that was a sign he believed her or was buying time before calling the nice men with a spacious van and butterfly nets. "Well, the car doesn't appear to be here any longer. You say you've got the license plate number. What I'd suggest is that I forward my report to the detectives in charge of that pending homicide. They can decide the best strategy going forward. Run the plate. See how this guy fits in, if at all."

"Can't you just run it now? Maybe we'll find out the guy lives around the corner, and it's all just a misunderstanding."

"Or maybe I'll wind up stepping on the toes of your homicide investigators and messing something up big-time. I don't think either one of us wants that, right?"

Not to mention that forwarding the report would be less work for you.

"You know, I shouldn't have even called. I'm sorry to have bothered you."

"So now you're saying you *don't* want to file a report?"

"I let my imagination get away with me."

"No offense, lady, but I don't want to learn next week that my failure to write down this license plate fucked up some shield's murder case. You know the name of the detectives involved, or do I need to look it up?"

Her cell phone rang. She recognized the prefix of the incoming number as Arthur Cronin's law firm. He was not going to like this one bit.

Hank Beckman finally made it through the knot of standstill traffic snarled at the intersection of Bowery and Canal Street. That neighborhood always brought a smile to his face. The coexistence of Chinatown dim sum restaurants, the remains of Little Italy, and emerging hipster boutiques and bars was at once bizarre and happy.

He'd been raised in Montana. After getting his undergrad degree and a CPA with the help of Uncle Sam, he'd completed the requisite years in the army and then put in for the bureau. New agents don't have the luxury of choosing their cities of service, but he'd assumed that the demand for a spot like Montana or Idaho—working bank robberies and gun cases—would be low.

But then thanks to Brad Pitt, Robert Redford, and a little flick called *A River Runs Through It,* suddenly every man with a midlife crisis and a fishing rod wanted to move to the northwest corner of the country. Small populations, combined with low crime rates, meant tiny field offices with few agents. Hank wound up with a job in the bureau, but an assignment in the Big Apple.

He'd planned on getting out as fast as he could, but he'd become accustomed to it faster than he'd anticipated. He bought the apartment near Prospect Park. The city wasn't an easy place to make friends, but Hank never really needed anyone's company. For a while, he felt like he was friends with some of Jen's crowd, but when she moved out, he didn't feel comfortable staying in touch. Then after her husband's plane crash, Ellen found herself a forty-year-old widow in Montana, living alone on a ranch. She said the sound of a new life in New York wasn't so bad. Two years later, she had the Upper East Side apartment with a view of the park from a terrace. Then within a year, she had met and was quickly engaged to Randall Updike, or at least that was the name he'd been using at the time.

Sometimes Hank wondered what would have happened if he hadn't run that background check on "Randall." Ellen would have inevitably lost the bulk of her money to Larson, he suspected. She would presumably have still been saddled with the clinical depression and untreated alcoholism that had led to her death. But maybe he would have noticed his sister's problems. If the man she loved had conned her out of her last dime, Hank would have known to watch out for her. He would have recognized the depth of the attack on her. But as it was, at the time, he had been arrogant enough to think that she should have been grateful to her little brother for saving her.

Now, as he made his way back to Brooklyn across the Manhattan Bridge, he was fairly certain that Alice Humphrey had spotted him but had not managed to follow him from the East Village. He was also fairly certain that Alice Humphrey—with her practical shoes and clumsy gait, a bit like a general stomping his way through a field—was not the same woman he had seen cruising in stiletto heels toward Travis Larson's apartment. He was profoundly less certain, however, about what to do with that puzzling piece of information.

CHAPTER
FORTY-TWO

Alice rose from damp moss beneath a towering mulberry tree, trying to shake the dirt from her ruffled skirt. She heard footsteps approaching.

"She went that way!"

It was a man's voice. Somehow she knew he was looking for her, and that she did not want to be found. She ran through the woods in red patent saddle shoes, watching the ground beneath her, aiming for flat patches of soil between rocks and entangled roots. She saw a spot of light up ahead in the clearing.

When she emerged from the trees, she recognized the backyard of her family's home in Bedford. The landscaped grass. Two hammocks beneath the willow tree. The swimming pool they rarely used.

She slid open the glass door on the deck and stepped inside the house. She felt taller now. Her saddle shoes and ruffled skirt had been replaced by her current-day blue jeans and all-weather boots.

"Mom? Papa? Ben?"

The kitchen was as she remembered it from her childhood: walnut cabinets, burgundy wallpaper, brass fixtures. She turned the corner expecting to find the living room, but instead she was on the set of *Life with Dad*. It was the pilot episode. She saw a younger version of herself on the sofa in a three-sided living room. The saddle shoes and ruffles were back.

The man who played her father delivered the setup line: "Don't look at me. My idea of the four food groups are spaghetti, ice cream, beef jerky, and beer." The set fell silent. "Your line, Alice."

She wanted to whisper to her younger self: *That's what you get when your mom is a dad.*

Then the line was delivered. A studio audience she couldn't see laughed, as required. Even at ten years old, she had known the line wasn't funny. She had known the laughter was feigned.

She heard the back door slide open behind her and moved farther into the house for a place to hide. She ran up the stairs, into her father's study, and slipped behind the steel gray brocade curtains. She peeked out at the decor that had caused such a ruckus between her parents. *It's my office, Rose. It is my one private space. Why can't I keep it the way I like it? For Christ's sake, it looks like a French whorehouse vomited on a Duran Duran video.* Her mother had insisted that her father get rid of the outdated wood paneling and shag carpet, replacing it with a black, white, and red color palette, glass and steel furniture, and Patrick Nagel paintings that would appear dated within a couple of years.

For some reason, Alice could not stop staring at the room. The black-and-white-striped wallpaper that her father had called schizophrenia-inducing. The sofa in the center of the room, whose red velvet grain she had run her fingers across so deliberately that day the police had come asking questions about Ben's keg party.

Something about that room felt so familiar. She'd known it in her childhood, of course. Standing there behind the curtains, she could even smell the remnants of her father's herbal cigarettes—the ones he'd turned to for years until he'd weaned himself for good when Alice was in college. But something about the room felt more current. She didn't want to stop looking at it. She wanted to stay there and remember.

But she heard the footsteps and accompanying voices headed her way. Their steps were deliberate now. In sync with one another. Step. Step. Step. Step. She heard a bell that rang with each approaching stride. Step/ring. Step/ring. The door opened, and she tried to make herself smaller behind her father's curtains. She took a deep breath and found comfort in the smell of her father's exhaled smoke.

The footsteps stopped, but the chime of the bells continued and became more aggressive and shrill. No longer a ring, but a buzz. Buzz. Buzz. Buzz.

Her eyes darted open to blackness, near total but for the digital display of her bedside clock and a sliver of light penetrating the crack in her curtains. She heard an urgent buzzing from her security system. Some gin-brined idiot on St. Mark's was leaning on the outside doorbell again, one of the many downsides to living in the middle of Manhattan's go-to neighborhood for early-twenty-something binge drinking.

She closed her eyes again and willed the noise to stop. It did not.

The parquet floor felt cold beneath her bare feet as she padded to the front door and held down the intercom button. "You're leaning on a stranger's doorbell, asshole. Go. Home."

She prepared herself for one of the usual retorts. "Bitch" was most common. Occasionally she got an actual apology. More than a few times she'd been invited to join the drunk for one last round. But tonight's visitor was not the usual fare.

"It's Jeff. Let me up."

She had just managed to tie her robe by the time he burst through the door she had left cracked open. She smelled alcohol as he slipped past her.

"It's almost one in the morning."

"I've been trying to call you."

"It's sleeping time." After one too many failed calls to Ben, she had decided that an Ambien sounded pretty good. Off went the ringer on her home phone, and off went the cell. She noticed the message light blinking on her answering machine on the kitchen counter. "What's going on?"

"Have you heard anything further from the police?"

"No. I was following your advice not to talk to them anymore, and they haven't tried to contact me anyway." She had half expected another visit from the detectives after she filed the report about the green Toyota, but the rest of the day had been uneventful.

"I hate to tell you this, but I think things are about to get worse."

"I don't think that's possible."

"Your gloves. Please tell me you have those gloves you love so much. The ones with the fur inside of them that you pretend is fake."

"Faux faux fur?"

"Yes. Please tell me you have those. Physically. In your possession."

"No. They went missing last week. I bought another pair but the fur's not the same—"

"The police have them, Alice. Or I assume they do. They showed me a picture of those gloves inside a plastic bag and asked me if you owned a pair like that."

"You're sure they're mine?"

"I wasn't until you just told me yours are missing. But, yeah, they've got that same pattern on them and everything."

"Crocodile-embossed," she muttered. "The police went to your apartment at one in the morning to ask you about my gloves?" She knew that what he was telling her was important, but she still felt groggy from sleep. She still pictured herself standing in her father's office, staring at the gaudy wallpaper.

"He showed up at a bar, actually. He said his name was Danes?" She nodded. "I assume he followed me to try to catch me off guard. Nothing like having a cop show up at your table at Temple Bar."

She knew the place. It had been one of their favorites when they first got together. It was the kind of place that people chose for dates.

"So did it work?"

"What do you mean?"

"Did Danes catch you off guard?"

"No. That's why I'm here. I told them I'd had conversations with you in a legal capacity and therefore would not be discussing anything with them. But it's not going to be that hard for them to prove those gloves are yours. And if they're asking around about those gloves, it's for a reason. They must have Drew's blood on them or something."

"You know what they say: 'If the glove doesn't fit, you must acquit.' "

"What is wrong with you, Alice? This isn't funny."

"At this point, it's actually pretty fucking hilarious. Of course they have my gloves. They were already missing by the time I found Drew's body, but you know what? I'm sure you're right. They've probably got Drew's blood on them—plenty of his DNA, and my DNA, and every other piece of evidence you could possibly imagine. Because that's how this is going to play out. Whoever did this to me, did it with absolute perfection. And I have no idea who did it. Or why. Or what any of it has to do with me."

"You don't have to go through this alone." He placed his hand on her wrist, but she pulled away.

"Of course I'm alone. You've been a good friend, but you know, this isn't happening to you. You're at fucking Temple Bar drinking champagne with a date."

He looked at the floor and swallowed.

"I'm sorry. I'm tired, and I'm scared, and I'm being a total bitch. Thanks for not digging my hole any deeper with the police." She walked to the front door and opened it. He pushed it shut.

"I didn't like being there with someone else."

"Where?"

"At Temple Bar. She was the one who suggested it. I thought I could be there and not think about you. I was wrong."

She felt a tear tickling her cheek, and didn't know whether it was there because of the stress of her current predicament or the memory of what her life had once been—her life with Jeff and the one she'd thought they'd always have together. He stepped toward her and ran his fingers through her hair. Placed a palm against the nape of her neck. It felt so familiar. They'd done this hundreds of times before. This part had never been their problem. He would pull her face toward his. He would kiss her lips, gently at first and then not so gently. He would know exactly where to place his hands on her body. The exact moment to lead her to the bedroom.

And she let it all happen.

For the first time in a miserable week, Alice felt a smile on her face when she woke up. Jeff rustled the curtains trying to pull his clothes on in the dark.

"Love 'em and leave 'em, huh?"

"I've got a deposition in an hour. I was trying not to wake you."

She felt warm beneath the comforter and pushed the covers down to her waistline. She looked up at him, squinting to protect herself from the sunlight penetrating the parted curtains.

"That is so unfair."

"What? I'm just lying here."

That was apparently all it took to persuade him to fall back into bed with her. A few seconds later, however, Jeff suddenly sat up in bed to face her.

"I feel like I need to apologize to you for this."

"What are you talking about?" She tugged at his elbow, trying to nudge him back to horizontal.

"I feel like I took advantage of you when you're probably in a fragile place."

"Fragile? Did you really just call me fragile?"

"No, because I have absolutely no desire to have my ass kicked. But I did wake up wondering if last night—after everything that has been happening to you this week—was the best time for, you know, *us*."

"I'm a grown-up, Jeff. I make my own decisions. And, in case you couldn't tell, I was definitely a willing participant in last night's activities."

"I guess I'm just surprised that you're willing to fall back into the same pattern that, at least at one point, made you so unhappy. I remember you telling me how unhappy you were, and that's not what I want, Alice. It's why I've tried—to the point of misery, even—to find another woman I can care about half as much as you."

She pulled the covers back up to her shoulders. "Not the best time to talk to me about other women."

"My point was that nothing ever works with anyone else, and it's because you and I always fall back into the same patterns."

"You really think it's the same this time?"

"Isn't it always with us? We've been doing this for years. And it never seems to be enough for one of us, so we call it quits. But then we see each other as friends, and it can never stay just-friends. And then we're back to being us again."

"It's always been enough for me, Jeff. In light of what I've learned about my parents' marriage in the past year, maybe I just wasn't trained to dream of the traditional wedding package and the kids in the yard with a picket fence. We've always been good friends. And there's always been love between us, no matter what phase of our continuing cycles we're in. That's enough for me. You're the one who needs something I can't give you, and I don't want to keep you from having everything you want: a woman who can be mother to your children and a family you can take care of for life. I have never wanted to stand in the way of that."

"Or maybe you were so convinced that I wanted all of that stuff that you pushed me away." She saw his eyes move to the clock on the nightstand. "I hate that I have to leave right now."

"We'll talk after your deposition. And only if you think we need to talk. Really, Jeff, I woke up just now feeling happy, despite all that's been heaped on me the past few days. You didn't take advantage of me. And I don't think there's a problem here."

"I'll call you when I free up. I want to see you tonight, okay?"

"Of course."

"And, just so you know? Right now? Looking at you and having been with you this week while all this hell has been breaking loose? I don't know why I ever thought there was something else out there for me to find."

CHAPTER
FORTY-THREE

The next time she opened her eyes, she felt groggy. She reached for the clock. It was almost noon. She didn't know if it was the sleeping pill, the sex, or an intense disaffection for her current reality that kept her in bed, but she decided in that moment that if she could stay wrapped in those blankets, with her head on that pillow, for the remainder of her life, that would be her preference.

The sound of her apartment buzzer pulled her from the fantasy of an eternal bed rest.

"Hello?"

"Let me in. Hurry."

She buzzed the security entrance and cracked open the apartment door, feeling a pang of guilt for being disappointed that it was Lily and not Jeff. She was scooping coffee grounds into a filter when she heard Lily's footsteps coming hard and fast up the hallway stairs. She sprang into the apartment and bolted the door behind her.

"I'm getting a late start, but I'll have coffee to offer in a sec. Don't freak out, but last night—"

"Shit, Alice, I am so sorry. We've got to do something."

She knew immediately, from one look at Lily's panicked expression. With that one look, she realized how stupid she had been to allow a moment with Jeff to escalate into an escape from reality. Jeff had come to her apartment in the middle of the night for a reason, and it had nothing to do with lost memories at Temple Bar or the ease with which the two of them could lose themselves in each other. *It's not going to be that hard for them to prove those gloves are yours.*

"The police questioned you, didn't they?"

Lily nodded. She looked like she might cry. "Fuck, I'm so sorry. They came to my office. And I freaked. I just answered. I didn't see how it could possibly matter. But then I realized: why the fuck would they be asking me about your gloves unless it mattered? And I tried calling you, but your phone's off." The words were spilling out of her. "And now they're here."

"What do you mean, they're here?"

"You weren't answering your phone, so I got down here as fast as I could to try to tell you. But there's a bunch of police cars downstairs, Alice. I saw them watching me when I was at the door. They were getting out of their cars when I walked in. I think—Fuck, Alice, I think they're here to arrest you."

Alice would subsequently try to remember her immediate reaction, but memory is a funny thing. It's as if those first forty-five seconds were forever lost. She knew she was muttering, "Oh my God," more than could ever be helpful. She vaguely recalled looking down to see what she was wearing and wondering how quickly she could change into real clothes.

But whatever mess was unfolding in her mind was instantly clarified when Lily grabbed her by the shoulders. "Alice, you need to get out of here."

She processed what Lily was telling her. Those gloves must have been the piece of rock-solid evidence they'd been waiting for, the thing that sealed those suspicions they'd formed about her on the first day. They were here to take her away. She heard Lily's words again, this time louder. "Get out of here. They don't know for sure you're home. Go out the freight entrance."

"I can't. I mean, I should call my lawyer. It's going to make me look guilty."

"They're not here yet. Just leave before they get here. There's no law that says you have to be home. I'll tell them a neighbor buzzed me in, and you weren't actually here. Just go. Come on, get moving."

Alice remembered what Cronin had said to her about clients who could make another life for themselves elsewhere. A passport, some money, and a private jet, he'd said. She had access to all of that. Her father could help her. If it really came to that. If it was necessary. But she wouldn't have the option once they took her into custody.

She was moving faster than she could think. She pulled on a pair of jeans and a warm sweater. She grabbed her passport from her jewelry box. Pulled her gym bag, already stocked with basic necessities, from the front closet. Stuffed her laptop in her purse. She started to reach for her bright blue coat when she stopped herself, opting instead for the nondescript black trench she'd stopped wearing a couple of years ago.

"Are they in the building?" she asked, tugging on the coat.

"I don't think so." Lily cracked open the apartment door. "Okay, it's safe. You need to hurry."

She grabbed Lily and kissed her hard on the cheek before making her way to the freight elevator. As she slipped out of the delivery entrance at the back of the building on Ninth Street, she was aware of the sound of sirens in the distance. At least, she hoped they were in the distance.

And she wondered whether she would ever get her life back.

PART III

MEMORIES

CHAPTER
FORTY-FOUR

Joann Stevenson hit the play button once again on her cell phone. She had heard this message so many times, her memory could pull up each syllable before it was spoken. She could hear the inflection of each word in her own mind. The pop of the *p* in the word *person*, followed by a slight giggle at the end of the sentence. She could almost picture a tiny bubble of spit form at the corner of her daughter's lip before she licked it away during the pause.

Hi, Mom. It's the daughter-type person. There was the giggle and the lip lick. *I know you've got the late shift tonight, but I just wanted you to know I'm home and ordered a pizza with the money you left me, just like in your note. Me and Sebastian miss you. See you tomorrow.*

The message was nearly a month old, but it was the only recording she had of Becca's voice. Oh, she had a few old videos from when she was a kid. Reciting the preamble of the constitution for national civics day in the first grade. Getting tangled up on the words "domestic tranquility": *establish justice, insure domestic chance hillary.* That truly painful solo from her otherwise adorable turn as the lion in *Wizard of Oz.* But the only sound she had of a more mature, teenage Becca was this twelve-second cell phone message.

Listening to her daughter's voice made her feel less alone. When news had gotten out about Becca's disappearance, she had been surrounded by well-wishers. She had felt cared for. Maybe even loved.

But now Mark was gone. She didn't blame him. It had been too early in a relationship to expect the man not to be rattled by the polygraph the police had asked for, not to mention her depression, anger, and utterly unpredictable fits of inconsolable tears.

The casseroles that had turned up on her porch with notes of kindness had tapered off. So had the phone calls from worried friends offering to search for Becca. Or to keep her company. Or anything else that she might find helpful. Now her boss was beginning to ask when she thought she might make it back to work.

She had never felt so alone. And so even though she had already memorized every word of this message, and the sound of each individual syllable, she hit play once again.

Morhart noticed that the gutters needed cleaning. It had stopped raining two hours earlier, but water was still dripping over the aluminum edge. Spikes of green had begun to sprout from the accumulated leaves.

He had stayed in Dover for a reason. After college, he could have moved down to the city. The economy was on fire back then. He could have gotten a job in the computer industry, or maybe even in finance. But he wanted to live in Dover. And even in good times, Dover didn't have cutting-edge jobs. There were teachers, doctors, lawyers, the service industry, and government. He went with the police department.

He had no regrets, but sometimes he wondered whether Dover was still the place he had resolved never to leave. In the Dover of his memories, two or three of the neighborhood men would have quietly taken turns attending to the clogged gutters of a distracted single mother struggling to work full-time and raise a daughter. The idea that these gutters would be growing trees while Becca Stevenson was missing? Well, that wasn't the way Morhart thought of the people in this community.

He was about to knock on the screen door when he caught a glimpse of her through the living room window. Joann Stevenson's face was somehow young and old at the same time. Ageless, he supposed. Her forehead was unlined, but her cheeks were beginning to sag, and creases had formed around her mouth like parentheses. Her face was broad, her eyes wide-set. She was an attractive woman, but not what someone might call *pretty*. There was a stillness to her expression—to her entire body—that made him think she had lived a longer, fuller life than other women her age. There was a depth to her that resonated in her very energy.

He rapped his knuckles on the screen and felt guilty when she jumped, the cell phone in her hand tumbling to the coffee table. She looked terrified when she answered the door, the way she did each time he'd come here since their first meeting. She didn't need to explain the expression on her face. She was a woman wondering if this was the day: Was this the cold, damp afternoon when a police officer would knock on her door and tell her that her daughter's body had been located?

He raised his eyebrows just enough to signal that today was not the day.

She handled the update as he knew she would. He had not seen her shed another tear since she'd learned about Becca's secret relationship with her biological father. He knew she wanted to cry. He could almost feel the emotion running through her body. He believed it was the reason why she sat with her knees pushed together and her elbows tucked into her waist, as if she could literally trap her feelings inside to maintain composure in front of a man who was still in every meaningful sense a stranger.

She nodded periodically, her lips pressed tightly, as he told her the news. The police in the city had made progress, but all of it was on their side of the investigation. He believed they might be announcing a murder suspect. They might even make an arrest. But so far they had been unable to determine why Becca's fingerprints had been in that gallery.

"If they arrest someone for killing that man, could that help us find Becca?"

"That's what I'm hoping, Joann." According to his agreement

with the NYPD, he could not disclose the details of the investigation, but he found himself wanting to tell Joann everything. "We've got to keep our fingers crossed that the arrest will put pressure on that person to open up to us about Becca. I'm really hoping that's how it plays out."

She nodded again.

"No one else seems to care she's gone anymore." There was no melodrama to her voice. It was almost as if she were talking to herself. Or maybe to little Sebastian, nuzzling his tiny dog face against the sofa cushions. "Everyone's moving on."

He found himself placing a hand in the middle of her back, then the other hand reaching for her knee. Just the outer edge. Nothing inappropriate, he would tell himself later.

"I'm not, Joann. I'm not going anywhere."

He expected her to break down, but she only nodded, her lips pressed together once again.

Thirty-three miles away, in the Thirteenth Precinct of the NYPD, Detective John Shannon waved his partner, Willie Danes, over to his desk and pointed at the computer screen. "I was taking another look at Alice Humphrey's Facebook page."

"You better watch it. Folks around here might start wondering whether you're developing a little crush on our former child starlet."

"Who's the one who found that profile she created under her alias?" It wasn't until Shannon discovered the Facebook profile for "Drew Campbell" that they could corroborate the rental agent's statement that a red-haired woman had been the one to sign the lease for the gallery under that name.

"The partner stumbles across one good find, and now I'm never going to hear the end of it."

"I think I've got another find to add to the growing list. Cute picture of her and her brother, huh?"

Danes bent over to get a better look. "Yeah. Adorable."

"Notice anything about the decor?"

The older brother, probably high school–aged, looked proud with his arm wrapped around his little sister. She was probably around twelve, still all arms and legs sticking out from her slender torso. They sat on a bright red sofa, a glass-topped chrome coffee table before them, black-and-white-striped wallpaper behind.

They had both seen that room before.

"What the—"

CHAPTER
FORTY-FIVE

Alice maintained a brisk but unexceptional pace down Second Avenue until she reached First Street, when she turned right and broke into a full sprint toward the 6 train at Bleecker. She scurried down the subway stairs and was about to swipe her MetroCard at the turnstile when she stopped herself. Could the police trace a MetroCard that had been purchased on an Amex? If they knew she was on the 6, couldn't they contact the driver to stop the train? She'd be trapped.

She searched her wallet for cash to buy a new card, but found she was down to her last $14. She wouldn't get far without more cash.

Ben's apartment was only five blocks away. She poked her head out from the subway stairs, searching for signs of police, then made her way south on Mulberry, turning on Spring Street, and then south again on Mott. She rang the buzzer, tapping her forehead softly against the door as she prayed Ben would answer. Two more attempts at the buzzer. Nothing.

She was about to give up when a heavyset man emerged from the building, lugging two overstuffed Hefty bags of garbage. The top of his bald head was sweaty despite the cold. The key ring clipped to his belt loop was worthy of a prison warden.

"Are you the super?"

He nodded as he turned sideways to maneuver his stomach and

the trash bags past her. Alice grabbed one of the sacks and helped drag it to the curb. "Thanks, lady, but condo only. No units on sale now."

"My brother lives here. Ben Humphrey?" She fumbled through her wallet to pull out her driver's license.

"Oh, yeah. From *Life with Dad*. I know all about his family. You're all grown up now, but, yeah, I can still see that same face."

"This is awful, but I managed to leave a file in my brother's apartment that I desperately need for a meeting I have in, like, less than an hour. And of course, with my luck, Ben's not home. Is there any way you can let me in?"

One of those people who paid cash for everything, her brother found the $400 cap on ATM withdrawals "miserly" and was in the habit of storing large amounts of cash in his dresser drawer. He jokingly called it his drug-dealer stash.

The super hesitated.

"It will take two seconds. You can even watch me go inside if you need to." She flashed her warmest, most trustworthy smile. If she had to, she could sneak the money while pretending to look for her file.

"No problem. I know how much Mr. Humphrey loves his sister." He was already flipping through the keys. They rode up to the fourth floor together. She could still hear the super breathing hard from the exertion of hauling the garbage bags. He slipped the key in the door, but the knob budged on its own. "What do you know? You didn't even need me."

"Ben?"

She knew her brother was in the habit of leaving the door unlocked when he was home, but she didn't think he was stupid enough to do so when he was out.

The place was messier than it had been three nights earlier. The kitchen cabinets were open. A stack of entertainment magazines had slid from the coffee table onto the floor. The bathroom door was ajar, and she could only imagine the filth to be found there. But she saw no obvious drugs or paraphernalia in view, and was relieved not to be confronted with undeniable proof that her brother was using again.

She walked directly to the dresser in the bedroom area of his loft and opened the top drawer. A pad of bills about an inch thick was tucked to the side of a row of neatly folded boxer briefs, one of the perks of sending laundry out for service. She shoved the wad of cash in her purse, not bothering to count. The police would know her brother lived nearby. The super would tell them she was here.

In her rush to walk away, she almost didn't see his cell phone on the nightstand. They would be tracking hers, but probably not his. An extra phone could come in handy.

Where was he?

She looked out the window, hoping to see him strolling toward the building, cup of coffee or bagel bag in hand. She couldn't wait here all day.

As she stepped away from the window, she caught a glimpse of the dusty framed photograph on the sill. It was one of her favorites as well—an eleven-year-old Alice decorating her napping teenage brother with a shaving cream beard while her conspiring father caught the footage. Her father might have hated his wife's penchant for mid-1980s decor, but Ben had loved it, sneaking into his father's office whenever possible to laze on the red sofa.

And then she realized why some of the photographs on the Hans Schuler thumb drives had struck her as dated. When she'd discovered those hidden images, her attention had been pulled to their most vile elements, and then immediately repelled. She had never focused on the background, but now she remembered. The pictures that had seemed scanned—the ones that appeared to be of a young girl and an older man—had contained images of steel gray brocade curtains, a red velvet sofa, and the black-and-white-striped wallpaper that her father had once called schizophrenia-inducing.

And now that she recalled the background of those horrible photographs, she understood her dream from the previous night. She had dreamed she was a child, standing in her father's office and not wanting to leave, because some part of her subconscious had known. In her sleep, she had been on the verge of figuring it out.

The pictures of that young girl with the older man had been taken twenty-five years ago in her father's office in Bedford.

Setting aside her guilt, she slipped Ben's cell into her purse. She'd explain it all to him later.

She left her brother's apartment in such a fog that she did not see the man step from the green Toyota and begin to follow her on foot.

CHAPTER
FORTY-SIX

As Alice watched clumps of hair fall from the scissor blades into the trash can, she tried to process the pieces of cognitive data that told her that the dark locks belonged to her. She had stopped herself before walking into Duane Reade. The chain drugstore would surely have security cameras stocked with tapes that could be handed over to the police department, revealing her purchases. Instead, she had opted for the smaller Ricky's beauty supply shop, where she had paid cash for a pair of shears, a bottle of "Temptation" brown dye, and latex gloves to protect her finger tips.

Scoring an hour alone in the Union Square hotel room had turned out to be easier than she would have thought. Just last year, she had read a crime novel in which the seemingly indestructible hero had slipped a few bucks to a New York City bellhop in exchange for a night in an unrented hotel room. The agreement she'd struck had cost her more than a few bucks, and had secured her only an hour of solitude, but the transaction had been in cash and had cost her only $40 of the wad she'd grabbed from Ben's dresser.

She bent over at the waist, blasting her hair with the hotel room's dryer, then flipped up to check out her newly shorn coif. She had remembered to dab some of the dye on her eyebrows with a Q-tip, just like the hairdresser had that one time in high school when she had briefly decided to be a brunette.

When she was young, her mother had said she looked just like Little Orphan Annie, only prettier. Now her trademark long red hair with natural highlights had been replaced by an abrupt, black—no, "Temptation"-colored—chin-length bob. She used another minute of her room time to line her eyes with the ninety-nine-cent pencil she had also picked up at Ricky's. She barely recognized the vamp gazing back at her from the mirror.

The tips of her hair were still damp against her jawline as she propped herself on the foot of the hotel bed, contemplating Ben's cell phone. By now, he had probably figured out it was missing. From there, he would have checked his stash of cash in the dresser. She should try to get word to him that she'd been the culprit before he called police.

The detectives might be monitoring calls to her parents and closest friends, but maybe she could call one of Ben's friends. As she scrolled through the list of Ben's recent calls, she saw a name that felt familiar. *Robert Atkinson.*

Where had she heard that name? She tried to jog her memory of Ben's acquaintances, but no one by that name came to mind. Then she remembered. The name had nothing to do with Ben at all. Robert Atkinson was the reporter who had been trying to call her all week. According to Ben's phone, the two men had spoken to each other several times, enough for her brother to have added the reporter's name to his phone directory.

She picked up the room phone and dialed 9 for an outside line, followed by Robert Atkinson's telephone number.

"Empire Media."

"I'm calling for Robert Atkinson."

"May I ask who's calling?"

"This is, um, a source on one of his stories." She wondered if the tidbits she had read in newspapers about journalists protecting the confidentiality of their sources was accurate.

"If you can tell me generally the story with which you were assisting, I can forward your call as appropriate?" The woman sounded young, perhaps in her early twenties, still at that period of life when every sentence seemed to end in a question mark, even when not asking a question.

"I'd rather speak to Mr. Atkinson personally."

"You haven't heard?"

"About what exactly?"

"Bob's dead. He was killed in a car accident last night on I-684."

Hank Beckman recognized the prefix of the 212 number on his cell phone screen as an incoming call from the NYPD.

"Beckman." He plugged his free ear closed with his index finger in an attempt to block the sound of traffic on Park Avenue.

Detective John Shannon did not bother identifying himself. "We were copied on an incident report filed by a Miss Alice Humphrey. She claimed a man in a green Camry was following her. She wrote down the license plate."

"Nothing illegal about driving around Manhattan." Supposedly the bureau's determination regarding his termination was still pending, but Hank could read the writing on the wall. He was for all practical purposes a free agent now.

"I hear your days at the bureau might be numbered. I don't know what you have in mind, but don't fuck this all up for both of us, Beckman."

"I tried to tell you: Alice Humphrey is not the woman I saw with Larson. I'm sure of that. You think you can just gloss that over?"

"The mountain of evidence I've got against the recollection of a burnout like you? I'm not losing sleep."

"Have you arrested her?"

"Not yet. We've got enough, though. The DA's office is working on the warrants now. I mean it, Beckman: stay away from the girl."

"Whatever you say, Shannon. You're the man."

He flipped the phone shut. A half hour on the corner was too much time in the damn cold. He was grateful for the burst of warm air when he opened the glass door of Union Bar. Ignoring the bartender's frustrated glare when he ordered tea, he made himself comfortable at a table for two in the corner, right next to the window with an unobscured view of the Park Avenue hotel Alice Humphrey had entered thirty-two minutes earlier.

Alice felt herself lose track of time in the void of the silent phone line.

"Are you still there?"

"Yes, I'm sorry. I just—um, I'm very sorry to hear about Mr. Atkinson's accident. Do you know what happened?"

"The police are saying he ran off the road, like into a ravine or something? No one even saw it happen. Someone passed the accident scene this morning and called an ambulance, but it was way too late. They don't know whether it was intentional or if he was drunk or if it was, like, I don't know, road rage or something. I heard the editor say the police think there's a possibility of foul play."

It was a long-winded and manic way of saying she didn't know anything yet.

"My name is Alice Humphrey. Mr. Atkinson had been trying for some time to reach me. I believe he was also speaking to my brother, Ben Humphrey. I was hoping to find out why he'd been calling me."

"Bob has—*had*—a tendency to be, like, really private until he was ready to go to print with a story? If you ask me, the writers can be a little cutthroat with each other. I think they get paid based on what's printed, maybe?"

"What is Empire Media? I'm not familiar with it."

"Sure you are, you just don't know it." She spoke like someone looking forward to announcing a joke's punch line.

"I don't understand."

"The *National Star*?"

"Ah." Alice did indeed recognize the name of the notorious tabloid.

"Exactly. No surprise the writers like to say they're from Empire Media instead. Sounds, you know, like, classier?"

"And you don't know what Mr. Atkinson might have been work-ing on that involved me or my brother? Maybe something involving a gallery called the Highline?"

"Sorry."

"Or perhaps Frank Humphrey?"

"Nope. Oh, wait, you're, like, with *that* Humphrey?"

"One big happy family," she muttered. "Do you know if Mr. At-kinson might have left some notes in his office that might explain why he was calling me?"

"We don't exactly give the writers offices, if you know what I mean? Bob usually worked at home. Here's the thing." She lowered her voice to a whisper. "You know how I said the police think there's a possibility of foul play? Apparently the passenger side door was open on Bob's car, and the keys were gone from the igni-tion. They also didn't find any sign of his briefcase, even though he always carried it."

"So the police think someone caused the accident to steal his keys and briefcase?"

"No, they said it's more likely someone came across the scene and stole the stuff after the fact. Can you imagine? Who would do something like that? But the police did ask whether Bob might have been working on something that could have created enemies. That's why the company had his cell phone calls forwarded here. His editor didn't want to miss out if Bob was in the hunt. Pretty cold, huh?"

Alice was thinking the woman was not a very discreet recep-tionist when she was struck by the irony that of the two women on either end of this phone conversation, she was the one who'd been out of work for nearly a year.

"Is it possible the editor knows why Mr. Atkinson was calling me?"

"Oh, no. I heard him tell the police that Bob had been even more intense than usual lately, but he has no idea what Bob was up to. He was like an old dinosaur around here and sort of did his own thing. I'm supposed to get the name and number of anyone who calls for him. Alice Humphrey, you said? And what number can he call you back at?"

"I'm traveling now," she lied, "so I'll just have to try again later."

"Okay, I'll let him know."

"Did Bob live upstate?" Maybe she could talk her way into the dead reporter's house to look for any notes he might have left behind, if whoever stole his keys and briefcase hadn't beaten her to it.

"I'm sorry?"

"You said that Mr. Atkinson's car accident was on 684. Did he live upstate?"

"No, he lives by Gramercy Park. I'm pretty sure he was driving home from Bedford."

"He had been spending time in Bedford?"

"Yeah. I overheard him on the phone a couple different times with the Bedford Police Department asking for some ancient police report. He said he was finally going to drive up there and find the damn thing himself. It'll be so sad if that's what ended up putting him on the road last night, you know?"

Hank was about to fetch some more warm water for his tea bag when he spotted the woman with short, chocolate-colored hair and heavily lined eyes emerging from the hotel. He was impressed by the transformation. The clothes were the same, but the long black coat and all-weather boots were practically a winter uniform for Manhattan's women. From the neck up, she was unrecognizable. The strawberry tone of her skin looked paler against the near-black hair. The style of her hair and makeup was different, too. Younger. Stronger. Edgier.

In fact, her hasty makeover had been so effective that he might have missed her if he hadn't spent so much time over the last two days thinking about the way she carried herself. The long red hair was gone, but that sheepish gait was unmistakable.

He left his empty paper cup on the table and headed south on Park Avenue, letting her maintain a half-block lead.

CHAPTER
FORTY-SEVEN

Alice caught a glimpse of her own reflection in the glass of the subway car's window and was startled. *Breathe,* she told herself. *You might feel like you are walking around Manhattan in a Halloween costume, but these people around you have no idea who you are or what you are supposed to look like.*

She had paid $20 for a new MetroCard. She would pay cash again at Grand Central for a train ticket to Katonah, one town north of Bedford. She hadn't figured out yet whether she would be brave enough to exit the train in the town where she had spent nearly every summer of her childhood. Surely the police would have someone watching her parents' house. And the locals might recognize her, despite this ridiculous haircut. She had every reason to stay as far away from Bedford as possible. But somehow she knew that whatever secrets Robert Atkinson had been searching for in Bedford would provide the key to the locks she felt tightening around her.

The 6 train stopped at Twenty-third Street. It was still early in the afternoon, so foot traffic was light. The young couple across from her moved toward the exit, waiting for the doors to part. The man pushed a loose strand of his girlfriend's hair behind her ear, and she smiled her thanks. Something about that simple act of thoughtfulness made Alice want to cry.

The couple stepped from the car, leaving her alone with the homeless man dozing in and out of sleep and a guy who seemed to think earbuds the size of pencil erasers could somehow shield the people around him from the rap music thumping from his iPod. The doors remained open, and Alice realized she was holding her breath again, waiting for the car to be sealed like a protective shell. She did not want to see a police officer step inside. And with both Drew Campbell and Robert Atkinson dead, she was beginning to wonder whether the police might be the least of her worries.

She allowed herself to exhale when the doors closed. She felt her core flex instinctively, muscle memory formed from years of subway transit, stabilizing her own body, preparing for the abrupt lurch of the train's movement. But there was no movement. The car remained still. There were no sounds other than the tinny rhymes leaking from the iPod guy's headphones and the quiet hum of the homeless man's snore. She was holding her breath yet again, wishing she had waited at Union Square for an express train.

When the car finally jerked forward, her body was unprepared. She slid all the way into the empty seat beside her, and had never been so thankful for the unceremonious wobbling of a New York City subway ride.

Just as quickly as she had calmed herself, she felt the hot rush of unmitigated terror when the sliding door at the end of the train opened and a man who looked like the driver of the green Toyota stepped inside.

She rose from her seat and walked hurriedly toward the opposite end of the car. She could hear his footsteps behind her and wondered if either the homeless man or the iPod guy would help her if she screamed. She pulled at the exit door, realizing she had never tried to walk from car to car on the subway and had no idea how to operate the sliding door.

She felt the man's hand on her shoulder. She turned and pressed herself against the door, trying to release herself from his grasp. She could still hear the homeless man's purr and the iPod guy's tunes.

"Help. Someone help?"

"Shh. Shh. It's okay. Stop. Just stop."

The man's palms were raised as if he was the one being attacked, but his face was completely calm. Something about his whispered pleas for her to stop resisting was comforting. "My name is Hank Beckman, and I believe you're innocent."

"So you actually *saw* the woman who was kissing Drew Campbell in the photograph the police showed me?"

They had completed the 6 train leg of the trip and were continuing their conversation on a bench in Grand Central Terminal, each of them telling the other a one-sided view of the events of the last few days. They were strangers, but somehow the simple fact that this man was an FBI agent who believed she was telling the truth allowed her to share every detail within her knowledge.

"You mean Travis Larson. There is no Drew Campbell. But, yes, I believe that the woman I saw at Larson's apartment was the same woman in that photograph. And I believe she was intentionally trying to look like you and had purchased the identical blue coat for exactly that purpose. The human mind is capable of greatness, but we have been trained to process information with efficiency, which can sometimes mean superficially. We grab on to salient identifiers, often at the expense of devoting attention to more nuanced details. It's one of the reasons why cross-racial eyewitness identifications are less reliable. We see a person of a different race and give disproportionate weight to that one distinctive visual trait without really processing the individual's true appearance."

"So it's not like this other woman is my identical twin?"

He shook his head. "Don't get me wrong: she certainly did resemble you. You probably could see the similarity for yourself in that photograph. But she and Larson were taking advantage of the fact that your hair, if you don't mind me saying, was the single characteristic that most people would identify first when looking at you. And I assume you bought that blue coat for a reason."

"It never fails to get a compliment."

"No surprise there. Your coloring—her coloring—with that bright blue? It's a knockout combination. Any chance that coat's a specialty item? We could start with that to track down your doppelganger."

"Mass-produced in China and sold at department stores all over the country. Sorry."

"You shouldn't have cut it, you know." He pointed to his head. "Your hair."

"The last thing I'm worried about right now are my looks."

"That's not what I mean. If you hadn't changed your hair, I'd be trying to talk you into going home. It looks really bad that you ran."

"I panicked. They had my building surrounded. They were coming to get me. I pictured myself being carried away in handcuffs, and I just couldn't sit there and let it happen."

"They weren't coming for you. Not yet, anyway. Shannon told me not an hour ago that they were still working on the warrant. It's definitely in the pike."

Lily must have seen a police car on the street outside her building and assumed they were there for her.

"If you go back now, though, they'll see what you've done to your hair. Changing your appearance is quintessential evidence of consciousness of guilt. That, combined with lies they caught you in about your relationship with Larson? They may as well have a confession."

"I never lied to them."

"But they think you did. And that new haircut of yours makes their version all the more likely."

"I think I liked you better when I thought you were trying to kill me."

"I'm just telling you how it is. So tell me what you're planning to do in Bedford."

She had already purchased a ticket in cash. The train was due to leave in twelve minutes. "I'm going to find out why Robert Atkinson was tracking down a police report from there."

"Why don't you just call your brother and ask him what he knows about Atkinson?"

"Because I have no idea how to get hold of him. He's cell-only, and I went and took his only phone." She was also increasingly convinced that he'd been holding something back from her since the very beginning.

"So you're going to march into a police station and tell them you're Alice Humphrey?"

"No. I'm thinking I'll say I'm a reporter following up on the story Atkinson was working on."

"And what if someone there recognizes you? I assume Bedford's a small place."

"I don't think I have any choice right now but to take a few calculated risks."

He rose from the bench without speaking, reached into his coat pocket, and dangled a set of car keys. "That green Toyota that's been tailing you should get us up to Bedford just fine. I'll pull in front of the exit on Lexington in about twenty. Don't go anywhere."

"Why are you doing this?" she asked.

"Let's just say I might also be in need of a few calculated risks."

CHAPTER
FORTY-EIGHT

J ust as Beckman had predicted, they pulled off 684 at the Bedford exit about an hour after crossing the Triborough Bridge.
The plan was for him to go to the police station to ask questions
about Robert Atkinson while she drove one town north to Katonah
to avoid the chance of being recognized in Bedford.

"Here." He handed her a cell phone. "I'll call you when it's time
to pick me up."

"Isn't there some FBI rule that says you shouldn't be handing over
your phone to a wanted fugitive?"

"Probably, but I think we can agree I've officially left the reservation. That's a disposable that can't be traced to you, so let's keep it
that way. Absolutely *no* calls to anyone you know. The NYPD will
be pulling their LUDs."

She thought about Jeff and how badly she wanted to contact him.
He was supposed to call her when his depositions were over, but she
had turned off her phone so the police couldn't track it. If he didn't
hear from her soon, he was going to think she was having regrets
about last night.

"Their what?"

"Local usage details. Incoming and outgoing calls. Just don't call
anyone but me, all right? I got one for me, too. The number's already in there as the last number dialed."

She fiddled with the keys to be sure she could find the entry. A chirp escaped from his coat pocket. "See? We're all set. Call me if there are any problems. Otherwise, you'll be hearing from me when it's time to pick me up. No speeding. Come to full stops. Don't get pulled over. That's how they caught Ted Bundy."

"Great. Now I'm being compared to a serial killer."

He rolled his eyes, and she smiled.

"You've told me everything you know? Absolutely everything?"

"Yes. Absolutely." She could tell from the way he looked at her that, once again, he believed her. "Agent Beckman?"

"Call me Hank."

"Thank you, Hank."

He got out of the car two blocks from the police station, and she crawled across the console to take his place at the wheel, waving before taking the direct route back to the highway, as cautious as a first-time taker of the driving exam.

Hank had never had reason to step inside the police station in Lolo, Montana, where he was raised, but he imagined it would have looked something like the one in Bedford. With clean concrete steps and upgraded glass windows, the building was not actually old, but had been designed to appear old-fashioned. Small towns did not want to admit that they were home to criminal acts and those who committed them. If they had to have a police station, better it at least be quaint.

A gray-haired woman sat at the desk nearest to an unstaffed reception window at the building's entrance. He tapped gently on the glass, and she let out a little yelp.

"Sorry, ma'am. I didn't mean to startle you there."

"No worries. Guess I let myself get carried away on my Sudoku." She made her way to the window, no doubt slowed by the fact that her chubby feet looked like two bratwurst forced into her hot pink pumps, color-coordinated to match her black-and-pink-flowered blouse. Up close, he could see that her reading glasses were bedazzled with rhinestones. The photo ID hanging from the New York Giants lanyard around her neck identified her as Gail Richards.

"I have an aunt who can plow through an entire Sudoku book in three hours straight, then still be searching for more. I tell her she needs to go to Sudoku rehab."

"Oh, don't I know it. What can I do you for today?"

He flashed his FBI identification. Before he could even get a word out, she was pointing to the back of the building. "Oh, I'll show you to the detectives."

"No, ma'am, this is more likely to be a matter for the folks who sit up here near the window. It's my understanding that a journalist by the name of Robert Atkinson has been trying to obtain a copy of a police report from you all. I believe it may have been a report from some time ago?"

"Oh my, yes. That's not a name I'll soon forget. He must have called me six different times. First he thought I had the name wrong. Then he said I had the date wrong. Then he seemed to think I was some silly girl who didn't know her way around our archive files, but I gave him some choice words on that one. Next thing I know, here he waltzes up to the window yesterday—right when I'm trying to close up for the night—claiming that someone's on the take. Someone destroyed records. Acting like we're Enron or something, standing around shredding documents just to keep them out of the hands of the important Mr. Atkinson."

Hank could suddenly imagine perky Miss Gail with the bedazzled reading glasses tearing out a man's throat if properly motivated.

"And what police report was he trying to obtain?"

"A nonexistent one, if you ask me."

"And according to him?"

She sighed at the mere thought of having to remind herself of the inanity of his request. "At first, all he'd give me was a date. April 18, 1985. Well, it was either late at night on April 18 or sometime April 19 or maybe early in the morning on April 20, which would have been a Sunday. But it had something to do with something that happened on April 18. I told him that we might not be a hotbed of crime up here, but we'd have more than one incident report on a spring weekend, that's for sure. I asked him for an address or a suspect or the nature of the crime, and he just wasn't willing to budge. Believe it or not, that was probably his first three phone calls. Then he finally calls back and tells me, fine, the name of the complainant would have been Christie Kinley."

Something about the name sounded familiar. He had taken in an ocean of information from Alice Humphrey in the last few hours, but he could hear her voice speaking a similar name during their manic exchange of data. Kinley. It was the last name that was familiar.

"Do you mean *Julie* Kinley?" He recalled Alice mentioning a plagiarism claim that ITH had settled with a woman named Julie Kinley. If the woman hadn't passed away last year, she would have risen to the top of his list of suspects.

"I was about to say, legal name Julie Kinley, but she was known as Christie. Trust me, that was a name I took note of. I thought maybe Atkinson was playing a joke on me, but apparently the mother named her after the actress Julie Christie."

"And you remember all this without notes." He tried not to go too heavy on the marveling tone, but knew he needed to make up for trying to correct her about the complainant's first name. "I'd like to have someone at the bureau with that kind of memory."

"You darling man, I can't even tell you what I had for breakfast this morning. This just goes to show you how that Atkinson fellow hounded me. But my job's my job, so off I go to archives, digging through the paper files. Some people aren't the best about their dates, you know. April gets in with August. May winds up before March. And I knew I'd never hear the end of it from this guy if I told him we didn't have the report when in fact we actually did. So, let me tell you, I *looked*. Hard. And there were no reports filed by Julie or Christie or anyone else named Kinley any time in 1985, or even the spring of '84 and '86, which I checked just to be clear. I did not appreciate him suggesting that I hadn't searched properly."

"That's where the choice words came in, huh?" He flashed a conspiratorial grin.

"Oh, don't you know it. Choice indeed. So choice you could cut them with a knife and eat them with Heinz 57 sauce. Don't tell the mayor, but I'm pretty sure I dropped some bombs you can't say on the radio."

"Sounds like Atkinson deserved it." He felt bad dishing on the man under the circumstances.

"Once I told him—in fine detail—just how thorough my work had been, I thought we were over and done with. But sure enough, he showed up here yesterday asking to see the chief. Like the chief of police is just going to march to the front window because Gail says so."

He shook his head at the insanity of the suggestion.

"Then he goes and accuses us of destroying documents."

"Us?"

"Well, and that was the thing, right? He was so sure records had been destroyed, but he refused to say how he was so certain they had ever existed in the first place. I finally had to get a sergeant to deal with him, but you *know* I was listening in."

Hank had no doubt at all.

"Sergeant Jenner's sort of shining him on a bit, basically trying to get rid of the man. But then old Atkinson blurts out that he knows the police report was filed because he'd seen it before. So the sergeant asks the questions anyone with half a brain would ask. If you read the report, why can't you tell us more about the nature of the crime or the name of the suspect or *something* to help us know what in the world you're talking about?"

"And what did Atkinson have to say about that?"

"Absolutely nothing. He left in a huff, yelling to the sergeant that there'd been a payoff. That the girl got paid. The cops had gotten paid. And he'd gotten sandbagged."

"Atkinson said that *he* had been sandbagged?"

"Yep. I remember his exact words. He said GD-it, but, you know, he actually said the GD part. He said, GD-it, that tramp got paid off. The cops got paid off. And all I got was f-in' sandbagged. But instead of f-in', it was—"

He nodded to make clear she didn't have to fill in that particular blank.

"Did Mr. Atkinson do something wrong?"

"No, ma'am. Why do you ask?"

"You never said why you were here. I figured he was in trouble. I'd be happy if I never had to deal with him again, that's for sure."

"I don't think you'll be seeing him around here any time soon."

Alice drove the route from Katonah south to Bedford just as cautiously as she had taken it northbound. Her new ally, Hank Beckman, took a spot in the passenger seat.

"So, bad news first: no police report."

When her new disposable phone had rung, she'd allowed herself a brief moment of hope that he might declare their mission accomplished. But when he told her to meet him outside the Shell Station off the Old Post Road, she could tell from his briskness that there would be no easy answers.

"After this week, only a photograph of me on a police report with someone else's name would count as bad news. Is there good news?"

"Not sure it's good, but I do have some information to heap on to the pile. You said your father—or ITH—settled a lawsuit with a woman named Julie Kinley?"

She nodded. "She accused him of stealing the story idea for my dad's first big film, *In the Heavens*. Art Cronin already checked her out, though. She died last year."

"Well, you know that police report Robert Atkinson was so eager to get his hands on? According to him, the complainant would have been one Julie Christie Kinley."

"Julie Christie?"

"Weird, huh? I guess her mother named her after the actress. Atkinson told the records clerk that the woman actually went by the name Christie, but her real name was Julie. That's what the settlement papers said, right? Julie Kinley?"

"Yeah." As her voice echoed in her own ears, it sounded vacant.

"Is something wrong?"

"I'm not sure. There's something about that name: Christie Kinley."

"It almost rhymes."

"I think that's why I remember it. I have no idea what this means, but I remember a girl named Christie Kinley who lived somewhere around Bedford. But she couldn't have been the woman who accused my father of plagiarism."

"How come?"

"Because she was just a kid. She was somewhere in between me and my brother. In fact, I'm pretty sure she came to our house a couple of times. She wouldn't have even been born when *In the Heavens* was made. Atkinson told the police that she was the one who filed the report?"

"Yes, Julie Christie Kinley. I assumed it was the same Julie Kinley who entered the settlement with ITH. I figured she'd gone to the police with her claims. People do that all the time, mixing up civil and criminal complaints. According to Atkinson, she would have filed the report in April 1985. April 18, to be precise."

"He knew the exact date?

"Not quite. The complaint had something to do with the night of April 18, which supposedly was a Friday, but the actual report could have been made any time during that weekend."

In April of 1985, Alice would have been in the sixth grade. Ben would have just turned sixteen. In fact, his birthday would have fallen precisely one week before the eighteenth, on April 11. And she knew without question that one week after his sixteenth birthday, on a Friday night, Ben hosted one hell of a keg party on the Bedford property, rowdy enough to lead two police officers to her family's home on Sunday afternoon.

Threads of information were beginning to weave together. She hadn't wanted to see the connections, but could not continue to deny the only explanation that made any sense.

"Did the records clerk say anything else about Atkinson?"

"Yeah. He was hurling accusations that someone with the police department had destroyed the report he was looking for. He said the tramp and the cops got paid off, and all he got was sandbagged."

"That *he* was sandbagged?"

"Fucking sandbagged, was I believe the exact quote."

"I think I know what that police report was all about. And if I'm right, that settlement with ITH had absolutely nothing to do with a stolen screenplay."

CHAPTER
FORTY-NINE

"**D**on't you need a search warrant or something?"

"The man lived alone, and now he's dead. Guess the super figured no one's left behind to yell at him for letting an FBI agent inside."

Hank used the superintendent's key to open the door to Robert Atkinson's Gramercy Park apartment.

"Either this guy's a worse housekeeper than I am, or I'd say that whoever removed those keys from his ignition has already been here."

Kitchen drawers were open. Sofa cushions overturned. Even the edges of the living room rug had been flipped.

"Maybe a little of both." Alice ran her fingertip across the dust accumulated on a student-sized desk in Atkinson's front alcove. She pointed at a dust-free rectangle about the size of a laptop. The power cord was still connected to the wall.

"So much for finding a computer with all of our answers written up in an easy-to-follow tabloid story."

"You've been pretty quiet since we left Bedford."

"So have you. Given what this day's been like, I figured you might want to be alone with your thoughts. You don't know me from Adam, after all."

"I know you're an FBI agent. I know that probably means you

have a theory—something to connect Julie Christie Kinley's police report, her settlement with ITH, and those photographs I found on that thumb drive."

"Anything I have to say would be conjecture at this point."

"But isn't that what investigators do? Conjure up possible explanations and then look for confirming or disconfirming evidence?"

"You said in Bedford that you thought you knew what the police report might have been about."

She sat on Robert Atkinson's faux leather desk chair. "The night of April 18, 1985, was precisely one week after my brother's sixteenth birthday. Our house there's on five acres of land. He used to get his friends together at the back edge of the property. At the time, it seemed like they were partying like rock stars, but it was probably pretty typical high school fare. My parents were sort of don't ask, don't tell about the entire thing. On that particular night, the party got so out of control, some girl got sent away to boarding school because of it. The police came to our house the following Sunday asking all kinds of questions about who'd been there and what happened."

She knew that Hank's silence was probably an interrogation technique he had learned in the FBI, but she didn't care. She continued with her story.

"They asked me where my father was during the party. I remember because I was so afraid he was going to get in trouble for something Ben had done—like trying to hold the parents responsible for underage drinking or something. I told the police that my dad had been in our screening room with me. He'd gotten an advance copy of *Goonies*. Mom had gone to bed early. Their friend, Arthur, was staying for the weekend, but *Goonies* wasn't exactly his bag, so he went out to the guest cottage. This was before my father stopped drinking. The truth was that he was pounding scotch after scotch after scotch. I tried to rouse him when I turned in, but he was totally passed out. I never actually saw him go to bed. I could still hear Ben's friends partying when I fell asleep."

Hank was silent again, but for some reason, this time she needed to be prodded.

"I notice you mentioned Christie Kinley, the ITH settlement agreement, and the thumb drive all together. Maybe part of you has decided that those pieces of information are all related to that weekend at your house in Bedford?"

"Don't you think so?"

"I'm asking you to say out loud what it is that you believe now, Alice."

"I don't want to say it. I don't want to believe it."

"It's just the two of us here. It's like you said—investigators look for confirming or disconfirming evidence. We'll investigate. To-gether. I'll help you. And if we disconfirm whatever possibility you're thinking about in your head right now, no one else has to know it was ever on the table."

She looked at her feet as she spoke. "I think my father had sex with Christie Kinley the night of my brother's party. I think he took pictures of them together in his study. I think she filed a police report, but that somehow my father made the case go away, paying her a settlement, using ITH for cover. And I think all these years later, someone's still very pissed off at my father, and at me for un-wittingly providing him an alibi. They made money through the gallery by selling child pornography on those thumb drives, then framed me for the entire enterprise."

She felt like she'd just released a hundred pounds of poison into the air, but Hank seemed completely impassive. "Okay, so let's start looking for evidence that cuts one way or another on that. Atkinson told the records clerk up at the police department in Bedford that he had been sandbagged. Maybe he was on to the story back when it happened, but got shut down."

No shock or judgment or drama. He had allowed her to voice what she'd been thinking without having to hear someone else ex-press how horrific the idea was.

"Where do we search, given that someone else already got to Atkinson, his car, and this apartment?"

"Whoever rifled through this place did it in a hurry. They prob-ably assumed that his briefcase and the computer covered what was there to find. But if Atkinson really was playing his cards close to his vest, he might have taken extra precautions. Let's see if the FBI hasn't taught me a thing or two about where people stash the good stuff."

Hank knew he wasn't the best investigator in the country. He was behind the curve on the technological advances that increasingly drove cutting-edge law enforcement strategies. And he didn't have those hyper-honed intuitions some investigators had about human motivations and desires. But he was good with witnesses. He knew how to handle himself in interrogations and interviews. And he was proud of himself for waiting on Alice Humphrey to articulate her suspicions about Christie Kinley, her father, those photographs, and the settlement agreement. If he had been the one to say it first, he just might have lost her.

He allowed her to help with the search, knowing that her forays into the apartment closets and under Atkinson's sofa and bed would get them nowhere. In many ways, this investigation really was hers. She was the one with her freedom on the line. She was the one who knew her father and the history that was indisputably tangled up with Travis Larson and the scam he was running at Highline Gallery. He was just there to supply the expertise.

So, in light of that expertise, he left the drawer-digging and cabinet-foraging to her while he looked. *Really* looked. He wasn't sure yet what he was searching for, but he'd know it once he saw it. A loose floorboard. An old coffee can in the freezer, despite a fresh bag of beans on the kitchen countertop. A slightly crooked painting that might be covering a vault in the wall. Whoever was here before them had already rummaged through the obvious places. He was looking for something so ordinary as to be misleading.

Atkinson's apartment was small, so the options were limited. He'd already checked the oven, the freezer, and the inside of the bread machine inexplicably stored in the front closet, probably a remnant from a past relationship like the waffle maker Jen had purchased for him just a few months before moving out of their place.

And then he saw it. On the floor-to-ceiling bookshelf next to the desk, Atkinson had crammed books, magazines, CDs, and DVDs. From what Hank could tell from the media setup in the living room, Atkinson had been a tech guy: plasma screen TV, sound system, Blu-ray, TiVo, the works. There was no ancient VCR in sight. But next to the desk, in the pile of chaos that had been pulled from the bookshelf, was an unmarked plastic videocassette case.

He pulled it open, and a tightly rolled bundle of papers fell out. Alice rushed over from the sofa, where she had been searching in the cracks beneath the cushions. He forced himself to hand her the documents. She deserved to see them first. If she didn't want to look, she could always decline. Instead, she took a seat on the hardwood floor and spread the papers out before her.

Alice felt sick. Literally sick. Not literally the way people nowadays said literally when they in fact meant figuratively—as in, "my head *literally* exploded." Alice felt *actually* sick. She took a deep breath and swallowed the bile she felt forming in her esophagus.

She could not stop reading the tiny sidebar column on the yellowed page of newsprint from the May 2, 1985, edition of the *National Star,* byline Robert Atkinson:

GUESS THE CELEBRITY

What A-lister (as in Academy Award winner) is at the center of a criminal sex investigation? That the cad is married to a beloved celeb is the tamest aspect of this emerging scandal. Sources tell us a fourteen-year-old girl claims this director sweet-talked her into his home and then forced himself on her. Charges have not yet been filed, but we anticipate that this scumbag will soon feel like he's in hell.

Inside the same rolled tube of documents they had found another sheet torn from the *National Star,* this one of May 9, 1985, retracting the earlier tidbit:

Last week, we printed a "blind item" suggesting that an Academy Award–winning director was being investigated on sex-related criminal charges. We did not name the individual in question at the time because the story did not yet meet our rigorous standards for publication. Unfortunately, the source upon which we relied for the anonymous "blind item" was misinformed, as were we. Readers should not attempt to surmise the identity of the story's subject, since the original story was not based on truth or fact. We apologize for our mistake.

"I'd say on the spectrum of confirming or disconfirming evidence, we've pretty much confirmed it."

"Or disconfirmed," Hank said, "if you believe the retraction."

"Of course I don't believe the retraction. The *National Star* was ahead of its time. You see these blind items all the time. They don't name the person so they can't get sued by a celebrity willing to spend millions of dollars on attorneys' fees. But my father has worked with an actor who sues tabloids for retractions every single time one of them publishes an article hinting he's gay. Well, guess what? The guy is for all practical purposes married to another supposedly straight actor. It's just like Atkinson said. The girl got paid off in a settlement. My dad must have bribed the cops to make the police report go away. And he probably threatened to sue the *National Star* once all Atkinson's so-called evidence had been wiped away."

"So that's why he said he got sandbagged. Maybe he finally figured out that his original story was actually true and was trying to get himself paid, too. Your father had all those tabloid stories come out last year. That could have been the trigger for Atkinson to start digging back into that night in Bedford again."

"That explains why he was calling me and my brother—to see what we remembered about that weekend."

Her father and Art's cover story that Kinley was a former employee was a classic move on their part: treat her like a child, while they pulled secret strings in an attempt to help her. They probably figured Arthur would come up with a solution without having to tell anyone about that night in Bedford. But *she* was the one who had been sucked into the Highline Gallery mess. She was the one who had found that man's body. And she was the one being investigated by the police. She had a right to know everything.

"Was Christie Kinley at your brother's party that night?"

She shook her head. "I was inside the whole time. But obviously Ben would know."

"We really need to find your brother."

Hank had been able to nudge her toward a vocalization of her worst fears, but this time she rambled out loud about Ben's various acquaintances without reaching the logical inference he'd been suggesting. He decided to give her one more push.

"How harmful would it be to your father if Atkinson had dredged up those old allegations?"

"To be accused of—*that*?" He'd been careful so far not to use the word *rape*, and she stopped before saying it herself. "Obviously that would destroy him."

Now he allowed the silence to fill Robert Atkinson's apartment again, waiting for her to draw her own conclusions.

"If you think my father had something to do with Atkinson's car accident, you're out of your mind. When all those women were coming out of the woodwork last year, he was totally unfazed. At worst, he might do damage control and pay Atkinson off, like he did with Christie Kinley, but he'd never resort to violence. Absolutely not. It's unimaginable. I would bet my life on that."

"So then who goes to the trouble of setting you up using pictures of your father and Christie Kinley, only to decide they don't want Atkinson's story out there in the public domain?"

"It has to be someone who's still angry about what happened that night in Bedford. It's like they're killing three birds with one stone. They get the money from selling the thumb drives. They fuck with me for creating an alibi for my father. And presumably they bring my father down in the process once the police figure out those pictures are of him—if they haven't already."

If he was willing to shift his focus from her father, what she was saying made sense. "Maybe whoever did this wanted to get back at you and your father, but without dragging Christie Kinley's name into it. If Atkinson had broken the story, Kinley's name would have been thrown into the mix. People then start saying she's a liar. Or that she was the seductress. And she's dead, so she can't even defend herself."

"Except what if she's not dead?"

"You told me she died last year."

"I told you that because Arthur Cronin tried tracking her down and only found a death certificate. But if Travis Larson can run around New York telling realtors and gallery owners his name is Steven Henning, and telling me his name is Drew Campbell, maybe he was working with a woman who decided she no longer wanted to be Julie Christie Kinley. Do you know how to find out if someone faked her death?"

"We'd need to track down someone who actually saw Christie Kinley's body." He pulled out his BlackBerry and started entering information with both thumbs. "Okay, I've got an obituary here from the *Lakeville Journal* last March. 'Julie Christie Kinley died peacefully in her family home in Falls Village.' "

Alice recognized the town name. "She must have left Westchester and moved to Connecticut at some point."

She had been fighting breast cancer since her diagnosis last summer. She was preceded in death by her mother, Gloria Barnes Kinley, and survived by her sister, Mia Louise Andrews. In lieu of flowers, the family requests that contributions be sent to the Susan G. Komen Breast Cancer Foundation.

"If she died in her family home, I guess we should start there." He looked at his watch. "By the time we get to Connecticut, it will be a little late to be knocking on strangers' doors to ask about a dead woman. It'll have to wait until tomorrow."

...

Alice knew they had reached the end of what could be accomplished today. They would have to start up again tomorrow in Falls Village. She could not recall another time in her life when she had absolutely nowhere to go.

"All right. You can use the bat phone to call me when it's time to leave the city."

"You can't go back to your apartment tonight."

"I know."

"So where are you planning to stay?"

"I stopped trying to plan anything about fifteen hours ago. That sofa you're on seems as good a place as any."

She could tell he didn't like the suggestion. She didn't want him to suggest his own apartment. She wanted him to be precisely what he seemed, a man who believed that law enforcement should stand for truth, a man who was willing to help her because it was the right thing to do.

"How about we make the drive tonight to avoid the traffic. We'll find a hotel up there to crash. Two rooms, of course."

It was the perfect suggestion.

They were halfway to Connecticut on the Hutchinson River Parkway when they heard the announcement on 1010 News radio. An arrest warrant had been issued for Alice Humphrey, the daughter of Academy Award–winning director Frank Humphrey, for the murder of a former boyfriend and business associate. The facts of the case were still sealed, but according to an anonymous source, evidence submitted in support of the warrant included sexual photographs of Frank Humphrey with an allegedly underage girl. It was unclear how the photographs were related to the murder allegations against his daughter. The reporter promised more details as they rolled in.

They drove in silence to Falls Village. As she fell asleep in a lumpy bed in a roadside motel, she had never felt so alone.

CHAPTER
FIFTY

Joann Stevenson felt like the wind had been knocked out of her. In the days that had passed since she'd last seen her daughter, she had learned to protect herself as she listened to the television. Hearing Becca described as a missing teenager—with all of the accompanying speculation about the dark possibilities—was not easy. But even harder were the nights when the newscasters said nothing about Becca during those thirty-second commercial teasers, a reminder to Joann that her daughter's disappearance was already turning into yesterday's story, surpassed by the latest home invasion or commercial fire.

What she did not expect during a commercial break from *Glee*—the show Becca had turned her on to—was the announcement that an arrest warrant had been issued for the murder at the Highline Gallery, or that the suspect in question was a woman—a former child actress at that. Nor did she expect the scintillating teaser that the woman's father and pornographic photographs of him with an underage girl might be involved.

She knew it was late, but called Jason Morhart anyway.

"Why didn't you tell me?"

"Joann?"

"That's right. Joann Stevenson, the white-trash woman whose daughter went missing, and no one had the proper decency to call to say an arrest warrant was going out. I had to hear about it on the news."

"It's on the news?"

She heard a television come on in the background. "You didn't know?"

"I knew an arrest might be coming soon. They're still not sure of Becca's connection to the gallery, Joann. Hopefully if they get this woman in custody, they can turn the pressure on for answers about Becca. Remember? We talked about this?"

"Did you know this movie director was involved?"

"He's the suspect's father. They're looking for the woman who was running the gallery where Becca's fingerprints were found."

"But they're saying the father took sexual photographs of an underage girl."

"That part was on the news?" The detail must have proved too titillating not to leak.

"So you knew about the pictures? I thought the picture of Becca was one she'd taken to send to that boy, Dan Hunter."

"The gallery was selling pornographic photographs—the picture that Becca sent to Dan was definitely not one of them. I'm sorry, but it was a detail I couldn't share with you."

"I mean, a man like Frank Humphrey must have access to all kinds of film distribution networks. He could peddle that smut all over the world."

"I can assure you, Joann, that the detectives in the city are absolutely positive that Becca was not one of the kids depicted in those photographs. And I promise you—I swear on my life—that I had no idea that they suspected this woman's father of being involved."

"I can't believe no one even called to tell me the arrest warrant was really happening. Jason, I heard about it on the news." She didn't like the shrill tone of her voice.

"They didn't call me either. I would've told you. I would have driven over there myself to let you know in person to expect the announcement. I'm so sorry, Joann."

"Is it too late?"

"You know you can call me anytime you need me. That's why I wanted you to have this number."

"No, I mean is it too late for you to come over here? To talk to me."

Jason knew it was probably a mistake, but he pulled on his coat and climbed into his truck.

CHAPTER FIFTY-ONE

The home in which Christie Kinley had supposedly passed away was a large yellow colonial with a wraparound porch and French doors. Alice guessed the lot was about three acres. She wondered if her father's money had paid for it.

The woman who answered the door was about her age. Her hair was pulled into a high ponytail. She was wearing running clothes and had her car keys in hand. "Let's go, Jenny. We're going to the gym. Little Kyle's going to be in the playroom, too. It'll be fun. Sorry about that," she said, lowering her voice to a conversational tone. "Getting a four-year-old in the car is a twenty-minute production."

Alice let Hank do the talking, since he was the one with a badge. He explained that they were looking for background information about the previous homeowner, Julie Kinley. They believed she still went by her middle name, Christie.

"She passed away last year. We bought the house in the summer and only dealt with the real estate agent. I've got a forwarding address for her mail, though. It goes to her sister, I believe?" She reached for the black metal mailbox affixed to the front porch and slipped out one of the envelopes awaiting pickup. "This looked like junk mail from her gym, but I forward everything just in case. You can take it if you want."

Alice saw a handwritten Brooklyn address on the envelope before Hank slipped it into his coat pocket.

"Do you happen to know the details of Ms. Kinley's passing?" he asked.

"No, I think I've intentionally kept my ears closed to that kind of talk in the neighborhood. I don't really want to know there was a dead person in my house. Silly, I suppose, but the house was all cleared out by the time we looked at it, and I like to pretend to think we were the first to ever live here. You might try Mrs. Withers next door. She's lived here forever and is one of those neighbors who seems to know everything about everybody."

Alice could tell that the woman didn't consider that trait a good thing.

They could still hear the mom yelling at Jenny to "hurry it up" as they made their way to the next-door neighbor's house.

Mrs. Withers was exactly what a nosy neighbor should be—a little plump with curly white hair, a kitchen that smelled like bread, and an ability to whip up mugs of hot cocoa, with marshmallows no less, for strangers who showed up without notice. She also liked to talk. A lot. And quickly.

"I always felt sorry for Christie. The cancer was like the icing on the cake, confirmation of that queasy feeling I had since I first met her as a teenager. It's like some people are just born with bad karma. I always hoped that something would turn for that girl. When Gloria died —"

"That was Christie's mother?" Alice was delighted at the woman's loquaciousness, but found it difficult to get a word in edgewise.

"If you could call her a mother. She was always flitting around, chasing after this man or the next. That's how she managed to have two daughters without ever having a man involved in any way except the bedroom, if she even bothered going to a bed. She was a groupie back in the sixties, you know."

Alice and Hank both muttered the requisite "No, we didn't," but Mrs. Withers had plowed on without them.

"Oh, she would talk about those days like she was Neil Armstrong, walking on the moon. She bedded Mick Jagger once, according to her. By the time she moved here, Christie was fourteen years old and already headed to rehab, but Gloria was still at it. She'd go down to the city and try to pick up these has-been actors at their old hangouts. She was one of those gals who thought a woman's only value was to land a man. She wanted those girls of hers to be famous, but never taught them a single talent or skill. In Gloria's delusional mind, they'd get by on their looks. But then Gloria had her stroke about eight or nine years ago, and Christie moved back into the house to take care of Mia."

"Mia is Christie's sister?" Alice remembered mention of a surviving sister in Christie's obituary.

"Yep, and Gloria screwed her up at least as much as she did Christie. When Christie moved back here, I thought maybe this would be her chance to have a better life, without Gloria hounding her about getting a husband locked down. It seemed like she might have gotten her head on a little straighter, but then she got the news about the cancer. Poor thing was too far gone by the time they caught it."

She finally paused, taking a sip of her cocoa as if they had been having an idle conversation about the relative merits of powder or liquid dish detergent.

Alice didn't know how to ask the woman whether she was absolutely certain Christie had really died.

"I imagine that's a difficult end to one's life," she finally said.

"Oh, it was horrible. You know, when Gloria went, it was from a stroke out in the yard shoveling snow. She just fell down and died. But we all had to watch Christie go. She got so thin because she couldn't keep any food down."

Alice looked at Hank, who also seemed disappointed. The deterioration this woman was describing did not seem like something that could be feigned.

"I think Christie knew when it was finally time for her to go.

She rounded up a group of people at the house so she could be surrounded by friendly faces. She told us to make it a potluck so she
could watch us eat." She smiled at the memory. "Then when she
was feeling tired, she called her best friend and her sister into her
room to hold her hands while she fell asleep. She never woke up."

"So you were actually there at the house when she passed?"

"Yes. I like to think it's because Christie knew I always hoped for
something better for her."

"You mentioned that Christie moved back into the house to take
care of her sister. May I ask if there's something wrong with Mia?"
Maybe she would know who might still hold a grudge about what
happened to her sister as a teenager.

"Well, it depends by what you mean by something *wrong*, I suppose. Supposedly she's a very talented photographer, but as my
granddaughter sometimes says, there's a screw loose in there. There's
a darkness to her. Very negative energy. Why do you ask?"

"It just seems a little old to be living with her mother." Even eight
or nine years ago, when Gloria died, the daughters would have been
around thirty years old.

"Oh, Mia's a youngster. She only needed Christie to stay with
her at the house for a few years, and then she moved down to the
city, so Christie had the house on her own. You know, when Gloria
moved in next door, she was just pregnant with little Mia. Christie
was already messed up, so I thought maybe Gloria wanted a second
chance. But then she goes and makes all the same mistakes with
Mia, starting with that name. Mia Farrow and Louise Fletcher. I
mean, naming your daughter after the crazy nurse in *One Flew over
the Cuckoo's Nest*? Talk about cuckoo. Mia Louise Andrews. The
dad was never in the picture, but I assumed that Andrews was the
father's name. Then Gloria told me years later after a few margaritas
on July 4 that she just made up the baby's last name. Maybe it was
for Julie Andrews? Who could really know with that woman."

"So, I'm sorry—Mia was born when?" The story was building in
Alice's head faster than she could process it.

"Well, let's see . . . Gloria wasn't even showing yet when she moved here in, it must have been 1985. The beginning of the summer. Early June, I think. She'd been having all kinds of problems with Christie. I said before she sent her off to rehab, but it was technically boarding school. Again, who knows how Gloria paid for that either. I never saw a woman other than a prostitute who found a way to pay so many bills without doing any other work than on her back. Oh lord, did I just say that?"

Alice knew precisely how Gloria had paid her bills. She needed Mrs. Withers to get back on track.

"Christie was sent away to boarding school?" Alice remembered Ben telling her that a girl at his party had gotten so wasted that her parents had sent her away to an all-girls boarding school.

"Yep, for girls only. I thought it might do her some good to be away from her mother, but she only stayed a year. You know, I even joked with Gloria that first summer that with Christie going away to boarding school, and Gloria having a little baby at her age, people might get the wrong impression."

Alice looked at Hank, who spoke for the first time since the cocoa had been poured. "You mean the neighbors might gossip that Gloria's pregnancy was fake, and that the baby was actually Christie's."

"I know, I'm just awful. But I was only joking."

Alice knew in her gut what the relationship was between Christie Kinley's sister and all of the questions she had been carrying around the last week. But that didn't stop her from asking the validating question.

"If you don't mind, Mrs. Withers, what does Mia look like?"

"Well, she's a lovely girl. It makes her penchant for these lowlife men all the more perplexing! She'd never bring home a nice guy like this one. But what does she look like? She's slender, you know. Very fit. One of those girls who carries herself well. And she has the most amazing red hair. Delicate features. Sort of a honey-and-strawberries kind of complexion. You know what, dear? I know this will sound like babble from an old woman, but if I had to say, Mia looks a bit like you if it weren't for that dark hair of yours."

CHAPTER
FIFTY-TWO

They were back at their motel outside White Plains, strategizing their next move.

"I know you're the one who's an FBI agent, but don't we have enough evidence to go to Shannon and Danes? I ran from my apartment because I knew I was in over my head. But with what we know now? I'm willing to go back to the city. I'll turn myself in if that's what it takes to make them investigate Mia."

"You can do that, but once you turn yourself in on the warrant, no one will be in a rush to exonerate you. You'll probably get slapped with a no-bail hold on the murder charge. The police will have passed the case on to the DA's office, so it will be clear as far as they're concerned. And the prosecutors will keep setting over your trial date until a judge forces them to fish or cut bait. It would be better to get them to drop the charges up front."

"You're a federal agent. Can't you just tell them what to do?"

He shook his head. "If only I could. Federal and state governments are separate sovereigns. Put it this way: the last time I talked to John Shannon, he basically called me a burnout and a loser. I can call them with this tip about Mia, but trust me: they're not going to listen."

"How can they ignore it? If we're right, Mia Andrews is my half sister." She cringed at the thought. "My guess is she had no idea that Christie was actually her mother, until Christie died. Maybe she found the settlement documents or something else that made her realize her sister was actually her biological mother. She has every reason to hate me and my father."

"Mrs. Withers did say she had a weak spot for dirtbags, which pretty much sums up Travis Larson."

"She has to be the woman kissing Larson in that picture. Plus she's a photographer. That can't be a coincidence. If she got part of the settlement money when her mother died, she might have been in a position to front the Highline Gallery operation. Like I said before: three birds, one stone. She makes money off the sale of the so-called artwork. She frames me. And she gets the pictures from my father's office in front of the police without ever having to name her mother as the girl depicted in them."

Hank had run Mia Andrews and learned that Mrs. Withers had not been exaggerating when she'd described the young woman as troubled. Two drug busts. A stop by police officers who suspected her of prostitution. The use of a false name and identification on the second drug arrest. According to Hank, she was precisely the kind of woman who might have crossed paths with Travis Larson.

"That's one version of the facts. But John Shannon and Willie Danes have spent the last week convincing themselves that you killed Larson and were the mastermind behind those thumb drive sales from the gallery. To them? Mia's existence will just be another motive for you to act out against your father and try to prove you could be independent. I'm sure the way they look at it, your slipping those pictures of your dad into those thumb drives was some Freudian act of revenge."

"Even the suggestion that I would peddle obscenity involving my own father—"

"I hate to say it, Alice, but I've seen people do much sicker things. And so have Shannon and Danes. All I'm saying is that the NYPD isn't necessarily going to shift their entire theory based on what we have so far. But that's not an absolute deal breaker. We just need them to be sufficiently intrigued to follow up on it. To be open-minded. But if I'm the one to call them, it's not going to happen."

Alice found herself thinking about the words her father had used to persuade her to call Arthur Cronin for help. He had quoted Malcolm Gladwell—something about "practical intelligence," "an ability to read a situation. To know what to say and how and when to say it."

"I know we can't call my friends, but what about my lawyer?"

"Is this your boyfriend, Jeff? I guarantee you they're pulling his LUDs."

She didn't feel the need to articulate the complications that made the word *boyfriend* a poor descriptor. "No. I told Danes the last time he tried to interview me that Arthur Cronin was my lawyer."

"They wouldn't have the balls to monitor his phone."

"Then that's who I think we should call."

"Alice. Where are you? I've been trying to cover for you with the police, but what the hell is going on?" Based on his secretary's urgency in transferring the call, Alice could tell Art had been waiting to hear from her.

"My friend Lily warned me the police were coming. I just couldn't let them take me. You know that I'm innocent."

"You don't look innocent to them right now. We need to negotiate your turning yourself in. Their case is probably shit."

"How are Mom and Dad holding up?" She wished she could make herself not care about her father. He was the one who'd created this predicament. But even though she knew he was a cheat and a liar, she had to believe that he had beaten whatever part of him had been with Christie Kinley that night when he had finally stopped drinking.

"I've got a public relations firm putting together a damage-control campaign about these old photographs, but he's more worried about you."

She noticed he was not denying that the man in the pictures was her father.

"I know about Christie Kinley, Art. I know she wasn't a former employee. That lawsuit had nothing to do with plagiarism."

"I'm sorry, Alice. I was the one who told your father I could get this mess straightened out without having to rehash these ugly details."

"A fourteen-year-old girl accused my father of *raping* her. It's more than just an ugly detail."

"It wasn't *rape*. The girl was drunk. Your father even more so. She was enamored with your father's celebrity. She set him up."

"I don't want to hear any of that right now."

"We should have been up-front with you, but your father wants to rectify it. He was absolutely convinced that the church protesting the gallery was behind this. He has given me a full waiver to discuss these matters not only with you but with the police or anyone else, if doing so would finally get you out of this jam. He's willing to let the chips fall as they may."

"Did you two know that Christie Kinley had a child nine months after that night in Bedford?"

"What? Where did you hear that?"

"Did you know or not?"

"Of course not! That was never an issue in the settlement. No one ever made such an allegation."

She explained the timing of Gloria's supposed pregnancy while Christie was sent away to boarding school. "It would explain why a red-haired woman who looks like me was spotted with Travis Larson. Can you please call the detectives and convince them they need to talk to this woman? Her name is Mia Louise Andrews. If they can prove a connection between her and Larson, that should be enough to convince them I was set up."

"The only thing those detectives want to hear from me right now is that I can bring you in on the warrant."

"Tell them I'll turn myself in if they interview Mia."

"The NYPD doesn't usually take well to blackmail."

"With your talents, Art, I'm sure you can get them to see it as a fair compromise."

"I suppose if they arrested you without following up on this angle, someone like me might use it to excoriate them in the media. A rush to judgment. Shoddy investigation tactics."

"See? I knew you'd come up with something."

"All right. Let me give these schmucks a call and see what I can do. Where do I call you back?"

She mouthed the request to Hank, who gave her approval to recite the number of her disposable cell.

"I'll call you back in twenty."

She looked at her watch. Twenty minutes before she'd know whether she was going to jail or—well, she didn't know the alternative.

Twenty minutes came and went in silence. After thirty, she tried Art, and then continued dialing every five minutes.

When her cell rang shortly before the one-hour mark, she picked up immediately, continuing her ritualized pacing of the narrow path between the foot of the hotel bed and the fake mahogany television stand. Art's voice sounded hoarse when he apologized for the delay.

"Jesus. I hope a screaming match wasn't involved."

"I'm sorry?"

"Your voice sounds like you've been yelling."

"No, but there's something I need to tell you."

"That does not sound good. The police wouldn't listen about Mia? Hello?" She looked at the signal bars on her cell. The call hadn't dropped. "Can you hear me? Art?"

"Yeah, I'm here."

"Seriously, you sound weird. If there's bad news, go ahead and give it to me. I can take it."

When he finally spoke, he was all business. "Okay, you need to pay very close attention. I want to talk to you first about where we stand with the police. And you have to promise me that you're going to follow through on whatever course of action we decide is best, no matter what. Can you promise me that?"

"Of course. Why wouldn't—"

"So here's the deal. I talked to Danes. He sounded put out. And very skeptical. But I got him to agree to a knock and talk with Mia Andrews—check her out, see what she might have to say about this matter."

"Thank God—"

"Not so fast. It was obvious he's only shining us on, which means he might believe any story this gal hands to him. It's always possible she's going to say something that actually hurts you."

"I'm willing to take that risk."

"Plus his agreement to check out Mia was conditional. He'll only question her if I produce you on the warrant."

"I don't want to turn myself in on the warrant until after they see Mia. What if I turn myself in, and Mia's off in Mexico with a fake name, never to be seen again?"

"Which leaves us in a standoff. Here's what I was able to negotiate: you agree to return from wherever you've been hiding. Once we're together in the city, Danes and his partner will reach out to Mia. Once the interview is over, he calls me, and I deliver you to them."

"What if they can't find Mia?"

"Then I made no promises. They'll have to keep looking for you themselves. What do you think?"

"What other choice do I have?"

"I can get one of my own investigators on it. We could put together what would eventually be our defense case, and present it to the DA's office to try to preempt an indictment. In the meantime, the longer you go without turning yourself in, the less likely it is they'll be willing to help you out. And to be honest, police pressure can be a lot more effective in getting a response than a private investigator."

"So basically I should turn myself in anyway, and if we go with Danes's deal, the police will at least be the ones asking Mia questions?"

"That's how I see it."

"All right. Let's do it." She swallowed, realizing that tonight she would probably be sleeping in a jail cell. "What's the next step?"

"Can you be in Williamsburg by six o'clock?"

That would give her nearly four hours.

"No problem."

"I didn't know how far away you were, so I asked for some time to make you available. Danes wants you near Mia's house so you can turn yourself in as soon as the interview's over."

"That quickly, huh?"

"They're worried you'll renege. I'll meet you down there. I think it's good for us to be close by. Hopefully, something will come of their talks with Mia, in which case we might be able to help tie up some loose ends. I'm looking at a map now. There's an intersection about a block from Mia's address. Rutledge and Lee. I'll meet you there a little before six. Now are you sure this is what you want to do?"

Of course it wasn't what she *wanted*. She wanted her life back. She wanted anything else but her current circumstance. "Yes. I'm sure."

"Okay, now remember that you promised not to change course, no matter what."

"Why do you keep saying that?"

"Because your father called me. He begged me for your number so he could tell you himself, but I was worried he'd lead the police right to you."

"You're really scaring me. Are they okay?" Hank mouthed a silent *What?* from the threadbare chair in the corner of the hotel room.

"They're fine, but it's Ben. His sponsor hadn't heard from him for a while and got worried enough to go by his apartment. He found Ben in the bathroom. There's no easy way to say this. Your brother was using again. He overdosed."

"Where is he? Did he go to the hospital? Is Down with him?" Despite Ben's at least initially regular attendance at NA meetings, he'd never found anyone with whom he was as comfortable discussing his addiction as Down.

"It wasn't just an OD. Ben's dead. They think it happened some-time yesterday. Heroin. I'm so sorry."

She remembered Ben's unlocked apartment. The unoccupied loft. The cracked bathroom door that she had never opened. Her ugly rush to grab his money and cell phone. Maybe if she had nudged that door. She imagined rubber tubing around her brother's bare arm, a syringe still hanging from his vein.

"Alice, I'm so, so sorry. You had a right to know immediately, but remember your promise. You need to focus on yourself right now—for the sake of your parents, if nothing else. They can't lose both of you."

From his choked-back sob, she knew he'd been holding himself together for her benefit, playing the role of the unflappable lawyer who was going to take care of everything. Practical intelligence, her father had called it.

She felt the phone slip from her hand before Hank grabbed her shoulders to break her fall.

CHAPTER
FIFTY-THREE

It was nearly four o'clock, and Jason was still pissed at those fat-slob NYPD-ers who had fucked him over. He also had a crick in his neck from spending the entire night tossing and turning on Joann Stevenson's sofa, unsure whether the lack of sleep was from the fact that he hadn't slept on a couch since college, or because he knew he had no business being on that particular one.

To top it off, Nancy had to go and say something about the fact that he looked exactly how he felt. "Holy moly, Jason. You're much too young to have bags under your eyes the size of mine. You've got to take care of yourself, honey."

"Just allergies, Nancy. Nothing to worry about."

He'd been steaming all day, but decided he had to draw a line in the sand with those detectives in the city. Willie Danes picked up after two rings.

"Danes."

"It's Jason Morhart from Dover. My victim's mom heard about your arrest warrant on the news last night."

"Now if only we could find the defendant."

He emphasized the last syllable to rhyme with *ant*, the way Jason noticed lawyers often did. He always thought it was a person's way of trying to sound like an expert.

"You should have kept me in the loop, Danes. Our departments had an agreement. Full exchange of all information. And you never told me anything about that woman's father being in some of those photographs. That's got my victim's mom all worked up about the pornography angle again. Her daughter being missing is bad enough. She doesn't need to worry about naked pictures of her getting distributed all over the world."

"Sounds like you're the one who's got yourself all worked up about the feelings of that girl's mother, Morhart. This is a criminal investigation."

"And it's supposed to be a *joint* one. Forget about the girl's family. *I* shouldn't have heard about a major development from the television. Did you forget who it was who told you George Hardy is Becca's father? Or who told you to look for Becca's fingerprints in the first place?"

"A lot of good that's done us. We'd actually have a pretty nice and neat case if we didn't have to explain what the hell your girl's prints are doing in that gallery."

"Jesus, Danes. Listen to yourself. I'm sorry if the truth is interfering with the tidiness of your murder case."

"Aw, crap. I'm being a jerk because I know we blew it. We got sucked into the momentum of things and were working overdrive on the arrest warrant. We didn't think to call you. Sorry, man. Honestly, though, we got nothing but conjecture about Becca. Our best guess is that Larson was grooming her for the camera, but either something went wrong and she wound up getting hurt, or hopefully she got spooked and ran off. Once we get Humphrey in custody, maybe we'll get a better read on the situation."

"Any thoughts on when that might be?"

"With any luck, it'll be tonight. Look, do you really want to be involved in this, even if it's not taking us directly into Becca territory yet?"

"We did have a cooperation agreement."

"I'll tell you what. I worked out this cockamamie agreement with Humphrey's lawyer for her to turn herself in, but first I promised to chase down some girl she thinks is her secret identical half sister or something."

"Her what?"

"It's nonsense, man, but that's the way this girl's been yanking our chain from the beginning. It's a box I got to check off, though, and Shannon's probably going to be tied up with the DA. We're trying to figure out whether we have any charges against the father, and then we can use those as leverage with the daughter. Think you can meet me in Williamsburg by six o'clock? Take a run at this mystery witness with me? It'll be a waste of time, but if you want to be in the loop, you and I will play Murtaugh and Riggs tonight."

"Only if you're the Mel Gibson one. Without the phone rage."

"Deal."

"Where's Williamsburg?"

"In Brooklyn, man. That's one of the five boroughs of New York City?"

PART IV

MIA

PART IV

CHAPTER
FIFTY-FOUR

Alice's disposable phone rang at 5:58 p.m. She recognized her surrogate uncle and now-attorney's voice.

"Where are you?" he asked.

"Outside a fruit market on Rutledge and Lee."

"Are you holding up all right?"

"No, but I'm here."

She had spent another two hours in the hotel room, overtaken by uncontrollable sobbing. Just when she thought she had no more left to give—the tears losing steam, her breathing returning to normal—she'd succumb beneath another oncoming wave.

It was Hank who had finally forced her into the car. He spoke more words during the drive to Brooklyn than he had since they'd met. He'd lost a sister. Her name was Ellen. He talked about her death and the way it tethered him to Travis Larson. About the phone call from the state police after Ellen's accident. About how he had to hang up on the trooper before learning the location of her body so he could run to the bathroom to be sick.

And then he said he'd never gotten past the guilt. That the responsibility for someone else's pain was a weight that could never be eased. *You feel responsible for Ben, but your parents feel responsible for you. Don't do this to them, Alice. Don't give up on yourself. Don't let them go to bed every night, knowing you're either a fugitive or in prison, and feeling like it's all their fault.*

So just as she had promised Art she would, she had pulled herself to-gether—for tonight. For now. Grieving the loss of her brother would have to come later. Hank had dropped her off at the intersection where she and Arthur had agreed to meet. There was no need to advertise to the NYPD that her plan had been assisted by an FBI agent. He promised he'd be circling in the neighborhood, waiting for her to call.

Art had apparently pulled himself together as well. "I got stuck in traffic trying to get out of Manhattan. I'm crossing the Williams-burg Bridge now. I don't want to risk screwing anything up, so I'll call Danes and let him know you're in place standing by. I'll be right there. If we're lucky, Mia will either come clean or at least act hinky enough for Danes and Shannon to clue in that she's behind this."

As uncomfortable as she had been with the status quo, she felt sick knowing that something was going to change tonight. Either the police would see her in a new light, or she would officially become a criminal defendant. "How are my parents?"

"It was, well, I'll go ahead and say it—it was a fucking hard day. But we're going to try to have something resembling good news for the Humphrey family soon, okay? I'll be there in a couple of minutes."

She squared her shoulders and let the cold in, just like Ben had taught her when she was little.

Jason was growing frustrated with the snarl of one-way streets that threatened to take him farther and farther from the address where he was supposed to have met Willie Danes two minutes earlier at 5:55.

He finally gave up and pulled in front of a fire hydrant on the corner outside Mia Andrews's building. If he got a ticket, he'd send it to the town to pay. Only one shoe had hit the asphalt before he heard a voice beckon from across the street.

"Dover can't buy you an official ride, Morhart?" Willie Danes stepped from a white Crown Vic.

"I like my own car."

"Whatever, man. Let's do what we got to do."

"So who's this lady again?"

"You know those old sex pictures taken in Frank Humphrey's house? The ones that got you all pissed off?"

Technically, the pictures were not the source of Jason's aggrievement. It was the NYPD's failure to tell him their significance. Whatever. He nodded.

"According to Alice Humphrey, the chick he was with was some girl at his son's birthday party. This woman who lives here is that girl's younger sister." Jason tried to process the connections between the players. "But Alice wants us to believe that she's not in fact the little sister. That she's actually the girl's daughter, which would make her Frank Humphrey's daughter also, which would make her Alice Humphrey's half sister. And supposedly that cluster fuck of a situation's enough to give this girl a motive to set up Alice and her father."

"So what's the plan?"

"We go through the motions. I made a deal with Alice's lawyer: we check out this Mia person, and Alice turns herself in. Pretty simple. I give it point-one percent odds that this girl is even relevant, and, if she is, I'd put it at ninety percent that she winds up helping us build our case against Alice."

"That's a lot of math, Danes."

"Yeah, that was a little fucked up. My point is, don't sweat it." A jingle escaped from the phone clipped to Danes's waistband. "Danes . . . She's nearby? You're not going to fuck me on this, are you, Cronin? . . . All right. I'll call you when we're done." He returned the cell to its holder. "We're all set. According to her lawyer, Alice Humphrey's waiting in the neighborhood to turn herself in. Let's see what this chick's got to say."

It happened fast. Faster than anything Morhart had been trained for at the Town of Dover Police Department, or in college, or on the basketball team at Linwood High. It felt like he was watching a video game rather than living the intentionally simple life he had created.

They had walked through the main entrance of the generic light brown brick apartment building. They took the two flights of stairs to unit #3B, Jason having to slow down for Danes to keep up. Danes was the one who knocked on Mia Andrews's door. Four beats with no response.

In retrospect, they had each waited to the left and right sides of the apartment door, respectively—not because they sensed any danger, but instinctively, the way you eventually learn not to stand too close to a top step. They were two cops paying an unannounced visit to a stranger. Without their brains even processing that simple fact, their bodies had known not to stand at the dead center of that door.

If they had, two police departments might have had funerals on their hands.

Four beats with no response. Then another knock, again from Danes. "Miss Andrews. The apartment downstairs is reporting a leak. We need to check the sink in your kitchen. Are you there?"

Jason would remember later the way Danes looked at him from the opposite side of the doorway and winked—as if the building leak was such a clever cover story. When he replayed those seconds in his mind, Jason could almost imagine Danes's winking eyelid returning to its place of rest, only to blink again when the first shot was fired.

They both fell to the ground so quickly that Jason hit his head against Danes's shoulder.

Two more shots, right through the door frame. *Pop, pop.* Jason had never heard a gun fired other than during target practice or hunting. The sound reverberated against the walls and ceiling. He found himself covering his ears, as if the noise were their biggest threat.

Danes was the one who returned fire first. Jason flinched as he heard more pops—these louder and closer—before realizing they were coming from Danes's Glock. He removed his own .40 cal Beretta from its holster and started firing through the door. He had no idea where they were aiming, but they both unloaded their weapons as they scuttled crablike across the floor toward the staircase.

He could hear his own heavy breaths blurring with Danes's panting in the stairwell once their weapons were empty. Danes was yelling radio codes that Jason used in Dover only in theory. He could smell fear in their perspiration. And then the hallway fell silent except for the sound of a child crying somewhere on a floor above them.

The first two pops could have been a car backfiring. Alice flinched at the noise, then forced herself to take a deep breath, realizing that her imagination was getting the best of her.

But the first two pops were followed by an array of firecrackers in quick, chaotic succession. She heard a woman on the street scream. A teenager crossing the intersection in front of her ducked into the fruit market, pulling the screaming woman with him.

But as other people ran for cover, Alice felt herself running into the street. They had driven past Mia's building when Hank dropped her off. She knew where the woman lived. She was absolutely certain the shots were fired there. Her feet were moving faster than she could think.

She heard brakes screeching next to her. Hank Beckman was jumping from his green Camry. "Alice! No!" But her feet were still moving. She was the one who had sent those police officers to the apartment. She had known going into it that Arthur had sold them on the idea by offering her up as the bait. Of course they had treated the entire enterprise as a joke. Of course they hadn't exercised precautions. And she should have seen it coming.

Hank reached for her arm and pulled her back toward his car. "Stop it, Alice. Just stop!"

She heard a yell escape from her throat—a primal sound that she never would have recognized as her own voice. In that one, prolonged cry, she felt the pain of what was happening now—harm to the police officers whom she'd sent into that apartment, perhaps the loss of any chance to ever speak to the sole person who might exonerate her—and the pain of what had already come to pass—her brother's death, the sight of Travis Larson's bloodied corpse. All of it rose at once and rippled through her body, releasing itself through that horrible sound. She felt herself shivering against Hank Beckman.

"Alice. Alice, is that you?" Beckman held her tightly against his chest, patting the back of her head, but someone else was calling her name now. She peered out across Hank's shoulder and saw Arthur crossing the street, car keys in hand. "I almost didn't recognize you with that hairdo. I saw a parking spot a couple blocks away and figured I better grab it. What is going on here?"

CHAPTER FIFTY-FIVE

Alice tapped her nails against Hank Beckman's steering wheel, trying not to think about the minutes that had passed since he'd instructed her to pull the car to the curb while he made his way into Mia's building. Arthur started to ask another question from the passenger seat, but she shushed him, wanting to focus on the silence that existed beyond the sounds of her tapping fingernails and the car's idling engine.

Silence was a good thing, she kept reminding herself. Silence meant no more gunshots. Silence meant Hank was all right.

Sirens broke through the hush that had fallen over the neighborhood since the gunfire. The sounds were muted at first, but grew louder, then stopped. Help had arrived. Whatever had unfolded at Mia's address, backup officers would be there by now, along with ambulances for anyone who was injured. It was another half an hour before her cell phone rang. She nearly dropped it in her rush to answer.

"Hank?"

"Everyone's fine."

"Really? Danes? Shannon?"

"Danes came with cooperating law enforcement from New Jersey. They're both absolutely fine. Not a scratch."

"But the gunfire—"

"Mia popped off a few shots when they arrived. They both returned fire. When backup arrived, they entered the premises and found the subject on the floor, dead from what appears to be a single gunshot to the face." Alice noticed that he had slipped into whatever sterile mode of speaking he had learned as an FBI agent. "It's unclear whether the bullet came from law enforcement or was perhaps self-inflicted when she realized she couldn't escape. The good news is, she was packing a .38."

She didn't understand the significance.

"That's the same kind of gun used to kill Travis Larson. They'll run the ballistics. This is the beginning of the end, Alice. This is a good thing."

"Did you see her?"

"Mia? Yeah, only for a second. Danes cleared me out pronto."

"What did she look like?"

"You don't want to know. Look: it's too early to be definitive, but I've been doing this a long time. My instincts are telling me we were right. This all still needs to play out, but we were right. You're going to be okay."

She felt herself start to cry and gave a reassuring nod to Arthur in the passenger seat. "So what do I do now? Do they still want me to turn myself in? I'm willing to. I'm ready to do it."

"No, but I think you need to come here. Danes found something he wants to show you."

"What is it?"

"I don't know, but he thinks you need to see it for yourself."

She and Arthur walked the quick block and a half to Mia's apartment. Hank met them outside, ushering them past a perimeter that a uniformed officer was beginning to erect with yellow crime tape. They stopped at the landing outside the building entrance. Hank disappeared inside, then reemerged with Willie Danes. For the first time since that initial meeting when she'd found Travis Larson's body at the gallery, he shook her hand.

"Once we were clear, we did a sweep through the apartment to make sure there was no one on the premises. This happened to catch my eye." Danes handed her a framed photograph. "It was on her dresser."

The woman at the center of the five-by-seven looked thin and pale, her hair like matted straw against her scalp. Five women surrounded her, trying their best to look celebratory. Two of them meant nothing in particular to Alice, but three were significant. One was sweet Mrs. Withers, looking very much the same as she had earlier this morning when she'd sunk those marshmallows in the hot chocolate. One was a relatively attractive younger woman—probably early twenties. She had long red hair with orange and blond streaks, and what Mrs. Withers had described as a honey-and-strawberries complexion. She looked like a younger version of Alice. The final woman had short, wispy white-blond hair and dark green eyes that penetrated the camera. Her long, lanky arms were wrapped around the frail-looking woman in the center and the red-head who was undoubtedly Mia Andrews.

In retrospect, the fifth woman in the photograph had been there at every turn of the previous month. She had been the one to initially tell Alice that Drew Campbell was too good to be true, only to encourage her to meet him when he called. She had been the one to tell Alice not to dig too deeply into the background of Highline Gallery. She had been the one to dissuade her from calling Robert Atkinson while the reporter was still alive to tell his story. She had been the one to inform the police that Alice owned a pair of crocodile-embossed gloves lined with fur that might or might not be real mink. She had been the one to encourage Alice to run from the police.

The final woman in the photograph—the one nestled closest to a cancer-ridden Christie Kinley as she hosted the final party of her life—was Lily Harper.

CHAPTER FIFTY-SIX

For two hours, she and Arthur had waited in Arthur's parked Lexus, intermittently running the engine for warmth, while Hank dashed back and forth between Mia's apartment and the car, assuring them each time that Danes had "promised" they'd be ready for her soon. But "ready" no longer meant an expectation that she would be turning herself in to face charges of murdering her supposed coconspirator and lover, Travis Larson. Now Alice the former fugitive was their best hope of understanding why Mia Andrews had opened fire on two police officers when they knocked on her door.

After two hours of waiting beyond the growing swarm of police cars, they finally received instructions to head up to the Thirteenth Precinct. Danes and the New Jersey officer who accompanied him would be required to follow protocol for an officer-involved shooting, but John Shannon would meet them there.

Hank smiled when he delivered the news that a patrol car transport would not be necessary. She was free to ride with her attorney. Hank would drive his own car. If she still wanted him. As a translator of sorts. But only if she wanted him to go.

It had taken nearly three hours for the three of them—Hank, Alice, and Arthur—to lay out everything she had learned about Christie Kinley, Mia Andrews, and Robert Atkinson: that night in

Bedford, the settlement and confidentiality agreement, Mia's birth while Christie was supposedly at boarding school, Atkinson's attempts to locate the old police reports. And, finally, Lily Harper, whom she had met at the gym six months earlier.

It was after midnight. Shannon had given her the option of going home for a few hours of sleep before resuming in the morning, but Alice had spent too many days without answers. If the NYPD had been slow to believe her in the beginning, the gunfire at Mia Andrews's home had kicked them into Alice Humphrey—exoneration overdrive. She was afraid that if she fell asleep, she'd wake up to a new reality. And she wanted to think about something other than Ben overdosing in his bathroom.

So now she, her lawyer, and her new friend, Hank, sat huddled around John Shannon's desk as they watched two uniformed officers escort Lily Harper into an interrogation room. Her once-trusted eyes remained locked on Alice as she walked the gauntlet, but Alice could read no emotion in them.

Once Lily was out of sight, Alice assumed her spot behind a one-way mirror, as Detective Shannon had instructed, ready to hear what her good friend had to say for herself.

Some facts simply could not be denied. Yes, Lily conceded, she knew Christie Kinley. They'd grown up together in Mount Kisco. Raised by her widower father, Lily had spent more nights at the Kinley home than her own. Practically a sister to her, Christie had remained Lily's closest friend until her death. And, yes, she had known and practically helped raise Christie's younger sister, Mia, and had watched her grow up into a troubled and yet nevertheless loved young woman. Lily's admission of these truths meant nothing to Alice. After all, Detective Shannon had already shown her the photograph they'd found in Mia's apartment.

But when it came to any involvement on Mia Andrews's part in the bizarre events at the Highline Gallery, Lily feigned ignorance.

"I'm very sorry, Detective, but if you could please slow down and show a little empathy here. Your officers just dragged me from my home with no explanation, and now you've told me that cops killed a girl who was practically my own baby sister."

Maybe Lily was the one who should have gone into acting.

"For the record, your honorary baby sister fired on them first, and the preliminary report from the scene is that she shot herself when she realized she couldn't escape. We are looking now for connections between Mia and Travis Larson, the man who used the name Drew Campbell when he hired Alice to work at the gallery. We will find those links, Lily. There's no doubt about it. Her fingerprints at his place, or his at hers. Phone records. E-mails. It will happen. And once we have that evidence, do you really want to be nailed down on your story that you had absolutely no idea that Alice's dream job had something to do with Mia and her scumbag boyfriend? If I were you, I'd start looking to help yourself."

"I never *met* Drew Campbell! I knew Mia was seeing a guy, but if it was the man who hired Alice, I certainly had no idea of that."

"Was Mia's boyfriend named Travis Larson?"

Someone who didn't know Lily would have said she answered without hesitation. But Alice knew her. Or at least she thought she had. And she could tell Lily paused.

"Yes, I met him. Once. Down in Williamsburg, for dinner." Dinner meant potential witnesses. Some facts simply could not be denied. "But how was I supposed to know he was the same guy who hired Alice? Are you sure Mia was involved? I can't even begin to wrap my head around this."

"Can you think of some other reason she might have opened fire on two police officers?"

"I didn't even know she owned a gun."

"Well, apparently she did, and it's probably going to turn out to be the same weapon that killed her boyfriend. You deny knowing anything about the gallery setup, so let's go back in time. What did you know about Christie Kinley's settlement with Frank Humphrey?"

"Nothing."

"This woman was one of your closest friends, and she never told you that Frank Humphrey raped her?"

Lily was thinking again. Mentally lining all the ducks in a row. How much could she deny? "I knew something bad happened to her. I wasn't at that party, or maybe it wouldn't have happened. But she told me the next day she got so drunk she blacked out. But she could tell—you know, from pain down there—that something might have happened. Something sexual. And then when she opened her purse, she found a camera and remembered the guy taking pictures. She must have grabbed it afterward when she ran out."

"So you knew about the pictures all these years."

"But I never saw them. I knew she was planning to go to the AV room at school to develop them, to get evidence against the guy. But then when I talked to her the next week, she said she didn't want to have to testify and all that stuff. She never told me who the guy was, but I just assumed it was one of the other kids at the party. A couple of months later, she said her mom was pissed at her for getting so drunk and was sending her away for a year."

"So you're trying to tell me that you didn't know Mia was Christie and Frank Humphrey's daughter?"

More thinking. More calculating.

"Let me give you some advice, Lily. If you think there is even the slightest possibility that what you say here tonight is going to get you out of this jam, you are absolutely mistaken. Tonight is just the beginning. Whatever version of events you give us tonight, I am going to search high and low for evidence that's either going to back that up or prove to me you're a liar. I've got an officer outside your apartment right now, securing the premises until we get a warrant. We will search your computer. We'll read every e-mail you ever exchanged with Mia. We'll check your search history and see if you've been Googling Frank Humphrey in your spare time. Or if you checked out Alice before coincidentally befriending her at the gym. So I would choose your next words very carefully."

She sighed dramatically, as if to acknowledge that this time, she was truly coming clean. "I had no idea about Frank Humphrey's involvement, or even about Christie getting pregnant, until after Christie passed away. I was helping Mia clean out the house to get it ready for sale, and that's when we found all the papers."

"What papers?"

"Everything. Gloria—that's Christie and Mia's mom, or I guess only Christie's mom—anyway, Gloria must have kept a file of everything, just in case. The photographs from that night. A copy of the police report Christie filed the day after the party. The settlement agreement. Mia's birth records. The formal adoption by Gloria. We were in absolute shock."

"And a couple of months later, you just happen to meet Frank Humphrey's daughter and become one of her closest friends? It sounds to me like you and Mia spent those months planning your revenge."

"It wasn't like that. Yes, I'd say we were both pretty angry. I mean, here's this grown man who fucking *raped* a fourteen-year-old girl and got off scot-free."

"It was your friend and her mom who decided to settle."

"Christie's mother was hardly a stable parent, and Christie would have known how badly her mother needed that money. And I'm sure Frank Humphrey's lawyer threatened to make those photographs public and to argue that Christie had been asking for it. So, yeah, she settled for the money, but it doesn't make what Frank Humphrey did right."

Alice hated that she found herself agreeing with her friend. She wanted so badly to believe there was an explanation for what Lily had done to her.

"Mia and I were both following Humphrey's sex scandals really closely—like maybe these tabloid stories were karma biting him in the ass. And one night when I was surfing the news about him, I Googled the daughter who had given him an alibi."

Even though the conversation in the room was being piped in through speakers, Alice leaned closer to the glass, as if proximity might help her understand.

"I found her Facebook page. It was so weird to think that this woman whose paths had crossed with Christie's so long ago was living just a few blocks from me. Her profile mentioned which gym she went to, so, yeah, I was curious. I wanted to know whether Frank Humphrey's family had any idea what kind of man he is. But then, you know what? Alice was just a regular person. And she wasn't exactly giving her father a free pass. I liked her. And she became my friend."

Alice wondered if Lily knew she was listening.

"You mentioned that you saw the settlement agreement."

"Yes."

"Then you would have seen that the agreement was between Christie and a company called ITH."

"Yes." Alice suspected that search teams at Mia's apartment would soon find that old file of documents, and Lily's fingerprints would be on them.

Alice saw a flicker behind Lily's eyes as she realized the mistake she had made. Lily had been sitting right next to Alice when she had given Detective Shannon a copy of her pay stub with the ITH company name on it. They had talked about that name several times afterward. She had to have made the connection.

"I went to Mia the next day and confronted her." Alice felt a scream building in her chest. This woman had played her from the very beginning, and now she was doing the same with Shannon. "She told me what she had done. Travis had a plan to sell porn without going through the Internet. I didn't understand why that would be profitable—"

"Because it was child porn, Miss Harper. Your favorite little sister was peddling child porn with her boyfriend."

Lily swallowed. "I had no idea, obviously. Mia made it sound like sex tapes or something. Travis had this plan, and she knew from me that Alice was in the art world and needed a job. She saw an opportunity to set Alice up as the fall guy. The money from the sales all got wired overseas. They'd run the scam for a while, then pull the plug and leave her high and dry."

"Did she tell you she killed Travis Larson?"

She nodded. "The protesters outside the gallery had him spooked. Alice was demanding to speak to the gallery owner. The press was trying to find the supposed artist. It would only be a matter of time before someone figured out what was embedded in those thumb drives. Travis was supposed to call Alice and calm her down, but Mia heard him tell Alice to meet the next morning at the gallery. She went there and confronted him. He was planning to double-cross her. He was going to blame everything on Mia and then try to cozy up to Alice in the hopes of getting into her family money."

Alice felt Hank's eyes on her. The plan Lily described sounded right up Travis Larson's alley.

"You told me you didn't know Mia had a gun."

"I meant that I didn't know at first. She told me all this after the fact."

"And from then on you decided you'd help frame Alice Humphrey."

"No, I did not. I was trying to figure out how to help her without turning in Mia."

"You ratted Alice out when we asked you about those gloves we found near the murder scene. Then you told her to run, pretty much guaranteeing her conviction."

"I assumed her father would hire a bunch of lawyers to get her out of it. I didn't want anything bad to happen to her. I know it sounds weird, but I do care about her. She's my friend. But Mia— Mia was . . . troubled. Seriously troubled, okay? But she was like family. I didn't know what to do. You have to believe me."

The tears that were beginning to fall seemed real, but Alice had one question for her friend that Shannon had not yet raised.

"Can I talk to Detective Shannon?" she asked.

Arthur Cronin was the kind of lawyer who had no qualms about tapping on the interrogation room glass. Shannon looked annoyed but stepped out of the room.

"I'm sorry, Detective, but she's lying."

"I know that. She's admitting only as much as she has to and dis-puting everything else."

"She wants you to believe that Mia did all of this on her own, and she only helped her after the fact. Mia Andrews wore my gloves and then left them near the crime scene with gunshot residue on them. But how did Mia get my gloves in the first place?"

When Shannon returned to the interrogation room to ask that very question, Lily Harper stopped crying and asked for a lawyer.

CHAPTER FIFTY-SEVEN

TWO WEEKS LATER

"I'd have to say this has been a much more pleasant visit than the last couple of times you popped in on me."

Alice poured coffee for Detectives John Shannon and Willie Danes, as if they were two old pals in her living room rather than the two men who had tried to put her behind bars for the rest of her life.

"Your hair's back to red," Danes observed, gesturing awkwardly to her head.

"Yeah, the bottled version for now. The red roots were poking through. I looked like Pepé Le Pew on acid."

"Again, we just really want to apologize, both officially on behalf of the NYPD, but also for ourselves. We realize in retrospect that you were trying to work with us. We were too convinced of what we thought was the truth to hear you out."

They had already given her a layperson's debriefing of the case. Mia Andrews's neighbors could place Travis Larson at Mia's apartment as early as eight months ago. That photograph of her kissing Larson—planted on "Drew Campbell's" fake Facebook profile for police to find—had looked candid but was one of sixty similarly staged images found in Mia's digital camera. Activity on Mia's home computer proved that the artwork supposedly by Hans Schuler was her own. She had also been the one to join a members-only message board catering to "specialty erotica," advertising the Schuler exhibit at Highline Gallery and promising "secret bonus photographs with no traceable downloads" for those who followed the posted instructions. The .38 she used to deliver a fatal shot to her head was the same weapon used to kill Travis Larson. Robert Atkinson's briefcase and laptop were also found in her apartment.

"Will you ever know for certain whether she killed my brother?"

Danes frowned. "We're sorry, Alice. Nothing in her apartment ties her to Ben. We did, however, find recent calls from your brother to a suspected dealer. We spoke to that individual, and he indicated that your brother had started using again. What happens sometimes is, if a person who had been using drugs stops—as your brother did—his tolerance goes down. If he slips and uses the same amount, what used to be an acceptable quantity is just too much."

"I see."

"I mean, it's possible she somehow mixed his stash with something purer. Or maybe she got there after the fact and rifled through the apartment, as you suspected someone had."

Or it was possible her brother was a junkie who had let the multimillion-dollar loft her parents had purchased for him go to shit before sticking a needle in his arm one last time.

"It's okay, Detective. I understand."

Arthur had advised her what to expect. This home visit was part of the department's overall damage-control strategy. The city's attorneys had probably counseled them to win her over in an attempt to forestall a lawsuit.

As far as she was concerned, however, there was only one thing she wanted from them.

"Why hasn't Lily Harper been arrested?"

Danes looked at Shannon, who decided to do the talking on that one.

"The statements she made before lawyering up have actually panned out. If in fact she did not know about Mia's involvement with your job at the gallery until *after* Larson was murdered, then she's not an accessory."

"She led you to believe I was a murderer."

"And unfortunately the law does not impose a duty upon people to come forward to us with the truth. Even if she knew Mia was responsible, she doesn't have to report her. The only affirmative statement she ever made to us was when we asked her to identify your gloves. She told us they were yours, which was, in fact, a truthful statement. Letting you hang in the wind makes her a shitty person, but not an accomplice."

Arthur had already tried to explain that aspect of the law to her.

"But how else could Mia have gotten my gloves? Lily must have given them to her, which proves she knew what Mia was up to."

The detectives exchanged glances again.

"Will you please stop staring at each other and just talk to me like a normal person? I'm not going to sue you, but I want you to be honest with me. I deserve that. At the very least, I deserve absolute honesty."

"You're right," Shannon said. "I'm sorry. Lily's attorney has an explanation for the gloves. You remember how you thought Larson first found you at that art showing because you had it posted on your Facebook page?"

She nodded.

"Well, the following night, you posted something about a killer pizza at a place called Otto?"

She remembered. "Clams. It was a clam pizza."

"Did you happen to check your coat?" She nodded. "Lily's lawyer pointed out that Mia could have worn her matching blue coat to Otto and pulled some stunt at the coat check about the gloves."

"Or, more likely, Lily knows I always check my coat because the bar gets so crowded, and she's had two weeks to think up a story."

"You wanted honesty, Alice, and I'm giving it to you straight. No bullshit. You've got a valid point about those gloves, but we're never going to know for sure. And no prosecutor's going to try Lily based only on our speculation about those gloves."

"So Lily walks?"

"We're pushing the DA to charge her with obstruction. We'd argue that her linking you to the gloves, knowing full well you were innocent, essentially obligated her to tell us the whole truth. She also counseled you to run, which we might be able to bootstrap into something."

"You don't sound optimistic."

"It's up to the DA. Even if we can convince him to file, she probably won't do time. And she'll haul out the sad story about her dead friend and her secret daughter and all of that in the process."

"At least there's some good news," Danes said, searching for a change in subject. "You probably heard that your father's in the clear."

Even though Alice's arrest warrant was promptly withdrawn, the affidavit filed in its support had been leaked to the media. An enterprising reporter at the *National Enquirer* had unearthed the old blind item by Robert Atkinson. It had taken the churning wheel of Internet news only three days to declare Academy Award–winning director Frank Humphrey a child rapist.

When the district attorney's office asked her father for a DNA sample, Arthur wanted to fight it. The statute of limitations on anything that had happened in 1985 had long passed. The government was just doing the tabloid media's bidding, Arthur argued. But for the first time in a long while, her father had done the right thing. He had made the decision with only one interest in mind—the truth.

"So does anyone even know who Mia's father actually was?"

The funny thing about the truth was its constant ability to surprise. Even though her father had been resigned to accept the fact that he had fathered the illegitimate child of a barely teenage girl in 1985, Frank Humphrey's DNA did not, in fact, match Mia Andrews's. Christie Kinley may have believed that her pregnancy resulted from that night in her father's office, but she'd been mistaken.

Danes shook his head. "Could be anyone in Westchester County, from what we hear."

"And how are *you* holding up?" she asked. She had been through hell, but Willie Danes was the one who'd been shot at.

"I'm back on the job, as you can see. The guy from New Jersey and I were both cleared in our involvement. It shouldn't have happened that way. If I'd been treating your information more seriously, we could have gotten her out alive."

"Well, it sounds like she was the one who decided how it would end. Your bullets didn't kill her." Ballistics tests had proven that Mia Andrews's own gun had delivered the fatal shot to her face.

"I suppose there's that. The irony is that she could've just run down the fire escape when we knocked. She must've assumed we'd brought the cavalry."

"The bigger mystery is what Becca Stevenson's fingerprints were doing in that gallery bathroom," Shannon said. "We haven't found a single piece of evidence to tie Mia to Becca, but, as of three days ago, the NYPD officially declared us uninvolved in her disappearance. The investigation is back in Jersey. Anyhoo, got any other questions we can answer?"

They placed their coffee cups on the table in synchronicity, and she could tell they were eager to put this case in their rearview mirror.

"Not right now, detectives, but I will certainly call you if I need anything. And I do appreciate your coming here."

They apologized once again as they made their way out the door.

She would have thought that the news about Lily not being charged would be the sour note ringing in her head after the detectives' departure. Instead, she kept hearing Danes's voice: *Your father's in the clear.*

Alice had been at her parents' apartment when Arthur had called them with the news. Her mother had actually let out a little yelp, as if the fact that her husband hadn't actually impregnated his rape victim was something to celebrate. At least her father had the decency to be somber.

On the same day he had agreed to the blood test, her father had paid her an unannounced visit to confess everything he remembered about April 18, 1985—which was very little. Mom had gone to bed early, annoyed at how much he'd been drinking at dinner. Alice broke in to point out the irony of that detail, given how their lives had played out in the intervening quarter century, but it was clear her father did not want to be interrupted.

He knew Ben and his friends were drinking out back, but the boy's sixteenth birthday had been the previous weekend, and it seemed like harmless high school mischief. Arthur called it quits shortly after dinner himself. Alice had been begging to watch the screening copy of *Goonies* he had scored from Warner Brothers, so the two of them had moved into the theater. His rendition was just as Alice remembered the night.

As her father slowly recited his version of the evening, she realized that he had somehow convinced himself that his baby girl had forgotten his pre-sobriety days. "I was upset with your mother, even though she had a point about the drinking. But knowing she was right, and knowing she had locked herself away in our room because of it, only made me want to drink more. To this day, I can't tell you what that damn *Goonies* movie is even about, I was so inebriated. I passed out. And don't get me wrong, it wasn't the first time. But I actually *blacked* out. I woke up in the morning on the floor of the theater, and I couldn't remember a thing. When I saw Arthur later, he made some remark about the girl being too young even for me, and I didn't even know what he was talking about. He told me he walked out of the guest cottage to smoke a cigar and saw me talking to one of the girls from Ben's party. Obviously, his comment was just a joke. As you know by now, Alice—and this isn't easy for me to talk about with you—but, as you know, I have not always been faithful, not even close. And Arthur knew that. But he was only kidding. Of course I would never even think of striking something up with a girl of that age."

She had wanted to yell at him. *But you did, Dad. And it's not "strik-*

ing something up" when the girl is fourteen years old. But she said nothing and allowed him to continue his monologue.

"And then the police came on Sunday and told me a girl from the party was claiming I raped her. She said I took pictures during the act. I went into my office, and my camera was gone. The girl said she grabbed it when she ran away. I didn't know what to say. I knew that if I told them I was too drunk to remember where I had been all night, they would take me away. That's when I found you in your room. I brought you into my office to talk to them because I knew you would tell them we were watching a movie. I knew it would be just enough of an alibi to keep them from arresting me. I called Arthur right away, and we wound up reaching a settlement with the girl and her family."

"Her name was Christie, Papa. Christie Kinley, but her real name was Julie."

"Alice, I know you've been angry at me for some time now, and I can only wonder whether you will ever forgive me after what happened to you because of my mistakes. But I am trying to make it right. That is why I'm doing this blood test. I don't want to cover anything up anymore. You may not know this, but I never took another sip of alcohol once those officers knocked on our door. Not one sip. Because the fact that I could have done something like that—that I'll never even *know* the depths to which I sunk that night—made me hate myself. And I never wanted to be whatever man I became that night, not ever again. But I realize now that I felt entitled all those years. Because I'd quit drinking—because I had put that night behind me—I felt entitled to indulge other vices. And I felt entitled because your mother and I—well, we have our issues. But I never realized that the way I've carried on all these years was not just a betrayal of your mother and our wedding vows—words we long ago wrote off as more aspirational than anything—but a betrayal of you and Ben, and of me as a man. And that's what I came here to say. That I'm sorry. That to put my own baby girl in jeopardy is the worst crime a man could ever commit. And that, even though I'm getting to be an old man now, I plan on changing. For the better. So that you will let me be your father again. You're all I have left now, Alice. I need to be your father again."

She had cried. So had he. Ben was gone. She wasn't. She had promised him that she would find a way to forgive him.

So she might be able to keep her promise, she had been avoiding all media coverage about the story. She did not need to see photographs of her father emblazoned with the words *child rapist*. Or of her mother: "What did she know?" Or even the one she had seen of her brother: "Did Daddy's secrets cause him to OD?"

But now, sitting in her living room, flipping through her beloved *Entertainment Weekly*, she was unexpectedly confronted with a sidebar about the case. She checked the date on the cover. It was last week's edition, before the DNA results came in.

RAPE, LOVE CHILD, OR BOTH?

Academy Award—winning director Frank Humphrey reportedly settled a lawsuit in 1985 arising from allegations that he raped a fourteen-year-old acquaintance of his children. Now sources report that Mia Andrews (below), who killed herself last week in a police standoff, may have been the daughter from that ill-fated night. Humphrey's son, Ben, 41, died of a heroin overdose the day before the standoff.

She found herself staring at the photograph of Mia. She wasn't her perfect doppelgänger, but there was undoubtedly a resemblance, enough so that even Alice had been certain that the grainy picture of Mia kissing Travis Larson was a doctored photo of Alice.

She opened her laptop and searched until she found a site that had published a photograph of Christie Kinley. She hadn't realized it until now, but Christie looked like a younger version of her mother, like all those other women who had come forward last year to claim celebrity mistress status. Was the resemblance between Christie and Alice's mother sufficient to explain the similarity between Mia and Alice?

Alice stared again at Mia's photograph. No, Mia looked like her mother's daughter, but she looked even more like Alice. And there was only one way that could be true.

She rifled through her purse until she found the business card that was first handed to her the day she discovered Travis Larson's body. She had hoped she would never need to dial this number again. Detective Shannon answered. "Hi, Alice. I can't imagine you missed us already."

"No, but I'm afraid there still might be one loose end."

CHAPTER
FIFTY-EIGHT

Jason Morhart managed to cram his truck into the hybrid-sized spot at the curb outside Bloomingdale's.

It had been three days since the NYPD had broken the news. They had wrapped up their investigation and were about to tie the pretty little bow into a nice, neat package without any explanation for Becca Stevenson's disappearance.

Sometimes investigations required you to look at a case through a different lens—to start over again with no assumptions and to rethink facts and events in a new light. Maybe if Willie Danes and John Shannon had done that when they first learned about Mia Andrews, the woman might still be alive, and Jason wouldn't be waking up in cold sweats every night wondering whether he could have prevented the shooting in Williamsburg.

But now it was time for him to take a fresh look at Becca Stevenson's disappearance. He realized now that he had stopped challenging himself for explanations the minute he'd learned about the fingerprint match in Highline Gallery. From that moment on, he'd been convinced that his case was inextricably entwined with the NYPD's. He'd allowed himself to become complacent, waiting for them to arrest their suspect, who would in turn point him toward Becca.

But now the NYPD had all of its answers, and he was the one left with questions.

Where was Becca? How had her fingerprints wound up in High-line Gallery? And the question he kept coming back to, the one he knew *had* to be answered: How could it possibly be a coincidence that the Reverend George Hardy just *happened* to be protesting that very gallery?

He found Hardy and his protesters outside the Little Angels store where they'd last spoken.

"Back down here again, are you?"

"We get a big reaction down in SoHo. People don't understand that yelling at us—calling us hate mongers and Jesus freaks—only makes us stronger. And only brings us more attention, which ultimately builds our flock. This spot here's been good for us, yes it has."

"I don't know if you've been following that story about Highline Gallery."

"A bunch of wicked sinners there. I knew it from the start."

"Here's the thing, Reverend. I suspect you love Becca."

"I surely do. She's my daughter. My blood."

"And I think you're worried about her. I also believe that you follow a higher law, something grander than man's law. Finally, I believe—no, I am *convinced*—that your decision to picket the High-line Gallery is somehow related to the fact that your daughter's fingerprints were found on the bathroom door of that building."

"That's a lot of beliefs you have there, sir."

"When I put all of those beliefs together, Reverend, this is the conclusion I have to draw: you are privy to information that you still have not disclosed to the police. At the time you held it back, you did so with the firm conviction that somehow you were protecting Becca. But now all this time has passed, and no one has heard from your daughter. My guess is, you're starting to wonder whether you did the right thing by her."

The reverend was silent.

"The NYPD is shutting down its investigation. That leaves me and my Podunk department the last ones looking for Becca. And my best lead is still that dag-nab fingerprint, which brings me right back to the fact you were protesting that very same gallery. If there's any more information to offer, sir, I'm telling you that now's the time to divulge it."

Hardy's eyes moved between Jason and his fellow protesters. "It's a bit nippy today. Maybe you know a place where we can get a cup of tea."

The two of them had been Mutt and Jeff on the streets of SoHo, with Hardy dragging around his sign and megaphone, and Jason's fanny pack broadcasting to all the world that he was either a cop or tourist. They did, however, manage to find a café with cups of tea. They were $6 cups of tea, but Jason could justify the expense if his instincts were right.

"You're a smart man, Mr. Morhart, and I can tell that you care about the well-being of my daughter."

"I do, sir. I want to find her and bring her home."

"I will tell you everything I know, but I will not allow you to judge me. I know in my heart I was trying to do right by Becca." He waited for Jason to protest, but hearing nothing, proceeded. "I was with Becca that night after she left her friend's house. We had arranged to meet down the street. That's what we had been doing. Mostly we would talk on the phone. And once she rode the train into the city—I believe she told her mother she was doing some kind of school activity—but I tried to drive out to Dover and catch a few minutes with her as I could. We'd leave Dover proper. See the parks in that area and whatnot."

Jason wanted to grab the delicate tea cup from Hardy's fingertips and smash it against his head, but he tried to remain expressionless.

"To understand what happened that night, you first have to know that the last time I had seen her was three weeks prior. That was the day she rode the train into the city. The plan had been for me to drive her back home after some sightseeing, but then she told me she was meeting some friends from school and asked me to drop her off downtown. I was uncomfortable dumping her in the middle of this hedonistic jungle, but she pointed out that if I waited for her friends to arrive, one of them might mention my existence to her mother. Frankly, I recognized that to be a bit of emotional blackmail, but I realized this was probably normal for a teenager, so I agreed.

"I am not, however, stupid. I cruised my car around the corner so I could make certain she was in the safety of a circle of suitable friends. Instead, I saw her talking to a man who was either locking or unlocking that gallery on Washington Street. A grown man. And rough looking."

"Travis Larson."

The reverend nodded. "Of course, I did not know his name at the time. Nor did I know the place was a gallery. It was empty. But I did see him open that door. And I did see my daughter walk into that building with him. She lied to me. My own daughter. She had me deliver her into the waiting hands of a grown man."

"When was this?"

He doodled on the table, counting days backward. "Six Sundays ago." Precisely three weeks before Becca disappeared. It was also the same date as the photographs Becca had posted on Facebook. Hardy concluded his daughter had lied, but she really had met her friends. Or at least, she had believed at the time they were her friends.

"Go on."

"So when I saw her that last night, I asked her about it. Oh, boy, was she ever angry that I watched her." Jason could tell from the man's tone that he admired his daughter's temper. "She swore up and down that she didn't even know that man. That she had to go pee and saw the man there at the store and asked if she could use the bathroom. According to her, she was in and out of there in a few minutes."

"That's *it*? We've spent all these days trying to find a connection between Becca and that gallery, and all she did was use the bathroom?"

"Well, that's what she would've had me believe."

He wanted the man to get to his point, but the reverend was obviously used to a captive audience.

"We went to the Dairy Queen off Route 15, and when she went to the little girls' room, I looked at her cell phone. Now, don't go judging me. She was only a child, and I bought her that phone for the purpose of communicating with me. I felt I was in the right. But when I looked in that phone, I saw the filth she'd engaged in. The dirty talk. And not just talk, I saw that picture. I saw that picture . . . of my own *daughter*."

Jason could tell where this story was headed. He wanted to jump into the narrative and stop it. He wanted to run inside that Dairy Queen and tell this man he was making a horrible mistake.

"What did you do?"

"I went to the car, and I waited for her. When she got in, I did what I thought a father should do. I told her she had sinned. That the Lord saw all. That peddlers of flesh would be judged both here and in the hereafter."

Based on what Joann had told him about George Hardy's reaction to her pregnancy, Jason could only imagine the insults this man must have hurled at Becca. A teenage girl who had always been described as fragile. Who had opened herself up sexually for the first time to a boy, only to have him turn her into a laughingstock. Who had recently learned that the mother she trusted had lied to her about the circumstances of her own birth. Who was only beginning to know the father she never realized she had, only to have him call her the ugly words Jason knew the man had used.

"Why didn't you tell anyone this, George?"

The reverend's eyes were puffy and rimmed with red, the result of sleepless nights, tears, and (Jason guessed) regular tips of alcohol. "Just wait for me to explain it my way, all right, son? A couple days went by, and I didn't feel right about how we left it. I tried calling her, but she wasn't getting back to me. I assumed she was mad."

"You didn't know she was missing?"

"Who was going to tell me? Certainly not that mother of hers. So I drove by that storefront again, thinking I might find that man. Confront him. Tell him to stay away from Becca. And by that time, it was no longer vacant. It had opened as what they were calling a gallery. I saw those pictures on display in there. A man biting himself. And you can't tell me that one with the girl's belly in it was of a full-grown woman."

"You assumed the man you'd seen at the gallery had taken improper photographs of Becca."

"Of course I did. I saw some with my own eyes. I thought about calling the police directly, but then I'd have to tell them Becca was in those nasty pictures."

"You were worried about her reputation."

"Among other things, yes, I was. So I did what my church does best. I brought attention to the issue."

"By protesting."

"Yes, sir."

"You thought if the press made the artist prove the age of the models in those photographs, you'd get the artwork removed without having to drag your daughter's name into the matter."

"I'm not a total fool, you see? But now here's the thing that's important for you to understand. I *still* didn't know Becca was missing on that day we were protesting. It wasn't until the *next* day that I heard about Becca's disappearance on the radio news."

"That was the day Travis Larson was found dead at the gallery."

"And I heard about that story, too. Do you see what I'm getting at?"

"You didn't say anything because you thought Becca might have been involved in Travis's murder."

"I saw her with the man. And the man was trouble. It stood to reason."

"But now the NYPD knows who killed Larson, and Becca didn't have anything to do with it."

"I'm aware of that, son. And that's why I've told you everything I know."

"On that last night with Becca, how did you leave things?"

Hardy was fiddling with the handle of his empty teacup. "Not well. She jumped out of the car. I didn't stop her."

"Where?"

• • •

Jason called his captain as soon as he was inside his truck. "I got a lead on Becca Stevenson. She was last seen distraught near the vicinity of the River Styx Road marina, over by Lake Hopatcong."

"This is a solid tip?"

"Like a rock."

"What was she doing way over by the lake?"

She'd been having ice cream with a man whose love she had wanted more than life itself. She'd been having ice cream with a man who dealt her fragile sense of self the final blow. "We need to get divers down into the water, sir."

His next call was to Joann Stevenson. It would be the second hardest telephone call he would ever have to make. The hardest would come the following morning, when he had to tell her over the phone that her daughter's body had been found, just to be sure she didn't hear it first from someone else.

CHAPTER
FIFTY-NINE

"This is certainly a lovely treat." Arthur Cronin was inspecting the pear-glazed pork loin the waitress had placed on the table. He waited while a second staff member poured a thin drizzle of sauce across the dish. "It's not every day that one of my favorite people invites me to lunch. And with such panache."

"Well, it's not every day someone saves me from life in prison."

"I never would have let that happen, sweetie, but in this instance, I'd have to say your friendly neighborhood FBI agent probably did more of the work than your Uncle Artie. Any chance of a love connection there?"

"He was just doing the right thing, Art."

"But, let me guess, he's called you a time or two to see how you're holding up?"

She smiled.

"Aha! I knew it! What about that schlub of yours? Jeff from Indiana, isn't it?"

"You know quite well that his name is Jeff Wilkerson."

"How is Mr. Wilkerson dealing with your new FBI friend?"

"We're not actually talking right now."

"The on and off is off again, huh?" He was talking between bites now. She forced herself to take a bite of her pasta. If she didn't eat, he might know something was wrong.

"Actually, Art, Jeff asked me to marry him."

He dropped his fork to his plate. "Get out of town! Wilkie finally manned up, did he? Where's the ring? Tell me the man bought you a ring!"

She whispered a shh. She had chosen this restaurant because she knew it would be empty, but even five tables away, a fellow diner could overhear raised voices.

"I politely declined."

"You finally figured out you're too good for him."

"No, but it wasn't right. It never will be." She felt funny talking to Art about her love life, but she needed the conversation to seem natural.

"Still that thing about the kids?"

"I guess my father told you about it."

He waved his hand with a *pssh*. "A long time ago, when you broke up for a while."

When Jeff had proposed, she had almost accepted immediately. But she wanted to make sure he had really thought about the decision. She did not want their marriage to be an impulsive reaction to the events of the previous week. So she had stated her concerns. "But you so desperately want children."

And he had answered, "I love you, Alice. I would sacrifice anything for you. Anything."

Sacrifice. To be with her meant he would not have children of his own flesh and blood. And she knew Jeff. He would always see that as a sacrifice.

Those were details she would not share with Arthur. "It just wasn't going to work out. We should have realized that a long time ago, but what can I say? We're a couple of idiots. I'm fine now."

She wasn't fine. She had lost her brother. And her best friend, Jeff. And her fake friend, Lily. And now she was here.

"I've been thinking over everything that happened, Art, and there's a couple points I keep coming back to."

"What's that?" He took another bite of pork.

"I know the DNA test said Dad wasn't Mia's father, but that doesn't change the fact that she looked an awful lot like me."

"There was a certain resemblance. Mostly just your hair color, though, right?"

"No. Our noses. And complexion. High foreheads."

"Seems like an overstatement, but what are you getting at?"

"How is it possible that Christie Kinley believed my father was the father of her child, and the two of us look like each other but aren't actually related?"

"I don't know, but my head's starting to hurt thinking about it. This is all over, Alice. Be thankful—"

"It hurt my head, too, Art. And that's why I couldn't let it go. You see, here's what's puzzling. Mia Andrews and I *are* related."

"What are you talking about? We did the postmortem DNA tests."

"Against my father, yes. But I contacted the NYPD. I had them test *my* DNA against Mia's. We have genetic similarities consistent with being half sisters."

"That doesn't make any sense. Wait—unless. Oh, my God. She was at the house during Ben's party. Maybe she and Ben—"

"I thought of that, too. That's why the NYPD compared Mia's DNA against Ben's. There was no match. Mia's related to me, but not to Ben."

"Obviously someone made a mistake. You're not related to that woman."

"Here's the thing: Ben used to joke that I must be adopted, with my red hair. Mom always told me that she and Dad both had redheads back in the family tree somewhere. Recessive genes etcetera. But then I remembered that picture you have in your office, the one of your nephew at the Yankees game. He also had red hair and a sloped nose, sort of like mine. And yours."

"Me? You think my nose is sloped?"

"Stop this, Art. It won't be hard to get a sample of your DNA. I hear we leave it behind everywhere we go. I'll have your DNA compared against mine. And Mia's. The truth is going to come out.

You were staying in the guest cottage that night in Bedford. My father didn't remember what happened because nothing *did* happen. He really was blacked out in the theater all night. Christie Kinley's mother had brainwashed her to adore celebrities. What happened? She was drunk and asked if you were Ben's famous dad?"

Arthur slammed his fist against the table but then lowered his voice to deflect attention. "Alice, you've obviously gone through something terrible. But that does not justify these allegations."

"My mother said she hadn't been a perfect wife. She obviously did something that made her feel guilty enough to suffer through my father's transgressions all these years. How long did the affair go on? Was it a long-term thing, or was I the result of a drunken one-night stand?"

"This is crazy."

He rose to leave, but she played her trump card. "The New York State Patrol is pulling camera footage from 684 on the night of Robert Atkinson's car accident. Once they find proof of your car tailing Atkinson's, it'll be over, Arthur. My guess is they'll also find a fingerprint or two in Mia Andrews's apartment."

"Next you'll be accusing me of being the second shooter in the Kennedy assassination."

"My guess is you were already in Mia's apartment when you called me to say you were running late to Williamsburg. You talked your way inside, probably armed, then found the gun she used to kill Larson. All you had to do was fire a couple shots when the police showed up, then finish her off with her own gun and plant it in her hand. Danes wondered why she hadn't simply run down the fire escape. I didn't realize there was one until he said that. You ran out and met me on the street as if you had no idea what had happened."

"I love you. In fact, I love you as though you *were* my own daughter, but this is insane."

"You're a lawyer, Arthur. You know how this will play out. The DNA tests *will* be run. Video of your car near Atkinson's *will* be found. And now that the police know what to look for, they *will* find evidence that you were inside Mia's apartment. And even if only *one* of those things happens, you will not be able to lie, or lawyer, or pay your way out of it. What did you tell me about those clients of yours who go fugitive: Are you ready to walk away from *your* home, family, and reputation? Oh, yeah, that's right—you pretty much don't have any of those without the Humphreys, do you?"

"I'm leaving."

"I can't believe you would hurt Ben. He loved you."

He breathed heavily, staring at her from across the table, then raised a single finger and pointed at her. "I did *not* harm your brother."

"How about it, Godfather? Now that I know your secrets, will I be the next one they find dead in my bathroom?"

"Ben was using again. Ben was a spoiled junkie. And I would never, ever—no matter what—hurt you. I practically raised you."

"Because I'm your daughter. I'm your flesh and blood."

She could tell from his breathing that he was having a hard time maintaining his composure. He nodded, but she needed to hear him say it.

"Mia and I were a DNA match," she continued. "I already know. I just want to hear it straight from you. That's all I want, Art. And then if you want to make a run for it, I'm not going to stop you. But the truth *will* come out."

When he finally spoke, he had regained the evenness of his breath. "I wanted Rose to leave him. When your mother found out she was pregnant, I mean. She said you could've been either of ours, but I knew how much he'd been gone. I could feel that you would be our child. And when you were born, oh, I was so certain. But Rose would never leave Frank. She worships your father. The artistry. The wit. The passion. She would taunt me with it when I pressed her too hard."

"And that night with Christie Kinley?"

"That was *not* rape. And I had no idea that she was only fourteen."

"You allowed my father to believe all these years that he was the one."

"I also got the lawsuit settled with a confidentiality agreement. And, frankly, if it took a blacked-out night and a good scare to get your father to stop drinking, I might have done him a favor. Frank would've died by now at the rate he was going."

She realized that the man could justify anything. "Please tell me the truth about Ben."

"I swear to you, as God as my witness, I had nothing to do with that."

"Did it ever dawn on you that what he learned from Robert Atkinson about our father was the breaking point for him? Maybe you were the one who put the needle in his arm, but indirectly."

"I never meant to hurt either one of you." He reached for his wallet, but she waved him off.

"My treat, remember? What are you going to do?"

He gave her a sad smile. "You know what? You would've made a good lawyer, Alice, because you're right. I kept digging further and further, trying to bury the truth from twenty-five years ago, but I made too many mistakes. You got me. Maybe I'll see you on the other side."

He was surprisingly peaceful as he made his way to the exit, like a man who had already weighed his options and come to terms with his choice. But Alice would never learn what that decision might have been, because undercover police officers—dressed as waiters, busboys, and customers—swarmed Arthur Cronin before he could leave the restaurant.

Alice reached into her shirt and peeked at the microphone taped to her left breast. She could have sworn that Art threw her a wink as his handcuffs clicked shut.

EPILOGUE

Alice was panting by the time she reached her turnoff from Council Crest Drive. The view from the backside of her rental house had made the west hills irresistible, but she had not taken into account the labor that would be required for even a twenty-minute jog in this neighborhood. She slowed to a leisurely walk, allowing her heart rate to return to normal and the breeze to dry the thin layer of perspiration around her neck.

Alice had always heard that the Pacific Northwest was the perfect place to spend a summer, but now she knew firsthand. She would never have dreamed of running outdoors in steamy New York City in August, but even uphill in Portland, Oregon, she had barely broken a sweat.

She pulled her mail from the curbside box. A. J. Benjamin. She'd changed her name six weeks ago but was still getting used to it. A. J. for her initials, Alice Janine. And of course Benjamin. A. J. Benjamin seemed like she'd be a brunette, so it was back to the Temptation Brown in a bottle. At least for now. Memories were short, though. In another year or two, when people had forgotten about that time a girl who looked just like her was in the news, she could go back to her natural hue. Maybe she'd even go back to the name Alice Humphrey. Until then, a name was just a name, as interchangeable as her hair color.

It was Tuesday, and she had just enjoyed an afternoon jog. In New York City, Alice had only been able to exercise in the middle of the day when she was unemployed. In Portland, she was now a once-a-week telecommuter. No pencil skirts and tailored blouses for this woman, at least not on Tuesdays. She ran her fingers across her laptop's touchpad, bringing the screen back to life, and carried the computer out to the canvas chair she'd bought for her deck. Voilà, she was at work!

For the seventh time, she checked the flyer she had designed for errors. The Portland Art Museum's distribution list was only a tiny percentage of the Met's, and this show—an overview of Edward Hopper's images of Portland—would not even warrant its own publicity campaign back in the city. But it would be one of Portland's most attended exhibits of the year. She wanted the flyer to be perfect.

When she was absolutely certain she was satisfied, she e-mailed the file to her boss, reminding herself to sign the message A. J.

She found a message from her father waiting in her in-box.

She was still trying to convince him that the name change had not been a rejection of him. A. J. Benjamin on the West Coast was the fresh start she needed. Ironically, she actually spoke to her parents more now than she had when they'd lived in the same city. Maybe it was because they all knew they had to make an effort.

"Alice"—A. J. was only for people in her new life—"I thought this might interest you."

It was a link to a wedding announcement from last weekend's *New York Times*. Joann Stevenson to Jason Morhart. She was a medical billing technician. He was a police detective in Dover, New Jersey. These weren't the kinds of top-tier pedigrees usually found in the Sunday Styles section, but no couple could top the poignancy of their backstory—falling in love as he risked his life investigating the tragic death of the bride's daughter.

"Get this," her father added. "Ron Howard's trying to buy movie rights. Love, Dad."

Her instant message account was blinking on-screen, one of the costs of telecommuting. But this message wasn't from one of her coworkers at the museum. It was from Hank Beckman. His termination from the bureau was official. Brooklyn was a little pricey for the proportion of his pension he'd been able to salvage, but a friend had suggested Portland as a nice compromise between the big city and the Montana town where he'd been raised. He was thinking of flying out next week to check it out.

"A 'friend' suggested this, huh?" She hit the send key.

"Maybe you should've been the FBI agent."

They had seen each other a few times before she'd been offered the job in Portland. But a few get-togethers that weren't even officially dates could not be the reason she turned her back on the opportunity for a new life she so desperately needed.

"I'll pick you up at the airport." Send.

She typed the next sentence and reread it twice: "I have a guest room. It's yours if you want it." Send.

She tapped an impatient fingernail against the teak arm of her chair, waiting for his reply. "Sounds great. Thanks."

Maybe the fresh start didn't need to be entirely new. She knew she still needed to work through the lessons gleaned in the past year. Her understanding of family had been shaken. When her brother had learned what he thought was the truth about their father and that night in Bedford, he'd fallen back into addiction rather than turn to her. Now Ben was gone. So was the half sister she'd never even known she had. Art was still fighting the charges against him, but would likely die in prison. She tried not to feel sorry for the man who had raped Christie Kinley, and taken the life of his own daughter. But then she'd remember that Mia was not Art's only daughter. No, she did not feel sorry for Art, but she might never be able to accept that her biological father was capable of the sins Arthur Cronin had committed.

And the only father she had ever known—having found forgiveness from his wife for so many transgressions—was still finding it in himself to forgive hers. But, no matter what DNA tests had to say about it, Frank Humphrey was still her father. She just had to find a way to convince him of that.

Those months when she had been unemployed, when she had wanted so desperately to be free of her family, she had made herself miserable. She wanted a job. She wanted her own money. She wanted a man. She spent every second of every hour of every day craving what she did not have. Wanting states of being she could not even identify. Wanting *something*. Something *else*.

Then two police officers showed up at her apartment with a photograph. That single image had been a wake-up call. In that singular moment, she had realized how much there was to appreciate in simplicity. Clean air. This view of Mount Hood. A pretty decent job in a nice place with good people, with one day a week when she could work on this deck in her jogging togs. Parents who loved her. A couple of new friends in Portland. Maybe another to add to the list if Beckman chose to move.

Nothing could be more than this.

ACKNOWLEDGMENTS

The idea for *Long Gone* came during one of my regular early morning strolls through New York City's West Village. It was early 2009, when each cold day seemed to bring a new wave of unannounced and abrupt business closures. The familiar diner that was there on Monday would be replaced by an empty storefront on Tuesday. I found myself thinking about the employees who had lost their jobs. I wondered whether they received any more notice than the customers. I wondered what it would be like to show up at work one morning to find your entire professional life . . . gone.

By the time I was ready to start writing, I'd been living with that kernel of an idea for nearly a year. I felt like I knew Alice Humphrey, her family, and the other people in her life. To my surprise, during those intervening months, I also kept hearing from a missing girl and her guilt-stricken mother. To my amazement, I realized they belonged in this book as well.

Careful readers will probably recognize shadows of other recent events on the pages of *Long Gone*. Fictionalized versions of real world stories, either those I encountered as a prosecutor or have followed from afar, often seep into my novels. These are, of course, fictionalized, as in made up and untrue, and should not be construed as a comment upon any actual person or event.

I am so thankful to the people who help me take the voices in my head and turn them into books instead of a trip to the mental hospital: At Spitzer Literary Agency, my tremendous agent, Philip Spitzer, and his associates, Lukas Ortiz and Lucas Hunt; and at HarperCollins, Jonathan Burnham, Heather Drucker, Mark Ferguson, Angie Lee, Michael Morrison, Nicole Reardon, Jason Sack, Kathy Schneider, and Leah Wasielewski. I don't have sufficient words of praise for the professionalism, dedication, and intelligence that my editor, Jennifer Barth, continually brings to our relationship. I'm forever appreciative.

Thanks as well to Carrie Blank, Jonathan Hayes, Nikki Jones, McKenna Jordan, Dan Judson, Julian Ku, Josh Lamborn, David Lesh, Chris Mascal, NYPD Detective Lucas Miller, Heidi and Greg Moawad, Gary Moore, Richard Rhorer, Anne-Lise Spitzer, and Richard Urrutia.

Finally, I am the luckiest girl in the world thanks to my supercool husband, Sean.

A SPECIAL NOTE OF THANKS
TO MY READERS

Once again, I want to thank my readers, without whom I would not have the privilege of being a published writer. Were it not for you, I might wake up one morning to find myself out of work like Alice Humphrey (albeit hopefully without the dead bodies and whatnot). Thank you for continuing to read and to support my work.

I've gotten to know many of my readers through my Web site, Facebook, and Twitter. I'm so appreciative of the community we have built online and thank Holden Richards at Kitchen Media and Catherine Cairns of Cairns Designs for their technical assistance. If you read my books and haven't yet connected to this community, I hope you'll do so.

Some readers have even accepted my ongoing invitation to serve as online kitchen cabinet, helping me think through decisions like *Long Gone*'s title and the always-stressful selection of a new author headshot. For their helpful (and fun) kitchen-cabinet comments during the writing of *Long Gone,* I thank the following readers: Alice Jackson, Alison Janssen, Alromaithi Mohammed, Amber McDonald, Amber York, Anastacia Kipp, Andrea Wilson, Andy Gilham, Angie Thomas-Davis, Ann Turner, Anne Madison, Anthony N. Smith, April Smith, Ashton Laurent, Aude Dupré de Boulois, Audrey Pink, Barb Juarez, Barb Mullen Gasparac, Barbara Bryan, Barbara Detwiler, Barbara Pease Claypool, Barbara Theroux, Barbara Vink, B. C. Creighton, Becky Cemper, Becky Doshier Gallimore, Becky Morganstern, Bert Shapiro, Beth Stack, Bev Murphree, Beverly Bryan, Beverly Vick, Bill Horn, Bill Strider, Bill Tipping, Billie Ruth Walker, Billy Bob Billy, Bob Campbell, Bonnie D. Tharp, Bonnie Graham, Bonnie Powell Morningstar, Bren Sugar, Brenda LeSage, Brent Watson, Brian Fingerson, Brian Shrader, Bridget Cagan Herron, Bruce DeSilva, Bud Palmer, Candi Hartley-Hall, Candice Lamb, Carl Christensen, Carmen Munger, Carol Clark, Carol Johnsen, Carol Maddox, Carol O'Gorman, Carol Pennell, Carole Sauer, Carrie Weston, Cassie Ane, Catherine Kit Smither Norr, Cathy Carmouche, Chad Huckabaa, Charlotte Gray, Chaun Santoriello, Cheryl Boyd, Cheryl Fortune, Cheryl Gladen, Chris Cooper Cahall, Chris F. A. Johnson, Chris Knake, Chris Ozment, Chris Starkman, Chris Toft, Christel Verret Mollere, Christine Caillet, Christine Pernetti, Christopher Clarke, Chuck Palmer, Cindy Daniel, Cindy Marshall Sabin, Cliff Miller, Connie Ross Ciampanelli, Connie Williams Claus, Constance McClure, Courtney E. McIntyre, Craig Pittman, Curtis Ensler, Cyndi Sieber, Cynthia Poley Parran, Dani Leonor, Danny Nichols, Daphne Anne Humphrey, Darcy Lafferty Justice, Daryl McGrath, Dave Davis, David Bell, David Booker, David Hale Smith, David Hansard, David MacClure Conrad, David Maidstone, David Pinter, Dawn Lattimore, Deb Gravette Threadgill, Debbie Ballou Sladek, Deborah Burge, Debra Belmudes, Debra Manzella, Den Terwilliger, Dennis Leleux, Dennis Siler, Diana Bosley, Diana Taylor, Diane Griffiths, Diane Quilghini, Diane Simmons, Dianne Wisner, Dick Droese, Dodie Osbourne, Don Boynton, Don Nations, Donna Bagdasarian, Donna E. Stephenson, Donna Reed Enders, Douan Thomas, Dru Ann L Love, Dudley Forster, Dwayne K Workman, Dwight Lee Spencer, E.j. Copperman, Elaine Roberts Razo Videau, Elena Shapiro Wayne, Elizabeth A. Olesen, Elizabeth A. White, Elizabeth Julia, Ellen Sattler Harpin, Ellis Vidler, Elyse Dinh, Erin Mitchell, Ethel Rodenberger, Eva Björnberg,

Evelyn Lavelle, Evelyn Petree, Faye DeBlanc, Fran Burget, Frans Carlson, Gabrielle Reynolds, Gail Mackey Pick, Garret Gannuch, George Reid, Geraldine Evans, Gerry Brown, Gianna Mack, Glenn Eisenstein, Greg Byington, Greg Skipper, Gretchen Gfeller, Gunter Kaesdorf, H. Lyndon Arledge, Harry Hunsicker, Hayden Wakeling, Heather Brister Megehee, Helen Pate, Helene Goodwin Clausz, Ilene Ratcheson Ciccone, Irja Orav, Isabel Leek, J. D. Rhoades, Jackie Schmidt, Jacqueline May, Jacques Stenvert, James Jensen, James L. Stratton, James R. Bradbrook, James Willis, Jana Johnson, Jane Davis, Jane Moran, Janet Anne Montz-Dubis, Janet Reid, Janice Gable Bashman, Jann Sherman-Lassman, Jay Drescher, Jayne Starkey, Jean Tate, Jeanne Adcox Lockett, Jeanne Bielke-Rodenbiker, Jeanne King Hendrickson, Jeanne Warpinski, Jeannette Badillo, Jen Forbus, Jen Sale, Jen Volz, Jenine Kerr, Jennifer Baxter Weil, Jennifer Billey, Jennifer Houlihan, Jennifer Hudson, Jennifer Little Beck, Jennifer Jones, Jenny Drew, Jenny Spiva Rainwater, Jerri Leppert Hernandez, Jerri Leppert Hernandez, Jim Cox, Jimbob Niven, Jo Ann Nicholas, Jo Johnston, Jo McDermott, Joan Nichols Green, Joan Tregarthen Huston, Joan Vernola, JoAnn Frazier Cole, Jodi Olson, Jody Bacon Sanders, Jody Daffinrud, Jody Maxwell, Joe Carter, Joe Messinger, John Borman, John Colgrove, John Corson, John Decker, John Elder, John Flynn, John Haragan, John Jones, John Montag S. J., John Sporri, Johnnie McHan, Jon Carnero, Jon Smanz, Jon Horton, Jon Jordan, Jon Schuller, J. Padgett, J. T. Ellison, Jude Hardin, Judith Hogan, Judith McCarrick, Judy Aschenbrand, Judy Bush, Judy Gehrig, Judy Peterson McAferty, Judy Waren Bryan, Jules White, Julie Donner Schuenemann, Julie Ebinger Hilton, Kara Hudson, Karen Allison, Karen Clarkson, Karen Clarkson Clay, Karen Olson, Karen Harvey, Karen L. Randall, Karen Linder Catalona, Karen Nason Abdulfattah, Kathleen Scurlock, Kathryn Casey, Kathryn Long, Kathy Collings, Kathy Goodridge Poulin, Kathy Hepler, Kayla Painter, Kenneth McAlister Sr., Kercelia Fletcher, Kerry Maddux, Kevin Eoff, Kim Bonnesen, Kim McCully Mobley, Kim Peifley, Kimberly Cook Wright, Kristen

Howe, Kristine Mosher Tarrow, Kristyn Broussard Moore, Lanie Accles, Larry Ober, Larry Chavis, Laura Bostick Weber, Laura Lippman, Laura Piros McCarver, Laura Taylor, Leah Guinn, Leigh Hunt, Lenice Wolowiec Valsecchi, LeRoy Spicer, Les Donaldson, Lesley Sacher, Linda Careaga, Linda Connell, Linda Flannery, Linda Gilmer, Linda Hammitt-Salmi, Linda Jo DuPree, Linda Langdon Floyd, Linda Mitchell, Linda Moore, Linda Napikoski, Linda Nichols, Lindsay Vail, Lisa Bischke Neumann, Lisa Fowler, Lola Troy Fiur, Lori Anderson Mills, Lori Taylor, Louis Hillary Park, Lovada Marks Williams, Lynn Ashworth Peters, Lynn Hirshman, Lynne Healy, Lynne Victorine, Maralie Waterman BeLonge, Margaret Bailey, Margaret Franson Pruter, Margaret Palkovits Weber, Maria Hoffman, Maria Johnson, Marilyn Hambrecht, Marilyn Parker, Marion Montgomery, Marion Shaw, Marissa Wiley, Mark Henderson, Mark Hendricks, Mark Lichtenberger, Marleen Kennedy, Marlene Greenberg Lamancuso, Marlyn Beebe, Marni Curtis, Martha McConnell Greer, Martha Stephenson La Marche, Martyn James Lewis, Mary Alice Gorman, Mary Espenschied, Mary Frances Bass Jay, Mary Hohulin, Mary Marino-Strong, Mary Olson, Mary Phillips, Maryann Mercer, Maryellen Hannah, Matt Shaw, Matt Wieland, Maureen Wiley Apfl, Melissa Towe Downing, Merle Gornick, Mev Wilson, Michael Bok, Michael Cotton, Michael Rosenthal, Michael Sladek, Michael W. Sherer, Michael Walter, Michell Verduzco, Michelle L Ross, Michelle Moran, Michelle Phillips, Micki Fortenberry Dumke, Mike Houston, Mike McPeak, Mitch Smith, Nancy Laughlin, Nancy M. Hood, Naomi Dorris Houston, Naomi Johnson, Naomi Waynee, Neal LeBaron, Nick Christie, Nicola Trwst, Nidia Hernandez, Nik Nikkel, Nils Kristian Hagen Jr., Nisha Sharma, Nita Lapinski, Owen Weston, P. J. Feinson, Paddi Burke, Pam Davidson Reimer, Pamela Jarvis, Pamela Pescosolido, Pamela Picard, Pat Neveux, Patricia Burns Porter, Patrick Riley, Patti James Anderlohr, Patti MacDonnell, Patti Neal Blackwood, Patty Luecke, Paul Deyo, Paul Feeney, Paula Daniel Steinbacher, Paula Friedman, Paula Rossetti, Penny Anderson McIntosh,

Pepper Goforth, Phillip Jones, Phillis Spike Carbone, Phyllis Taylor Malone, Rachelle Gagné, Ramsey Burton Doran, Raymond Benson, Raymond Fundora, Rebecca S. Autrey, Rebecca Turman, Rebecca Woodbury, Reggie White, Renee James, Rhonda Leach Peterson, Rich Maxson, Richard Dory, Richard Reed, Rita Messina, Rob Friedman, Robert Carotenuto, Robert Carraher, Robert F. Klees, Robert Gooch, Robert Hartman, Robert J. Scheeler, Robert Ray, Roberta Boe, Roberta Clardy, Robin M. Healy, Robin Parsons Eastwood, Rocky Romeo, Rod Viator, Ron Cervantez, Ruby Jordon, Russ Cashon, Ruth Jordan, Ruth Miriampolski, Ruthie Vescoso, Sal Towse, Salli Schwartz, Sally Fortin, Samuel Perry, Sanam Dowlatdad, Sandie Herron, Sandie Hinkle, Sandra Cranmer, Sandra Jean Krna, Sandra Lee, Sandra Speller, Sandy Ebner, Sandy Plummer, Sara J. Henry, Sara Johann, Sara Thomas Simpson, Sara Weiss, Sarah LaPorte, Scott Irwin, Seale Ballenger, Shannon Anderson Crable, Shannon Keane English, Sharon Brown, Sharon Faith Graves, Sharon Swanson Magee, Shaun Slaathaug, Shawn McMichael Orgeron, Sheila Dawson, Sherree' Scarlott, Sherri Merkousko, Sherri Young Coats, Sherrie L. Saint, Sherry Chaffin Rasmus, Sheryl Cooper, Sheryl Ditty Hauch, Shirley Grosor, Sidney C. Mansfield, Siobhan O'Shea, Sita Laura, Stephanie Glencross, Stephanie Mary Haskell Gleave, Stephen Scarbrough, Stephen Tremp, Steve Gonzales, Sue McLauchlan Faulkner, Sue Stanisich, Sue Torf, Sue Young Fulks, Susan Abe, Susan Anderson, Susan Lowe, Susan Marsh, Susan P. Bagley, Susan Purins Meuckon, Susan Ransom Grimes, Susie Cowan Hudson, Suzanne C. Dubus, Suzanne Collier, Suzanne Sheppard, Suzanne W. Goldstone, Suzee Neal, Tanya Currin Faucette, Tasha Alexander, Ted Myers, Tena Clark Faruque, Terri Bischoff, Terry Boatman, Tim Busbey, Tim Hanner, Tina Tenley, Tina Warren, T. J. Carrell, Tolfe Lee Albert, Tom Russell, Tommye Baxter Cashin, Tony Sannicandro, Tori Bullock, Traci Boeh Wickett, Traci Hohenstein, Trena Klohe, Trudy Peltier, Tyra Bradbury, Veronica Piastuch, Vickie Parshall, Victoria Waller, Viola Burg, Wallace Clark, Wallace Henry

Wyeth, Walter Caldwell, Wayne Ledbetter, Wayne M. Blake, Wendy Brown, Wendy Hall, Will Thomas, William Brennan, William Bruner, and William Penrose.

I apologize for omitting names of other kitchen-cabinet participants, as I surely have, but please do know how much I appreciate your ongoing online support between books. See you on the interwebs!

ABOUT
THE AUTHOR

Alafair Burke is the best-selling author of six previous novels, including *212*, *Angel's Tip*, and *Dead Connection* in the Ellie Hatcher series. A former prosecutor, she now teaches criminal law and lives in Manhattan. *Long Gone* is her first stand-alone thriller.